# THE GREY HENS

# THE GREY HENS

## Isabel Contreras

The Book Guild Ltd
Sussex, England

The Book Guild Ltd
25 High Street,
Lewes, Sussex

First published 1995
© Isabel Contreras
Set in Baskerville
Typesetting by Acorn Bookwork, Salisbury, Wiltshire

Printed in Great Britain by
Antony Rowe Ltd.
Chippenham, Wiltshire.

A catalogue record for this book is
available from the British Library

ISBN 0 86332 967 5

This is for Bobo.

*"Pero yo ya no soy yo,*
*Ni mi casa es ya mi casa —"*

– Federico García Lorca,
*Romancero gitano*


*Mis gracias a*
  *Señor Plácido Domingo*
*por el título de éste libro.*

# 1

Unless you are a singer or an impresario, it is unlikely that you would know how to find the Drach Agency. The Royal Borough of Kensington & Chelsea certainly have their problems, and often whip past the little cul-de-sac carrying bins and refuse-sacks from the more obvious frontages of Kensington High Street, without a glance down the alleyway. Bobby Drach and several co-tenants made their protests at regular intervals, and then an enormous vehicle called Dennis would block the entrance and obscure the brief glimpses of red buses.

'I bet the buggers will be round like greased lightning just before Christmas,' Bobby remarked gloomily to his partner.

Standing at the second floor window, he watched the removal of bulging black sacks from the cul-de-sac, and uttered a sarcastic cheer as the last one was shoulder-hoisted and borne away.

'And of course, they'll come banging on the door for their little seasonal pressie, won't they,' he added.

'So what will you tell them?' murmured his partner, her head submerged in *Kobbé's Complete Opera Book*.

'To fuck off. Illiterate peasantry!'

He turned away from the window, snatched the *Financial Times* from Ez's desk. Her wooden magpie fell over as the paper caught the side of its beak. Ez stood it upright on a ledger.

'Good boy,' she said absently, patting it. Bobby eyed her over the pink sheets. Ruffled them irritably. 'Where the fuck is the Arts page today?'

'Same page as the TV programmes.'

'I know that, duckie . . . Jesus wept! Look at the column inches on this bespectacled twat! No wonder the country's in a bloody mess.'

The cul-de-sac and the façade of the Agency were, like Drach himself, somewhat misleading: the interior presented another picture altogether. The small suite of offices had been transformed two years ago by an Italian firm of designers called Sweet Sistine; and, based on Bobby's own modus operandi, was furnished with leather armchairs for bodily comfort and Dalí prints of the Crucifixion for mental stimulation. There was a general lack of enthusiasm for the blue cherubs on the ceilings, and even less of it for the life-size sculpture of a Roman god in the reception area. Bobby had named him Jock.

'Because,' he explained glint-eyed, 'he reminds me of my schooldays. I had a playmate called Jock.'

'A bit well-developed for a schoolboy, isn't he?' Ez mused doubtfully.

'I was thinking more about Jock's father,' and the pouches beneath his eyes stretched gleefully, 'but I can't remember his name. Anyway,' prodding the Roman god, 'we can use this bit as a hatstand.'

A sudden roar jolted Ez from her perusal of *Kobbé*.

'I don't bloody believe this!' and Bobby slammed the *Financial Times* down, stabbing a plump finger at the Arts column. 'That critic must have the brains of a fucking wombat! Have you read it?'

Ez shook her head solemnly. He snatched the paper back, quivering. 'What a load of pretentious shit! Just listen to this!' and began to parrot a thin aristocratic accent. '"Apart from a discernible waver in the upper register and fading breath control, especially in the Donizetti *L'amour qui m'a tourné*, the recital was warmly and deservedly applauded. This seemingly ageless master –"' Bobby stopped, and yelped. 'Seemingly bloody ageless, that peroxided old fart? His pianist deserves a military medal!'

Ez sighed, ran a hand through her tangled screen of curls.

'Italian bastard!' and, as the *Financial Times* skidded back across the desk, 'Bloody Vito Lavagna!'

She lit a cigarette, and watched his tall well-fed shape fold itself on to the arm of a chair, grey and silver hair shining with gel. Tired eye shadow rested in the creases of his lids. He looked despondent. But then, she mused, he always did whenever Lavagna paid a visit to London.

'Do you know him by any chance, Robert?'

'What? Know him? That tuneless prick? No I do not, thank you very much!'

He returned to her desk, picked up the newspaper again. Peered at her over the edges. 'Yes!' he snapped suddenly. 'I knew him. Years ago.'

'And?'

'And what, you nosy mare?' He folded the *F.T.* and hit her lightly on the head with it. 'Don't just sit there prying, get me some coffee!'

'I shall ask Julie to get some coffee,' she said with dignity, 'not being your maidservant myself.'

'That fat-arsed silly cow,' sulked Bobby, as Ez giggled and pressed a button on her desk. 'Julie? . . . Robert says you're a silly cow with a fat arse, and could we have two coffees, please?'

Julie appeared in the doorway. She was tall and dressed in red wool, hand-knitted.

'I don't know why you bother with that intercom thing,' she snapped, 'I'm only about nine feet away!'

Bobby gave a little skip towards her, hands outstretched. 'Darling, Ezita was telling naughty fibs, I never said you were silly or fat!'

Julie said briskly, 'I heard you. The door's open. Coffee, was it? Both with?'

The phone chirped on Ez's desk. Anna, from reception. 'Yes, he's here . . . Who? . . . Okay, I'll tell him. Thanks.' She cocked an eyebrow at Bobby. 'Your client's here. Rodrigo Kaffner.'

Bobby patted his hair, shot his cuffs, called 'Julie! Forget mine in here! Two coffees to my sanctum, if you please, on a bloody tray this time, with cream and sugar and teaspoons, and the sugar in a fucking bowl not in the bag!' Sighed, glanced in the mirror, gave a little twirl. 'Ezita, don't forget we're lunching at the Colorno, one-thirty, and do something with your hair for Christ's sake, you look like a flat-chested mop. And make-up, especially round those enormous eyes of yours. Emphasise your good points, darling, I've told you before.'

'Oh go away! Julie? Where's my coffee?'

An angry blur of bright red flashed through the outer office. 'Sorreee! Ain't got four legs, you'll have to wait!'

'Ooh tra la and fuck a brush!' sniggered Bobby, and took a last lingering look in the mirror. Composed himself into executive urbanity.

Ez was laughing and reaching for the phone. 'Don't be so vulgar, Robert, she'll get used to us in time! Now what did I do with Tom Patna's number? . . . it was here a moment ago.'

'That silly cow couldn't get used to going for a quick piss,' then 'And don't forget. Colorno. Half-past one. And we're walking there. If Kaffner decides to join the Agency, I might even treat you.'

'Good. I shall have the most expensive gourmet item on the menu.'

'No such thing at Colorno. You can have an extra breadstick.'

'*Grazie.*' She began to punch out a number and waved to him.

*   *   *

Bobby paused in Reception as they set off for lunch at their favourite Italian restaurant, and glared at the carrier bag hanging from the Roman god's private parts. Ez tittered as he glanced round for Anna.

'Where's that lop-sided cow gone now?' he snapped, and removed the offending bag, dumped it on his receptionist's desk. 'That bit is for hats!'

Laughing, they strolled up the cul-de-sac towards the August warmth of the High Street. Bobby remarked how clean and wide the alley looked without the knotted black sacks. Companionably they threaded their way through substantial pavement traffic towards Church Street, avoided a three-wheeled shopping trolley, and had an altercation with a young Arsenal supporter who shouted 'Watch where you're going, grandad!'

'Makes me the same age as your goalkeeper, then, doesn't it, chocolate drop?' snarled Bobby, and gave the football scarf a tug before darting out of reach. 'God, my legs ache!' groaning, as they headed up Church Street towards Colorno.

'Roberto, we've only been walking for five minutes!' giggled Ez.

He stopped to look in the window of an antique shop. 'Holy bloody Mary, what a nice way to make a living! Look at that for sheer poetry . . . one blue curtain and a chamber pot on legs! Must've taken them ages to plan that.'

'So!' Ez said as they smiled and walked on, 'Now that we've got Kaffner on our books, does he have any idea of the kind of starter-engagements he needs?'

'All fixed up,' smugly.

She stared at him. 'What do you mean, all fixed up? You only saw him a couple of hours ago!'

He grabbed her arm. 'Christ, look at that! Only August, and Colorno's got its summer awning out already! I see that gash is still there, don't Italians know how to use a bloody needle and thread?' He grinned at Ez. 'Like I said, Kaffner's fixed. The Festival Choir wanted a baritone for their *Dream of Gerontius*, so I've got him the job. Poor sod doesn't realise yet that it's Elgar; he's lived with bloody Rossini for so long he thinks it's another one of his. Oh – there's Aldo! – Coo-eeee!'

Ez Pepper cast a glance at her spasmodic reflection in a toyshop window as an automatic reflex, but saw only a creamy leisure suit and sunny shadows.

Bobby said out of the corner of his mouth, 'Shouldn't bother, duckie. Your beak's shiny, and your hair is in knots. As usual. Let's hope the sun's in Aldo's eyes, otherwise he won't let you in.'

'What on earth is he doing?' she whispered as they climbed the steps towards him. Five wide steps, black and white mosaic, red borders.

Aldo was trying to scratch the middle of his back with a fork.

'*Buon giorno!*' cried Ez gaily. 'You want a hand, Aldo?'

The Italian gloomily handed her the fork. 'Is not easy to reach, *Signorina* Eliza. Oh, *grazie!*' and he leaned blissfully against the palm tree in its wooden tub.

'Do you serve meals here?' Bobby asked acidly.

'*Scusi, Signor* Roberto . . . see, there is the new menu!'

Ez gave him a final searing scratch with the fork. 'The what?' she asked.

'Is new idea. My wife she say it will save money-spending if we not use a printer,' and he smiled proudly as they gazed at a large blackboard by the front door.

Aldo Gabinetto was basking in his wife's new prominence. 'You

11

like? Mirella say to me, Aldo, this is my best writing, I do it in chalking, like schooldays.'

'What the hell's this?' Bobby stabbed a finger at the board.

'*Spaghetti Napoli, Signor* Roberto.'

'It says Spetti,' Bobby said.

'Oh come on inside!' and Ez caught his hand. 'I want to talk to you about something important. Aldo, what's the Italian for 'important?' '

Bobby groaned. Aldo grinned; *Signorina* Eliza was always the same, asking questions, jotting his answers down in her notebook. She scribbled down *importante* and followed Bobby to their usual table.

'Come on, Aldo, chop chop! Carafe of house red, if you please!' Bobby looked with satisfaction round the deserted restaurant, neat and homely, decorated to match the Italian flag. Smiled at Ez. 'What do you want to talk about that's so *importante*?' He chortled as he felt her foot trying to reach his ankle.

*       *       *

'It's like lunching with a child,' he said, frowning with distaste. 'Crumbs on your mouth, pasta sauce on your fingers . . . and stop doodling with that bloody breadstick!' Stared closely. 'Jesus Christ, what's that?'

'What's what?' putting the breadstick apologetically on her plate.

'That bloody muck on your face! I've only just seen it now that you've pushed your hair back. You been sweeping chimneys?'

Ez tittered. 'Eye make-up.'

'You apply it, darling, with a small brush, not a dumper-truck. Aldo, do we get coffee in here, or shall I put a call through to Brazil? . . . Thank you . . . Now, Ezita, what was it you wanted to —'

'Sssh! What was that word Aldo used just then when the tradesman came in?'

'Darling, you said you had something important to tell Bobby,' patiently.

'Not to tell you. To talk to you about. Aldo!'

12

Bobby sighed. Aldo hurried across, '*Sì, Signorina* Eliza?'

'What did that word mean –' notebook poised, '– it sounded like *vaffanculo?*'

Aldo stared, shocked. Then he leaned over and whispered in Bobby's ear before retreating behind the small cocktail bar in the corner.

'Well?' impatiently. 'What did he say?'

Bobby grinned. 'It's a command for you to go and do something to yourself.'

'Go and do what, for heaven's sake?' Her pen was poised and waiting.

'Depends on whether you prefer the word screw or fuck.'

Ez wrote it down. 'Thank you, Robert.' She returned notebook and pen to her capacious shoulder-bag. Looked at him severely through her nest of smashed ringlets, as Bobby called them. 'Vito Lavagna,' she said firmly, wielding her teaspoon.

'More coffee with your sugar?' acidly watching her. Then, resignedly, 'What about him?' She had, he knew, expected him to rear back in horror. He smiled at her expression when he didn't. Said slowly, 'I think it must have been that phrase the guy used in the *F.T.* – "a seemingly ageless master". All of a sudden, it got me thinking about him. We were at grammar school together, Lavagna and I. And I suddenly thought, those two schoolkids are now in their bloody sixties. Jesus!'

'At school together?' She stared at him. 'Where?'

'Canterbury.'

'The Kent Canterbury? What on earth was an Italian boy doing there?'

'They needed him to make ice-cream! Silly cow . . . he was brought up in Kent.'

'Go on.'

He shrugged. 'Why the interest?'

'Bobby, he's an enormous star –'

He grinned. 'Was, Ezita, was, until wrinkles and years took him over. Why? Were you by any chance wondering if the Drach Agency could lure him away from EMI?'

Another spoonful of brimming brown sugar. He shuddered.

'Not really. Were you friends for a long time?'

13

'Long enough. Fifteen, sixteen years, something like that.' He sat back, his eyes thoughtful. 'In that time, of course, Vito discovered that he'd got a bit of a voice, and we went to Italy – Vito to study, and me to tag along on the fringes, as it were.'

'Where did you live?'

'Together, mainly,' and he smiled at her expression which ranged from "of course" to "yuk". He beckoned to Aldo. 'Come on, Ezita – workies! I'm due in bloody Chichester. By the way, where's Jake today? Haven't seen him.'

Jake Bonny was their senior assistant. 'He's in France,' said Ez casually as Bobby slid his credit card on top of the bill.

'What the fuck's he doing there?' sorting out pound coins for the tip.

'I sent him. That Danish soprano, Kilde Samso, requires asylum from her current agent, and, as she's at the Paris-Opéra this week, I thought Jake could make himself useful.'

Bobby laughed appreciatively, pushing his chair away from the table. Then, horrified, 'Christ, Julie's on her own! Hurry up and finish your bloody sugar!'

On the way back, sleeves rolled up in the warmth, Ez persisted 'So why did you and Lavagna split?'

'Because.'

'Because what?' irritated.

'I thought . . . well, that he was after someone else.'

'And was he?'

He shrugged. 'I thought he was, that's the main point. Now shut up!'

'Why don't you ring him, for old times' sake? Congratulate him on his last review?'

'Why don't you step under that fucking bus?' and quickened his pace.

Julie was in Ez's office, unloading two parcels on to the desk. The magpie lay beak-down beside them. 'Came after you'd gone,' she puffed.

'Glad to hear you did,' murmured Bobby. 'First time for you, was it?'

Julie stood the magpie upright and breathed dangerously. 'There was a phone call for you as well, Bobby. A Mr . . . .hang

14

on . . .' racing back to her room. Yelled, 'A Mr Scott Crushley!'

Bobby's facial muscles tightened. 'And who the merry fuck is he?'

'Dunno. Didn't give his number, said you knew him, and that it was very urgent.'

'I've never heard of the silly bugger!' as Ez tittered.

'Scott Crushley,' asserted Julie, returning with her notepad.

'Nothing else? Nothing, no teensy weensy clue for Bobby?'

Julie sniffed noisily. 'Nope.'

'Scott Crushley,' said Ez helpfully.

'Stop that feeble sniggering!' He glared at Julie's back as she retreated. Then thumped the desk. 'Christchristchrist! She's not only a walking disaster, she's also stone deaf!'

He circled the desk. 'I'm off to Chichester. If Mr Scott Crushley phones again – you're in charge! Good afternoon!'

\*　　\*　　\*

The only sound in the quiet room was of gently-frying wasps. And a piano.

When the clicks began, Ez uncurled herself from the old settee, allowing folders and photographs to slide to the floor. She plucked the record from the turntable and examined its surface. Her collection of 78's was diminishing week by week. Goodbye, *Moonlight Sonata*, even if it was only the first movement. She returned it to its torn cover.

Nearly half-past eight, and heavy rain had darkened the evening quickly. Three wall lamps gleamed, and in their light the carved wood of the sideboard shone. At night, she thought smugly, you'd never know that it had woodworm.

Earlier, she had washed her hair, and already the long thick strands were curling. She put out her tongue at her reflection in the mirror as she padded on bare feet across the landing to the kitchen. Her favourite caftan, pale mauve and grey and silky, swirled round her ankles as she filled the kettle. Bobby had said that a truly sophisticated person would possess a percolator, that only a twat would have a battered kettle and refer to it as 'my friend'.

15

As she waited for her friend to boil, a careless heap of granules and sugar waiting in a mug, she hummed to herself, mind fixed on the music library she was building. Singers, either known or just beginning to make their mark, were all to feature in it. In the beginning, a hobby and fascination. Now, detailed and loving research, as though one day they would all become clients of the Drach Agency. Ez liked to be prepared.

The kettle was beginning to rumble. She looked out of the kitchen window into the early darkness. The window overlooked the sloping glass roof of her landlady's conservatory. Rain trickled down it busily, gurgled in the guttering. She was content. The upper floor of the house was hers. Her landlady lived downstairs, a partially-deaf octogenarian called Ada.

Dear Ada, sometimes calling up the stairs 'Would you like a sherry, dear?' and then Ez more often than not would join her in the downstairs lounge for a glass of sweet González Byass. Ada's late brother had been a Reverend, and an old lectern and bible stood dusted in the corner. Bobby referred to him as John Bunion, and called the landlady 'Sexy', to Ez's irritation. Smiling now, she made her coffee and stirred until it swirled vigorously and lapped over the top.

Voices below. Then footsteps coming up the stairs. She peered round the door.

'Ezita!' cried Bobby, his hair distorted by wind and rain. 'Sexy Ada let me in, got oodles to tell, is that coffee you're making?'

'No, I'm boiling a few hamsters for my supper. Want some?'

He followed her into the kitchen, watched her switch on the kettle and hunt for another mug. Eyed the jar of granules.

'I said coffee,' he pointed out, 'not that cheap shit. Never mind, it will have to do. Proceed!'

'I'm most grateful,' and she rattled a drawer of cutlery. 'How was Chichester?'

'Satisfactory, if you can put up with bloody church spires and poor beer.' He winced, watching her. 'Not too much of that dung in mine, thank you, Bobby doesn't want ulcers.'

She smiled as she fetched milk from the fridge. 'Guess what! Julie's Scott Crushley turned up on the doorstep yesterday – and yes, we do know him. Usually as Ascot Rush-Leigh.'

Bobby groaned. 'I told you that cow was going deaf! Go on, what did he want this time? Another engagement to be cancelled just as the fucking curtain's going up? Trapped his cock in the door?'

A giggle. 'It's his mother.' She handed him his mug.

'Oh bloody hell, not again! Why doesn't he shove her in a bloody sack and leave her on the motorway?'

'He can't do the *Don Giovanni* in October.'

'Now isn't that a surprise! Why not? Has Mummy taken a dislike to Mozart?'

She mopped a pool of milk from the work-surface. 'He's bought a dog.' He stared at her. 'It barks,' she added.

'What? A barking dog? Does God know about this?'

She laughed as she switched off the kitchen light and shepherded him across the landing to the sitting room. 'It was to be company for his mother, but the damn thing won't stop barking, and not only the neighbours but also the police are complaining, so Ascot's decided to spend more time with both mother and dog. He'll be in your office at ten sharp tomorrow, to explain.'

'Oh thanks a trillion! Partner!'

She followed him into the quiet room. 'Neat and tidy as usual,' he commented sourly. Then, 'Great Christ! What's that?'

Ez grinned. Pulled a low table in front of the settee, picked up some of the fallen folders. 'Ignacio,' she said.

He approached the sideboard cautiously. 'It's a bloody teddy bear!'

'Yes, Robert. I know it is. A friend brought him from Spain.'

'What the fuck is it wearing?' peering at the smirking bear.

Ez smiled. 'It's a matador bear. In a suit of lights.'

'Shit.' He prodded it gingerly. Ignacio, some three feet high, swayed. Bobby sniggered '*Olé, torero*! God, I bet your friend looked a prat coming through Customs with this!'

He sank on to the settee. More glossy photographs slid out of their folders and on to the floor. He picked one up, scowled at it. Martes. Modesto Martes. A bloody Spanish nightingale. He waved it at Ez. 'When I was in Austria earlier this year,' he informed her, 'these were being given away free in supermarkets. His bloody face was everywhere. Conceited twat. I don't know why he doesn't simply shove his cock on a stick and wave it around, then we could all see what the fuss is about!'

She chuckled, said 'Never mind about Martes, you said you had lots to tell me.' Watched him as he suddenly got up and went over to the tall fireplace and leaned against it, staring at the ceiling for a moment.

'You've got a cobweb up there,' he murmured, 'thick enough to hang a man.' Then abruptly, 'I rang the Dorchester yesterday.' Continued with studied indifference 'Vito Lavagna's staying there, you know. He always does when he comes to London.'

'You rang him! You actually rang him! Come on, tell me!'

Bobby's chin lifted a fraction. 'They put me through to him, of course.'

'And what did he say?' Her eyes were alight.

'He told me to fuck off.'

A burst of laughter. 'He didn't!'

'Oh yes he did, until I nipped in quick with the nickname I gave him all those years ago, and then,' slowly, smiling, 'he asked how I was, and I congratulated him on his recital reviews, and . . . well, I ended up going round there to his suite for a chat.' Cleared his throat. 'Bit awkward to start with. Years in between. But, well, like that cobweb of yours,' nodding at the ceiling, 'once you remove it, everything's clear again. I tell you, Ez, it was quite something. Lump in throat time.'

He drained his coffee and shuddered daintily. And without preamble, asked 'Are you free tomorrow evening?'

She laughed, waved a folder at him. 'As usual!'

'Good. Got anything decent to wear? And I don't mean that cast-off Oxfam rubbish you go for, I mean decent as in attractive.' He frowned. 'Not that bloody purple thing with the decayed otter round the hem; and certainly not the dark green –' He stopped abruptly, hoping that she hadn't heard the last bit.

She hadn't. Looking interested, she asked 'Why? Where are we going?'

'Out to dinner. Il Finocchio. For nine o'clock.'

'May I know what the big occasion is?'

'Oh nothing,' airily, 'just dinner. You and me and Vito.'

18

Dark grey eyes at full stretch. Excitedly, 'Is this something to do with the Agency?'

'Not quite the way you think, darling, Vito's got a perfectly good manager already.'

He examined his fingernails. She wasn't going to like the next bit. Not at first. He looked at her warily. 'Vito dropped me a hint – a teensy weensy one – that a friend of his, a certain Spanish tenor, is not intending to renew his current manager's contract later this year. And Vito would like to sound us out, professionally speaking. Then he may – or may not – talk to this friend.'

'Who? Who is it?' Ez jumped up, her face full of light.

Bobby felt a little sorry for her now that the hook had been swallowed.

'Come on, who is it? God, is it Martes? Modesto Martes?'

'Your brains,' he said with deliberate emphasis, 'are on the same level as the neckline of your dark green dress.'

She stared. Then smiled. 'Dark green dress? What on earth made you remember that? Dear God, I haven't worn that since we went –' Horrified. 'Oh no! You don't mean Contreras!'

He almost wished that he didn't have to nod. Almost. He watched gleefully as the heart-shaped face slowly filled with a dark flush.

'None other. Dear old Pepe.' He pronounced it Paypay.

'Oh no, Bob!'

'Oh yes, Eliza! So, come on – what will you wear?'

She sat down abruptly. It had been Bobby's fault in the first place, the dark green dress. That, and the brooch.

*    *    *

The memories were vivid. The press reception had been at full swing when they eventually arrived and pushed their way through the crowd and flashing cameras. Their new star, Ulla Schinke, was laughing and tossing her hair, red with excitement.

'We're bloody late, I knew we would be, you and your damn fussing!' snapped Bobby Drach. 'This is supposed to be OUR reception, we should've been here long before that German canary appeared!'

Ez stood on tiptoe, looking for the eminences. There should have been four of them, including the hazel-eyed *Fraülein* Schinke, breathtakingly soprano and one of the Drach Agency's well-nurtured protegées; snatched from a low-key production at Glyndebourne by the lordly director of Decca, Byron Larch, and with the Agency's blessing, now contracted to sing in Verdi's *Requiem* at the Royal Festival Hall, with three international names.

'It's not my fault!' waving to various acquaintances. 'You chose the damn dress, not me!' She felt her heel catch yet again in the hem.

'Wear the dark green silk, Ezita,' peering in her wardrobe. 'I know it's cut very low and you don't wear a bra to boost it up a bit, and why should you, after all? Why put a couple of little poached eggs in a roasting-pan? OUCH! . . . don't hit Bobby, not while he's thinking . . . .Hah! Got it! Drach to the rescue!'

And the following day, he had triumphantly slapped a small box on her desk. The box was elderly, and had a torn corner. The name "Harrods" slanted in faded gold across the lid. She opened it warily. Inside, beneath a layer of lint, lay a brooch. She didn't gasp with pleasure.

Prodded it. 'What is this?' coldly.

'A brooch. For your dress, duckie. Like it?'

She lifted it from its nest. It didn't sparkle or glitter. It lay in the palm of her hand: a very large flower with six petals and a centre, dull silver with a few black streaks of age.

She started to giggle. 'It's bloody awful! I'm not putting this thing on!'

Then Bobby had looked sad, lowering his head, saying quietly 'It belonged to a very special lady, Ez. My auntie Janey,' which had stopped her giggles somewhat but not the doubts. 'It's bloody ugly!' Then, seeing his bowed head, 'Well . . .' She turned it over. 'The pin's bent!'

'I can straighten that for you!' he snapped.

Well, she sighed, as everyone waited for the three famous singers to appear, he'd done his best. She could feel it bobbing awkwardly against her cleavage, two of the sharp petals harassing her skin.

Then loud applause and shouts as the French soprano, Bo Lehatz, finally appeared. Behind her, the American bass Lemuel Doe, chiselled white Apache face, mane of famous hair. Bo Lehatz scowling viciously as another man joined them.

'That's Pepe Contreras,' Bobby whispered, nudging her.

She had heard his Christmas album, made, so it was said, against his manager's better judgement. Bobby had bought a copy as a joke, and insisted on playing it in his sanctum on Christmas Eve.

'This is operatic culture at its finest,' he informed the staff. 'Christ Almighty, I've heard things sung better by half-pissed Greeks at funerals. Just listen to that effortless bleating, children! Sing-along-a-Paypay . . .'

Trying to ignore the petals of her brooch, Ez looked at the Spanish tenor as he dodged around smiling, greeting, waving. Thick black hair, eyes with heavy lids, a hooked nose. He was touching Ulla Schinke's arm, introducing her to someone.

'Come on,' said Bobby testily, 'let's get into the fucking limelight before that sallow-skinned git snatches it all.'

At the reception afterwards, drink in hand and bonhomie rampant, Bobby submitted beamingly to interviews, told Ez to circulate discreetly, and was now engaged in serious conversation with Byron Larch. Larch wore a denim suit, and Bobby was interested in the stitching. He caught up with her just as she was approaching a noisy knot of males, which included the Spanish tenor. He was telling some kind of anecdote, gesturing dramatically. Then the group exploded into appreciative laughter, and Contreras flung out his arm, laughing with them.

Bobby said 'Right, one more gin and tonic, then we can push off.'

Ez stayed where she was. Her breathing stopped, then resumed with shallow caution.

'Come on! What's the matter, do you need a piss or something?'

She said nothing. He peered at her white face. 'Ezita?' Put out a hand.

'Don't touch me!' biting her lips, hard. Then 'Bobby . . .' A whisper, and still motionless, '. . . the pin.'

'Eh? What pin?'

'The brooch pin.' A slim hand gingerly clutched his sleeve. Her eyes, dark and swimming, focused on a small trickle of blood. 'Bobby, the pin came loose −'

The silly mare's going to pass out, he thought. 'Ezita, don't make a bloody fuss here, come and sit down!' Jesus!

'The pin!' Her eyes swivelled to his face. 'It's gone right into my −'

He followed the slight distraught gesture of her hand.

'Oh sodding Christ!' Agitated, 'Can't you pull it out?'

'I daren't, it's already bleeding, it might spurt out all over the place.' A quick nervous sob.

'How the fuck did it happen? It was alright a moment ago!' His voice had risen hysterically. Contreras and the man next to him turned round.

Ez mumbled dizzily, 'Mr Contreras threw out his hand and it hit the brooch, I told you the pin wasn't safe!'

Pepe Contreras looked at them both, his eyes going to the clutched cleavage. He asked politely, 'Is there something of wrong?'

'Wrong?' screeched Bobby. 'Yes, there is something of wrong! You have seriously wounded the lady, you clumsy −'

'Bobby . . .' faintly.

'Sorry? I have what?'

'Why the hell don't you watch what you're doing? I only hope someone can get it out pretty damn quick before she bleeds to death! Is there a sodding doctor in this mob?'

Ez saw a pair of brown eyes which were out of focus. Several interested people were now closing in on them. 'Bobby, just get me away from −'

Growing concern, 'But what is it that I have done?'

Bobby took a deep breath. 'Her brooch,' he said loudly. 'You flung out your bloody arm and knocked the pin right inside her −' He cupped his chest on the left hand side. 'Savvy?'

'*Dios mío*! Here, *Señor* Drach, let me −'

And she heard nothing, just a buzz and someone saying 'Oh dear!'

Afterwards, at home, memory hazy, she lay on her old settee

22

with Bobby trying to tip Amontillado into her mouth.

'Say again, Roberto,' she begged weakly, 'You mean that he actually −?'

Bobby nodded. 'In a quiet room, though, very private.'

She struggled to sit up, the gauze and wadding already beginning to come adrift.

'Bugger the quiet and private room! Did he or did he not take off my dress?'

'Well. Nearly.'

'What do you mean − nearly?' It was a shout.

Bobby winced. 'He slipped the top part down over your shoulders so that he could get to the pin . . .'

'And where the hell were you?'

'Holding his jacket. It's alright,' he added hastily. 'He didn't see much. He just removed the brooch and put his handkerchief over your tit. Then the doctor came.'

She began to howl quietly.

\* \* \*

Now, she began to laugh. Bobby looked relieved, slapped his knee. 'After all, it was nearly two years ago. After all the tits he's seen, he's not likely to remember one little flat one, is he?'

A cushion flew. 'Well now,' rubbing his plump hands, 'how about a drop of something stronger, to wish ourselves luck tomorrow? Got anything in the sideboard?'

'Mmmm? Oh. Yes, there's some dry sherry, I think.'

He bent down, peered in the cupboard.

'Christ!' He pulled out the bottle and held it up to the light. 'What vintage is this? Nineteen hundred and Noah's Ark? It looks like bloody vegetable oil.'

He screwed off the cap and sniffed cautiously. Enraged, he shook it.

'What were you keeping this for, a suicide attempt?'

She giggled. 'Let's try it, anyway. It was a very expensive bottle,' lamely.

'The bottle may well have been. It's the liquid inside that bothers me.'

23

The sherry gave a loud cluck and began to trickle reluctantly down the neck.

Bobby handed her a glass, quarter full. 'You first,' he said. 'I want to see what happens!'

Smiling, Ez said 'Here's to Vito Lavagna!'

An answering grin. 'And luck to the Drach Agency!'

# 2

Funeral. Hot. So hot.

With relief, she walked into the cool length of the room, her detached feelings seeing again the white walls and wide shuttered windows, the mosaic of the floor and its splatter of green rugs. Not one out of place. As always. A perfect setting for formal occasions. Polite and interested silence in the alcoves, one of which contained a black crucifix. Shining tamed plants in tubs, freshly sprayed that morning, the earth smelling strong. And one token ashtray, black like the crucifix.

Judit slowly removed her gloves.

Funeral.

The day of. One of the half-open shutters let in a small breeze collected from the density of trees beyond the balcony.

Pepe followed her slowly, his dark jacket hooked over one shoulder.

'Thanks for coming,' he said, and dropped the jacket onto the gold tapestried sofa. She looked at him, thought of taking off her hat but didn't.

'I was glad to,' she said matter-of-factly. Dear Lord, she thought, he looks so tired.

Dear Lord, he thought, how long is she going to stay. He sucked on his bottom lip, the movement pulling at his flesh and making his eyes larger and sadder.

'A drink, perhaps?'

Judit nodded, and he walked over to the lacquered cabinet below the crucifix.

'Vodka?'

'No. No thanks. Perrier, please,' smiling as he turned slightly to look at her over his shoulder.

'Things are different now,' she added lightly, and sat down on the sofa, automatically picking up his jacket and folding it neatly.

Frowned inside, knowing that black didn't suit her in spite of green eyes and pale hair that looked like watery sun.

He handed her the drink. 'Thanks for coming,' he said again. 'We appreciate it.'

Irritation flared, and she held it back with difficulty.

We. The corporate We. Pepe, Alfredo, *Papá* Gualterio. And, of course, until her death, María Magdalena.

The conglomerate We. Anyone else, including Judit, once wife of Pepe, mother of all his stillborn children, was hardly ever given a union card. Except Mina, of course, Alfredo's wife. Smug limpet. Damned living children, both boys. Healthy.

She kept her voice soft. 'It was a shock. When Alfredo rang, I couldn't understand what he was trying to say to me.'

Pepe finished his whisky, looked at his watch. And then voices in the vast hall echoing, loudest of all that of Gualterio, the family patriarch. A throat full of gravel and phlegm as usual. Judit tensed, carried her glass to the lacquered cabinet and refilled it. Tried to resist the vodka, poured it carefully into the Perrier.

Several dark-clad people came through the archway into the sitting room, all talking at once, one cousin sinking on to the first chair she saw, sighing and rubbing her ankles. Two maids hovered, one with frizzy braids, the other with two hair-clips and a busy face.

'Pepe!' Gualterio nearly always roared. If he lowered his voice at all, it became a mutter hard to hear. 'Isn't it time you and Josep were off?'

Pepe smiled, nodded, joined the group of mourners with the smile frozen. His father scowled across the room at Judit.

She thought: María Magdalena Contreras. Dead skin and bones in a box. Aged forty-seven, unwed, quite ordinary. Had a part share in a dressmaker's shop. Her swift needle used as much at home as it was in the narrow premises in Barcelona. Unofficial mother to the family. Unknown, except to them and a few friends. Or rather, had been until a Spanish newspaper decided to get a different slant on her famous brother's life by interviewing the plain modest sister.

They had found in Magda an uncompromising sweetness of nature and a closeness of mouth. She was also extremely un-

26

photogenic, which didn't endear her to the *prensa amarilla*, nor did they take kindly to her uninteresting life. It was sad that the only photograph they had published showed two black moles on her hand. Of course, no-one had known then that this was to be the birth of others, the skin cancer that killed her.

Judit felt the vodka easing her throat muscles, and risked a glance of scorn at her former father-in-law. She knew that he enjoyed referring to her as "my ex-daughter", sometimes rubbing his hands gleefully as though he'd removed a dead fly from the window sill. Bastard, her look said. Arrogant sagging-skinned bastard. Sixty-five now, and still with the sense of humour of a silly child.

Pepe was nibbling a polite sandwich, talking to a red-eyed cousin. She saw him look again at his watch, but discreetly, out of his cousin's vision. The cousin wasn't bothering to wipe her tears away. He nodded and shook his head as if listening intently to the sobbed memories.

Judit's drink was nearly finished. She gently eased a little more vodka into the glass, but made sure that bubbles of mineral water could still be seen.

She didn't see Gualterio glance in her direction and nod briskly to his eldest son. A hand fell on her arm.

Pepe's brother Alfredo. Oddly like him in looks. She tried to picture this industrial chemist in stage make-up, groaning dramatically over a new blackhead spoiling the beauty of his profile. Her snort was muffled. Mina had not, obviously, been able to convince him about his haircut either. *De estilo erizo*, the family called it. Hedgehog-style. Short bristles, some prematurely grey.

'Hello again,' she said pleasantly. 'It went well, don't you think? Quiet. Just as dear Magda would have wished. I'm only amazed that the press didn't turn up for the occasion!'

Alfredo Contreras made sure that she knew he was gripping her arm for a purpose, but said politely, 'Josep issued a statement to *La Vanguardia* and *El País* a few moments ago, when it was over.'

He delicately removed the glass from her hand. Not unkindly, he suggested that she said her farewells. Josep and Pepe had a plane to catch.

Judit frowned. 'Plane?'

'They're going to Italy for a couple of days. For a break, you understand.'

*     *     *

A holiday, he thought. A small break to reassemble himself. Then rehearsals would begin. Another *Traviata*. A pity it wasn't the *Requiem*. It would have been a second epitaph for Magda.

His travel bag was ready, just her photograph to add to it, that and his Vick inhaler. There was already one small likeness of his sister in his wallet, which he called his mascotograph; taken on her nineteenth birthday, her hair already knotted at the back, thick eyebrows poised on the edge of yet another household worry.

He kissed the larger photograph, borrowed from the family album, tucked it inside the bag. Magda. Not only had she been his guiding force, not only had she sat up long into the nights patiently writing out chunks of libretto and copying bars of music in her neat hand ('You see, Pepecito . . . here . . . and here . . . are the ideas you had yesterday, now you can see them and judge'), not only had she consulted tirelessly with tailors, ensured proper diet and throat exercises ('It doesn't matter how late or early it is, how bored you become'); not only those things, he thought now, but also the biggest thing of all. And he went still.

Magda hadn't known or understood a single note of music. An occasional tuneless murmur in church, or tapping her fingers to some melody in her mind as she waited for the iron to heat up; and she could tell the difference between a viola and a violin if they stood side by side. And there the sister of Contreras reached her limits.

Jaw clenched, Pepe zipped the bag. At least his father wouldn't be alone; Alfredo would be there, and Mina and their two boys. For himself, two or three days in Vito's home, peace and understanding. Some untaxing music, a few old friends. Shorts and Campari. Silliness, like too much wine and trying to shin up the malevolent palm tree by the terrace, and Vito's wife noisily encouraging every painful scrape on the rough bark.

And then there was Josep to sort out. He supposed he should

feel guilty, thinking of Josep in this way. He shrugged, dropped the inhaler into one of the pockets of the bag. Josep Gusano.

Josep. Cautious and fussy. As old as Gualterio. Fussy friend, fussy manager. I don't advise the Rossini – La Scala had trouble with that director last year. I have consulted with Decca, and if you go ahead with that Puccini album, I can foresee disaster. Fussy.

Pepe was beginning to crave a new head, new ideas. Fresh slants without "your career will suffer" writ large on a staid forehead. A new man would be just as loyal as Josep Gusano. With the money they got out of him, it was guaranteed.

He grabbed the bag, leaving his dark suit and shirt for Ana to collect later. Closed the door of his hideaway and walked quickly along the tunnel to the main house. The door opened at the far end, Alfredo coming to help, late as usual.

'Only one bag, *hombre?*' taking it from him.

'Isn't it shocking, and me going off on a world cruise.'

A thump on the shoulder. 'Sure you've got everything? Wallet, fly-spray, spare set of genitals?'

Pepe snorted. Alfredo followed him into the hall, deliberately swung the bag behind his brother's knees.    'If you bloody well do that again –!'

The brothers smiled at each other. Gualterio, on his third cognac, boomed 'About time, *coño!* Josep's got the cab!'

Alfredo winked at Pepe. 'Oh, is it catching?' Schoolboy sniggers.

'Stupid buggers! When are you due back here?'

'Monday. Probably quite late.' The laughter over, he added 'Will you be okay?'

Gualterio eyed him. 'We'll be okay.' An embarrassed choke that left a blob of spittle on his lip. 'Too bloody noisy round here for us to be anything else, damn kids all over the place.'

Alfredo said in his ear, 'Gently does it, *hombre*. Rest yourself, okay?'

Josep Gusano was anxiously waiting in the taxi. 'The plane leaves in just over an hour,' he fussed. 'You've cut it fine.'

The taxi had been Josep's idea. The private car with Moncho driving was too well-known.

29

'Yes, I know,' Pepe said evenly. 'The delay was due to my sister's funeral.'

He hadn't intended the sarcasm, for Josep had loved Magda too. But now, with the past months of her fading from them and this day merging together, his mind was a battleground. Hot sun, a mass of large flowers, prayers, mourning cards, her abandoned outdoor shoes, the tempting vision of Vito's villa.

Josep said 'Sorry, Pepe.' Fidgeted with his briefcase.

The taxi curved its way through the outskirts of the city. They went past the dressmakers' shop where Magda had worked for so many years, the same place to where he had nervously gone one evening so that she could take him to his first singing lesson with *Señora* Capall. He was glad to see that the shutters were closed: a black ribbon fluttered on the door.

Josep was talking, the sound of a bee trying to find pollen. Bologna, next March, two performances not one, yes next March, haven't you been listening.

Pepe frowned. His mind itched. Another project to think about, a new one, of which Josep knew nothing. Money, basically. Money that could be used. In Magda's name. Last night, he had thought about it for over two hours. He would talk to his father and brother, when he returned home from Italy.

He closed his eyes and allowed Josep to see to the rest of the day.

\*       \*       \*

Vito Lavagna, in his maroon silk dressing robe, picked up his wristwatch from the coffee table and squinted at it.

He was obliged to.

The watch was an American import into Europe, the entire face showing a map of the world. It was difficult to read the time from it, especially when the minute hand was suspended over New Zealand. More especially, Vito detested the constant TV adverts announcing its arrival in the Community, with the wristwatches dancing round to a voice-over by that fat Italian idiot, Pio Fazzoletto. *Nessun* bloody *Dorma*. Ruined it for every other tenor.

Vito's American wife had bought it for him in a rush of

homesickness. He looked at it again. Was that half-past six or half-past Atlantic Ocean? The salon clock had stopped: and after the recent press conference, only a waiter remained in the suite, clearing the debris.

'Excuse me!' Vito gave his public smile. 'Do you happen to have the right time?'

'Awfully sorry, sir, I don't wear a wristwatch on duty.'

That figured.

He would take a chance. It certainly felt like half-past six. If it was, Pepe should be there by now. Should be showered and rested and lying on Vito's favourite recliner on the terrace. Keta would be fussing over him, perhaps the radio was at his side, softly on. Pepe was reasonably fluent in Italian. Fluent, but sometimes inattentive, with a tendency to pronounce the Italian 'z' as a Spanish 'th'. Pepe himself averred that his great grandmother had once been attacked by an Italian kitten, and that this had engendered an hereditary neurosis.

Vito touched his blonde moustache, gave it a thoughtful rub. Checked the dialling code. Picked up the phone. The cigar in the ashtray oozed blue smoke into the sunlight. It had stopped raining at last. Very nice if you were a flowerbed, he thought. Sometimes he wished he was, or at least something equally stationary.

Travelling was beginning to make him remember his birthdays. Christ, Lavagna, you'll soon be sixty-four! He shuddered, heard his phone in Turin begin to ring.

He smiled broadly. 'Hello? Keta?'

His wife's light voice answered with a pleased 'Hi, Baby! How are you?'

'Mighty fine, honey!' imitating her accent. 'Is he there, darling?'

'Large as life, prone on the sunbed, wearing your shorts.'

'Tell the parsimonious bastard to go buy his own! And how is my little Keta coping?'

'Vee, you don't cope with Pepe, you just pat him on the head, tell him he's looking as handsome as a day-old dog, and then tank him up with Chianti! I'm missing you – will you be home tomorrow?'

'God and the Holy Alitalia willing. I've got quite an interesting evening planned here, by the way, something to do with Pepe.

31

Give him a yell, sweetheart, I need a word with him. I'll speak to you later.'

'Okay!' and he heard her call to their guest. 'On his way,' she said softly. 'He's awful tired, Vee; losing Magda has hit him real hard.'

No time to re-light his cigar before Pepe picked up the phone. '*Ciao*, Lavagna!'

'*Muy buenas tardes*, Contreras! How did it go, old friend?'

A small thoughtful pause. Then 'Oh . . . you know . . .' Embarrassed laugh. 'I'm not used to real-life tragedies. Kept expecting Magda to come in and soothe all thc weeping relatives. Anyway, thanks for this interlude, *amigo*.'

'Don't mention it. Which reminds me, did I hear my wife correctly? Are you wearing a pair of my shorts?'

A snigger. 'I'm trying to! What were they originally, spare curtains?'

'Unlike you and others I could mention,' acidly 'I don't believe in advertising. I like my balls to breathe, thank you.'

Laughter. 'And did Keta also tell you that she's given me free rein with your 1970 Chianti?'

'My sympathy has its limits, songbird! By the way, how's Don Josep?'

A groan shivering down the line. 'Still fussing. Keta showed him to his room and he's been holed up there ever since. He's off to Bologna tomorrow, *gracias a Dios*. Christ, Vito, it's like being in a straitjacket! I keep thinking, roll on October when his contract runs out; and then I have to stop and wonder – who next? What then?'

'*Momento, amico*, keep my shorts dry.' Vito rubbed his moustache again, briefly wondered if the hair conditioner was really doing it good. He said grandly, 'Do you know, I may be able to help you with that little problem.'

Hopefully, 'You're going to kill him?'

'Not worth the bullet, old dear. No, I've recently run into an old chum of mine from, oh years ago; having dinner with him tonight, as a matter of fact. You know him, I think, or at least know of his Agency. He did say something about having met you a couple of years ago. Robert Drach.'

'Hang on . . . the name rings a bell . . . Two years ago? Can't recall what that was about, but . . . Oh shit, of course, the Drach Agency! Ulla Schinke! God yes . . . You say he's a friend of yours? I've heard it said that Drach is very pushy and persuasive when it comes to grabbing out-of-the-ordinary engagements for his clients!'

'And vice versa! He's just signed the Rossini-mad Kaffner and promptly shoved him into the *Dream of Gerontius!*'

They chortled together nastily. 'You say you're seeing him when?'

'This evening. A quiet dinner, with him and his partner.' He coughed. 'I may as well come clean, Pepe. I did outline your problem – in the vaguest terms, of course – when we were chatting the other day. He's interested, as far as it goes.'

'Shit, Vito, I'll have to think about this. What I know of him is good, excellent. A bit eccentric, perhaps, but after Josep . . . Look, *amigo* – sound him out further . . .'

A pause. Vito could imagine him tapping his fingers on Keta's brown address book by the phone.

'Vito? . . . Like I say, talk to him about it by all means, then when you get here we can have a chat, and I'll maybe try to fix up a meeting with him when I return to Barcelona. Okay?'

Pepe scored his thumbnail along the brown address book, then glanced at the terrace door, where Keta was signalling. 'Vito, Keta wants a word with you.' He grinned into the phone. 'I think she's going to tell you that Fazzoletto is arriving later this evening . . . .' He heard a rude noise from London, and sniggered.

Vito squawked 'Pio? Arriving where, for Christ's sake?'

Pepe bowed to Keta who scowled at him. He said, 'Arriving here, *amico*. Don't worry, I expect he'll bring his own shorts! Here's Keta – see you tomorrow. And thanks.'

He wandered back to the terrace, his sister resurfacing painfully after the interlude. A fresh bottle of Chianti had been opened, and he poured steadily.

Carried the glass of wine to the balustrade. Through the thick leaves of the fig trees and the malevolent palm, he could see clear sections of fast-dusking sky.

Sipped. Raised his glass.

*A ti*, Magda. *A ti*.

*   *   *

Bobby was waiting for her outside the restaurant. The brisk damp wind had scooped his hair sideways. He spoke to the taxi driver, handed him something.

'The tip, darling, the tip!' he hissed, taking her arm. 'What did you intend paying him with – your body?'

'Good evening, Robert,' pleasantly.

Il Finocchio, although a restaurant of elegance and expensive seclusion, had one drawback. The cocktail bar was situated in the basement of the property next door, and could only be reached from the street outside, a descent of several worn stone steps.

Ez and Bobby negotiated them into the faint sound of chamber music. It was a small curved room with framed tapestries of herbs on the walls, and no cooking smells. A darkly-suited man with a severe smile intercepted them.

'Excuse me, *signor*, do you have a reservation?'

'Guests of Mr Lavagna,' Bobby intoned grandly. 'The name's Drach.'

'Ah yes, of course, sir.' The smile was carefully prised apart. He consulted a grey book connected by a chain to his wrist. 'For nine o'clock. Gioacchino!' Snap of fingers.

A young man appeared with efficient daintiness. Ez handed over her cloak with relief, as did Bobby. It was warm in the bar.

They stared at each other. Bobby grimly ordered two sherries, and they sat down.

Ez giggled. 'Isn't blue a lovely colour?'

'You silly cow!' he hissed. 'Why didn't you tell me?'

'And spoil a lovely surprise?' Another snort. '*Grazie!*', beaming at the waiter.

'Thank you.' Bobby nodded stiffly to acknowledge his drink. 'The Bluebell Girls!'

'Behave yourself, you sound like a hysterical hen! Actually,' with a genteel sip from his glass, 'I think my shirt is slightly darker.'

'It's exactly the same!'

Bobby, in a similar midnight blue suit and pale blue silk shirt, smiled for the first time. 'Mine is better quality,' smugly. Then he leaned back, looking officious.

'Don't forget: when Vito arrives, no asking him damn-fool questions, no scribbling in that bloody notebook of yours, and no blurting out the circs under which you once met Contreras!'

'I'm not likely to do that, am I!' scornfully.

'I'm just saying, that's all. If you've got to look like a bloody golliwog, at least try to be a well-behaved one.'

'Am I allowed to speak to him at all?'

'Occasionally. I shall ring my little bell at the appropriate moments.' They grinned at each other. Then Bobby frowned suddenly, pointed his finger. 'What's that bloody mess on your face again?' He dabbed at the dried mascara traces with a serviette dampened in the sherry. 'Are you using a vibrator when you put your make-up on? Christ Al-bloody-mighty!'

The stern major domo appeared at their table. Allowed himself a smile of courtesy.

'*Signor* Lavagna has arrived in the restaurant, sir. Perhaps you will permit Gioacchino to escort you both . . . ?'

'Certainly, certainly,' Bobby said graciously, and assisted Ez to her feet. 'Come along, infant. Lead on, Jokyonio!'

\* \* \*

It was almost half-past eight before Keta was able to rejoin him on the terrace. She sank into a basket-weave chair, gipsy skirt swirling, thonged sandals, red hair scooped back. 'Whew! That's Josep fed and my article written! You okay, *caro*?'

'Mmmmmm.'

The Chianti bottle was almost empty. She tipped the remaining drops into her own glass, raised it to the stars. 'Cheers!'

'Mmmmm.'

He was stretched out on the recliner, a blissful smile on his face. The portable radio was switched on, and one of his bare feet flicked up and down to the beat of the music.

'What's this you're listening to?' She reached for the knob, turned up the sound. His eyes closed, he groped for the Chianti.

35

She grinned, handed him the empty bottle.

'Thanks,' he murmured. '*Aida*. From Rome.'

'Damn it, I'd forgotten the broadcast was on this evening! How's it going? There's been one helluva stink about it in the papers. Imagine having huge wild animals in a theatre that size!'

'Camels and cheetahs,' he sniggered. 'Cherri sounds in good voice, the rest not far short of bloody awful. Bottle's empty!'

'Yes, sweetheart, and it's gonna stay that way until you've eaten! Pio shouldn't be long now.'

'He's exactly what I need at the – *Momentito*! What was that?'

Shouts from the radio, an excited presenter.

'I think he said –'

'Ssssh!'

'This is madness! This is sheer madness! *Dio mio*! Nunzio Natica has fallen . . . The gate of Thebes is beginning . . . oh my God! The orchestra is running, this is indescribable lunacy, the orchestra pit has been invaded . . . One of the cheetahs is now – oh my God! – two of the cheetahs are now –'

Pepe started to titter, upended the empty bottle, poured air into his glass.

Keta was listening enthralled.

'. . . still no news of Cherri de Canasta since she was taken to the . . . The producer is now appealing for calm . . .'

'Silly bugger,' murmured Pepe. 'Appealing for calm, with cheetahs going mad in the pit?'

'I wonder what happened to Cherri? Hope it's nothing bad,' Keta said. Shrieks continued to blast from the radio. Then another sound overrode them, bigger by far.

They automatically looked skywards.

A very low-flying helicopter, nose almost vertical, edging over the fig trees.

'Pio!' laughed Keta.

'Fazzoletto,' beamed Pepe, and waggled his glass at the sky.

# 3

'This is Dante's *Inferno*! This is the *Inferno*!'

Pepe turned down the volume of the excited little radio as Keta flew from the terrace. There came swirling sounds of laughter from the villa, noise erupting.

His foot caught the empty Chianti bottle, and he watched it spin slowly, frowning as faint strains of music once more emerged from the radio. For some reason, the beleaguered orchestra had returned and was now playing Mascagni's *Intermezzo*. . . . Mascagni? He scratched his chin. Verdi had obviously walked out of the theatre clutching his programme.

And then Pio Fazzoletto, a coloured avalanche in huge paint-smeared jeans and silk scarves, burst on to the terrace grinning through his beard and carrying a frayed plimsoll which he tossed in the air, throwing his arms wide with a shout

'Pulgarcito!'

'Sperm Bank!'

And they embraced, slapped hands, embraced again.

'Christ, it's good to see you!' and Pepe's smile was broad, delighted.

'Would I have missed the chance? Would I? Shit, you little bastard, you're looking tired! . . . KETA!' A roar. 'Where's the booze? My throat's as dry as a sixty-year old whore!'

He kicked off the remaining laceless plimsoll to join its fellow, crunching the wickerwork of a chair as he sat down. Placed his foot on the empty bottle. Keta, beaming, indicated to the hovering valet that La Scala was required. This was Vito's name for a massive drinks trolley, a converted eighteenth century sideboard. She then discreetly disappeared to supervise the removal of Pio's paraphernalia from the vestibule.

A silk square, crimson and white, slid from the cliff-size shoulders as he leaned forward without the grin. 'Well, how did it go? Everything peaceful as it should be?'

Pepe nodded, 'Thanks. Yes.'

A hand covered his own, squeezing hard. 'Adriana and I made a prayer together at the same time as the ceremony. She sends her love.'

'Thanks,' grateful and touched.

'Poor little girl. You'll miss her, *amico*.'

Pepe's lips pulled together. Said wonderingly, 'It hurts.' Then he jumped to his feet as La Scala rumbled on to the terrace.

The valet, Ferruccio, out of breath, announced that supper was prepared and would be delivered to the *signori* forthwith.

'*Bene!*' called Pio, and rubbed his hands gleefully. 'What are we having?'

'Chickens,' Pepe said without enthusiasm. 'Six of them.'

'Good, good! You not having anything, Pepe? Hey, Ferruccio, any gin in that temple?

'*Sì, Signor* Fazzoletto,' opening one of the doors. 'What would you like with it?'

'I'll have a large gin topped up with a medium gin, if you please!'

Pepe dived for the Bacardi as the radio once again rattled with shouts, 'The police are . . . !'' 'The cheetah seems to be . . . !' 'The *maestro* is not . . . !'

Pio guffawed. 'What's this, my friend? The Rome cock-up?' Then 'Shit, should've phoned Adriana the minute I arrived!'

'How is she?' Pepe smiled at his friend's look of newly-wed anxiety. Pio had been married for years, but his expression never changed.

'Fine, fine,' beaming. 'Only two months to go!' He extracted himself from the chair. 'Ke-TA! I need your phone, *pronto!*'

Pepe groaned. 'Dear God, how many will this be?'

Pio threw his head back, laughed in sheer delight. 'Six? Seven? I lose count, Adriana loses count, even the kids lose count, God be praised! . . . Back in two shakes of a priest's cock, *amico!*'

Pepe tittered to himself, levered up the ring-pull of a can of Coke. He heard another bellow, 'Keta! Phone, please, my little swan will be worried!'

Adriana, thought Pepe, lowering himself back on the recliner:

38

half as tall as Pio, sweet-faced, tough as an army corporal.

He lay back, watching the stars.

Was that Magda up there amongst them? He couldn't remember seeing the one on the left before. It certainly looked new.

*   *   *

During the meal, Vito asked 'Do you two always dress alike?' and smiled.

Ez was sipping his choice of wine thoughtfully, admiring the fresh fur deposits in her mouth and wondering why she had been wasting it all these years in her lavatory bowl and waste pipes.

Bobby sniffed but said magnanimously, 'Eliza does try to copy me, she admires my taste.'

'Especially in jewellery,' Ez said acidly.

'Jewellery?' Vito fingered his gold bracelet. 'My wife writes about jewellery, of the antique kind. She's a freelance journalist,' he added. 'You may have read some of her articles? Keturah Parker.'

Wife? Ez felt Bobby's toe on her ankle. Hiding her confusion, she said blandly and tactfully, 'Keturah Parker? I didn't realise that she was your wife, *Signor* Lavagna,' which was true enough.

She smiled, placed her hand over her wine glass as the bottle hovered above it. 'That's a fascinating name – Keturah. It's from the Bible, isn't it?'

'You may well be right. Not surprising,' laughing, 'my father-in-law was a preacher before his retirement.'

'Keturah,' Ez nodded. 'One of Abraham's wives. Book of Genesis.'

'Don't you know the chapter as well, dear?' Bobby asked sweetly.

'Twenty-five.'

He scowled.

Vito said, 'I had a word with Contreras this evening, by the way, Roberto, and –' He paused as the waiter uncorked a fresh bottle. 'Yes . . yes . . . that will do nicely, thank you . . .' Sipped, nodded. Continued 'Poor fellow, he's at a low ebb at the moment.

He lost his sister recently – the funeral was today.'

'That's sad,' they said together.

'Only forty-seven, poor girl. You could say that Magdalena took the place of the mother; two younger brothers to look after, you know. Pepe was six when his mother died, and Magda –' He smiled. 'She made a very devoted and energetic little mother to them both. So, poor Pepe has lost two people really, not simply a sister.'

Bobby looked sympathetic, trying to remember what it was like to have a mother, and only succeeded in recalling his own shouting at him 'No boy of mine is going out wearing my bloody lipstick! Buy your own!'

'However,' Vito said, 'that did not prevent us from discussing his future when his current contract with Josep Gusano runs out later this year. The snag is –' leaning forward '– that dear old Gusano is an old friend of the family. At college with Pepe's father. Been with the boy since his career began. But –' He sighed, gestured with his fork, 'Contreras needs change. Gusano is not only a man with a blindfold, but his ears are deaf. Pepe wants challenge. A repertoire to excite the mind. More recording work.'

Ez asked 'More recording? Like Modesto Martes?' And they all grinned.

Vito said 'Martes would record anything that bloody moved. Rumour has it that whenever he takes a bath, there's a sound engineer perched on the soapdish with a mike, just in case.'

He smiled benignly at the titters from his audience.

Bobby asked, 'So what happens now – regarding Contreras?'

'As I told you, he's resting at my villa for a couple of days before returning to Barcelona. I shall see him tomorrow, and I'll mention your suggestions and so on,' providing that Fazzoletto has buggered off, he added silently, 'Then I propose, if I may, Roberto, to give you a ring on Sunday evening and let you know how the land lies. If he wishes to pursue it further –' He shrugged lightly with a "don't blame me if he doesn't" smile, 'he will want to meet you and discuss the matter, of course.'

He looked at Ez. 'Have you ever met him, Miss Pepper?'

Ez ignored Bobby's snigger. 'Only once,' she said airily, 'and only briefly.'

After supper, Pio began to sing.

Pepe sniggered, and tried to balance the coke tins one upon the other. Pio asked 'Wha' doing tha' for?' then continued with *Celeste Aida.*

The cans fell over. 'Cher-ist! Won't stay up.'

The singing ceased. 'Mine does. Adriana hasn't complained, anyway.' Light giggles escaped through the beard.

Pepe frowned. Sat back on his haunches. 'Did they catch the sheetahs?'

'Wha' sheetahs?'

They uttered little whimpers. A nest of silk squares surrounded Pio's feet. His friend leaned over and began knotting them together. Gazed at the sky. Pio asked, drinking his gin, 'Did they say wha' happened to Cherri?'

'Nope. Jus' that she'd hurt her back an' wrist and was in a clinic.'

So we don't know wha' happened to her then.'

'Nope.'

They fell silent. The stars beat down through the fig trees. Inside the villa, there was music as Keta patiently waited for them to stagger to bed, and in the long meantime listened to Shostakovich.

'Pio?'

– three silk squares knotted so far and carefully laid in a line.

'Wha'?'

'Would you say that eggs were born?'

'Born? Where?'

'Not where. When. When they come out of the hen.'

'That is chickens,' firmly. 'Hey! Wha' the fuck are you doing to my scarves?'

'No, fat sod, chickens are inside the eggs.' He finished tying number four to its companions.

Pio reached for the bottle. 'Then,' he pronounced, 'that is called being born. Eggs are born!'

'*Vwan* eggs!'

'God bless'em!'

Keta stood by the terrace door, watching them drink toasts to eggs. Went towards the kitchen to superintend the coffee blender.

\*     \*     \*

Eve Tinker's bookshop was deserted.

Apart from Eve herself, that is, on her knees beside an open crate. The small shop was stuffy in the heat, dust particles gleaming and fading swiftly in the sunlight.

She had tried propping the door open, but the slightest breeze from the street made it squeak. The single shopfront window which yesterday had looked flatteringly clean and clear in the overcast weather, now looked smeared and misty.

Still kneeling, she ran a duster along the shelf she had made ready for the new consignment. Twice she sneezed, straight brown hair swinging.

The old-fashioned bells jangled.

Ez came in breathless, 'Hi, only me! God, it's hot,' and Eve without looking up said 'Hi', and swore as two of the new books refused to stand upright. Abandoning them, she struggled to her feet, wiped her hands on her jeans.

'Is this a social visit?' and disappeared into a tiny room and began filling the kettle. 'Tea? Coffee?'' she called.

'Yes, please. It's both – social and business.'

Eve peeked round the door. 'Yes please to what?'

Prowling round and peering at the bookshelves, Ez said 'To whatever it was you offered. Have you got any Spanish books?'

'Tea I offered, or coffee. Yes, there are some over there, by the Penguin placard.'

'Tea, please. What sort are they?'

Eve shrugged. 'Phrase books, your hundred best bullrings, how to deep-freeze octopus . . . something like that, anyway. Ages since I checked out that corner.' She returned to the kitchenette, muttered 'Come on!' to the kettle, found two cups. Ez pounced as Eve reappeared with a rose-patterned tray and the tea.

'Yip yip! You clever little bookseller, you!' and triumphantly brandished a fat and heavy dictionary. Delightedly, she dumped it at Eve's elbow.

'I'll take it,' she said grandly. 'Kindly charge it to my account.'

'You haven't got one!'

'Oh. Charge it to someone else's then.'

'Bloody idiot!'

As they sipped tea, Eve asked 'What's the dictionary in aid of? I thought you knew Spanish.'

'Rusty. Very rusty. Last time I studied it was when I was going out with Lewis. Remember him?'

'The one with the hat? Can't think what you saw in him, he'd got a nose like a bloody overflow pipe.'

Ez snorted. Then said, 'This is something to do with the Agency, I might need to brush up my vocabulary in a hurry. This tea is foul! How's Clair, by the way?'

Clair was sixteen years old, the daughter of Eve.

Eve sighed, wagged her hands wearily. 'Oh . . . you know. Keen on everything that costs a lot of pennies.' She brightened. 'That reminds me – she wants you to do some more embroidery for her, if you've got the time. She's bought a new t-shirt, wants a fancy slogan or something on the back. Would you?'

'Tell her, no problem.' She crammed her purchase into her shoulderbag and hoisted it off the counter. 'And it won't cost you any pennies!'

The doorbells jangled as Ez stepped happily into the street which smelled of next door's fresh bread.

*     *     *

It hadn't all gone according to plan.

The day had started off well enough. Vito had spent the flight to Italy happily perusing his worn libretto for *L'Elisir d'Amore*, re-reading his pretentious margin notes from years ago, shaking his head in amusement. Then Gaetano had been waiting for him at the airport, ready to whisk him home to Keta. The Ferrari had been cleaned and briskly polished, a new flag fluttering on the bonnet.

43

And, as he entered his vast seraphimmed hall, he could smell coffee freshly perking and a hint of something gently cooking with herbs. Oregano he could detect above all.

'I think I shall drop a line to the Prime Minister,' he smiled, his arm around Keta's shoulders. 'Alitalia was bang on schedule!'

'Which Prime Minister, Baby?' kissing his cheek, 'There've been at least two new ones since you left on Monday!'

'A-ha! Thought I recognised the baggage-handler! And you –' holding her at arms' length, 'are looking good!'

'So are you, darling. Nice and relaxed.'

'It's been a pleasant few days,' he admitted, reflecting that the nights had been good, too. He peered past her. 'Where's Pepe?'

Keta smiled. 'Where do you think? With Pio. They're having a game of ping-pong on the terrace.'

He scowled briefly. 'I'll just have a quick shower before I say hello. How is he – Pepe?'

'Relaxing,' she laughed. 'Letting it all hang loose!'

'God!'

And he ascended the sweep of staircase smiling to himself.

Good to be back. He soaped himself with vigour, relishing the familiar smell of natural perfumed warmth in the room around him. He had already showered twice since his companion had left the hotel suite in the Dorchester. Water ran into his smiling mouth. God, the things you could do with a hairbrush and comb! He regretted not asking the man's name.

Towelling himself dry, he found that he was humming *Nessun Dorma* under his breath. Fuck that! Bad enough knowing that Fazzoletto was bouncing around on the expensive Grecian tiles downstairs, without bringing his bloody aria into the bathroom.

Good enough guy, though. In small doses and preferably at a distance. Pio tended to fill a room like a giant colourful plant. Small doses, that was the thing.

He dropped the towel on the floor, unscrewed the cap from his new skin revitalizer and gently massaged the liquid into the numerous body creases, tapping the flat stomach with pride. *L'Elisir d'Amore*, his next engagement. As Nemorino. Young peasant boy.

44

On with a youthful shirt and cotton slacks, final glance in the mirror. A quick nod, and then he was ready to sally forth to the table tennis tournament on the terrace. And tournament it would be, for Pio. Went through life expecting rosettes and bloody banners. Good enough guy, though.

As he emerged from the cool peace of the villa, a white ball whipped past him, and Pio's thunderous chuckle and terminating squeak echoed, followed by 'That's the one, *coño*! Beat that!' and he jigged from foot to foot like a child.

Pepe had a towel round his neck, and he was laughing.

'Hi!' called Vito, the ball spinning between his feet.

'Hi, Bum Lover!' cried Pio.

Pepe hid his face in the towel, but he was still grinning as he dropped it on a chair and headed across the terrace, hand outstretched.

'Welcome back, Lavagna! Good trip? Keta says you had good reviews, in spite of your pianist!'

'Carlatti's a fine musician,' protested Vito, shaking hands, trying not to scowl at Pio who was smiling jovially. He had a noisy smile, too, he thought sourly. The greeting had rankled.

'He would be,' from Pio, clapping him briskly on the back, 'if they took his piano away! Christ, when he plays a trill, it sounds like a JCB lifting concrete!'

Keta slipped nimbly between them. 'Drinks, boys? Or coffee?'

The table tennis players suddenly remembered that they were hot, exhausted and parched, and sank on to the sunloungers with dramatic groans.

'A long long long Bacardi,' pleaded Pepe, legs sprawled, a fresh graze on his knee. Adding 'With iced Coke, iced lemon, iced straw and iced ice . . .' and started laughing again.

Vito stared at him. Pepe caught his eye and his tittering grew until he had to clutch his stomach. Pio's head was in his hands, shoulders heaving, sounds of spasmodic tweets.

Keta put a sympathetic arm around her husband's waist. 'Drink, Vee? Pay no attention to these bums; they've been like this since yesterday.'

'S. . .sorry,' gasped Pepe, eyes brimming, as Pio uttered a high whine and slid from his perch.

'Something funny?' asked Vito, patting Keta's hand as she passed him a Campari and soda. He watched, a disbelieving schoolmaster, as Pio thumped the ground with his fist.

'Just two kids, Baby. Call it relaxing.' She added in a whisper, 'Pepe's so much better today, Pio's done him good.'

'Has he!' Vito's voice was sour. 'When's he going back to dear little Mother Earth? Goodness me, he hasn't become a father for at least nine months! Is he getting bored with it?'

'Shut up, you idiot! Adriana's pregnant – I told you!'

'God, that's wonderful!' viciously. Stared at the recumbent howling monster on the terrace. Shuddered. 'Poor cow!'

'Vito!' A sharp tap on the hand. Then, 'He's leaving us before dinner, darling. His pilot's picking him up around seven.'

Ah. Yes. Pio's new toy. The helicopter. It was painted blue and gold, and reminded Vito of a Fabergé egg.

'What a bloody shame,' he murmured.

'Hey, Vito!' Pepe called. 'You want to hear the news from Roma?'

Vito sauntered over, noting subconsciously the good-shaped bare legs, the sports shirt clinging to damp muscles. With full awareness, however, he also noted the body of Pio. It had elected to remain on the tiled floor with its back propped against a low wall, its splayed feet displaying disgusting plimsolls. Its hand held a tumbler raised to the sun, whisky and lemonade twinkling and glaring into Vito's dark glasses.

He sat down tidily in the nearest chair, took out his cigar case.

Pio's hand shot out. A finger beckoned.

'Would you care for a cigar, old friend?' sarcastically.

'*Grazie*. How noble!'

'So – what news from Rome?' lighter clicking, glancing at Pepe. Pepe was rubbing the graze on his knee. 'Eh?'

'News from Rome, you said.'

'Did I? Ouch, this is bloody sore! Keta, have you got anything I could rub on it?'

Pio grinned over his drink, burped loudly. 'What the feather-brained Miss Contreras meant was – last night, Zero fiddled while Roma burned!'

'You mean Nero,' Pepe, looking up from his kneecap.

46

Pio sniggered. 'Fiddlesticks!' and uttered a delighted roar. 'Get it? Fiddlesti–'

Pepe's foam rubber cushion hit him full force. 'Shit, be careful of my belly, there's an innocent child in there!'

Pepe cackled.

Vito closed his eyes. Then, with restrained venom, 'What happened in Rome?'

'*Aida* did.'

'Yes, thank you, Contreras, I know *Aida* was on there. Any more news?'

The two tenors continued with their mirth. Unperturbed dragonflies hovered above the carafe of iced water.

Keta said smoothly, 'The performance was a shambolic mess, darling.'

'You mean there really was a fire?' horrified.

'No, no, that was Pio being silly. It seems that one of the cheetahs was a female on heat –'

Pio uttered a lascivious growl, licking his lips.

'Shut it!' barked Vito. 'So, what happened?'

'What the fuck do you think happened?' hooted Pio. His large plimsolled foot hooked itself round Pepe's ankle. 'Hey, Pepita, get on all fours and I'll show him what that naughty boy-cheetah did!'

Keta continued, unblinking, 'The scenery was destroyed, and poor Cherri was taken to the clinic with a nasty back injury, Natica had cuts to his head, eight policemen were –'

'Any other members of the cast hurt?' His voice was sharp.

'The gate of Thebes came down on some of the Ethiopian slaves, and several had to be treated in hospital –'

Louis. Was that why there had been no answer when he rang this morning? Oh dear Christ.

Keta looked at him steadily, with sympathy. 'None of them was badly hurt,' she said, and touched his hand gently.

\* \* \*

'You want to start what?'

Vito, syphoning soda into the fresh orange juice, turned to stare at the guest who was his friend.

47

Pepe smiled. He had showered away the Bacardi and table tennis, dropped the borrowed shorts into a linen basket, and was now stretched at ease in his favourite black jeans and black shirt, savouring the wide leather armchair and the quietness of Vito's den.

Amidst the Florentine splendour of the villa, this room was plain and dark brown, an oasis in rugged lamplight. Pepe remembered how Judit had hated it, preferring instead the Italian renaissance cherubs and gilded joys of the rest of the house. He remembered, too, the copycat cherubs she had tried to import into their own family home: the fury of his father, 'Get them out of here! Nothing but irreligious little buggers covering their gnat-sized nothings with dimpled fingers!' And, seeing her flushed rage, 'If you like babies so much, try producing fat living ones of your own! Get your bloody womb seen to!'

Winced now at the memory of the subsequent frantic hands clutching him at night and her breath stinking of Gualterio's brandy. Quickly he leaned forward to pick up the glass of orange juice, his shirt riding out of the waistband.

'A research foundation for skin cancer,' he repeated quietly, and cocked an eyebrow at Vito.

The clock on the mantelshelf began to chime softly in B minor.

'Alfredo and I,' he continued, 'read up everything we could find on the disease. He knows more about the scientific facts that I do; but what I *can* do about it is to provide money for research into it. It would be for Magda, the foundation, and in her name. And, *amigo*,' smiling now, 'in order to do this, I need many more appearances, different venues, than Josep Gusano is prepared to give. I have to spread my wings, to publicize the Fund. Vito, I'm forty years old, and I'm not going to achieve my goal if I allow myself to get stuck forever with neat recitals, *Traviata* and bloody *Carmen*! I need, in other words, Robert Drach. My thoughts are now very clear on this. With Josep, I feel like a rented robot. With Drach, somehow, I don't think I'd get the chance!'

Vito laughed. 'To judge from what they were saying during our dinner together, you most certainly wouldn't!'

They grinned across the lamplight. 'So – what's his partner like? Young, old, what?'

'Mid-thirties, I'd say . . . hard to tell. Bright, as full of curiosity as a magpie. Name's Eliza. Eliza Pepper.'

A snigger. 'Pardon me?'

'Pepper. As in *pimiento*, old boy.'

'Name doesn't ring any bells,' and he sipped his drink, lost in thought. Probably one of the pastel-frocked brigade who had petrifying urges to bring Puccini to the people, let's do him in modern English, shall we. – or even worse, one of the panting kind ever alert for a personal glance from Contreras, better still for his zip to break. He snorted. What the hell did they think he'd got in there, a set the size of bagpipes?

Vito was laughing at the expression on his face. 'A million lire for your thoughts, old friend!'

'Save them for my Magda Foundation, *hombre*!'

Before his eyes could cloud with thought again, Vito asked cheerfully, 'How's the love of your life these days? Bionda Merdina?'

Pepe scowled. 'Cooling, if you must know. She's got a nasty habit of talking to the press when she's had a glass of bloody champagne. Vito – get back to important matters – is Drach prepared to discuss this?'

'I told you – I'm ringing him tomorrow evening. I think you should meet and talk, at least. You've nothing to lose – and nor has he.'

Pepe frowned. Eventually he said 'I go home tomorrow. Then I have several free days before rehearsals begin on bloody *Traviata*.' A rueful smile. 'Alfredo and I are going to sort out Magda's things, her documents and so on. I wonder if . . . . Vito, do you think you might ask him to come out to Barcelona for a day or so? Perhaps he could overnight it, then we could talk at our ease. Say Wednesday to Thursday? Josep will be out of the way, and I can talk to my father beforehand and put him in the picture. Could you ask Drach to do that?'

'Consider it done. I'll contact you after I've spoken to him.'

Then he excused himself and went thankfully to the telephone in his music room.

49

Scanned the piece of paper in his hand. Dialled. He waited, his mouth puckering when no-one answered.

Louis. Ethiopian slave.

Worried, he hung up.

# 4

On a warm and perfumed Sunday morning, Modesto Martes was waking up with a sleepy smile and thinking 'You lucky girl' as the dream-maiden slowly faded. He gave his long legs an ecstatic stretch under the thin sheet.

His wife was still asleep, lying on her side, a hand tucked beneath her cheek. On her bedside table lay her spectacles, large lenses, gold rims. The lenses were automatically beginning to darken in the sunlight.

Modesto wriggled carefully out of bed and went quietly to his *en suite* bathroom. Stealthily. He must keep Mimosa in a good humour. Imperative. This Sunday must be as placid as possible, at least to start with.

The bathroom was long and broad, the children called it The High Street. The shutters framing the arched windows were open to the air, a dove pondered and pecked on the nearest sill. There was a smell of cooking honeysuckle.

The toilet rested at the top of three mosaic steps patterned with Egyptian gods. Here we go, thought Modesto, coronation time. He sat for a while, whistling, trying to decipher the time displayed on a lopsided clock on the wall opposite. It was shaped like a Disneyland fish. He eyed it with disfavour. Mimosa had brought it back from Florida for the kids, years ago. Only the Americans could make white look garish.

Still whistling, he cleared the steps in one jump, grinning at the notice on the wall in his youngest daughter's block capitals: 'Now wash your hands.' Underneath, his son had added 'Then rinse your balls.' Smiling, he showered vigorously, muttering Keep Mimosa in a Good Mood. Thank Christ the kids were here, they would help take the edge off any unpleasantness.

Mentally, as he shaved (but not too closely, still holiday time, remember), he went through the list of his immediates. Recording session tomorrow, *Carmen, olé*. Thank you, Deutsche Grammophon. Couldn't the silly bastards simply re-release his previous version in the run-up to Christmas? – oh no, not they, they wanted this one to be superphonic and fresh and digital, plus a brand-new Carmen. Portuguese. Pretty good, actually. Pretty! He grinned. It was not a wolfish grin. Mimosa did not allow wolfish grins.

He widened his eyes, checked the lower lids. Yes: Optrex time. Mustn't allow the old twinkle to disappear, it would be needed before the day was out.

Bloody *Carmen*. He essayed a guttural French 'r' as his eyeballs swivelled the Optrex. It still came out like the growl of an Hispanic terrier. But, after *Carmen* – and here he started whistling again – off to New York. Should be a masterpiece, this *Butterfly*. Not that it was his favourite rôle by any means. Pinkerton scarcely dominated the action, after all. Nevertheless, it should be an intriguing production at the very least, with Tim Divine in charge of everything but the wiring. He only took a few days longer than God with his creations. Modesto smiled happily. My darling Cherri as Butterfly. Funny, even kitted out in kimono and rice powder, Cherri de Canasta still managed to look as if she were playing full-back for the Wallabies.

Modesto frowned suddenly. He hoped that she would be fit enough to do the bloody thing after that *Aida* farce in Rome. He had sent flowers and a loving message to the clinic in Naples, but so far there had been no word from either Cherri or her manager-husband. Musing on this, he dressed quickly.

The family Martes were waiting for him as he strode down to the terrace, all sitting round a white table to enjoy breakfast together. It was shady against the heat already lashing up from the valley.

His two daughters were laughing at a photograph in a magazine, bare tanned legs kicking. Sara was seventeen, Isolda fifteen, brown-eyed, black hair pulled back from their faces, pale nail varnish. His son, christened Modesto but known as Gruñón because he had been a surly baby, was twenty-five. Tall like his father, bespectacled like his mother, nibbling a croissant and reading the business section of the Sunday paper.

Mimosa proffered the jug of orange juice. Modesto kissed her cheek, said no thanks, coffee for me. Mimosa looked relaxed, as though breakfasting together happened every day of the week. Her blouse hung loose over her jeans, heavy breasts outlined beneath the floral pattern.

Checking the coffee pot, she said merrily, 'Looks as though we shall have a blisteringly hot evening!'

She beamed at them all. This last evening of the holidays (or Papadays, as the children called them) was, as usual, to be privately special. Tonight, a barbecue. Here, at home. Just family and a few friends, and Gruñón's latest girlfriend Marisol, who bit her nails. About sixteen of us, she thought. A nice family size.

Modesto's heart plummeted.

Sara said, 'About eight o'clock, *Mamá*?'

'Oh, any time after half-past seven, darling.' She glanced round happily. 'Oh it will be so nice, all of us together!' She smiled at Modesto, who was staring at his coffee. When he failed to join in the burst of enthusiasm around the table, she looked at him sharply. 'Desto?'

Reluctantly, he lifted his gaze. 'Er . . . sorry, *querida*? . . I . . . what did you say?'

The eyes narrowed. 'I was saying, darling, that this evening will be nice. The barbecue.'

Silence. Then 'Er . . .'

Isolda cried 'You hadn't forgotten, had you, *Papi*? Your last evening?'

'We are waiting,' Mimosa said. Her tone was not friendly.

'Of course I hadn't forgotten!' he blustered. 'As if I'd miss my last Papaday!' They all smiled. Mimosa remained watchful, pushing her black fluffy hair off her forehead.

Her husband glanced at her, then said jovially as his heart fluttered, 'There's just one little thing, though . . . Er . . . one tiny change to our plans . . .'

'*Papá*!'

There came a time for honesty, after all; so he folded his napkin and grinned nervously. He coughed. 'Well . . . I think I forgot to tell you, darling . . . there'll be one or two extra guests at the barbecue.'

'Who?' with fading sweetness. 'Who are the one or two?'

'Oh. Well, perhaps three or four . . .' as Mimosa stood up. She was smaller than any of her children. 'Or five.' Then very hurriedly, 'The thing is, we're being filmed.'

Eruption of noise, laughter, protests. And the calm ice of his wife, 'We are being WHAT?'

'Filmed,' he said in a low voice. Tried to take her hand. It was snatched away.

'I see.' She circled him with the coffee pot.

'*Mamá!*' The girls hastily left the table. Gruñón folded his business section.

'*Querida mía . . .*'

'Don't you *querida* me, you snake! Explain! Explain this – film!'

He set down the cup of coffee. 'Please, little Heart! It was an idea that Decca had –'

'*Que se joda* Decca!'

'– it's to be a video. Me. At home with my family.' Pleading, 'After all, Fazzoletto did one for last Christmas –'

'*Que se joda* Fazzoletto!'

'Just a few shots?' he begged. 'Look, darling Sweetness, it will only be for a few minutes, half an hour, perhaps an hour –'

'And maybe the whole bloody evening!' she screamed.

'Informal shots,' he muttered.

'Oh yes? How bloody informal? Tell me! Informal diamonds and my informal satin bloody ball gown? And our friends – tie and tails? And what about Uncle bloody Pablo belching his way through God knows how many bottles of Rioja? What do we do with him, parcel him up and pretend he's the laundry?'

He glanced swiftly and admiringly at her heaving chest. 'Tiger Cub –'

She began to prowl. 'Going to be filmed as it informally happens, is it? Like dear twinkling Modesto, Family Man, holding a grilled steak in front of the cameras in his three-hundred-guinea suit and bloody gold cufflinks? While I –' dramatic scream '– have to draft in bloody chefs to do the real work in case Decca –' she spat on the ground 'daren't let you get actually dirty on nasty charcoal?'

54

She gasped for breath. Their children peered cautiously round the terrace door.

Modesto began visibly to panic. 'My Heart, my Bundle-bunny! I swear to you, only half an hour . . . We shall wear our oldest clothes . . .' And he folded her in his arms, whispering love, nuzzling her ear and making her spectacles tip upwards. Their children smiled at each other.

Her eyes swam. She sniffed. 'Only half an hour?' she murmured.

'Half an hour, my precious duckling. Less, perhaps.' Optimistically. Decca had said three hours, plus re-takes.

'Bit of a short video, isn't it, Father Dear?' from Gruñón, grinning.

'They're filling it in with clips from my operatic scenes!' he snapped.

'Well . . .' Mimosa began, knowing that there really wasn't any choice. He kissed her round upturned face. Plucked the glasses from her nose, kissed its tip.

'*Querida,* let's go and choose something for us to wear this evening. Mmmm?' He raised a dark eyebrow suggestively.

Mimosa giggled softly. They left the terrace, arms around waists.

Sara hooted 'Isn't it pathetic?'

Isolda said, 'Do people still do it at their age? Yuk!'

Gruñón said thoughtfully, 'Last time I did it, it only took me ten minutes. I wonder if there's something wrong with me? It takes Dad ages!'

*   *   *

Bobby Drach smiled involuntarily as he straightened the white linen runner on his side table. Ezita had embroidered it for him, an extra birthday present last year. He loved her embroidery.

'But not,' he had insisted, 'any flowers or those bloody autumn leaves. Something classy. Something different for Bobby!' – and as a result, his glass now stood upon the opening bars of the *Marriage of Figaro* overture, giant-size. Clever little mare, he grinned, loving it.

He checked his watch against the grandmother clock by the door. When would Vito ring? He hadn't promised any particular time. While he waited, he listened half-heartedly to a CD of Patna and West's latest musical offering. Friends and stable-mates of the Drach Agency, this was their version of the ballet *Coppélia*, a musical set in Wigan in the 1930s and involving (as far as he could make out) rival shoe shops. To his surprise, Nathaniel West had not filched anything from Delibes. A touch of Schubert, perhaps, quite a lot of Stravinsky and Prokofiev, and a whole chunk of Wagner's *Lohengrin*, but definitely no Léo Delibes. Tom Patna had even disguised the title. *Coppolia*. Very good. How the fuck had they managed to get two of their musicals on Broadway? Money-spinning cretins.

When the phone rang, the line was poor. Crackling.

'. . . bert! . . . thing okay with . . . ? . . . job getting through!'

A long buzz intervened.

'Vito? Good of you to ring! I'm fine – how are you?'

'. . . getting . . . However! Not to worry! . . . like to know . . . says about Wedn . . . .fixed?'

'Pardon? Fixed? I can't catch what you're saying!'

'. . . uck it! . . . Wednesday till Thursday . . . elona. He says he'd ra . . . can . . .'

Bobby gritted his teeth, feebly shook the receiver. 'Sorry, Vito, the line is piss-poor. Is this something to do with Contreras?'

'. . . is! What the . . . think . . . So, if . . . flight . . . .fax his secretary . . . 988 . . . airport.'

Fuck British Telecom! Bobby grabbed his pen. 'Vito, before this bloody line drowns in the sea, let me check that I've got it right so far. Are you saying that Contreras wants me to go to Barcelona, this Wednesday?'

'. . .s.'

'What?'

'YES!' A clear shout.

'Bloody hell, you nearly deafened me! Quick, before the bugger goes again – yes, fine for Wednesday, no problems.'

'Until Thursday, stay overnight. At least you've got the lively Miss Pepper to hold the fort for you! Here's the number to fax his secretary . . .' Waited while Bobby repeated it, then added 'He'll arrange for you to be met at the airport, okay?'

'That's great, Vito, many thanks. By the by, any chance of you and I meeting up in the near future?'

After a brief chat, he scribbled on his pad, picked up the warm phone and dialled.

'Ezita?'

Her voice stung his eardrum, loud and clear. 'Hi, Bob!'

'Ez, Vito's just phoned, Contreras wants us to fly out to Barcelona on Wednesday, through Thursday! How about that, then?'

A silence. Then 'Us?'

'Of course us!' impatiently. 'You're the bloody ideas wizard, he'll want to know what we can fucking well offer, won't he!'

'But –'

'But what, you stupid mare? Thought you'd be thrilled right down to your gusset!'

'Bobby, I am!' Then, 'Suppose he –'

'Suppose who?'

'Contreras. Suppose he remembers about that brooch?' Her voice contained an anguished quality that made him snigger quietly.

'I've told you before, he didn't have time to notice your bloody face, and that flat tit of yours is hardly likely to have stuck in his mind, is it? What do you think he's been doing for two years – going round in a bloody dream singing *Someday I'll find you?*'

A reluctant laugh. 'Well, if you think . . .'

'I do! So, if you cover the buggers up properly, there'll be no problem. Now! – may I arrange to fax the Holy Contreras tomorrow?'

Later, he poured more soda into his glass.

Then stared thoughtfully at the room. Just lately, an idea, usually half-buried at the back of his many other ideas, had begun to wade to the surface.

He frowned. Should he?

A silly idea. And yet. It made him feel oddly excited. Bold, even. A surge of enthusiasm and a nice glow inside him. He added extra Scotch to the extra soda.

Why not? He raised his glass in salute. Why the hell not?

The old aunt dressed in black whispered, 'I shall cry for her.'

Pepe patted her hand, did not see the arthritis nor her pain as he touched it.

'So shall we all,' he murmured, then hugged her to him. She had been taller than he, once. Now, his mother's sister was small and therefore a stranger.

'Thank you for coming, Aunt Pilar,' he said. He realised that it must have been a hard journey for her, nearly a hundred kilometres from her home in Tarragona. A lonely home, indeed, where the doctor called more often than the postman.

She kissed Pepe's cheek twice. She was the last of the relatives to leave, having stayed on with her brother-in-law and her ghosts. Now it was Tuesday, and a car waited in the drive to take her gently home.

After she had gone, Pepe went slowly into his music room. Sat down at the piano. His fingers were soft from the heat and Aunt Pilar's hand cream, and he flexed them irritably.

*La Traviata.* Thank God it was at the Liceo. Home-base for the first run of the season, where he could sink into the peace and stone walls of his private quarters when he wasn't at rehearsal or on music call.

He felt restless, reluctant to have deep thought; examined his thumb with care, nibbled a patch of dead skin, wondering what was suddenly so strange in the familiar room. He looked around, vaguely puzzled.

Usual things in usual places. Music stand. The thin sofa with its black and green throw-over, black and white chequered floor. The ghastly print by Joan Miró which his brother had given him as a reminder that things could go dreadfully wrong if you tried hard enough.

Bookshelves neatly stuffed, libretti, manuscripts. A tree in a brass tub, eighteen glossy leaves shaped like spoons, one yellow-tinted and ready to drop off.

All was the same as before. Even the dying leaf had been hanging limply for weeks.

Then the oddity struck him, and his jaw tightened. There was no libretto of *La Traviata* waiting for him on top of the piano. Oh Magda!

Oh Magda. She had never failed in all the years to have the libretto of his next opera waiting for him. On top of the piano. He touched the empty space gently.

Footsteps behind him, ringing on the tiles.

'She'll be next!' his brother announced cheerfully. 'Poor old Pilar.'

Pepe looked up and grinned. 'Merry little sod!'

'Aren't I just! Anyway,' shoving his brother along the piano stool so that he could sit down, 'it'll either be her or you – can I be there when you tell Gualterio about Josep?' He tittered.

Pepe thumped his brother's thigh and stood up, his attention briefly caught by the fronds of a palm outside the window, dipping rapidly in a gust of breeze. Went restlessly to the shelves to hunt down *Traviata*.

'Don't know why the hell you didn't tell him last night, when we were talking about Magda's research fund,' Alfredo continued.

'Just shut your mouth and stick to your bloody test tubes! . . . Jesus, how did this manage to get so dusty? I must use the thing every other month,' finding the libretto and flicking it along the top with his finger.

Alfredo played an arpeggio then launched into a syncopated 'Baa baa black sheep', crying 'Listen, world, I'm as musical as my brother!' And as Pepe started to laugh, he asked 'So when is this new wizard Drach coming to see you?'

'Tomorrow,' dropping *Traviata* on the sofa. 'Vito seems to think a lot of him.'

'His capabilities or his balls?'

They snorted. Alfredo added 'Good job you'll be tucked away in your kennel, *hombre*, just in case he fancies you!'

The kennel. Naturally. Affectionate nickname for his uplifter of spirits and private headquarters, the kennel. Attached to the main house by virtue of an underground tunnel, it had originally been an escape anyway, for the beleaguered President of the Catalan Government, Lluís Companys, back in 1934. Living in the big house himself, his declaration of a Catalan Republic had ensured him becoming a reluctant target of the Federalists.

House searches were frequent and upsetting, he found, and the hidden *casita* was useful. Even its tangled gardens were closed off from the main estate by a fourteen foot stone wall which played host to ivy and giant brambles. Since those days, of course, there had been many renovations, although the walls still staggered under their dark burdens and the gardens grew almost as they wished. The tunnel itself was now paved and lit, with four small alcoves on either side, each containing a religious painting and electric votive candle.

And the kennel, with its octagonal hall and small pugnacious rooms, maintained its seclusion as it always had. Only one telephone, only one bedroom. Not even Judit had shared that bed, let alone possessed a key. Nowadays, Mina and Ana (the chief domestic and general friend) kept it aired and presentable for its part-time recluse.

Alfredo had stooped down to tie his shoelace. Looked up, grinning. 'He could easily fall in love with you, you know – you're so pretty!'

Pepe gave him a shove, Alfredo lost his balance and swore.

Pepe snapped his fingers, 'Come on then, walkies! Good boy! *Tus tus!*'

'You stupid bugger!'

Laughing, he got to his feet, put his arm round his brother's shoulders. 'Let's go and see if Mina's got some coffee for us. Then, I suppose, we ought to go up to Magda's rooms and make a start. What sayest thou?'

In a faint voice, 'Yes. Right. I suppose we must.'

Somewhere in the upper regions of the house they could hear their father bawling 'Take your bloody dirty shoes off that! Now!' and young voices protesting.

'Isn't he a sweet little grandad,' sniggered Alfredo.

Another bellow echoing, 'In Africa, they make pies out of little boys like you!'

'I don't know why you and Mina want them to have a classical education,' mused Pepe. 'They could learn everything from Gualterio. Africans eat boys. They never taught us that at school.' He sniffed loudly and suddenly. His brother jumped, 'Christ!'

Pepe said, 'Shit! Don't say this catarrh is starting again! Why does it have to come on at rehearsal time?' He gave a lusty experimental snort.

'You,' said Alfredo affectionately, 'need a woman.'

Pepe stared at him. 'What's that got to do with my bloody catarrh?'

'Nothing. Just thought a bit of bull-running might take your mind off it, that's all.' Clapped his brother on the back. 'Which reminds me – how's Bonker Merdina these days?'

A frown. 'Shut it!'

Alfredo tittered.

'I said shut it!'

Alfredo did a little dance. 'Ooooh, Bonker, you little teee-aser! You've broken my zip again, that's the third one this week!'

'SHUT IT!'

'Open wide! That's it! Ooooh, Bonker, look at this, you'll need both hands!'

Laughing and jostling, they made their way to the family sitting room. Mina, slim, wavy hair neatly shaped, was poised on the sofa with the coffee-pot at hand. She smiled to herself as she heard Alfredo exclaim 'Honestly, it would do you good, one of those ripe frisky tarts by the fish market! Christ, she'd chew the hairs on your belly!'

They came in, grinning, and Mina composed her face into wifeliness.

'Good – just in time for coffee,' she said brightly.

*   *   *

Modesto Martes rang that evening.

Pepe had just finished his supper of Camembert and pickled gherkins, relaxing alone in his kennel and pouring over printed copy, biro busy, savouring the white wine as he rolled it thoughtfully round his tongue.

'Hi, Modesto! How goes it?'

A long groan. 'Bad. Very very bad.'

Pepe, alarmed, 'Are you sick? Mimosa? The family? Your voice?'

61

'The voice, God be thanked, is well.' He ignored the other questions. Then rapidly, '*Hombre*, does the name Catalina Lucha mean anything to you?'

Pepe frowned. 'Can't say it does. Why? Who is she?'

'She's a soprano.'

'Oh isn't that good news? Nice to know they're still around.'

'This is serious!' A touch of impatience. 'You're sure you haven't seen her, heard of her? She's an American.'

'So? Do a Columbus – go discover her!'

'Look, Contreras!' threateningly. Then, 'God, it would be helpful if someone had seen the cow! Thing is, I'm off to New York in three days' time, for Tim Divine and his "dee-fini-tyve" version of bloody *Butterfly*. . . .'

Pepe laughed. 'So where does this Lucha fit in? Is she a replacement?'

A groan. '*Exacto*! She's in for Cherri, God help me. Cherri's still pillow-propping after her accident in Rome. You hear about that? Jesus, it's landed me well and truly in the shit!'

Pepe masked his glee. 'Why, exactly?'

'Oh God, if only you'd been able to tell me. . . .'

'Tell you what, for heaven's sake?'

Low voice, terrified. 'How dark she is.'

A titter. 'Pardon me?'

'Pepe!' Laboured breathing. 'Pepe, she's a coon!'

'You what?' sniggering.

'A coon! They've given me a fucking black minstrel! What I want to know is, how bloody black? I mean, Christ Almighty, I can't sing Pinkerton with a negro Butterfly!'

'A . . .' Pepe doubled up.

'Jesus, how can they do this to me? Pepe, are you listening? . . . It's *Butterfly* we're doing, not *Porgy and* fucking *Bess*! . . . Oh stop howling, Contreras, it's not funny! And you know what is even worse? She is –' lowering his voice, '– a Met Pet!'

That silenced the laughter from Barcelona. 'Dear God!'

Met Pet. The dreaded awesome sobriquet. Met Pets were the darlings, the favoured, the pampered. Met Pets belonged to the city of New York, in the custodial care of the Lincoln Center. It was rumoured that they were tested for voice at three months old and then removed from the world until they eventually emerged, small armies of them, as copybook Otellos and Toscas, with beards or daggers and uniformly word-perfect.

Modesto said miserably, 'Mimosa says it's divine retribution.'

The Barcelona laugh was back. 'Why? What have you been up to?'

'God! The other evening I landed my entire family in a load of steaming compost, my friend! Decca came to film our private barbecue. They arrived just before six, Mimosa was still in the bath or shaving her bloody legs or something, nothing was set up, steaks still de-frosting, you name it; and then they didn't bloody well leave until two in the morning! Mimosa was going crazy, I thought she'd have my balls on the griddle; Gruñón and I got half-pissed in front of the cameras . . . Bloody hell, and now a coloured Met Pet! I wish I was a sodding taxi-driver!'

So do I, thought Pepe nastily as he murmured consoling noises and replaced the receiver.

He wandered out on to the old terrace which ran three quarters of the way round the kennel.

At least Macho Martes hasn't got Josep and Gualterio to contend with, he brooded. Nor a dead sister, whose sorted documents and effects were entirely devoted to Pepe Contreras, and led Alfredo to say in awe 'I come to the conclusion, brother, that you – to Magda – were life and dreams and God. That's one hell of a responsibility for you, *amigo*,' and he had shuddered.

And then the interview with his father, who held no such views on his youngest son after the revelation that Josep Gusano had to go.

'You fucking seven-day wonder! Want to bury him like we buried Magda, do you? Think that singing and whoring and Pepe are what life's all about, you pathetic little bastard? Eh? Friends and values and affection can all go take a bit at hell – is that it?'

Angry hands, holding the bottle of brandy, pouring. 'You addle-brained runt! That man –' slam of bottle hard on table '– that man has been with you since you started! You conceited prick, he's guided you, brought you the best offers, the best bloody Houses, protected you from yourself – and now you suddenly decide that he isn't up to the bloody job! Your brains exist only between your legs!'

'Thank you, Father. You have been most understanding.'

*　　　*　　　*

'Look!' cried Ez in exasperation, 'Just because you used to do costume for the Amateur Dramatics lot in Dorking, doesn't mean you can start telling me what to wear!'

'The Ammie Drammies were in Guildford, duckie, not Dorking.' Bobby picked up the magpie from her desk and examined its beak. 'And as far as *you're* concerned, I have a right to know. I don't want you turning up at the airport looking like something out of the bloody *Jungle Book*, nor engaging our host in small talk wearing one of your spot-the-tit outfits. I want to know because I want to sleep peacefully tonight. Bobby doesn't need nightmares at a crucial time like this!' He scratched at the magpie's beak. 'What's this?'

'What's what?' rummaging through her drawer.

'This red mark on Giacomo's beak. It won't come off.'

'Oh, that. It's nail varnish. Julie spilt it.'

'Christ Al-bloody-mighty, two clumsy cows in the same office!' He went to the door. Paused. 'So what are you wearing?'

'Oh not again!' Then, sweetly, 'Do you really want to know? Well – one of my outfits is from Marks and Spencer. Polyester. Size 10/12. Pink. They're called pyjamas.'

He made a swift gesture at her just as Julie called from the outer office, 'Robert! There's a call for you – shall I put it through in there?'

'Who is it?'

'A National Opera Company.'

'Oh how very succinct! Thank you, Julie.' Glared round the door at her. 'Which bloody National? English, Welsh or bloody Scottish?'

'Sorry, didn't catch that bit. But they say it's urgent.'

'Shit, I bet it's the English, everything's fucking urgent to them! Put 'em through to my den, will you, Bobby's bottle of Scotch is down there.'

He exited, saying loudly, falsetto, 'Oh Mr Drach, is it in so-and-so's contract to have a piss at ten o'clock in the morning?'

Ez and Julie giggled.

Tuesday afternoon. Not as warm as it had been, a stiff goose-pimpling breeze that drove the cul-de-sac smells through the open window.

Ez smiled to herself. This morning, she had made a frenzied search of her favourite Oxfam shop for a new outfit. Some of the creations had been beyond belief. The shop assistant had grinned at her, 'What's the big occasion this time, Ez?'

She was dubious about the assistant's eventual persuasive choice. A rich chestnut camisole top and matching pleated-front wide trousers in a flimsy silk that the assistant called "faille". There was also a bronze belt. 'This ensemble belonged to Lady Irene,' the girl said confidentially. 'We get a lot of her stuff, she's very generous to us.'

No wonder, thought Ez, and bought it. At least the neckline was modest, and the garments were lined. That should please Bobby, at any rate.

# 5

On Wednesday morning, a hot still day in Turin, cooler here in the valleys, Keta stood frowning by the open door of the music room.

It was nearly midday, and when Vito was at home they liked to have an early luncheon together.

He had been closeted in there for hours, since daybreak, with his score and libretto of *L'Elisir d'Amore*. He adored Donizetti to the point of worship. Vito Lavagna, the eighteen-year-old, had dragged his friend Drach from concert hall to opera-house in 1948 to listen to anyone or anything that was commemorating the centenary of Donizetti's death. Even the aftermath of the war had not stopped the music.

Vito now considered that the acid-tongued composer kept both voice and passion young, whatever the mirror said if the sun was too bright. He ran his fingers across the piano keys, humming under his breath, re-thinking Nemorino. Suppose, this time, he were to –

Phone. It sounded sharp and off-key. Peevishly, 'Lavagna!'

'It's Louis.'

The peevishness vanished, something flooded inside him. 'My dear boy! How are you? Did you get my wire?'

'I got it. I'm okay, just a bit shaken. No structural damage.'

'That is a relief! I was worried about you.'

'When do we meet again?' brusquely.

'I've been thinking about that. Look, I'm off to Salzburg on Friday, *L'Elisir*. We go into rehearsal at the weekend. What are you doing between now and then?'

'Very little. I'm not Vito Lavagna.'

Vito said soothingly, 'Are you okay for tomorrow sometime?'

'I suppose. Does the "sometime" mean half an hour in your precious company, or may I count on more?'

'Louis, Louis,' murmured Vito placatingly. Out of nowhere, a faint tingling round his thighs. He glanced at the framed calendar on the piano. 'Could you get away tomorrow afternoon until early Friday morning? We could hop off to the lake villa. I'll give them a ring and let them know I'm coming, if that's —?'

'That would be okay,' softly. 'A whole night, Vito . . .' Laughed loudly into the phone. 'I'm back in my usual doss-house; will you pick me up and drive us down there?'

'Well. . . .' Vito frowned. He didn't like driving.

'Pick me up, and I'll drive. About two o'clock?'

'Make that three.'

'Fine. See you.'

Louis hung up, abrupt as usual. Vito squeezed his thighs together. When he opened his eyes, Keta was walking into the room, smiling.

'You're getting careless, Baby,' she said smoothly. 'The door was open.'

'Is lunch ready?'

She nodded.

He left the piano and put his arm through hers. 'I'm hungry!' he laughed.

It was true. There was something about Donizetti that put him in a happy hungry mood.

*　　*　　*

Their seatbelts were fastened, the aircraft slowly pivoting to point towards its take-off zone.

Ez had been late arriving at the airport. 'You stupid mare!' he had snapped, grabbing her arm and hustling her through the crowds to the check-in desk.

'Oh I do beg your pardon!' sarcastically, watching her overnight bag disappear down the chute. 'If I'd known there would be so much traffic between Putney and Heathrow, I'd've got up earlier and built a special motorway!'

He didn't relinquish her arm until they were safely aboard, and even then he fussed over the belt and double-checked it.

'I don't think I shall fall out of the plane!' she remarked acidly.

'You? You'd fall out of your own bloody coffin!' he hissed. Then eyed her carefully. 'Actually, you don't look too bad. I like the suit.'

It was the colour of pale stone, short pleated skirt, dark orange blouse. She stuck out her legs and waggled her feet at him, grinning.

'Oh Jesus! Fucking trainers!'

'Better for travelling in. Don't worry, I've got some high heels in my bag, I'll change them before we get there.'

'You'll be lucky, your bag's in the luggage hold. What are you going to do, ask the fucking pilot to stop and hover while you go and look for it?'

She tittered, then said pleasantly, 'I meant, you idiot, that I'll change them when we land. I'm sure the car will wait.'

Bobby grinned suddenly. 'We'll be landing at the right bloody airport for you, won't we – it's called El Prat!'

As the aircraft swayed and lumbered to a halt, and the whine of the engines increased, he said, 'Heard the latest on Rush-Leigh? As well as cancelling *Don Giovanni*, he can't do the *Magic* bloody *Flute* in November, either! His mummy told me that on the phone. Mummy rang me because that squint-eyed twat of a baritone was too busy to tell me himself. You know what he was doing? He was out, picking fucking wild mushrooms! Oh sympathy for Bobby!' as Ez creased, 'And God help that bloody Spanish onion if he tries to muck us about like that!'

\*     \*     \*

The stewardess had served coffee. Ez unwrapped the cubes of brown sugar with enthusiastic abandon.

Bobby seemed restless, hadn't commented on the sugar, drank his coffee quickly and now waited for the stewardess to reappear. It was bright like a still day above the clouds. The scheduled flight, although it was August, was only half-taken, and snacks and drinks were plentiful.

Bobby was taking a break between emotions. Several times now, since Sunday evening, he had taken out his idea and looked at it closely. Furtively, at first; sometimes a nervous laugh.

68

Sometimes, bravado. Then again, a sarcastic smile as he returned it to his inner mind. Yet it didn't quite fit back there. Jagged, almost. Sticking out. Whatever it was doing, he decided, it wasn't about to disappear.

Smiled to himself, almost relieved. Then saw Ez unwrapping her fifth sugar cube.

'Nice to see you taking all those health warnings to heart,' he said. 'You really might live quite a long time. Sugar with everything. Ciggies. No bloody exercise. And,' triumphantly, 'you like fried bread!'

He beckoned the stewardess, waved his cup aloft. Was rewarded by a pleasant smile and swift service.

'Nice little bum,' he commented as the trim figure walked back down the aisle. 'Didn't you hear what I said, Miss Health Freak?'

'No,' responded Ez. 'Bob, I've been thinking,' sipping her coffee thoughtfully. Swallowed too fast, choked. Then 'Something Vito said, about Contreras wanting to –'

'Funny,' he interrupted. 'I was just thinking about him myself.'

'Who – Vito?'

'Yes. Look, Ezita –' He faced her suddenly. His look was surprisingly intense.

She stopped sipping.

He sighed. 'Ez, I. . . .'

She resumed sipping. Said sympathetically, 'It's okay, talk about him if you want to. I'll listen.'

Far from looking grateful, he scowled instead. 'When I said I was thinking of Vito, I didn't mean in that way!'

'Oh, pardon me!'

With difficulty, he switched on a smile. Ez eyed him with distrust.

He squinted out of the porthole, then faced her again.

'Ez, I wish . . . no . . . What's the fucking word I want . . .?'

'Which one would you like?' giggling.

'Shut up! Have patience with Bobby –' Then, 'Ez, I'd like to follow Vito's example.'

Sipped. 'Thought you already had.' The corners of her mouth lifted.

He gritted his teeth. And as the aircraft ploughed steadily on course, he said cautiously, 'Get married, I mean.'

Her laughter pealed, joyous and unrestrained. 'Oh Roberto!' Coffee slopped into the saucer.

'Shut up!' fiercely. 'Stop making that bloody noise, they'll think you're being sick!' Defensively, as her eyes brimmed with more laughter, 'Vito got married – why not me?'

Sudden stirrings of shock. 'Bobby? . . . You *are* joking . . . ?' Bobby with a wife? Giggles threatened. Her coffee swirled as she wielded her spoon again, eyes fixed on his face.

'Why the hell should I be joking? I didn't hear the world laugh when Vito got married! Many of us do.' His voice was stiff.

She touched his arm with affection. 'Of course they don't laugh. It's just that . . . oh come on, Bob, we've know each other for years, it's such a strange idea, coming from you.' His profile remained frozen. She took a deep breath, tried again. 'Is it anyone I know, then! Have I met her? Is it Miss Summers, the architect?'

He turned his head. 'Miss fucking Summers? Christ!' shuddering. He stared past her. 'It's you I'm talking about, you silly mare!'

Saucer met cup head-on, brown warm stains jostled on the pale skirt.

'Me?' Incredulous, she gazed at him.

'Ezita!' His fingers curled round her wrist. 'Can't you see? We're already partners, good friends. We're always over at each other's place, why can't we live in just the one – mine – and share the same name? Christ knows we're fond enough of each other. And there'd be no complications, our relationship would be, well, you know, we'd be free in that sense,' he finished lamely. Added, 'You've got coffee all over that nice skirt!' His eyes were wet.

She said 'Oh Bobby . . . God! . . .' And again, 'Oh Bobby!'

Trap her while she's dumbfounded, he counselled himself. 'Just think it over, sweetie. Please? It honestly does make sense for us. Think about it, take your time.'

Worriedly, he cast his mind over his flat. Only one proper bedroom. Shit, hadn't thought of that. Oh well, there was always the little spare room. She'd fit into that nicely. 'Promise me you will think it over? Carefully?'

'Well . . . okay . . . but . . .'

He put his finger to his lips. 'Don't say anything more. You know now. Just mull it over, right? Now!' briskly, 'what the fuck are we going to do about that skirt of yours?'

*   *   *

Which was why she was still wearing trainers when they were paged at the airport, plus her jeans and a blue t-shirt which had the word *Adagio* embroidered on the back. Luckily, the promised car was late in arriving, due, the driver said, to a pothole and an injured donkey.

Bobby looked at him disapprovingly. He was not attired as a chauffeur should be. He came, instead, equipped with a cheerful smile, striped shirt and slacks, and looked a little surprised when he saw Ez.

'Good days!' he greeted Bobby. '*Señor* Drach? . . . And, pardon me, *Señorita* –? Don Pepe did not say a *señorita*,' and he grinned appreciatively at Ez, grasping her overnight bag.

She glanced at Bobby with dawning suspicion, but held her tongue while they were being settled in the Mercedes by the still-grinning driver, who announced that he was Ramón but please call me Moncho, everybody –

'*Gracias*, Moncho,' Ez said, and perched herself on the edge of the back seat, quivering with rage.

Bobby was smirking. He felt wonderful, even though the car needed a good wash and the exhaust bounced up and down even when the car was stationary.

As they left the airport perimeter, he said possessively, 'You look like a bloody urchin! Whatever will Contreras think? Why in the name of fucking Christ are you so clumsy?'

For a moment, she gave her full attention to the passing city and its lost but healthy palm trees. Then, pleasantly, 'Robert? Would you please tell me something?' And before he could blink, continued smoothly, 'Such as why you didn't tell me that I was not invited here? Such as why, when I didn't want to come in the first place because of that bloody brooch, you told me I had to? Damn you, Bob, it's embarrassing enough without being an unexpected guest as well!'

71

'Temper, temper!' patting her hand. 'They won't bat an eyelid. These Spaniards run their homes like hotels, how do you think the tourist trade started?' Unrepentant, he glanced at her shirt. Open neck, the three buttons unfastened.

'Fasten the bottom one, there's a good girl, we don't want Paypay peering down there and remembering, do we?'

Silently, she returned to the passing view, fuming. Marriage? Marriage! Jesus, it was laughable! Button this, alter that, your shoes are dirty . . . Hysteria threatened, and she snorted into her fist as the scenery gradually changed. Now the road became a single lane, and there were fields in which nothing grazed. Just two giant billboards, one per pasture, depicting a black bull and the legend "Veterano".

Bobby nudged her and pointed. 'Is that where they put retired bulls?'

'It's an advert for brandy!' scornfully.

'Eeeew, silly me!'

What can't be cured must be endured, she thought grimly.

Her attention was drawn to the narrowing of the road as it curled upwards. Then a dusty sign, which said "Sant Moiseps".

'Is that another brandy?' whispered Bobby.

Gradually, along each side of the road, appeared high pink-washed walls, occasionally broken by black iron-rodded gates. A police motorcycle lay outside one of them. It all seemed deserted, no-one passing by. Just the quick glimpse of palm trees soaring tall above the walls. And then came a massive wall, split neatly by double gates, gold-spiked. They stood open, and beyond them they saw a tall fat house with ornate balconies, shuttered windows. Ez smiled dreamily at it. She saw beyond the shutters – to the darkness of tiled floors, the tinkling of a fountain in a cool courtyard, a beautiful lady reclining in dreamlike solitude.

She tapped Moncho on the shoulder. 'What house is that?' pointing.

'Is not a house, *señorita*. Is the canning factory.'

She subsided, clutching her shoulderbag. The car revved, and they were climbing still higher. Far below, and in the distance, was the city with its glimpses of busy ocean. Moncho turned sharply to the right, on to a track that made them bounce.

'Is there!' he said, and indicated another long high wall with foliage hanging over the red-tiled top. More wrought-iron gates. Ez thrust a hand through her jumbled hair, tugged at the bottom of her shirt. As the car neared the gates, Bobby hissed 'I can see your fucking nipples through that shirt! Do something!'

'Like what – cut them off?' she hissed back.

He thought grimly, when we're married, you are going to start wearing a bra, madam!

Moncho slowed down, spoke into a handset. Then the gates opened slowly, as though they could change their minds if they wanted to. And now a dim drive, glorious vigorous trees miles high and touching; shrubs bursting.

'Fulham Road,' muttered Bobby.

Then they saw the house, plain and two-storeyed, solidly cream, mossy red tiles on the bits of visible roof. Heavy front door, a flight of sandstone steps leading down to the drive which here was broad with tyre-marks in the gravel.

Moncho eased the car to a halt, and Pepe came down the steps to greet them.

Bobby scrambled out, smiling, holding out his hand. 'Mr Contreras! Good to see you again!'

'Mr Drach! How kind of you to come at such short noticing!'

They shook hands. Pepe thought with relief, you're not a complete stranger after all, I recognise your face.

He put a hand on his guest's shoulder. 'You must feel in need of a washing and a long drink after your trip! Please, you must remind me – where did we meet, you and I?' and they went towards the steps, Bobby saying 'That would be most welcome, thank you, most kind. We met, in actual fact, at a press conf –'

A yelp. And Moncho saying, 'Please, let me help you, *señorita!*'

A breathless 'Oh bloody hell! . . . Thanks, Moncho . . . Oh God! Now look what's happened!'

Pepe had turned to stare, taken by surprise. His lips twitched, raised an eyebrow at Bobby. His driver was on his hands and knees in the gravel, searching.

Bobby said coldly, 'Please do forgive this, Mr Contreras. That – is my partner, she insisted on coming with me. Ez! What the hell's going on?' And he hastened over to the chaos, Moncho looking up

73

and smiling weakly, Ez dishevelled and clambering out of the car, her bag spilling its contents.

'I told you to fasten that bloody button!' he snarled under his breath.

'It bloody came off!' she yelled in his face, 'when you shot out of the car nearly taking my bloody bag with you! . . . Oh . . . *gracias*, Moncho,' as the driver got to his feet and handed her a hairbrush and a lighter. Pepe was grinning.

'May I introduce my partner,' Bobby said grimly. 'Eliza Pepper.'

'Oh God,' wiping her hand over her head and squinting through the curly tangles. 'Er . . . how do you do?'

He pretended to peer closely as if bird-nesting, brown eyes laughing, grey ones large and riveted. Took her hand, he cool and scented and clean, his guest not, encircled by half-heard voices and the dying stink of petrol fumes.

'Welcome,' he said, the vaguest of memories stirring.

'Thank you,' wanting to lower her gaze. Somewhere, Bobby coughed.

'Is my pleasure.'

'Thank you.'

Riveted.

When their hands fell apart, he could have sworn before God that her fingers were still with his.

*       *       *

Bobby was elated. It showed in his stride as he headed along the carpeted corridor towards the room that now housed his partner. It showed in the clean cut of his white dinner jacket and in the hair which had been combed until it shone like Lehar's waltz in the gleam of the bracket lamps.

It showed despite meeting a mouse called Roberto earlier in the day, which had hunched and sniffed on the staircase, noisily cheered on by two small boys who looked like Pepe in embryo. He had, indeed, assumed they were his sons until a neat and pretty woman suddenly appeared and apologised in English, rounded up both mouse and the boys and explained that she was Pepe's sister-

74

in-law and they belonged to her, all three.

'Sweet. Quite, quite sweet,' Bobby had murmured, feeling sick as the smallest child seemed intent on getting him to examine the mouse more closely.

'*Se llama* Roberto,' said the five-year-old Pau.

'What a bright little boy! He knows my name already,' beamed Bobby, and backed away. He later complained to Ez about the mouse.

'You'd think,' he said, 'that in a house like this and with all their money, they could afford to rid themselves of bloody mice! Don't they have pest controllers in Spain, for Christ's sake?'

Ez had already been introduced to Roberto the mouse; she smiled sweetly and said nothing.

Bobby's elation had begun to soar in the afternoon. Despite the frostiness from Ez during the car journey (which he ascribed to a natural fluster following his proposal, and, accordingly, nervous tension), he sensed something different – thoughtful – about her during the business meeting and the drinks that followed their arrival. He caught her smiling to herself, a dazed smile he thought, and rubbed his hands.

Robert and Eliza Drach. He winked at her across the room.

She sat in an armchair in the formal sitting room. Pepe, in there for the first time since the day of the funeral, noticed that there were more potted plants in the room now. Less people, more leaves. He liked it.

He sat with Roberto on the long sofa,wanting to talk for hours with Ez Pepper and cup her face in his hands. Talking for hours, however, was all very well in his head. He found it difficult to do more than smile feebly at her after their hands had dusted briefly when he gave her a glass of Amontillado.

Forty years old, going on sixteen, he frowned. Taking a deep breath, he asked her 'Er . . . .?'  She smiled, tried to think of an answer.

Pepe interrupted his next remark with a loud sniff, followed by an equally noisy swallow.

Bobby frowned. 'Caught a cold, Mr Contreras?'

'Er . . . no, not at all. Is my catarrh. Sorry!'

Bloody hell, thought Bobby. Doh re mi fah sniff.

Pepe said, hitching his jeans, 'You will please both join us, the family, at dinner this evening?' looking at Ez.

'That's very kind of you,' she murmured, and wondered if Christmas trees felt this way when their lights were switched on.

'Delighted!' said Bobby briskly. 'I've already met your sister and her two children. Quite charming.'

'Mina is my brother's wife –'

'Good. Good. Ez, don't get your cigarettes out in here, there's a good girl . . . So now, Mr Contreras, you were saying –?'

Why are you sitting over there, *Señorita* Pepper? I want to feel your knee and your foot beside mine.

She wanted to finish her sherry so that he could refill it and hand it to her again.

As Bobby dressed for dinner – the couple of hours stretched out on the bed had refreshed him – he reflected that the discussions had been smooth and generous on both sides. Ez had, thankfully, cast off her bemused look and had generated sparks with her ideas after Paypay had outlined his plans for the Magda Fund.

Yes, he thought, examining the fit of his jacket in the mirror, the Drach Agency could arrange a lot for the fund-raising, not just recitals, something a little more adventurous to interest and ti-tillate the public. All in all, a satisfying kick in the teeth for the likes of Modesto Martes whose only likely attempt at fund-raising would be for a gold statue of himself in Madrid's main plaza. Probably with champagne pouring out of its cock. He sniggered.

No-one had mentioned Josep Gusano. That was Paypay's business. It had been enough to see the eagerness on his face when Ez sat beside him, and the attention he gave to their ideas. All in all, he considered that they had presented their new canary with a very attractive package. He only wished that Ezita had taken the trouble to pull off the thread of buttonless cotton dangling down her shirt: their host had definitely noticed that, kept looking at it fascinated by such sloppiness.

Luckily, he had not dwelt on the matter of their first meeting, merely nodded and said 'Ah yes, Verdi's *Requiem*', and did something acrobatic with his mouth. That catarrh, probably.

And of course, Ez knew when her part in the talks was over, and had excused herself when finance became involved, asking

76

politely if there were any books she could browse through, something to do with a Spanish poet called Lorker. Paypay had gone out of his way to escort her to the library. Good-mannered.

*     *     *

Pepe stood up at once.

'Books? Certainly, please I show you where. You like reading?'

'Does she like reading!' snorted Bobby, taking a sheaf of papers from his briefcase. 'You can't move in the girl's flat for bloody books!'

And none of them are getting a home in mine, he thought. Perhaps one or two of her favourites, but that is it. And if she wants to hang on to that fucking Ignacio, it can go in the little spare room and sparkle in there.

In the library, she looked around and glowed. 'This is lovely!'

'Lorca I cannot vouch for,' watching her, 'but you might find something to give pleasure. My sister read a great deal, so did my mother. All their books are here, I think too the poetry.'

'You won't mind if –?'

He touched her arm, and she tried to drop her gaze. 'I don't mind what you do.'

'That is kind of you. Thank you.'

'Is of my pleasure. I would stay to assist, but Roberto will –'

'Yes, of course. I'll be fine. Thank you.'

'Well, then, I will . . . .' He went to the door. His hand made a vague gesture, then he said quickly, 'This evening, perhaps, after we have eaten, you would allow me to show you around? The gardens, yes?'

'I would like that,' catching her breath.

'Is good.' Smiled and returned to his new mentor in the sitting room.

It was an enchanting library, she thought, dazed. A bowl of fresh roses and wet leaves, the smell of old and new and battered books. A folding ladder with three steps leaning against a black desk. Nothing to sit on, other than a broad window seat. She began to browse, thinking about their walk after eating.

It was nearly an hour later when Pepe returned to the library and found her curled up on the window seat, face buried in a book which had a torn cover and patches of sellotape across it. She heard a catarrhal snort as he came in, and smiled at him over the book.

'This is terrific,' waving her hand around the room, 'Thank you again.'

'Pepe,' he added. Then musingly, 'Or is it Paypay?'

She chuckled, he smiled and sat down on the window seat, leaning over to look at the book in her hands. Her fingers, ringless, he noticed. Nails short, one bitten. One finger, the smallest one, had a distortion in the joint that made it curl slightly. Two freckles on the back of one hand.

'You have found Federico García Lorca?' and studied the wrist. A fading scratch.

'Part of him,' she smiled. The blueness of his chin and jaw intrigued her, the tooth that jutted forward slightly. She handed him the book.

'May I call you Ez?' as he studied the battered cover.

'Yes,' simply.

'*Gracias*, Ez.' Their eyes met over the sellotaped book, then he returned his gaze to it and smiled suddenly. Opened it, laughed, pointed to the inside cover. He said 'Look at this – a proud student!'

She bent to look, his fingernail had something black wedged inside.

'Josep María Contreras,' she read aloud,'*de 9 años, su libro.*' Glanced up at him. 'Yours?' she asked.

'Is mine! Magda – my sister – bought it for me. I wanted to be a composer then, and thought to set poems to music, and so she give me this . . . er . . .'

'Anthology?'

'Ah yes. *Exacto.*' Nodded slowly. 'Magda believed that this would give me good choices of poems for music fast and slow.' His smile was gentle, reflective.

'And did you? Set any of them to music, I mean?'

The smile became a rueful grin. 'Poor Lorca, poor José Zorrilla! No, I decide songs had to be, for me, sung not written.'

'And Josep? Is that your real name?'

'Pepe is the shortness of Josep. I think in English is Joe.'

She smiled. 'I think I prefer Pepe,' she said.

*     *     *

Bobby rapped on the door, eyeing the thickly-carpeted corridor with approval. Nice to see that they had covered some of the floors properly at least.

'Come in!'

He stood still at the sight of her.

'Jesus Christ! You almost look like a bloody woman! That is nice, nice, nice!' and he prowled round her, fingering the material of her chestnut-coloured ensemble.

'Why, thank –'

'Who went with you to choose this? Somebody with an eye for style, couldn't have been Eve, she was born in bloody jeans, that one. Who?'

'Lady Irene,' smoothly, unaware of her glowing eagerness.

'Who the fuck's Lady Irene?' suspiciously. 'Nice belt, too.'

'Bobby,' she interrupted with a peal of laughter, 'what is that perfume you're wearing?' She collapsed on the bed, fanning the air.

He scowled, and sniffed the inside of his wrists. 'It's called bloody *Scheherezade*. Friend of mine brought it from Paris. God!' He sniffed again, grinned reluctantly. 'No wonder the French have outdoor urinals if their piss smells anything like this! Do you think anyone will notice?' anxiously.

Another shriek of laughter.

He said bitterly, 'Let's hope they've all got bloody blocked noses like Sniffer!'

'Don't call him that!'

He suddenly glanced down, narrowed his eyes. 'Can you tell me why you've still got bare feet?'

'Oh. Well, my shoes got wet.'

'Wet? Where the hell were they?'

'In the bathroom; I put them too near the shower. Don't worry, I left them on the balcony to dry.'

79

He bustled outside, picked them up, examined them.

'Still damp, but they'll have to do. Put them on, you clumsy mare – Sniffer's sister will be here soon to take us down to dinner!'

'Sister-in-LAW! How many more times? And stop calling him that!'

He smirked as she tussled with the damp shoes. 'Very wise.'

'What is?' tugging.

'The heels aren't very high.'

'What did you think I'd bring – stilts?'

'No, I was just thinking. You wouldn't want to tower over dear old Paypay, would you? I mean, he isn't exactly a bloody sky-scraper, is he? More like your average rockery gnome – you careless cow!'

He ducked as her hairbrush caught him at the side of the head.

*　　*　　*

The meal was long and gentle, and Ez thought how like dark lakes their eyes were in the candlelight.

The patriarch, Gualterio, had arrived some minutes into the first course, acknowledged the introductions with a nod before falling on his food as though conversation was time-wasting. Ez could see no resemblance to either of his sons, for he was built tall and wide like a bear. Someone, perhaps as a joke, had placed a branch of candles close to his place setting, and the folds of his face were barely discernible.

'Don't your children come down for dinner?' Ez asked.

Mina smiled. 'Lluís and Pau? Sometimes. But not tonight. They have no English yet.'

'Lluís knows a very good word in English,' from Alfredo.

Mina cast him a warning glance. Turned back to Ez. 'And my father-in-law speaks mostly Catalan, not Spanish.'

'Not tonight he doesn't,' Alfredo said, and peering towards the end of the table, spoke to his father in Castilian. Ez smiled, en-tranced, as Gualterio replied, 'Go to hell, you burbling fart.'

Alfredo said to her, 'He says he will do his best.'

She caught Pepe's eye. He knew by now that Ez and Spanish were no strangers.

His breath too was caught. His mouth lifted. Eyes, he thought, fringed and lovely, grey thought-filled flowers, eyes that . . . 'Oh sorry, Roberto, you were saying?'

This is wonderful wine, she thought. And stole glances at him as Bobby monopolized him throughout the second course.

The girl's in a daze, thought Bobby, taking crusty bread from the proffered basket. I'm glad I asked her. Very, very glad.

'Well, naturally,' he continued to Pepe, 'If you can. . . .'

His eyes are two browns, amber and chocolate, she marvelled.

Alfredo, in his dark blurred English, said to her 'Excuse me, may I ask something?' and at her nod, dug his toothpick into the damask cloth.

'So,' he said. Paused to consider English syntax. 'You are named . . . Eeliza.'

She said she was, looking at the short bristles on his scalp.

The toothpick carved an ornate "E". 'Is from where, then?'

'Sorry?'

'Eeliza is from the where? Ez, I see, is short for that. Is Eeliza of an Eelizabeth?'

'Well,' panicking a little, 'it can be, but Eliza is my full –'

The toothpick snapped. Mina frowned, 'Alfredo!'

'Sorry,' selecting a new one. 'How then is Eeliza not of Eelizabeth?'

She heard Pepe chuckle as he poured more wonderful wine into her glass.

'*Gracias,*' she murmured, her fingers on the spiral stem.

'*De nada,*' and he slowly removed the neck of the bottle from her glass, and knocked it against a bowl of white flowers. Red drops fell on the cloth.

'Pepe!' from Mina.

Bobby said, 'The thing is, Pepe, when these fellows tell you that. . . .'

Alfredo eyed his brother, watched his eyes and hands. You randy bastard.

'I think,' he said firmly to his lady companion, 'that the Spanish is much better for you. Isabel. Is good sound, yes?'

'Yes,' she smiled.

Bobby called to Mina, 'I think you'll find that Persil is very good for the stains,' nodding at the spilt wine. Ez tittered faintly at the expression on Mina's face.

'I shall remember that,' she said politely. 'Thank you.'

'Don't mention it.' Turned back to Pepe, frowning. Clumsy idiot. He was staring into space now instead of attending to what was being said. Bloody artistes. Minds like sodding gauze.

Alfredo persisted 'Do you mind if we say Isabel? We can short it if you wish, to Isa. Is okay?'

'Is fine!' she laughed.

Bobby asked, 'What's all this about, then?'

'My name,' she said, not looking at him.

'Isa,' said Pepe quietly.

'Yes,' she replied.

*   *   *

Mina coughed delicately, to attract everyone's attention. 'Have we all finished eating? Papaterio? Would you care for coffee?'

'Bollocks to that muck,' screwing his napkin into a ball, 'Where's the brandy?'

'Papaterio!'

'Good idea!' Alfredo said eagerly. 'Would you like a cognac, Isa?'

'Thank you, yes,' Bobby cried with enthusiasm.

They adjourned to the family sitting room and relaxed, an immediate haze of cigar smoke from Gualterio. Mina and Ana bustled with glasses.

Alfredo intercepted his brother. '*Momentito, hombre.* A word.'

They went towards the terrace door.

'Well?'

Alfredo pointed down with his unlit cigar. 'Your enthusiasm is showing, brother!'

'What?'

'Your fun-fountain. Harness it, for Christ's sake, or wear a bloody skirt!'

'Oh Jesus!' He turned his back and adjusted himself, wincing, hearing Alfredo's snigger.

'Everything alright?' asked Mina brightly.

'Fine, fine,' said Alfredo, 'Just Pepe trying to stand out in a crowd as usual, isn't that right, *hombre?*' slapping Pepe on the shoulder.

'Shut it!'

Mina frowned, ushering them back to the inner circle of the room, where Gualterio was reluctantly replying in Castilian to a question from Ez.

When everyone was seated, a toast was proposed by Pepe. He informed them, smiling, hand on Bobby's shoulder, that he and the Drach Agency of London were in business together as from October. He repeated it in Spanish for his father, and watched his face carefully.

Gualterio drained his brandy. Stood up. 'I'm tired,' he said. Nodded to the guests, and left the room muttering *'Buenas noches.'*

Bobby hardly noticed. He was, instead, realising how it must feel to be a king.

A satisfactory, a tremendous, conclusion. And Ezita looking like a dewy-eyed Jersey cow. He sipped his cognac, enjoying the attention he was receiving from Alfredo and his pleasant wife. He would like Ez to look like this. Calm and neat.

Pepe said to her quietly, 'You remember? About the gardens?'

She stood up instantly, smiling. 'Of course I do.'

Bobby looked up sharply. 'What's this? Walkies?'

'Well . . .' Ez looked at Pepe.

Smoothly, he said 'I wish to show Isa something of interest in the garden, Roberto –'

A cackle from Alfredo. A glare from his brother.

'– and so, if you would excuse us?'

'No need, no need!' exclaimed Bobby, putting his glass down. 'I'd love to see round your garden, Pepe!'

'Why don't we all go?' suggested Alfredo, straightfaced, and took Mina's arm.

'Oh bloody hell,' moaned Pepe, and hissed a word in Catalan to his brother which evoked a gleeful cackle, and 'Pepe!' from Mina.

Ez was trying not to laugh as they all trooped on to the terrace and down the steps. Bobby was cupping her elbow, Pepe trailing miserably behind. They all paused for a moment, looking at the

83

long curving path ahead; lanterns shone on the granite, making it sparkle round the shadows.

'Something of interest, you said?' from Alfredo, his shoulders shaking.

'Yes, is it something I've missed?' Mina asked eagerly.

Oh shit. He thought desperately. Put his hand lightly on the chestnut-coloured silk in front of him. Her back responded, and his hand stayed. 'Er . . . Isa is very keen for Spanish poetry,' he improvised. 'Lorca, you know? I thought she might wish to see around, and know some of the history of this place. Spanish Civil War,' lamely.

'Did Lorker start it, then?' Bobby asked with interest.

'*O Dios mío!* . . . No, Roberto, he died during it.'

'In this garden?' impressed.

Alfredo doubled up, squawking. Even Mina was beginning titter.

God Almighty! He mumbled something, and Bobby nodded, satisfied. Ez dropped back a step, and their hands were not surprised when they met suddenly and held.

'Isa?' as the merry trio walked ahead of them, Mina saying something about the statues attracting too much ivy, 'Isa, tomorrow morning – my lawyers will be meeting with you and Roberto, and then I go for a medical check –'

'Hey, brother! What's the name of this fucking bush? Roberto wants to know!'

'Alfredo!' Then 'Pepe!' as her brother-in-law responded with acidity, 'I have no bloody idea! Tell him it's a sodding king-size saucepan! Anything!'

Ez giggled, and he tucked her hand firmly against his side where she felt the suede of his belt.

'There won't be much time to talk, Isa, not then. But I shall be in London on the fourteen of September –'

'The fourteenth?' Her eyes shone. His face was so close, so nearly –

'Pepe? You won't forget your appointment with Don Salvador tomorrow?'

'No, Mina. Thank you.' With his free hand, he touched her mouth. 'I go to the Royal Albert Hall, is a recital. Will you come to where I shall be staying −?'

'Ezita! Translation please, sweetie! Alf doesn't know the English for − what was it you said, Alf?'

'I said *cojones*,' Alfredo chortled. Mina slapped his arm.

'That's the one − co-honnies! Ezita?'

She felt Pepe's cheek against hers. He was tittering. 'Don't you dare translate that!'

'Sorry, Bob − perhaps it's botanical.'

'Mmmm, could be. He said there were two of them growing somewhere.'

A squeak from Mina. Ez was laughing helplessly, Pepe and Alfredo making funny noises. Bobby scowled at them all. 'I bet you do know, you silly mare!'

'I'll tell you later! Pepe −'

'I will telephone you before then. But, please, will you come?'

'To your recital? Of course I will.'

'Not to the recital.'

'Oh?'

For a flying instant as they looked at each other, their lips almost touched. He took a step back. '*Cristo*! . . . er . . . what were we . . . Oh, yes. No, not at the recital, I mean to my hotel. Isa, I shall be staying at the Grosvenor, we will be able to talk and −'

'Yes,' quietly.

'Oy! Prima Donna!' from Alfredo. 'How much further do you want us hike along this bloody path? Should we have brought a packed breakfast?'

Mina giggled, then said 'If you have seen enough, Roberto, Isabel, perhaps another cognac before we say goodnight?'

'Excellent idea, Mrs Mina!' and Bobby walked back to join Ez, who was amiably talking to Pepe. Good girl, be friendly to him, keep him happy!

Later, on the way to their rooms, he said 'That word Alfredo said − co-honnies. Tell Bobby what it means; I'd like to grow some in my window-box, Alf says they last for years.'

'Balls,' she said succinctly.

'There's no need to be fucking rude!' he snapped, and bade the future Mrs Drach a curt goodnight.

# 6

Holst's music for the planets soared through the chamber's shadows, trumpets bouncing through the arches and down to the marble floor.

Louis wished that he was deaf.

Vito, enjoying it immensely, chewed on his cigar and remained sprawled on the embroidered bedcover. He liked the music and he liked the bedcover. He and Keta had bought it in Istanbul, a tapestry of gold and pink, surreal roses and irises and little faces that peered through them. Voyeurs, he supposed.

His hand vaguely conducted the hidden orchestra. Someone, he reflected, had once used the iris as a symbol of sexuality. Probably a poet trying to make excuses for himself and earning fame through self-pity. Nothing honest about poets. Cloaked everything in an effort to reveal themselves. He brushed some ash from his robe.

Louis said loudly, 'It's like being in a freezer!' and sat on the bed, his face irritated. 'Where's the heating in this rat-hole?'

'Dear Louis, when villas were built in the eighteenth century, they turned their noses up at central heating and opted for Nature's north-westerlies instead. I told you – put something on. Plenty of my stuff in the closets over there,' and he waved a hand towards the shadows.

Donizetti from tomorrow. He suddenly remembered something he'd read in *La Stampa* the other day, and began to laugh. Oh yes, indeed: an interview with Modesto Martes, confirming that he would be at La Scala later in the year for *Otello*. Claiming that he preferred Verdi to Donizetti, though yes, he would like to do Nemorino at some stage, and no, he did not consider himself too old to tackle the role of young peasant boy.

The interviewer had added 'Martes admits to being fortyish.' His laughter increased. Fortyish? Oh sure, like Mussolini would one day be canonized. Spanish sod.

'Something funny?' Louis from the closets.

'What? Can't hear you!'

'Then turn that fucking music down!'

Vito smiled, turned it to full volume.

Louis came back to the bed, wrapped in a dressing-robe of pale satin with a fur belt.

Vito looked at it smiling. 'That's one of Keta's,' he remarked.

'So?'

'Oh, nothing. Nothing.' The music ended. Vito lazily reached over and selected another tape.

'Must you?' yelled Louis as Mussorgsky crashed into the arena. Then put his mouth to Vito's ear. Licked. Said 'There was a ghastly pink rabbit in the closet.'

'Oh?' and fingers began to stroke the shine on Keta's robe.

Louis said coldly 'A fluffy one with a bow-tie. Why doesn't she grow up? She's old enough to be a fucking grandmother!'

The fingers ceased stroking. 'I would advise you – again – not to make remarks of that kind about Keta.'

'Oh shit, don't tell me it's see the holy bridegroom time! What, exactly, has that red-haired lesbian got that I haven't? Apart from the obvious.' His thumb traced a circle round an exposed navel. Vito blew a faint breath upwards which touched and tickled his moustache.

'Well?' viciously, and the thumb gouged.

'Christ! . . . Nothing, dear boy. Nothing at all.'

*　　*　　*

Curled up on her old settee, she rested her head against Ignacio and pondered on the word 'yesterday'. Her cup of tea was cold, a hand stroked a small book. Almost dawn, the room was as cold as the tea.

Yesterday was . . . the last glimpse of Pepe signing on the dotted line, bidding them *adiós* before departing for his medical appointment, a wave over his shoulder as he and Federico the secretary left with the two attorneys.

Yesterday was . . . the flight home, her thoughts ignoring coffee and sugar, staring out at a sky that did nothing.

Bobby had sighed. Reaction setting in, he thought. All the excitement over the Contreras deal, plus being able to practise one of her languages. And all that foul wine last night. Mouton Cadet on the label. Sheep urine inside. He sighed again, as she twisted an unwrapped sugar cube round and round.

It must be like this, training a young dog. But he would say nothing at this stage, plenty of time for gentle guidance later, when he proposed properly. In a few days' time, he thought.

Said aloud, 'I'll ring Alan tomorrow.'

She turned her head, abandoning the clouds parked below. 'Who's he?'

'Oh, sorry, I was forgetting you'd only met him a hundred times.' Barked 'The bloody lawyer, you silly mare!'

'Lawyer?' dreamily.

'Remember them? Dark suits and a nasty habit of bleeding poor buggers like me dry? God Almighty!'

'Sorry,' she smiled. Their lawyers, of course. Messrs Osgood, Hutchinson & Webb. Alan Osgood dealt with the Agency's European contracts; a thin pole of a man whose hobby was collecting mediaeval musical instruments.

'I've got the most magnificent theorbo!' he had exclaimed on one occasion.

'Lucky you,' Bobby retorted coldly, 'I have to make do with the one God gave me.'

Now, happy that he had her attention, he continued 'We need his doodah for the contract, then he can deal direct with those dagos we saw this morning, after he's seen Sniffer. Did he tell you he'd be over for a recital next month? Him and that Spanish mezzo, Bragas.' He sniggered. 'Good luck to him! She wants her hubby Felix as the pianist, Sniffer wants his own man. León something.'

'León Salvaj,' she murmured. Closed her eyes.

Poor cow. Probably a hangover. But – be kind, Bobby. He reached into his jacket and pulled out a thin package wrapped in newspaper. Dropped it in her lap.

'Here – wake up! Pressie for you.'

She focused on it slowly, stared at him. 'For me? Oh Bob, that is sweet of you!' fumbling with the wrapping.

He said acidly, 'Don't thank me, thank Sniffer. He said to give it to you on the plane. Probably a bloody bomb. Oh – and do be careful with that expensive paper, won't you? He might want it back.'

Cartwheeling heart; unwrapped on her knee was the anthology Magda had given him when he was nine years old. And inside the cover, a piece of folded lined notepaper. Her smile was so enormous that she was sure her face wasn't wide enough.

'Christ!' exclaimed Bobby, picking up the battered book with its peeling sellotape, 'This must have cost him a bloody fortune! Set you back a few thousand at Sotheby's, this would.' Then, 'Ooooh look, genuine torn pages!'

She looked at his note, a page torn from an all-purpose jotter.

'Isa, for you I have drawn the line! You will see it. Isa, do not of forget, I will telliphone.'

A large 'P' followed, and a squiggle.

She smiled, touched it. His handwriting was no different from that of the nine year old Josep. She frowned then, trying to work out the first part of the message, wishing that it was in Spanish so that she could understand it.

Bobby was turning the pages of the anthology. 'What the fuck did he give you this for? It looks like bloody poetry. Here!' and he pointed to the opening line of a poem. 'What the hell does this mean?'

She suddenly felt full of spirits, alive. She pretended to study the Lorca, then announced 'It means: "I love your green balls, you dwarf." ' Tittered behind her hand.

Bobby said plaintively, 'Isn't that bloody typical of poets? Who's he supposed to be addressing, then, a fucking runner bean?'

'You mean you didn't know?' She smiled gently. 'Oh dear. You see, Robert, in Spain all male children are born with green genitals. Something to do with the trade winds, I think. It only lasts for a few weeks. This, you see, is a poem to a newborn baby.'

He looked at the page in wonderment. 'Well, you learn something every day, don't you! Do you mean to say that Sniffer and his brother used to have –' He stopped, looked at her shaking shoulders. Bawled, 'You stupid cow!'

And now, on the settee, chin resting on Ignacio's head, she chuckled again, this time thoughtfully. Outside, a few birds began their chorale, the first light in the avenue flickered off.

That laughter had been the birth of her idea. 'Poems set to music. I wanted to be a composer then.'

Poems. And music. Lorca and Zorrilla his favourites, as she lay in a waking dream of him. Obviously, she couldn't do it herself; the only music she had ever written was a melody for her viola, and her music teacher had played it solemnly on the piano first, before pointing out that Beethoven had beaten her to it and used it in his third symphony.

No. She couldn't do it for him. But Tom Patna and Nathan West could.

Then she was on the settee, reading eagerly. Lorca: Bobby's 'Bollocks Ode' as he had started to call it. Lyrical beauty. She read it now as if it were a song. Perfect for a tenor voice of his *legero* quality.

Then some of the other poems, perhaps, they could go with it. Say eight. An album, Patna for the lyrics. Pepe could do one side in Spanish, the other in English, dual market. Perhaps promote it, a studio recital for television. His own trademark, a take-off for his fund-raising.

Then excitement, turning the pages, searching for Zorrilla. She found his poem, *La Siesta*, languid, gentle. This would be a delight for Nathan, the rhythms were already there.

And suddenly, Pepe's message, 'For you I have drawn the line'. There it was, the line. In *La Siesta*. Same blue ink, large 'P', squiggle.

Underlined:  '. . . *duerme entretanto*
        *que yo te velo: duerme*
        *que yo te canto.*'
She kissed the sellotaped page.
    'Sleep, meanwhile,
    As I watch over you. Sleep,
        while I sing to you.'
Without fuss or thought, she was in love with the magician. The last street lamp died, and a milk float clattered.

*     *     *

The telling had been done, and Josep Gusano was dumb-founded.

'I find this hard to believe,' he said quietly.

Pepe refused to look anywhere other than at Josep's eyes. His own were solemn and determined. And so was his mouth as he said 'I mean it, Josep. You are a friend and part of this family, I revere all that you have done. But now . . .' and his hands flickered, 'now there are hills I must climb, don't you see? For Magda. My next birthday brings me to forty-one, and then I have what? Fifteen years to sing? A few more, if God is good. I must take long strides now, old friend, and I don't think you could match your pace with mine.'

'You have always been at liberty to stretch your pace.'

'Yes,' impatiently, 'but the fault in that, Josep, is that I need a manager who will encourage me to do that! I say to you frankly, you are forever blocking my ideas, putting your hand on my pen if I wish to sign 'yes', telling me over and over that the time is not right, the venue is not right, the hour of the day is not right! And I have been lazy, unthinking, did nothing. Now, there is the Fund to work for, and I will need every promotion and kick up the arse I can take! . . . No, *amigo*, I need a go-getter, I want for Magda portions of the pie you would only insist were trivial and might give me stomach-cramp. I need Drach. I cannot turn this chance away. I'm sorry.'

Josep folded his jacket over his arm. Stood up slowly.

'So be it, Pepe. I don't know Drach personally, all I know is that his way is not mine. But he is good. Very good. I wish you luck, every success.' Held out his hand.

Pepe shook it firmly, eager to be gone.

*     *     *

Before most of the household had stirred, Federico Golpe was hurrying down the tunnel towards Pepe's kennel. He didn't care

91

for the tunnel, being somewhat claustrophobic, nor did he like the smug religious paintings in the alcoves. Sometimes he didn't rate his employment as Pepe's Barcelona-based secretary very highly, either, especially at this hour of the day.

In answer to his triple knock, Pepe opened the door, unshaven and wearing nothing but a plain wrap that reached his knees, hairy legs bare and displaying a prominent blue vein. He was flexing his nostrils.

'Telegram for you, Don Pepe,' handing him a yellow sheet, 'and the –'

'*Gracias*,' and shut the door.

He caught sight of the sender's name, grinned. Poured himself a cup of weak coffee.

Fazzoletto. Hardly the most succinct of wire-senders.

'Greetings, Pulgarcito! Am heading off for Paris today, *Bohème*. Did I tell you they've paired me off with that bitch, Lehatz. Three perfs only, tickets still available. After this am set for the Zarzuela Madrid, only hour's flight from you, can I pitch my tent with you for day or two? Send to Paris-Opéra if poss, name of hotel escapes me, bet it's a Frog Hilton. Adriana sends love, looks enormous, aren't I a clever boy. Saw your lady Merdina in Milano, rumour has it you've neglected her for so long she's started wearing knickers, can this be true.

*Arrivederci*, Pio.'

Pepe sniggered to himself, went into the den to dictate a brief yes you fat idiot, and made a note to warn Mina.

Showering, the reminder about Bionda Merdina lasted in his mind only slightly longer than the first bubbles round his feet. Inside himself, he could hear a giggle, see eyes like doves, a face the shape of his heart.

Whistling *Rule Britannia*, he decided suddenly that Teresa Bragas could have her own way as far as the recital pianist was concerned. She could have bloody Felix. In future, though, Roberto Drach would be told to make damn sure that it was León Salvaj on the concert platform with him.

*     *     *

The first thing that Pio Fazzoletto did on arriving in a hotel suite was to perform a simple ceremony. This consisted of hunting through his bags to find his coat-of-arms; and, having found it, to kiss it, hum a few bars of *O Sole Mio* and place it tenderly in a prominent position in the lounging area.

It had been made for him years ago by a fellow student at the Academy in Bologna. The student had had a cunning way with ceramics, later abandoning music for pottery but unfortunately losing most of his fingers in an accident with a buzz-saw. Now, on a warm Paris afternoon, Pio stood it carefully on a cocktail cabinet, after removing a framed map of the city which he dropped into a waste-paper basket. He grinned at it lovingly. It was gleaming white with a solitary minim engraved upon it. The minim contained a leering face. Underneath was the motto

*CANTARE! MANGIARE! FOTTERE!*

His prized possession now established, Pio unwound the swathe of silk scarves from his shoulders and lowered his bulk with distrust on to the chaise longue. Eyed the usual complimentary bottle of *vin rouge*, and put in a quick call to his wife, beaming like a happy child at the sound of her voice. Hung up, reassured that all was well. She was certainly big in the belly this time. Shyly, he thought to himself that maybe his sperm was getting bigger. He'd thought of mentioning this to the gynaecologist but was too embarrassed. There was nothing in Adriana's text books about it. Nothing under "s" for supersperm.

He sat back, yawned. Paris. He hated it. Pio, he reflected, is not a happy person. Not to mince the meat, Pio is in fact pissed off.

Paris. Doses of unending servility and fawning. Of course, he was used to that wherever he happened to be, but here the doses came in dollops of *crême* and he yearned for someone to shout go screw yourself you fat tuneless cretin, as the audience sometimes did at La Scala.

He eyed the bottle of wine. Château-something. To read some of these labels, you'd think France had more bloody *châteaux* than trees. This particular wine had already been uncorked – 'To let it breathe, *Monsieur*,' smiled the waiter, fawning.

'Very interesting,' Pio had murmured in Italian, 'A bottle with lungs. How clever!'

'*Merci, Monsieur* Fazzoletto,' fawning.

'*Vaffanculo!*' offered Pio, wishing that he would. He tittered.

Started scowling as the wine breathed. Somewhere in one of his bags was the libretto of *La Bohème*. His enthusiasm for this production had nose-dived and hit the ground when he learned the identity of his new Mimi. Mimi: defined as seventeen years old, frail, consumptive, beautiful. So what had they given him this time?

Bo Lehatz. 'The brightest star in our cultural heavens!' screamed *Le Figaro*. God help the rest of the poor sods, thought Pio. Rubbed the thickly-bearded chin and narrowed his eyes. Bo Lehatz. Thirty-three, thin-lipped, thin-voiced, a body more at home in a mortuary. Had an aversion to singing in Italian, turned every "r" into that sickly French gargle. Off-stage, supercilious, stalking around with her retinue making loud remarks about her fellow singers.

He waved the waiter away, then dolefully poured himself a glass of Château-something. After the first eight swallows he began to enjoy it. While he drank, he read Pepe's wire which had been smoothly despatched from Opera House to hotel.

Pio grinned. Good! Lodgings solved, plus Ana's cooking. He would ask her to concentrate on geese this time. Spanish chickens tasted as bland as grass and cream cheese.

Re-filling his glass, he ambled into the bedroom, knowing what he would find. Yes, there it was. A bloody duvet, with a tidal wave of lace. Bloody Paris. All this and Bo Lehatz. Still, he reminded himself, even hell had its bright spots. And Buzzer Ahmet was one of them.

*       *       *

The Paris-Opéra had been lucky to get the Bangladeshi conductor.

Buzzer Ahmet had many forthright views on opera and its rôle in the musical scheme of things, and refused to conduct more than four a year.

He had come from Bangladesh via Australia some twenty years ago, a young stern and even-tempered conductor named Zubair Ahmet, who gradually became known to those in his world as Buzzer.

As Pio mused and drank wine five floors above, Buzzer walked purposefully through the hotel foyer. He was a man of medium height, strongly built, with compelling eyes in an astonishingly pale face, and a voice that was crisp and accustomed to speaking several languages.

An excited voice behind him stopped Buzzer in mid-stride.

'*Monsieur* Ahmet! *Maestro!*'

The hotel manager. Buzzer tried not to frown. He timed his engagements with precision; the orchestra would already be assembling in the House. His eyebrow raised itself in query, nearly disappearing into the neat shock of black hair.

'*Maestro!* There's an urgent phone call for you – you may take it in my office – it's from Dacca!'

Dacca? From home? Buzzer burst through the door. His father was ill, had been back in hospital for some days. Snatched the phone, barked 'Ahmet!'

'Hi,' came a lazy voice. 'Glad I caught you, Buzz. Can we talk sometime this evening?'

Buzzer glared at the hovering manager. 'Decca!' he hissed as his heart rate slowed.

What the hell did Decca want now? More importantly, what did their chief pain-in-the-crotch Byron Larch want!

'Hello, Byron. This evening? Sorry, I'm tied up.'

'Untie, old boy.'

'No can do. Tomorrow lunchtime?'

'Can't you –? Ah well, that will have to do. Must see you before I go back to London, new idea's come up.'

'My suite, tomorrow, half after midday.'

A new idea's come up, mimicked Buzzer as he hung up. He hoped it was a damn sight better than the last one – standing in a bloody barge on the Thames trying to conduct the *Water Music*, violinists all over the place and third trumpet being sick.

He stepped into the waiting taxi, then cleared his mind of everything but the work in hand.

Buzzer gazed out at Paris with undisguised pleasure.

*　　*　　*

'Isabel?'

'Pepe? Is that you?'

'I think so. I am looking round to see. Yes, it is me!'

'Your voice sounds different on the phone.'

'Yours does not. It smiles at me, like before. Are you alone?'

'Yes, Roberto's in Liverpool. Just me and Julie, our secretary.'

'Isa, I too am mercifully alone at the moment. Just imagine! – no Alfredo, no Roberto! What on earth can we say, now that we have not interruptions? . . . You are laughing!'

'I was remembering!'

'What were you doing when I rang?'

'Having coffee and looking at an awful photograph of you in today's paper.'

'*Cristo*, not the one with teeth?'

'The one with lots of teeth.'

'Even badder! What is my photo doing there in your newspaper?'

'Sitting there surrounded by newsprint.'

'Very funny, Isa, very funny! It is a review?'

'No, sir, it's an ad for your recital in London. Roberto's going to it, to the recital, I mean . . .'

'Isa, would you like to come too? I can get you the ticket –'

'I'd . . . well, I'd love to, but –'

'You would sooner wait until the fifteen. So would I. If you were out there –'

'I wouldn't hear what you were singing.'

'Nor would I, then *Madame* Bragas would give me looks to freeze my back-spine! Don't laugh – she is a melodic piranha fish. Isa, you are still giggling! Look, *querida*, can we sort out the fifteen, please?'

'Sorry. I am just so happy. Yes. The fifteenth. You will be at the Grosvenor Hotel?'

'The Grosvenor, yes. Until the sixteen, the Sunday. Do you know it?'

'Sunday? Of course I know –'

'The bloody Grosvenor, you *cucufato*! It is spelt G.R.O.S.V.–'

'I know how to spell it, you – what was that word you used?'

'*Cucufato*. It means a nutcase, a raving idiot nut.'

'Ah. Not a fat cuckoo, then.'

'Most certain not! You are slender and just nice for my hand around your waist.'

'Am I?'

'Oh definitely, *Señorita* Isabel! . . . God! . . . er . . . what were we saying?'

'*Cucufatos* at the Grosvenor.'

'Ah, *sí, exacto*. So, on the fifteen, Saturday evening, I am free as a bird –'

'Why are you giving a recital on a Friday?'

'Holy shit, Isa, does it matter! Listen, will you! I shall send a car to your apartment, and then Enrique, who travels with me, he will bring you to my suite. And we shall talk and have supper together, no Roberto, no Alfredo. The car will pick you up for me at seven, okay?'

'Okay, *señor*! Pepe? Thank you for the anthology . . .'

'Did Zorrilla give you my message?'

'Yes. He passed it on to me when I couldn't sleep. It was beautiful.'

'He is good companion. And a musician with words. Look, I must go, Isa . . . You will not forget? Saturday?'

'Not for one second.'

'Until the fifteen, Grey Eyes.'

'Until then.'

* * *

It was just as Fazzoletto had feared. He had already had nightmares about the first rehearsals, when his head and stomach were growling with wine: and God bless 'em, they had all come true.

If this was *Pagliacci*, he thought, I would be dressed up as a

97

fucking clown and no-one would take any notice. Here, I am made to look like one without the costume, *grazie* to that skinny nasty-tempered bitch. If she were chopped into little pieces, she wouldn't make even a saucerful of bloody pasta.

Again, Buzzer Ahmet was the saving grace for Pio. He knew exactly what he was doing and exactly when to do it; nor did he insist on his singers going full voice at rehearsal during the early stages. And he had worked with Bo Lehatz before. Apart from Buzzer, the rest of the production was pure shit. His Marcello was a nervy Bulgarian called Roic, who had been living on and off with a girl from Glasgow; as a result, his Italian had a certain spikiness to it. Pio thought it was like adding vinegar and chives to pure cream.

But, inevitably, it was Lehatz whom God had sent as a reminder that Pio had not been to Mass for months. She stared down her nose as he walked on stage for the first sing, remarking to her voice coach that Mimi would never fall in love with a fat hairy bastard like that even if she were as drunk as a kite.

'*Buon giorno*,' as civilly as he could.

'*Bonjour*, Fatty.'

She glared down at Buzzer, shirt-sleeved and waiting in the pit, his desk lamp gleaming. '*Maestro*, this is to be *La Bohème, n'est-ce pas?* Not a burlesque?'

Her voice coach giggled.

Buzzer's face was cold and empty. 'Your entrance scene, please, Miss Lehatz.'

'That's where you drop your fucking key in the dark,' Pio said helpfully.

'Fat dog turd!'

'Careful! Don't waste that lovely voice of yours, we might need it to sharpen pencils!'

'Mimi's entrance scene,' announced Buzzer, level-toned.

'Mimi's entrance scene!' bawled Pio. 'Someone stand behind me with a shovel in case she hits a right note!'

'*Va te faire enculer!*'

'Sooner do it that way, *mon amie*, than with you!'

Buzzer raised his stick, and the orchestra obediently launched into the opening bars of *Colonel Bogey*.

'Now!' he said sternly when the laughter had died down, 'May we begin?'

'*Si, Maestro.*'

'*Oui, Maestro.*'

'Your poor bloody husband!'

'Fuck off, gas balloon!'

*　　*　　*

Vito, slumped in front of the dressing-table mirror, silently informed his sweating reflection that he was heading for some kind of trouble.

Louis was in Salzburg with him.

He should not have been within multi-miles of Salzburg. Vito knew for a fact that Louis and other members of the Reggio Bettino Choral Society had been scheduled this week and the next for chorus work in *Nabucco* at the Sydney Opera House. Instead of which, he was in Salzburg doing sod-all other than lurk around the sets of *L'Elisir d'Amore* with a peculiar intensity that had taken him by surprise.

He, smiling, told Vito as they drank rich creamy coffee at a pavement table that he had pleaded a neat case of bronchitis.

Vito had looked worriedly at him, squinting through the sun in his eyes.

And Louis laughed. 'You really should have been born a girl, Lavagna! A scared little girlie!'

'Be quiet, damn it!'

'A little girlie. Like you were last night, crying fat tears when I stopped working your balls! Next time, Miss Lavagna, when my teeth are grazing in your balding pastures –'

'Shut-your-mouth!' glancing fearfully around the café.

And after that, he was supposed to emote as a bloody lovesick peasant boy! Vito pushed away the few flowers he had picked up from the stage after the performance, reached for a fresh chunk of cottonwool.

Louis. Off-key complacency surrounding him. Vito dabbed at the perspiring makeup, meeting his own gaze in the mirror. A still moment. Louis was a vortex. He nodded to himself. Beware,

99

Lavagna. Ditch him. Send him on his way with a diamond-studded flea in his ear. If you can. If you want to.

Impatiently tore off more cotton wool.

* * *

Bobby Drach was happily selecting mushrooms from an open-fronted shop in Kings Road. Must be the right size; look at those skinny buggers shoved right to the front, God Almighty, they had to be joking!

His fingers swooped behind the large price marker and found the fresher ones. Good. A lot more clinging compost on these. Humming under his breath, he handed over the bag for weighing, then flagged down a taxi.

Tonight, Ez was coming to dinner. Nothing unusual about that, she often did.

Nothing unusual. And he was nervous.

Calm down, fruitcake, he cautioned himself as he bustled around the kitchen in his apron, scattering knives and having to shut cupboard doors twice. The trouble with you is, you're rushed off your size nines these days; up and down to bloody Liverpool wishing that conductors were an endangered species, especially that stupid bugger who had assumed that the Drach Agency mezzo's red rash meant an allergy to Debussy.

And then there was the forthcoming arrival of Sniffer to these shores and more legals to contend with; oh bloody whoopee, hours with Alan Osgood and his theorbo.

And then there was Ezita, going from bad to zero, pestering Nathan West about some lunatic idea she'd had about the Bollocks Ode, plus a silly smile on her face most of the time, saying 'Oh – sorry?' whenever she was spoken to.

But tonight – dinner at Bobby's, just the two of them. This is the big league for Bobby, he beamed, chopping onions, smoothing them into a bowl. He knew she liked his Beef Stroganoff. The steak was marinating. Soured cream in the fridge, those bloody over-priced mushrooms peeled. Salad tossed until the lettuce screamed. Yes, the big league, rinsing his hands under the tap.

Me Bobby. Me – husband. Christ! His titter was nervous as he sorted out cutlery. God, I hope she's in an adult mood tonight, ready to cope with all the plans they would have to make. I hope she's thought it over very seriously!

Jesus! – I hope she's bloody remembered!

# 7

'Seen Martes's latest write-up for *Butterfly*? Pretty starry. Let's hope that Snifferkins does the same for us!'

Ez, perched on the kitchen table, indicated that she had not seen it. Bobby was feeling a little irritable. Not only had she arrived early when he was still in his apron and his hair in a mess, but she was also wearing his unfavourite colour of rose pink. Okay for roses but not for leisure suits, in his opinion. And her hair! Snaking all over the place, the sort of thing you see on the end of a long handle, resting in a bucket.

Furthermore, tremors were attacking his soul. Was he doing the right thing? What if she said yes? Suppose she said no?

'In the *Financial Times*,' nodding his head towards the draining-board, where the paper lay submerged beneath onion skins and mushroom stalks. 'They were bloody quick to review it, I must say – only six days after the bloody performance.'

'There's been nothing at all in there about Pepe's *Traviata*,' she complained, swinging her legs. A wooden spoon fell to the floor.

'For God's sake, give the *F.T.* a chance – they've already done one opera review in seven months, we mustn't expect miracles from their bloody arts critic. Pick that spoon up, I need it!'

'What's for dinner?' breezily, watching as he grabbed a spatula and stirred the contents of a round pan. 'Is it Stroganoff?'

'Of course it's bloody Stroggy! What did you think it was, egg and fucking chips? And stop lurking there like a stick of rock, make yourself useful! . . . Oh Christ, the butter's burning! Bobby mustn't panic, Bobby mustn't let this silly mare put him off!' His fingers flew from switch to switch, 'Shit, I've turned the rice off now!'

'Do you think Bobby ought to phone the fire brigade?' tittered Ez as blue smoke sputtered round the frying-pan.

'Fuck off! Get the salad from the fridge, it's already been tossed –'

'Must've been heavy for you,' she murmured.

'The salad, you dozy bitch! . . . .Christ, these onions are going black! Plates, Ez, quick! Bloody hell!'

They ate their meal to a background of Beethoven quartets, Bobby relaxing gratefully with his wine.

He pointed a fork at the panelled wall behind her, 'That's new.'

She turned and eyed the Goya print in its gilt frame. 'It's . . . well, it's a bit obvious, isn't it?'

'Oh dear, and there was silly me thinking that paintings were there to be seen! How naïve of Bobby!' He glared as he reached for more salad. 'And what would be your own idea of the un-obvious, mmm? A bloody stuffed bear in sequins?'

'Shut up,' laughing. 'Oh Robert, that was a lovely meal – thank you.'

The point of no return, he said to himself, as they adjourned to the buttoned leather armchairs in the lounge. He poured out cognac, said 'Coffee later.' Took a deep breath, held it while he counted three. Said quickly,'Ez, you know what I asked you on the plane. A couple of weeks ago. Have you given it any thought?'

'About the Lorca poem and Nathan West, you mean?'

'Christ Almighty! When we were on the fucking plane going, not coming back!'

She sipped, eyed him. 'Oh. Yes. Of course . . . . . Oh Bobby . . . I feel very flattered.' Large eyes solemn. 'But –'

The "but" caught him unawares. 'But? But what?'

She looked down, concentrated on a large button on the arm of her chair. Cleared her throat. 'Oh my dear friend, dear Bob, I couldn't have really said yes before, let alone now. Not since –' She bit her lip.

Pounced. 'Not since what? Come on, tell me! You've been drifting around like a fart in a storm for days! Jesus, don't tell me you've suddenly got yourself a bloody toy-boy!'

She smiled unwillingly. 'No. . . .'

'Then what? Why? Who? Someone you met while I was in Liverpool?'

'No. Before that.' She smiled softly. Took a breath that raced. 'It was when we were in Barcelona.'

He shook his head and swallowed at the same time, spluttering, eyes watering. Then, 'In Barcelona? I don't get this, Ez. We were only there five bloody minutes, and you were with me the whole . . . Oh no! Oh Jesus fucking Christ, no!' His hand thumped the arm of the chair. 'Not bloody Sniffer!'

'Stop calling him that,' automatically.

'This is bloody crazy! I always knew you were soft in the head, but this . . . This is the daydream of the bloody century!' And, as she shook her head, 'Of all the wild ideas – to pick on that fucking hook-nosed midget!'

'He is not a midget!'

'You could put the little sod on your sideboard –'

'– he's well over five –'

'– and forget to bloody dust him! Of all the ridiculous –'

He got up stiffly and headed for the Courvoisier. 'Eyes the colour of old shit! A brother who looks like Mrs Tiggywinkle!' He spun round. 'Ez, look, darling, you've got a crush on him, on his voice, it'll go off, and when it does –' Gripped her hand. 'Then we can talk about our own –'

It was her smile that halted him. A smile that the Electricity Board would charge extra for. And her 'Bobby, it isn't just me.'

His jaw slackened. 'You mean that he . . . as well as you . . . ?'

She nodded slowly, the smile quivering then brightening again. So bright, indeed, that he found himself hugging her and patting her on the back and mumbling 'But how?' and 'There, there!'

Her laugh shook. 'We've hardly had time to think, to talk; but he rang, while you were in Liverpool. Bobby, we both know. That's all there is to it. It was so fast, as though it was there all the time and the hell with the introductions!'

Bobby perched in wonderment on the arm of her chair, ruffled her hair.

'I think I've lost my voice!' he said loudly.

She giggled.

'That's better, that's more like my Ezita! . . . But honestly, I don't know what to say. You and old Sniffer. Christ!'

*       *       *

Of all the passengers on board the TriStar, only Martes was nervous.

He sat in the private cabin with his Swiss-German manager, and even Klaus Ruwald was saying nothing to break the twitching silence.

Martes chewed his lip, stared at his feet, had wayward thoughts that trailed like ants back and forth until he wanted to howl.

'Shall I order something to eat?' Ruwald asked suddenly.

Modesto eyed him and shook his head. Glanced out of the porthole, his face creased with panic.

All he was sure of was that Mimosa would kill him. And he would die seeing venom and not love on her little round face.

He re-crossed his legs, fingers tapping. *Herr* Ruwald started to speak again, then changed his mind.

Modesto closed his eyes. God God GOD! How could he have been so crass, so sick in the head, so idiotically sick in the balls? He thumped his knee in frustration, and again Ruwald looked up from the paperwork spread neatly on his coffee tray.

'Might I suggest something?' he asked quietly.

'No!'

Ruwald shrugged. Cleared his throat, then said 'Perhaps, then, you might care to discuss the Gala we're to do next January?'

'No I bloody wouldn't!' Modesto flared. 'I'm already in the middle of one farce, I have no wish to talk about another!'

'It's in a good cause,' said Ruwald undeterred.

'I don't care if it will save the bloody world from starvation! I am not doing it, and that – is – FINAL!'

'Oh but you are,' Ruwald said smoothly. 'The contract was drawn up: you signed. I merely thought you might wish to discuss the programming.'

'Well I don't! I don't want to hear about it, I don't want to talk about the bloody thing!'

'It's for orphans –'

'Fuck the orphans!'

He glared down at the useless clouds. Disintegration, he thought. The symptoms were there. Total disintegration. I and my balls are going mad.

105

GOD! He switched his gaze to the inset lights in the ceiling. One of them was hissing. Like Mimosa, when she was angry. God!

I have never been weak before. Tempted, yes. But never weak. Yes! – he could start off by saying that to Mimosa! Mimosa, I have never been weak in my life – you know that, darling.

His shoulders slumped. If Mimosa already knew . . . the newspapers . . . God! . . . if she knew, he wouldn't get beyond 'Mim' before she savaged his throat.

Klaus Ruwald was beginning to feel pity. Sometimes Martes could be a flamboyant show-off, leering and winking suggestively, posing; but there was justification for that in his headline-catching career. His bedtime habits, on the other hand, had always been as secret as a freemason's left leg. And he knew Mimosa Martes well. Beneath that small exterior lay a minefield, bang bang bang if she was ever stepped upon. God alone knew how many pieces of Martes there would be to shovel up and auction.

Pleased with this analogy, he rang the bell for the steward. His client looked more than ready for a generous Glenlivet.

Modesto chewed his nail. So much for jokes! Coon this, coon that, Christ, then in she walked in a one-piece jogsuit of clinging crimson, trainers that had never hit a pavement, and silk-black hair smoothed away from her face. That face! Skin the colour of a sunbathing peach, smooth and sleek, ebony eyes slanting and smiling and –

He moved sharply in his seat. Oh God, that was all he needed to plead his case: begging for mercy and understanding, and getting an instant hard-on whenever he thought about her! God!

Two large Scotches arrived, and miniatures of soda. Eyed his Rolex watch. Only two hours before the plane touched down and Mimosa took off. God!

'The critics were as one in praise of your Pinkerton,' said Ruwald.

'My what?' Martes jumped, his drink lurching.

'Pinkerton. Your performance. They loved it.'

'Oh. Yes. Pinkerton . . .'

So did I, Christ forgive me! Lucha, my Butterfly, those gorgeous knowing eyes, soft buds that were lips. She'd deliberately teased him in her kimono, pulling the front suggestively, and giving his balls a pat during the love duet.

'*Herr* Martes? If I may . . . this Charity Gala in Seville. *Herr* Lavagna has finally agreed to take part –'

'Oh bloody hell, that's all I need!'

'– and the organizers wish to know if you'd be prepared to take the baritone role in the *Pearl Fishers* duet –'

Modesto's eyes lit up briefly. 'Sure. No problem.' He was never averse to surprising the world with his vocal accomplishments in another range.

'– to Lavagna's tenor.'

'NO! I am not singing with that clapped-out old arse-vandal, and that's final!' He buried his face in his hands. GOD! What was he going to do? He permitted himself one last ray of hope. She might not have heard . . . nor seen . . . nor . . .

The ray flickered and went out.

\*　　\*　　\*

Nathaniel West gave a sweeping bow and presented Ez with the folder.

'There you are, milady: signed, sealed and delivered. Do I get a kiss?'

'Oh Nat, bless you!' Hugged him excitedly. 'You're a genius!'

He snatched another kiss before she escaped. What was it about her that made him wish he was a kid again, running wild in the sun?

'And please give Tom my thanks when you see him,' she laughed breathlessly. Asked, 'What did he make of the translations I did for him?'

Nathan said reflectively, 'He had a few spots of bother. Like having to neaten up the phrase "Under the gipsy moon, things are watching her and she does not see them." He had to fit that to four crotchets, three quavers and a half-bar rest! Will Contreras settle for "Gi-i-psy moon, wa-tchi-ing"?'

They laughed. She opened the folder eagerly. The music and lyrics had been set and printed, neatly bound, smart title-page. Her first dream in clear detail.

107

'Oh Nat! Thanks so much. Well? What do you and Tom think of it, as a serious project, if Contreras likes it?'

'We like it a lot, Ezzie.' Which was true. He and Patna had been amused, then intrigued. And found themselves spending hours on the damn thing and discussing the future possibilities. Now, at her insistence, he sang part of the melody for her, major key, change to minor, where it stayed for as long as he sang. She could hear the words in her mind, fitting like mittens to the music.

Bobby swept into the room, frowning at the cigarette smoke, and peered over Ez's shoulder. 'Oh – is this the Bollocks Song?'

Ez giggled. Nathan merely said 'Must love you and leave you – give my regards to Contreras, will you, darling? Tell him Mozart would have earned *muchos* guilders for this work of art!'

'It's probably Mozart's anyway,' said Bobby caustically.

Nathan took no notice. 'Ezzie, let us know if Contreras likes the whole concept, will you? I've got a feeling this could be bonanza time!'

* * *

Mimosa was on the balcony of their bedroom. She leaned on the rail, closing her eyes and breathing in the fragrance of jasmine and honeysuckle. She couldn't imagine life without it. She had been born in the garden of her parents' home, and the whole of her forty-four years had been spent within the smell of it.

Below her, on the terrace, her son Gruñón waved an envelope, yelled 'Post!'

It was already vividly hot, and she took the letter with her into the shade to read it. Fumbled in the pocket of her robe for her glasses.

'Is Dad coming home today?'

'What?' peering at the envelope. 'Oh, yes. Sometime this evening.'

The postmark was Barcelona. She opened it, and pulled out a newspaper cutting, prodded inside for an accompanying letter. There wasn't one.

She looked at the clipping. A photograph. With *New York Times* and the relevant date added in biro at the top.

A photograph. She stared at it. Modesto. Well, obviously. He'd been in New York, and he had a habit of being photographed. She looked at his beaming face shown in three-quarter shot; casual shirt open to the waist, the medallion he always wore. She carefully followed his arms from the broad shoulders to where the hands rested. One on the woman's breast, the other under her chin.

The woman. Profile. Head tilted, a curving smile. Skinny blouse opened nearly as far as Modesto's shirt.

Underneath, a paragraph.

*CAUGHT NETTING A BUTTERFLY!*

"Modesto Martes in an intimate moment with American soprano Catalina Lucha, at the Late Late Club. Miss Lucha smiled 'Desto and I are real close'. There was no comment forthcoming from Mr Martes, who later left the nightclub with Miss Lucha in a private limo. The couple are currently appearing in Puccini's —"

'Anything wrong, *Mamá?*'

She turned over the cutting. Sellotaped to the back was a different piece of newsprint, this time from Madrid's *El País*. The *Servicios* column, where both men and women advertised their charms and sexual preferences and telephone numbers.

Years ago, a young giggling Mimosa and her girlfriend had dialled one of the numbers at random, hanging up with shrieks of laughter before the call could be answered. Years ago. And like a familiar echo, the current ad stared at her:

"Manolo, high quality, athletic positions, hotel or domicile, please ring me." The advertiser's name had been crossed out, "Modesto" printed neatly above.

'*Mamá*, what is it?'

She handed the cutting to him. Stared up at her son as he looked at the *New York Times* and the local delicacy on the other side.

He shouted, 'What the hell is this supposed to be? What bastard — oh don't cry, please don't, oh bloody hell!'

The tears were silent, looking at Gruñón white-faced.

'Dammit, Dad wouldn't do this to you, not to you! Of all the wicked —'

Wide-eyed, she stood up and took a deep shaking breath.

'I'll kill him!' she screamed. 'I'll make him wish he'd been born a rat in a research laboratory! God in Heaven,' shaking her fist, 'I'll split the bastard open so wide the blood will fly upwards, you hear me, Gruñón? – there'll be nothing left of him! I'll tear out his vocal chords one by bloody one and put them in a dish of BLOODY ACID!'

And she collapsed sobbing at her son's feet.

Their daughter Sara came running, '*Mamá*, what on earth –?'

'Help me get her to her room,' pleaded Gruñón from his painful kneeling position, 'she's had a shock, some bugger sent her this,' and he thrust the paper into her hand.

Sara was rooted, staring at her father and the woman who smiled at him.

'Don't just stand there, girl, help me with her!'

She bent down, gripped Mimosa's hand. 'Come along, dearest, come and lie down, I'll bring you some nice iced tea, then we can talk if you want to. Come, darling, come with Sarita.'

Mimosa allowed herself to be guided to the bedroom, leaning against her children, sobbing bitterly.

Later, propped up on the pillows, Gruñón and Sara hovering anxiously, she said icily, 'He is banned from this house.' And 'Sara, get his suitcases, please. Pack them yourself, don't ask the maid to do anything.'

'But where shall I put –?'

'Put them in the courtyard where his car usually stops. That will do. He will know.'

They tiptoed away, anxious backward glances.

Sara said, 'I'll stay within call. You do the cases, you're used to packing men's things. Then I suppose we should call the police . . . Oh *Papá*, how could you?'

'God help the silly sod!' said Gruñón, and went to pack.

*       *       *

'I shall require a modest funeral,' Buzzer Ahmet advised his wife, watching her finish her steak.

Fancy Ahmet, syndicated photographer, pealed with laughter.

110

'Oh come on, Buzz, it isn't the end of the world! Just one simple photograph, that's all, and it'll be me doing it – Byron and Decca were very specific about that,' and she reached over for his sautéed potatoes.

'Didn't PanAm feed you?' he enquired bitterly. 'Allah-God, woman, my soul is distraught enough after Fazzoletto and Bo Lehatz, without this!' He poured more wine for them both. 'I'd sooner talk about my funeral, if you please. The catering will be up to you, of course. But as far as the eulogies are concerned, I want it dignified and simple, as befits a man of music.'

'Such as the coffin passing beneath an arch of solemn batons?'

'Something like that. But a simple service, non-denominational, and a little music to send me on my way.'

'Mozart's *Requiem*, do you suggest, darling?'

'Tut tut, no. Nothing so obvious. I was thinking more of, say, Haydn. His symphonies.'

'Which one? He wrote 104 of them.'

'All of them, please. And I'll have those bastards Byron Larch and Pio Fazzoletto standing there the whole bloody way through, holding my remains between them!' He leaned forward, said urgently, 'You're sure it will be you and no-one else taking that photograph?'

*      *      *

'Christ on crutches, this'll wipe the twinkle out of his eye!' and Alfredo Contreras howled with laughter, waving the daily paper at his brother.

They were in the sitting room of Pepe's kennel. Mina was bustling in and out of the bedroom supervising the items he would need for the two-night stay in London, automatically taking over Magda's role.

Pepe said 'What will? Who?' as he rummaged through the bureau drawers for a missing manuscript.

Alfredo sniggered. 'Pretty-boy Martes! Just look at the picture they got of the stupid bugger! Surely he knew the gents of the press would be following him all over New York? Must have brains made of wool!'

111

Mina peered over his shoulder at *La Vanguardia*. 'Oh, that one. Modesto,' she informed Pepe, 'in a rather intimate moment.'

'Intimate!' scoffed Alfredo. 'If it grew any bigger it would poke her eye out! Christ, look where his hand is! It's worse than the photo of him on the back page!'

Guffawing, he tossed the paper to his brother.

Pepe laughed with delight. 'So this is the coon he was so scared of! – I told you about that, remember? No wonder he looks so smug!'

'Pepe, please! Don't use that word!'

'Eh? Smug?'

'She means "coon" brother. Nowadays, one has to say "less pale" or "sun-kissed", or some such fucking rubbish!'

'Alfredo!'

Pepe read the article, tittering. Then, 'Wonder if Mimosa's seen it yet?' And went back to the bureau, clearing his throat noisily.

Alfredo's laughter rose again. 'What do you think she'll go for first, *hombre*? His throat or his cock?'

'Judging by that photo, I'd say his –'

'Will you both please shut up? Alfredo, I won't warn you again! One of these days the boys are going to hear you, and – Pepe, what are you hunting for?'

'A torn copy of *Cielito Lindo*, and Tosti's *Farewell*,' sadly, reflecting that Magda would have had them ready for him, neatly waiting on top of his music case. No bureau-hunting with Magda in charge.

'They're on top of your music case, on your bed,' Mina said smoothly, wrapping a bow tie in tissue paper.

Pepe glanced at his brother, saw that he was still perusing *La Vanguardia*, said hurriedly to her, 'Thanks. And could you pack some silk pyjamas as well, *querida*, and that black wrap?'

She eyed him. 'Silk pyjamas? But you don't usually –'

'Yes I do! Sometimes,' frowning at her to lower her voice.

'Very well,' thinking how shifty he looked. She returned to the bedroom, stealing looks at him through the open door.   Alfredo's eyes had narrowed. Put the newspaper down. 'Alright, little bro, who is it this time?'

Pepe spun round. 'What the hell are you talking about?'

'You! Taking all your silks and satins with you − don't tell me that dear Bonker will be in London, too!'

'Bionda will not be in London. Now shut it!'

A gleeful titter. 'Bet she is! All ready and waiting to spread her legs!'

'Bionda is God knows where, *amigo*. And she doesn't spread her legs, as you call it!'

'What does she do, then? Make you sit up and beg?'

'Look, our relationship is strictly professional −'

'Tee hee! So that's what they call it these days . . . used to be called shagging when I was a lad!'

'Boys!' Mina, red-faced.

'Shut your bloody foul mouth, brother!' Pepe angrily slammed a drawer. 'I won't have you saying things like that about her!'

'Oh sorry, I'm sure. Won't even mention the bloody whore again, oh dear me, no! Not one more word about the most sought-after backstage shag on the planet, not one − Ouch, you bastard!'

To the sounds of tussling and grunting, Mina quietly made coffee in the little kitchen and brought the tray into the sitting room. Her husband was gingerly touching his mouth, Pepe slumped in an armchair looking vicious and out of breath.

She poured daintily.

Alfredo smiled sweetly, abandoning his sore lip. 'This silk pyjama thing. Serious, is it? Another professional relationship?'

The silence was grim.

'Come on, baby brother! . . . .Mina, have you packed his silk knickers as well?'

Pepe glared. Then suddenly rubbed his nose, scratched his chin, looked at his sister-in-law. 'As a matter of fact . . . I've got something to, well, to say. To you both,' scowling at Alfredo.

Mina looked up from her inspection of the coffee-pot lid. Alfredo assumed a solemn expression which made Pepe's reluctant mouth twitch.

'This . . . er . . . trip to London.'

'Yes?' in unison.

'Well. Look, you'd better know, I suppose. The thing is, I shall be seeing someone −'

'I knew it, I knew it!' Alfredo crowed.

113

'Shut it, *coño!*' He sipped the coffee, burning his lips. Tried again. 'I'm meeting someone. Someone who may be – no, is – special. That is to say, there is or could very possibly be, something between us.'

Mina said blankly, 'Between who?' while Alfredo choked on his coffee.

'Between me and this girl I'm – Mina, you may become a widow in two seconds, just as long as it takes me to flatten that bastard!'

'Sorry. I am now mute!' handkerchief over his mouth, muffled laughter.

'Mina, if things work out, I want her to come and stay here with us, live with me, I mean live here with us. But with me. If she'll come. Do you understand?'

Alfredo removed the handkerchief, consulted the ceiling. 'Ah yes, isn't this one of Einstein's abandoned theories? If the son of the hippopotamus –'

'For the love of God, this is serious!'

Mina said gently, 'Then it isn't Bionda Merdina?'

Pepe exploded, 'Jesus, no way!'

'Why on earth not?' Alfredo mused. 'She'd fit in very well. She could cook for us – that would be nice – and serve cauliflower cheese in between shags –'

Pepe stood up.

'– and if Gualterio was in a bad mood, she could calm him down with a verse or two from *O mio babbino caro*. Make him as sweet as a kitten, that would.'

Pepe tried without success not to laugh, failed, and sat down. 'You bloody idiot!' Then quietly, 'I'm being serious. This girl – she isn't in my profession, well, that is to say, she is, but in a different –'

'Now parse that sentence and break it down into its grammatical components, there's a good boy!'

'Bloody hell, I'll kill –'

'Alfredo! Pepe, dear, who is she? Have you mentioned her before?'

Pepe said hesitantly, 'You've met her, actually. Several weeks ago. Eliza. Eliza Pepper. Isabel.'

'Isabel? The one with *Señor* Drach?'

114

'Great gods, yes, you did have the heat for her, didn't you?'

He sat back, let it all wash over him.

Then, 'You mean you want her to live here with you, in the kennel?'

'Please understand, I can't be sure of anything yet, Mina. She may not want to come. She has her career in London, she may not want to give that up. I just don't know yet. I'm just warning you, that's all. But – if she does come –' He smiled, slow and sweet, 'then yes, we would use the kennel.'

Alfredo opened his mouth and Mina placed her hand over it.

She said thoughtfully, 'She would . . . yes, she'd be okay to have around, she'd be fun, someone to talk to.' Smiled. 'She'll be welcome, Pepe.' She then released Alfredo's mouth. 'Speak!' she hissed.

'Well, *hombre*, if you're as sure as this . . . Look forward to seeing Isa again!' and he stuck out his hand. It was shaken solemnly.

Alfredo added, 'Poor bitch!'

\*     \*     \*

The phone rang as Pepe was still sorting out his music, his mind an assortment of Catalan songs, Isabel, and the doses of catarrh mixture to be taken before he went to bed.

'Hello?'

'Pepe? Pio.' No preliminaries. 'I'm in Madrid. Look, I'm waiting for my flight to be called, I have to be *molto rapido*, understand?'

'Pio,' patiently, 'I know you're waiting for your flight, you're coming here for a couple of days, remember?'

'Pepe. Please, *amico*.' The voice wavered.

'Sperm Bank? What is it?' He must be mistaken; the sound that came down the line was a sob. 'Pio?'

'It's my Adriana. I've cancelled Madrid, I'm heading for home now, I'm in the departure lounge . . .'

'For God's sake, *hombre*, what's happened?'

'My Adriana. A message came through to the Zarzuela when we arrived in Madrid,' – a definite sob, '– she lost the baby, Pepe, they now fight to save my Adriana, oh God, my little girl!'

Shocked, Pepe heard the phone clatter. Then another voice on the line, one that Pepe knew well. Bruno Busoni, Pio's general factotum. '*Signor* Contreras?'

'Bruno, what the hell's going on?'

'He can't talk any more, *Signor* Pepe, he is passing out. His secretary had a message on her desk, about the poor little *bambino* and *Signora* Pio. Is very grave, very sad. I have cancelled at the Zarzuela, we go home *pronto*. I have tried to reach the clinic, but can't get through. I will ring you when things are more clear, yes? Now I must help *Signor* Pio, he is collapsed with shock, you understand?'

'Dear Christ!'

Dazed, he returned to the den. Drank wine without tasting it, thought of the bounding love contained in the brilliance that was Pio. And all of it for Adriana, still holding hands like teenagers.

Dear God, let her be getting well even as I stand here helpless.

He wanted to weep for his friend.

# 8

'OUT!'

'Please! *Querida!*'

'OUT!'

'My dearest!'

'OUT OUT OUT!' and Mimosa slammed the door behind her. There came the sound of a key turning fiercely in the lock.

'Mimosa!'

He stood in the middle of their bedroom, his hands spread in a helpless litany.

'Mimosa, listen to me – please!'

Martes had been overwhelmed by fear and anger at the sight of the suitcases in a neat row in the front courtyard, five of them when there should have been at least twenty; and he had burst at a run into the villa and up the central staircase, his thick trainers silent except for sharp squeaks where carpet gave way to parquet.

Mimosa was in their bedroom; had whirled and fled when he appeared, screaming her first 'Out!'

'Mimosa! My dearest love!' He went closer to the locked door.

'Out!'

'Not until we sit and talk!'

'If you're not out of there in two seconds, I'll . . . I'll drown myself in the bloody bath! I MEAN IT!'

Something snapped, and he yelled back 'You're not in the bathroom, that's my bloody dressing-room!' He heard low angry muttering, then something hit the door.

'Darling, will you please listen to me? Mimosa? My love? Please?'

He pressed his ear to the door. Muffled weeping. 'Just for three minutes? Please, little dove, just long enough to hear my side of it? *Querida*, I shall go on to our balcony. I shall put our chairs side by side, I shall pour you a Martini, and we shall talk. Together. Then you can judge for yourself. Don't condemn me unheard, Mimosa!'

Silence. 'Mimosa, for Christ's sake, who do you want to believe, me or the bloody press?'

Silence. Then he thought he heard the key squeak a little. 'Dearest, I shall be on the balcony. For five minutes. If you don't come to me, I . . .' He uttered a choking sob. Just one, just loud enough to penetrate the stout door.

A voice behind him whispered, 'Come on, Dad, you can do it better than that!'

'Fuck off!' hissed Modesto to his son. Gruñón did so, grinning.

Modesto scowled at the dressing-room door and went on to the balcony.

* * *

At the private and woodlanded clinic on the outskirts of Bologna, a huge bearded figure, eyes hollow, face and shoulders sagging with fear and weariness, was being greeted by incomprehension.

'But *Signor* Fazzoletto,' protested the receptionist, one hand on the bell to summon the duty physician, 'what is it you're saying?'

'My wife, damn you! Adriana! Where is she? How is she? Take me to her!'

Bruno Busoni put his hand soothingly on Pio's arm. 'Calmly, my friend.'

'Get your fucking paw off me, Busoni! Where is my wife?' he yelled, and the scared blonde receptionist pressed the bell for the second time and kept her finger down.

Pio slammed his fist on the desk. 'What are you – a southern-born cretin? My wife is in here, damn you, my wife –' He broke off, sobbing noisily.

'But *Signor* Fazzoletto –'

'What the hell is going on?' demanded a stern voice. The physician, in his dressing-gown, marched up to Pio and looked angrily at the girl.

Pio had slumped into a chair, huddled over one of his shawls.

'I think there's been a mistake, sir,' began the girl.

Bruno said, 'We had a message while we were in Madrid to say that *Signora* Fazzoletto was here, and in danger of her life after losing her child.'

Pio looked up, gripped the doctor's hand. 'Please,' he whispered.

The grip was painful. The doctor tried to retrieve his hand but failed. Instead he winced, said gently '*Signor* Fazzoletto, your wife is not here. I saw her just two days ago, and she was fine. Absolutely fine. She is not here. Do you understand me? She – is – not – here.'

In wonderment, Pio gazed at him like a trusting child. 'Not here?'

'Definitely not here.' He glanced at his receptionist. 'Brandy!'

Pio's shoulders began to take a rest from heaving. They went still. Then 'The phone!' he bellowed. 'Let me ring my home!'

'But of course,' smoothly, rubbing his squashed hand, 'You may use the one in my office, but please, have a few drops of brandy bef–'

'Where is it? Which room is your office?'

'Through here, but please, do not ring while you are in this state, the shock to your wife –'

Pio snatched the phone, thrust it at Bruno. 'Dial!'

'*Signor* Fazzoletto, I really would urge you to calm down before you speak to –'

'Bruno! Do as I say!'

Adriana Fazzoletto was appalled and then amused. 'Yes of course I'm here at home, *caro*! Look – shall I describe the room to you, if you don't believe me?'

'Home, Bruno!' commanded Pio afterwards. 'My God, whoever did this will pay! You hear me, Busoni? I swear I'll tear the bastard into so many pieces that even pecking chickens wouldn't find him! Did you hear me and witness that? It is my oath, Bruno!'

And they departed. Pio also asked Bruno to arrange for flowers to be sent to the receptionist.

*     *     *

The view, it seemed to him, had never looked so beautiful. It held everything he loved. Away in the distance, the peaks of the Sierra de Guadarrama, and somewhere in the blue haze on his left, the solidity that was Madrid. He smelt the jasmine, and saw through passionate eyes his serene gardens, distant olive trees, the three remaining outer walls of a Moorish fortress sharp against the sky. He smelt the hush of the vista.

He hadn't been able to find the Martini. Found a bottle of Ochoa with a rotting cork instead, fishing out the largest pieces from the glass before handing it to her.

'What was it you read, exactly?' he asked swiftly, wishing he could staple her to the cane chair before she could fly away.

She didn't look at him, stared instead towards the Sierra. 'Enough,' she said.

'Which newspaper?'

'Oh, going to sue them, are you?'

'I JUST WANT TO BLOODY . . . I just,' lowering his voice into a mellow key, 'want to know which gutter rag you suddenly decided to read, *querida*.'

'I wasn't reading a newspaper.'

'Eh? Then how –?'

'This!' she screeched suddenly, thrusting her hand into her pocket (Christ, she's got a gun!), and slapped the cutting on to his knee. Snatched back her hand. 'It came by bloody post!'

'Oh shit.' The *New York Times*. The photograph. Or one of them. Lucha's blouse: the vivid orange one, he recalled, cheese-cloth, with a slightly-torn washing instructions label on the inside.

Mimosa impatiently indicated that he should also look at the reverse.

He paled, quickly. 'Christ in Heaven, you mean some bastard sent you this anonymously?'

'No – your Aunt Juana sent it!'

'Oh, did she? How is she, it's a long – Oh. I see. Sorry. God, my precious Wonderface, this is wicked filth! How dare they do this to you?'

'What about YOU? What you have done to me!' And she began to sob again. He knelt beside her, urgently '*Querida mía*, I swear on the Holy Book that I never did anything with this

120

woman! I never laid a . . . Mimosa, I love you, I would never dream of . . . Not with anyone else, my beautiful swan! Never!'

She was sniffing, trying not to look at his panic-stricken face. 'Gruñón sent for the police, they took the envelope, I wouldn't let them take this, Sara made them photograph it instead, but what's the point, if every bloody newspaper . . .'

'Oh darling, darling!' The base of his spine was beginning to go into seizure, but he dared not relinquish his post. 'Mimosa, will you listen if I tell you –?'

'Tell me.' She gulped her wine.

He gingerly rubbed his back. 'Well. Remember how I dreaded doing the bloody thing with her, me with a black Butterfly?' He sighed as she nodded. 'I've got to be honest with you, darling, she is beautiful. The sort of beauty that is born once in a hundred years. We were all stunned by her. I can't describe the effect she had on everyone.' He restrained another sigh. 'Mike – he was the chief electrician – used to complain that whenever she appeared, his erection got in the way of the cables.'

He heard, above his bowed head, a muffled titter.

'Anyway, she'd got a voice, not as brilliant as I'd been told, but a fine top register.'

(Oh God, my back is going to split in half.)

'Fine top register,' she prompted him sarcastically.

'Oh yes . . . Well, apart from rehearsals of course, we did have coffee together, a couple of dinners with Tim Divine and his lady. That photo – that was taken as we were about to leave the dance-floor. She wanted me to go back to her apartment, but I said no, of course.' (Oh my knees, Christ, they've gone numb!)

Her lips tightened.

'Don't grim your mouth, sweetness,' he whispered in his pain.

'It says that you and this woman left the nightclub in a private limousine!'

'Well I didn't! I put her into the bloody thing and went on to another nightclub with some of the cast.' (I'm paralysed, I can't move my dead legs.) 'Mimosa, I swear to you, I never never touched her!'

'Oh really? And what were you doing in that photograph? Measuring her for a dress?'

'Trick of the camera,' he muttered. Thank Christ it wasn't the full-length one she'd seen. Difficult enough explaining away a hand clutching a lady's breast, without that. Angrily, 'Dearest, please believe that what I say is the truth!'

She stood up, went thoughtfully to the balcony door. He tried to rise, eagerly, but the pain made him screech instead. She smiled down at his agony. 'You will, of course, sleep in another room. Luisa will fix one for you.'

He gazed at her in disbelief. 'In another –?' He struggled to get up, clutching at the chair. 'You can't mean that! Rosebud, please! I've been longing for you, praying to be home with you, to hold you!'

Before she slammed the balcony door, she said sweetly, 'Then you'll just have to have wet dreams, won't you? Dearest?'

*    *    *

The little Italian lady shrugged.

'I have told you a million times, I did not take that message! That one did!' pointing to a slightly younger version of herself.

'Ah yes – you were at lunch, you say, *Signora* Fegato?'

Muttering, 'Shall I recite the damned menu?'

'*No. No, grazie.*' The inspector turned to the other woman. 'You do not work for *Signor* Fazzoletto?'

'No thank you! I am a friend of *Signor* Busoni, and I was waiting for him when the phone rang. That one –', pointing to *Signora* Fegato, 'had already sloped off for lunch, and there is then, you see, only me in the office, so when the phone rings what am I to do, ignore it, tell it to bugger off? No, I answer it politely, as politely as one can when one is not paid for doing so, and I say "who is speaking" and this voice starts to tell me –'

'Just a moment, please, *Signora* Frittomisto! . . . *grazie*! The voice on the phone – was it a man or a woman?'

She shrugged. 'Difficult. Very difficult. It could have been a high-voiced man or a low-voiced woman.'

'I think we're on to something here, sir,' sniggered the sergeant.

'This person, the one on the telephone,' the inspector continued icily, 'spoke in which language?'

122

'In Italian. Very bad Italian. But,' proudly, 'I understood it!'

'Naturally. You're from Naples!' said *Signora* Fegato.

'Milanese cow!' spat *Signora* Frittomisto.

'*Signore! Per favore!* . . . *grazie.* Anything else about the voice, the accent?'

'I would say most definitely a Spanish accent.'

'Strange, that, in Madrid,' murmured the sergeant.

'The voice – was it clear, loud, as though the person was speaking locally?'

Another shrug. 'Clear enough, but sometimes when I speak to my son in England from my home in Napoli, the line is just as clear as if he were in the next room, and my Antonio laughs and says *Mamma*, we . . .'

He nodded, and signalled to his sergeant to take over. Serve the funny sod right. If this were a complaint by anyone other than God Almighty Fazzoletto, it would be recorded and then torn up into a hundred pieces. After all, what harm had been done? None, except to prevent the fat bastard earning yet more lire when there were so many starving people in the world, including himself.

He bade the ladies a courteous good-day and left the interview room.

\*　　\*　　\*

Smiling to herself, she smoothed Clair's t-shirt across her knee, rummaged through her sewing-basket for a large needle.

He was here. Pepe. And already in bad odour with Bobby Drach. His phone call had been quite succinct.

'Yes, he's been, yes he's signed! Sort of. Would you do me a favour, Ezita? When you see the illiterate sod tomorrow, ask him if he ever went to school. Tell him that signing something means joined-up writing and not fucking block capitals, and also remind him that he spells his surname with an 's' on the bloody end! Osgood's balls are jangling like carriage clocks. If it's all too much for him, tell him an 'X' will do, and I'll witness it!'

Pepe was here. He would be singing now.

Ez, still smiling, licked the end of the embroidery silk and dreamily poked it at the eye of the needle.

*　　*　　*

When Pepe Contreras opened the door of his suite, two voices spoke simultaneously from the region of his knees.

'*Perdóneme*, Don Pepe,' Enrique said, holding a leather folder.

'Hello!' grinned Ez, sitting back on her heels, clutching sheets of manuscript, 'Sorry, we were –'

'I hit the lady,' offered Enrique.

A raised eyebrow and a twitching mouth that said 'You did what?'

'I hit –'

'No he didn't, he was carrying this for me, and I tried to take it from him just as he was knocking on –'

'First it was Moncho, now it is Enrique! How do you do it, Isabel?' and laughing, held out his hand to help her. She scrambled to her feet, bits of fluff clinging to her black trousers, and took the folder from her smiling escort. 'Thanks, Enrique – my fault!'

'My pleasure, *señorita*,' and he glanced at Pepe with envy. Her smile, he thought, was like a candle with three wicks. She looked like a small matador in her crimson blouse and black waistcoat.

'Would you care to come in?' smiled Pepe, still holding her hand. 'Thanks, Enrique,' over his shoulder.

'Yes, *gracias*,' beaming.

Enrique had been a good companion in the car, telling her first of all about Barcelona and then about the village that was his home, and how happy he was that portable bullrings were now available so that he and his village could enjoy good *fiestas* without travelling for miles. Until he had met the Sainted Arpeggio, he said twinkling, he had wanted to be an impresario of the bullring, king of the *corrida*.

Pepe closed the door. They looked at each other. '*Hola*,' he said gently.

'Hello,' wonderingly. Then thrust the assembled folder at him. 'This is for you,' shyly.

'That is most kind. *Gracias*,' taking it without looking at it, gazing at her.

She pushed a hand through her hair. 'It only seems like five –'

'A lifetime! I cannot believe you are here! You look very pretty.' A broad smile, then 'Come, let me give us a drink.'

He put the folder on a table by the door, and escorted her into the salon. It was broad, high-ceilinged, in shades of mauve and blue-grey, and her eyes registered with surprise an upright piano in an alcove, concealed lighting directed upon it. The sofa to which he guided her had a plump look, velvet feel, banks of cushions. She sat down and smiled up at him.

'Amontillado?'

'Please,' and watched him moving around the bar, muttering to a bottle as it clattered on the tray. Pale brown slacks, cream shirt with the collar turned up, top buttons unfastened. He handed her a brimming schooner and sat beside her, a pale liquid in his own glass that sparkled.

'To you, Isa!'

'To you, Pepe,' and they sipped in a token gesture. Her shoulderbag keeled over on her knees, and he took it from her, grinning, placed it on the floor. 'Please, no more spillings!'

She laughed with him over the rim of her glass. 'Thank you for sending the car and Enrique,' she said, 'but when I go home, I'll –'

'Isabel?'

'Yes?'

'Are you as nervous as I am?'

'Yes,' lowering her gaze, frowning busily at the fluff on her knees.

'Is like pulling a Christmas cracker and not knowing if it will bang.'

'Yes.'

'Isa?'

'Yes?' looking at him again.

'Do you know any other words?'

She gave a small laugh, spluttering into her sherry. 'Sorry,' she said, 'but it's never been like this for me. There's so much to say –'

'All the past years ago to talk of. Forty of them for me! You know,' leaning back into the depths of the sofa, 'if you were a tree,

I could cut you in half and count the rings to discover your age!'

'You blessed idiot!'

She was still laughing as he took the glass from her and put it with his own on the knee-high table.

* * *

The clock in the salon had an infinitesimal tick. That is, if she heard it at all. To stop this feeling would be like hanging clothes out to dry in a still mist. It was devastating, the heavy buzz inside.

'Dear God,' he said, and rubbed his hand over his hair. Less sleek than she remembered it, then realised it was freshly-washed.

She pulled back a little, her eyes and his magnetised.  'Pepe?' in wonderment.

'Shut up,' he whispered. His mouth again, hers opening, his tongue like a warm spear. 'Dear dear God,' he said again.

There were too many buttons around, she thought wildly, what the hell did I put this waistcoat on for?

'Pepe!' gasping, 'that button belongs on the blouse, you're pushing it through the wrong −'

'Shit!' and the kissing stopped as frantic fingers sought the right apertures. He moaned 'Jesus Christ, I need a road map!' Her laughter snuffled into his mouth. 'Isa, help me!'

'Look!' she tittered, 'you're unfastening my blouse and buttoning my waistcoat!' She collapsed against his chest, shoulders shaking.

'Isa, for the love of God, my thumb's trapped!' and his laughter met hers as they sank into the cushions helplessly.

'If your brother was here now −'

'Oh shit, don't mention Alfredo, if he were here now I would − what is the English? − ah! Yes . . . I would knock his breeze!'

A shout of laughter that made his ears ring. 'You would what?'

'Knock his breeze. Isn't that what you say?'

She touched his shadowed jaw, ran her hand across his hip. 'I haven't heard that expression before,' she said solemnly.

His hips moved. 'It means − oh God, Isa! − something you build with, and you hit it down if you are angry with a person . . . Isa, your hand is . . . Oh Christ!'

126

She smiled wickedly.

He kissed her eyelids, just as she gave another yell of laughter. 'Bloody hell!' he swore, rubbing his ear.

'You know, I think my Spanish is better than your English, Contreras! Do you mean breeze-block? To knock someone's block off?'

'What?' concentrating again on the blouse. 'I said nothing about blocks! Look, what's the Spanish for –'

'How the hell do I know, you're the Spaniard! Hang on, my dictionary's in –'

'Fuck your dictionary!' Guided her hand, and beamed. Removed the willing waistcoat, and critically examined the buttons of the blouse.

'Breeze,' he muttered. 'You build with it.'

\*     \*     \*

'*Querida*, some time ago, you said that when you go home –'
'Did I?'

'Mmmmm . . . *tu boca* . . . .'

'*La tuya* . . . Oh yes . . . when I go home tonight –'

'You ARE home! Did I not say? Where I am, so is your home. Thank God, is end of the buttons . . . Do you understand?'

'But –'

'You are not thinking of staying with me tonight?'

'I wasn't sure what to think.'

He lay full length on the sofa, and pulled her down on top of him. 'We will get some things clear,' he said.

'Yes.' Kissed his bottom lip lightly, feeling his body clench.

'Oh God! . . . First of everything, you are with me tonight.'

'Yes.' Now his chin.

His hand moved jerkily between them, tugging at the blouse. 'Second,' as she chased his smile with her mouth, 'you will stop wearing buttons of clothes! Bloody hell, Isa, is easier to go in Fort Knox . . . Mmm-MM! . . . is nice . . . Where was I?'

'On secondly.'

'Ah. Third – why did you not bring your bag?'

'What?' She prised herself off his chest, stared at him. 'I did!'

'Not that one, *cucufato*! I mean for travelling with.'

'Travelling with?' She sank back upon him with shocks of sparkling delight, and he blew a strand of her hair from his mouth.

'Of course for travelling with. Tomorrow, you *idiota* . . . Er . . . what are you doing?'

'Your shirt – it puzzles me. Most shirts have buttons from top to bottom. Yours doesn't. The buttons stop. Here!' Her finger prodded his diaphragm.

'Christ, don't do that! Not yet . . .' A sudden screech. 'Isa, for the love of –'

'Sorry,' she snorted. 'I must cut my nails.'

Another long kiss. Then, 'What do you mean – tomorrow?'

'*Carita mía*, perhaps I am not clear to you. Tomorrow, we fly home to Barcelona. You, me, Enrique. We stay at my home. Do you never listen? I have said, where I am, is your home. You think I go away and leave you behind until my work brings me to London again? . . . *Querida*, if you do that, I shall lose control of . . .'

'Barcelona?' She finished unfastening his belt, let it dangle. He arrested her arms and sat up, struggling to arrange her on his knee.

'That is what I said. Tomorrow, our flight home is at, I think, five o'clock afternoon time. You will stay until Wednesday, then we both leave at the same time – I go to Zurich for *Carmen*, and you will have a week to see to your affairs here before returning to Barcelona. That is where we are to be living.' He frowned. 'Did I not say this before?'

She shook her head and made the happiness fizz.

'I really thought I had! I have said it in the head so many times that I think it is real!' He caressed her collarbone. 'I shall telephone Mina in the morning, so that the kennel is ready for us.'

'Woof!' she giggled weakly.

He kissed her, smiled jauntily. 'The kennel is my *casita*, my little house, is very private to me. Alfredo gave it the name of *perrera*, the kennel. He says my name should be Pepe Perrera on the billings, it has a better ring.'

The next kiss took longer to finish.

'Bloody thunder!' he gasped. 'Isa, do you think is time that we –?'

'I was beginning to think I'd have to carry you, Perrera!'

\*       \*       \*

'Christ! What was that?'

He sat up in bed with difficulty, and listened. He could hear her laughing under the sheets.

'Ssssh! What the –? Isa!' He shook the nearest moving mound. 'I can hear some clatters and whistling!'

Tangled hair and bright eyes emerged. 'Whistling?'

'Sssh! Listen!'

Silence. 'I can't hear anyth–'

'There! You see?' as a door closed loudly in the salon.

'Who –?'

'I don't know! I am going to find out,' sliding away from her. Then slapped his forehead. 'Isa, are you wearing a wristwatch?'

'Yes, of course. Why?'

He snatched her wrist.

'Ouch!'

'Sorry . . . Oh bloody hell! Is ten o'clock! That is the time I ordered our supper – they have just delivered it! Bloody food, at a time like this!'

Giggling, 'Can't you ask them to bring it back later?'

'This is the Grosvenor, Isa, not McDonald's.' He rubbed his face and looked sorrowful. 'Are you hungry?'

'Absolutely!' and she leapt neatly out of bed before he could move. She slipped her arms into his black silk wrap and smiled at him.

'Come on, Contreras! Food!'

\*       \*       \*

Mina had obviously forgotten to pack his pyjamas after all. Wearing his underpants and a scowl, Pepe inspected the supper trolley, glancing at the Asti Spumante with a thin-lipped

'Sparkling piss! I ordered Nuits Saint Georges!' and watching Ez as she fetched the folder they had both forgotten.

She curled up on the sofa with it, tucking his wrap round her knees. Had she eaten today? She couldn't remember. Perhaps the boiled egg had been yesterday.

'*Qué tonterías!*' he suddenly snorted, waving a lid in the air. 'Look – a silver cover, to keep the salad warm!'

'Efficiency is the Grosvenor's watchword, I seem to remember,' she murmured, looking at the manuscript. He poured the shining wine.

'To you, Isa *mía.*'

'Pepe. My love.'

They sipped together, eyes reflecting each other, lost. She handed the folder to him. 'This is for you.'

He took it in his hands, kissed her. Opened it, a child on Christmas Day, read the dedication, another kiss. Then he stared at the manuscript. The title page stared back at him –

A Gipsy Romance
by Patna & West
from Federico García Lorca.

Then he was at the upright piano, playing the melody slowly with his right hand, reading the words aloud. He nodded, stopped, began again, shook his head, stressed a word, added a note of his own, muttered '*sostenuto, sostenuto*', then continued nodding and playing. And suddenly spun round.

'Isa, this is – *mierda*, what are the words? – this is special stuff! How in hell did you get them to do it? Is *fantástico*! Of this I could make something!'

She smiled, charged with pleasure, 'Nathan was pleased with it, too.'

'It was all of your idea, this Lorca?'

She nodded, going to the trolley and spearing an anchovy. Carefully, 'Nathan and Tom and I thought – if you agreed – perhaps more poems, Lorca, Zorrilla, Bécquer, for an entire album: half in Spanish, the other side in English. They'd be delighted to do it. Pepe, it would be unique, no-one's done it before. And it could start your Magda Fund! Yes?'

He hugged her, eyes sparkling more than the wine. 'We plan it on our way home tomorrow, *querida!* Isa, any more ideas like this? I like what I hear, is just what I need, is fresh, like a —'

'Breeze-block?'

Squealed as his arms snatched her away from the supper trolley.

'You may finish your anchovy,' he said sternly, 'then we return to bed.'

'Oh dear! Suddenly I have the most frightful headache . . .'

'And suddenly I have just found two aspirins in my hand!'

And they were laughing, overjoyed.

*    *    *

Somewhere in the night, she woke with a hollow feeling in her throat and lay in his warmth for a while, puzzling about it. Then realised with surprise that she had not had a cigarette since waving goodbye to Ada. The luminous dial on her watch told her that it was three o'clock in the morning. A cigarette. To go with her thoughts.

Carefully she wriggled away from his arm. He was lying on his back, small bubbly sounds coming from his mouth. In his sleep, he cleared his throat, swallowed noisily, turned over. She smiled a fountain of love. Pulled on his black wrap once more and tiptoed into the salon.

The lamps from the avenue below cast enough light to see furniture shapes and her shoulder bag still on the floor. She lit a cigarette pleasurably, waved the smoke vaguely away. Shouldn't really be doing this. Looked around. No ashtray. Bloody hell. The scarcely-touched trolley had been removed, not even a saucer left that she could use. Suddenly remembered the bowl of flowers on top of the piano, a curved dish with long-stemmed anemones. Ez switched on the concealed light and perched happily on the stool with her back to the keyboard, the dish on her knee. Whenever she tapped the ash, it hissed in the petals.

I think my body has just been born. I hope it is born every single day of my life.

The surge of him inside her, huge hurting flowers of their own that needed more hurt, petals that were hard; and that gradually

131

fell off one by one as their shuddering began to ease.

'Never never in my life before never,' he had gasped, while her eyes were bemused and drenched. '*Nunca en la vida, princesa mía!*'

I love you, she whispered to the room, stretching her legs in a spasm of sudden joy. But. Barcelona. To live there. Her flat, the books, the Agency. Bobby.

Oh bloody hell – Bobby! The idea was enormous, to lose familiar nights of eager planning, getting a project up and running. And Bobby, my only family.

The sound of dripping water broke into her thoughts. That, and the slimy wetness of over-soaked stems.

'Oh shit!' and she scrambled from the piano stool, ramming the anemones back into the shallow bowl, using the hem of his wrap to mop the carpet. She pushed her cigarette into the flowers, replaced the bowl on the piano. The cigarette hissed and died.

A thought surfaced. If this was indeed the start of a life with Pepe, could she not persuade Bobby that – No. He'd never go along with that, he'd call her a grab-happy bitch and wave her goodbye. Being in love, she decided, could also mean being in deep manure.

So much talking to do. So much they would have to th–

'Isabel?'

She jumped.

Pepe switched on the nearest lamp, a ridiculous carved unicorn with its shade dipping like a hat about to fall off. She blinked, saw something red.

'Sorry, *querido*,' she said.

He sat beside her on the stool and sniffed the air. Smiled. 'You are being very good with the smoking,' he said. Stroked her knee firmly. Then, 'You are wet!'

She smiled sheepishly, kissed his newly-grown bristles. 'The flowers,' indicating the bowl on the piano, 'I was using them as an ashtray, and . . .' She shrugged, feebly. '. . . and there was a bit of mopping up to do. Sorry!'

'More spillings!' he grinned and bent over to pick up an anemone from the carpet.

She giggled faintly, seeing that his buttocks were bare. A large dimple in the left one. She thrust a fist to her mouth; he was wearing something red in front of himself, tied apron-style around his waist.

'What on earth have you nearly got on?' Her laughter was muffled.

He straightened up, glaring, holding the purple flower. 'Is your blouse. I could find nothing else, my wrap had disappeared again, and my pants are God knows where!' and he slowly began removing petals one by one, never taking his gaze from her, '*Me quiere . . . no me quiere . . . me quiere . . . no me —*'

'Of course I love you, you —' and squeaked as his hand moved up her thigh.

'I was,' he said solemnly, 'dreaming about you, *querida*.'

'What was the dream about?' she whispered, transferring her hand to the front of the apron-blouse and stroking the bulge.

'God! . . . er . . stop that! Jesus!' He closed his eyes. 'In the dream . . . Holy bloody Mary! . . . in the dream . . .'

'Hurry up!' She gave him a gentle nip. He uttered a ringing screech.

'Bloody hell! Okay . . . in the dream, you were gutting a fish.'

'I was what?' She stopped what she was doing.

'Gutting a BLOODY FISH!' he roared, and imprisoned her hands, grinning suddenly at the wrap which had fallen open. She glanced at her goose-pimpled breasts, tried to free her hands. Unrepentant, he touched them with his thumb, and began humming a melody. 'You know this tune?'

'No I do not! Will you let me fasten this damn thing . . .' as Bobby's reference to poached eggs flew through her memory.

'Oh,' nonchalantly, 'I really thought you might. Is from the *Requiem*, by Verdi.'

'You think my body needs a requiem?' tugging furiously at the wrap.

He threw back his head with a happy yell. 'Miss Broken Pin, I presume?' bowing.

Her mouth fell open. 'Pin? . . . Oh no! You DO remember!' Scarlet, she tucked the black silk into place. 'Pepe, stop laughing!'

'Dear God, your language on that day! You were nearly fainted, so white in your face, but you still tell me to go and pickle my balls!' He doubled over. 'Oh Isa *mía*, how could I help but fall in love so quick?' He picked her up suddenly.

'I never told you to pickle –'

'Oh but you did!' And their mouths were together and he muttered 'Unpickle them, woman!'

\*     \*     \*

Pepe said, after breakfast, 'The car will take you to your apartment, then we shall come for you just after two o'clock. Will that be enough time to pack what you need?' At her nod, he kissed her. 'Now I must telephone Mina,' happily.

And afterwards, dressed in her creased crimson blouse, Ez rang Bobby Drach.

'What the fuck do you mean, be at your place by midday?'

'Please, Bob? I have to talk to you.'

'Suppose I say no?' He sounded grumpy. A hangover, she guessed.

'Please? And could you bring a good-sized travel bag with you, mine's too small.'

'I thought Sniffer went everywhere by car?'

'Ha ha, funny man! Bobby, please. Look, I'm going to Barcelona later today, and –'

'Bloody Barcelona? How long for, may one ask?'

'Until Wednesday,' and waited for the roar to subside. 'Yes, I know we should be in Swansea, damn it I'm sorry, can't Jake go with you instead?'

'Bugger Jake, this is your job, not his!'

'Bobby, I'm sorry, but this is important. I've got to talk to you, understand? Will you come to Putney or not?'

Thoughtful pause. Then grudgingly, 'Alright, Bobby will be there. About midday. And with a generous travel bag. Christ, you're only going for three nights, surely even Sniffer won't need as many condoms as that?'

She turned frantically to see if Pepe was in earshot of the voice. He was standing right behind her, grinning, making a thumbs-up sign. She giggled.

'Oh Bobby, thanks, you're a –'

'I know, I know. Consider it done, you cheeky mare. See you

134

later. Love to Sniffer. You'd better wrap him up warm, there's a nasty wind blowing from the east. Don't want our Little Precious sneezing his way through his next fucking *Mattinata*, do we?'

Later, as they drank coffee and cream, he said 'Enrique will be here for you soon,' with a slow smile that made her skin feel like electric fur, 'so before he is coming, please give me your fingers, *querida mía*.'

She recognised the signet ring, the one from his little finger. It was gold, with a diamond-shaped piece of jet. He had bought it, he told her, on his eighteenth birthday and had vowed on his mother's memory that one day it would bear a real diamond. Then laughing, confessed that he preferred it as it was. Now he pushed it painfully over her knuckle.

'This is to bind us, *mi alma*. Promise you will wear it?'

'I love you, Perrera,' she whispered, and kissed it.

# 9

Most people know that her earliest ambition was to be an international wrestler.

But not with women. With men; more spunk and muscle, she said. And with three brothers who all grew to manhood via years of bruises and twisted ligaments, no-one had doubted her for a minute. Much later, when her biography was written, (with the title *High over Down Under* and a best-seller), all three testified to her ability in the art and her physical dedication. Only the discovery of her voice and the athleticism of her vocal chords had saved mankind, or so asserted her youngest brother Peter, by then a physiotherapist in Adelaide.

Cherri de Canasta had worked lovingly and hard for her acclaim. Her physical strength had stood her in good stead for the unending hours of practice and rehearsal, the months of travel without a pause. Modesto Martes, an ardent fan, once remarked that de Canasta was the only singer in the world who could still grin like a silly beacon when her feet were twisted with cramp and her eyes dizzy with B flats.

She had worked throughout the summer this year, a schedule culminating in Rome with the ill-fated *Aida*. She seethed with impatience as her back slowly improved, but then began to laugh at the absurdity of it, and made jokes about cheetahs banging away to the sound of Verdi, even drew cartoons which she sent to her brothers. Now, she was completing the healing process in the company of her husband at their apartment in Naples, planning her role as Desdemona in October.  Plus dieting. She had to be willowy for the part, she decided. Her husband disapprovingly watched as she ate baby-sized portions of muesli for breakfast, tiny steaks with raw onion for dinner. This was simply not his wife; though he had to admit that her brown hair shone and the rather plain face had acquired a strange attractiveness.

She swore to herself, mumbling dialogue between Otello and Iago, slashing a bright red mark at the side of her entrance cue.

Francesco Giormani looked up from his airmail copy of *The Times* and said 'I see your boys lost again!'

'You what? . . . oh bugger this pen! You got a biro over there?'

'Yup. Catch!'

She tested the pen in the margin of her libretto. 'Which boys?'

'Rugby boys. By – let's see – seven points to thirty-three, against the All Blacks.'

'Jesus bloody Christ! Isn't that just a score for heroes? That bloody full-back needs a whip across his arse! Kick a penalty? No way, mate, he's bloody blind in daylight.' She hummed a few bars under her breath, 'Nah nah NAH! C sharp, you cretin, C bloody sharp! And that flamin' hooker's older than my granny, oughter be in a field, grazing. Does sod-all.'

Francesco grinned. An American with Sicilian forebears, he got on well with this vigorous wife.

'Here, Frankie, pass me the phone, will you?' Still perusing *Otello*, she held out her hand.

'Who're you calling on a Sunday morning?'

'Moddie. Want to tell him I'm fit and ready for Verdi, no probs with the start date. Ta!'

Just a few kilometres outside Madrid, the phone rang as Mimosa was arranging fresh flowers.

'Hi there, Mimsy! How are you? Is old Laugh-a-minute there, by any chance?'

Mimosa switched her surly Spanish thoughts to English, 'Hello, Cherri, good to hear you! How are you now?'

'Fighting fit, ta, ready to tackle anything. How's Moddie? Say, wasn't that a hoot in the papers? Jeez, how did he explain himself when he got home?' Cherri's voice bubbled with mirth.

'Please, Cherri, I don't want to talk about –'

'God, that photo in the evening paper here, it looked so funny, Moddie pressed up to La Lucha closer than a shirt on a bloody ironing-board! Laugh? I thought I'd pee myself!'

'Please, I –' Her voice filled with tears.

'Oh shitteroo, I'm sorry, Mims.' Concern, then sudden laughter again. 'Come on, when you think about it, he made himself look a proper comedian!' A boisterous snigger. 'Can't you just laugh it off?'

'He said there was nothing to laugh off.'

'Well he would, wouldn't he? Didn't you ask him about that interview Lucha's understudy gave to the *Tribune*? About him kissing Lucha's toes in her dressing room? You oughter to think about changing the shape of his – Mimsy? Hello? . . . oh bugger these continentals, we've been cut off!'

Her husband said 'If I were you, I'd button my lip!'

She stared at him. 'What are you tweeting about now? You shouldn't listen in on girl talk, mate, Mimsy's a friend of mine, she needs all the support she can get! Damn it, I'll have to try again later.'

Somewhere in a dusty valley near Madrid, a door slammed.

*     *     *

Bobby Drach had been taking tea with Ada before Ez arrived home, sipping daintily from a china cup and wondering how much longer he had to keep up the inane conversation with the deaf bugger. He had awakened that morning with severe tooth-ache and was scarcely in the mood to listen to her bleating about the new central heating in her fucking church, not when he faced the torture of a visit to the fang-mender. Besides which, he'd already asked her twice if he could use her toilet and she hadn't heard him. He was, therefore, happy to see his partner when she poked her head round the door to announce her arrival, and he raced upstairs to her bathroom without the usual preliminaries.

When he emerged, Ez was in her sitting room examining his travel bag.

'My best one,' he informed her, 'so don't gum bloody labels all over it!' He looked at her closely. 'You look what is usually called happy,' wanting to use the word incandescent instead.

She grinned, taking a bottle of wine from the cupboard. 'Thanks for coming, Bob. Will you uncork this, please, I must go and change.'

He inserted a corkscrew rapidly. 'Sooner have this than Ada's bloody Earl Grey.' Cocked an eyebrow. 'And where exactly did your blouse spend the night? On a roller-coaster?'

She blushed. 'Mmm − it is a bit creased, isn't it!'

'Nothing that five ironings won't cure, dear. By the by, did you tell Ikkul Larynx about his signature?' Watched her as she shook her head. Sighed. 'I see. You mean you were bloody coupling all night!'

'Bob, please!' reddening still further.

He poured the wine as she went to change, calling after her 'Good job you arrived when you did, I was about to piss all over Sexy's cut moquette!'

Tittering, she struggled into a brown leisure suit, the un-accustomed ring snagging in the cuff and pulling a thread.

Bobby eyed her as she returned to pack the borrowed bag, carefully placing Lorca in a separate compartment. Drank his wine as she pulled a dusty duffle-bag from a cupboard. 'What the hell do you need that for?'

She grinned at him, blew some of the dust away, and removed Ignacio from the sideboard.

Bobby stared, horrified, as she placed the bear inside and covered his head with a folded scarf. 'What's this − bloody playtime?'

'He's going home,' she said solemnly.

'He's going home!' he mimicked. 'Christ, you and that illiterate bloody crooner are made for each other, you both belong in a fucking asylum!'

She sat beside him and picked up her wine glass. 'Robert,' she said, 'the key word was "HOME".'

'I'm not deaf! Got its passport?'

'Bob, I'm trying to tell you something.' He looked into grey serious eyes.

Tersely, 'I'm listening.'

'Pepe wants me to go out there, to Sant Moiseps. To live.'

'Well of course he does,' unamazed.

'What?' It was her turn to stare.

'Ezita darling, not everyone suffers from dying brain cells. I didn't think he was merely after a one-night screw, not unless he was bloody desperate, and from what I hear, duckie, he most certainly −'

139

'Bobby!'

'– isn't. So the question is,' pouring more wine, 'do you want out as far as the Agency's concerned?'

'Oh Bobby, no, I don't! But how can I –?'

'Darling, work doesn't stop at Heathrow, you know. You'll be with Sniffer, you can represent him from Barcelona, can't you? My Spanish rep!'

And he spluttered wine as arms flung themselves around his neck. 'Come on, you silly mare, you didn't really think that Bobby would let you go, did you?'

'Robert Drach, I love you!'

'So marry me!' and they looked at each other, then smiled. He cleared his throat, said 'Yes. Well. We'll talk about this seriously when you get back . . . .O-ho! Just a minute! What the hell –?' and he grabbed her hand. 'Shit my drawers, what's this meant to be?'

'It's his ring,' grinning.

'Oh, isn't it just out of this world!' His mouth curved downwards. 'Christ, he's a generous bugger, is old Sniffer! First a battered poetry book and now a tin ring! You can tell he's one of the highest-paid fucking canaries on the planet, can't you? What's this polished bit of crap in the centre? A sultana?'

'Bobby!' trying not to laugh but failing wonderfully.

He gazed heavenwards. 'I can see, Eliza, that you are going to bleed the poor sod dry. What's he taking you HOME in – a patched-up air balloon?'

'Shut up,' giggling. And they drank the wine as they edged their way round her future rôle in the Agency and somehow got on to the subject of teeth and the awful cost of getting fang-holes filled and she gave him an aspirin.

Finally, burping genteelly, Bobby went to the window. 'What time are you being collected, duckie?'

'Soon!' exultantly, rummaging in the bureau for her passport. 'Sod it, where is it?'

He said cheerfully, 'Don't see many of those in SW15, do you?'

'See many of what?'

'Bloody long limos. Wonder if it's anyone important? . . . No, I can see Sniffer in the back!' Sniggered as items flew from the bureau, 'Bloody hell, where's my passport? I only had it the other week!'

'Second drawer, right hand side,' still looking with interest out of the window. 'Oh fuck me, don't say Caruso is actually getting out! Christ, he is – walking through your front gate like an Ordinary Person! My my! ... What's he poncing around in a cloak for, in the middle of the bloody day?'

He opened the window. 'Oy, Batman! She's up here!'

'He's coming in? Oh bloody hell, if Ada gets there first . . .' And Ez flew down the stairs.

Bobby tittered as voices rose from the porch below, 'No, he isn't from church, Ada!' and 'Pardon me?' three times from Pepe. Ez must have poked him hard in the back, for the tenor bounced up the stairs two at a time, looking breathless.

'Nice concert on Friday, Pepe,' Bobby greeted him. 'Bragas and her pianist were excellent, I thought. Ez, did you remember to pack clean knickers, sweetie?' as Pepe glared.

'Bobby, will you shut up!' hissing, watching Pepe as he stared round the sitting room.

He nodded slowly, smiled at her and said 'Is nice here. Is what you call –'

'A hovel,' supplied Bobby briskly. 'Here's your duffle-bag, darling, couldn't find your Wellingtons and sanitary towels, sorry!'

'Stop it, you clown!' hugging him tightly as Pepe picked up the travel bag.

'God, look at that for strength,' murmured Bobby. Then loudly, 'Have a good trip, you two.'

Suddenly slapped his forehead, hastily reached inside the jacket and waved two pieces of paper. 'Before you go, Pepe, your signature on this, if you please, you printed it last time . . . That's a good boy! . . . Wasn't difficult, was it? And this one,' as Pepe frowned, trying to read it, '– oh don't do that, duckie, you'll get nasty lines on your face – see what you think of this when you've got a moment. It's a Charity Gala concert in Seville, next January. If you want it, I've got you a header on the bill. Here – take it!'

Pepe looked surprised. 'Yes, I have heard of this. Isn't Lavagna going to be there?'

Bobby beamed. 'That's how I knew about it. So, think it over, dear, let me know later. As for you,' hugging Ez once more, 'be back bright and bloody early on Thursday morning, otherwise I shall stick teensy pins in your poached eggs!'

'Poached eggs, did he say? *Huevos escalfados?*' murmured Pepe in the car.

'I'll explain later,' nestling against him.

Enrique, in front with the driver, smiled and studied Putney High Street.

\*       \*       \*

Strolling in the garden after a light and companionable lunch, Keta and Vito were each thinking about Berlin.

Vito occasionally twisted off a dying leaf from the abundant shrubs, as conscious of imperfections in Nature as he was in his own music. Keta's dark red hair gleamed in the light, newly-rinsed and glossy.

She persisted, 'Are you sure you won't mind if I come with you, Baby?'

His fingers halted their mini-harvest, and his smile was forced.

'Of course not. If you're sure you can stand it – I'm pitched at the Anton Bruckner again!'

She laughed and affected a shudder. 'My God! Remember when their central heating broke down?'

'January 1987,' he said promptly.

'And the snow! My God, the snow!' Then, as they wandered past the fountain, its cold drops spraying the fins of a large stone fish, 'You're sure it won't be a problem, if I do come?'

He shook his head. No, there wouldn't be a problem. There would be two. Louis, and –

'You'll like Gianni,' he had whispered during their last night in Salzburg; and his smile was faint in the dim glow of the bedside lamp. 'And what is more, Gianni adores Berlin. So we'll all be happy. Won't we, *fanciulla?*'

He tried to avoid the lips, asked 'Who is Gianni?'

Then thighs moved and Louis said 'Tut tut, what a time for questions,' and the sliding began and there was no

'. . . so nice to see Monda again!'

'What? Sorry, darling –' and tried to listen to his wife.

Berlin and Louis, *Lucia di Lammermoor* and Monda. And now Keta and Gianni.

Really, he reasoned quickly, I should be quite content. Another Donizetti, and with him this time, dear Monda Ballena. They all, with affection, called her 'The Wailing Wall', eighty-three kilos of pure soprano, warm and naive when it came to humour, an imperious flashing of ring-laden fingers and a haughty head if she felt disinclined to be warm. Solid Spanish flesh, subtly-scented.

One thing was undeniable; if Monda caught Louis lurking near the dressing-rooms, she would have him tossed out before he could say 'Hi.'

He grinned. Must warn the dear boy.

'It should be fun, all of us together,' he said drily.

\*　　\*　　\*

'Welcome back, *hombre!*'

Alfredo Contreras slapped his brother's outstretched hand, casting a sly glance at the smiling face. 'You,' he continued, handing Pepe a glass of freezing white wine, 'are looking decidedly well. The air in London must agree with you!'

'How kind of you,' and he continued to smile, looking down the curve of his nose, eyelids hooded.

'Christ!' his brother hooted, 'Have you seen him, Mina? He looks like a reptile who's just been at a nest of lady snakes!'

'Alfredo, don't start that again!' Mina, trim in her cherry-red dress, smartly stepped between them. 'How was the recital, Pepe?'

She quickly cast an eye over the family sitting room to see if she had missed anything. She had; Pau's train engine and Alfredo's monthly science magazine.

'Oh, reasonable, I believe. Considering a couple of minor irritations.'

'What irritations?' Mina stuck the magazine in a rack, and the engine in a cupboard with the rest of the train.

'Teresa Bragas for one, and her pianist-husband for another. As usual, I had to carry the whole thing while Bragas stood there missing her cues and fiddling with her bloody skirt. As for that diabetic fart Felix –' He shrugged. Scowled. 'Jesus, don't we have a better wine than this? It's over-chilled and tastes like tap water!'

Alfredo pointed to the bar. 'Too far for you to walk, is it? Or has my brown-haired sex-kitten been sucking too hard?'

'It doesn't sound too promising for you and Bragas in *Carmen*,' Mina laughed, enjoying her tap water.

'Oh, that's different, *querida*. Teresa makes a supreme effort to sing when she's got scenery to flounce around in and a crowd of extras to mask her ineptitude. What do you mean, *coño* – *your* sex-kitten?'

'I re-christened her, didn't I? I'm entitled! Without me, you'd still be trying to wrap your furry yellow tongue round "Eeeliza". Where is she, anyway?'

'Exploring the kennel and getting changed.' He crossed to the mirror above the fireplace and stuck out his tongue. 'No way is this yellow and furry!'

'I'm the scientist, and I say it is! Let me look at your testicles, Don Pepe – if they match your tongue, you've either got dry rot or woodworm.'

'Alfredo! No, Pepe, don't hit him, I need him to serve the drinks.' She suddenly put a hand to her mouth. 'Lord, I've just remembered! Pepe, I must have a word with you later. About Judit.'

'What? What about her?' He looked quickly at the door.

Lowering her voice, 'She came round here this morning – I'll tell you later when we get a few moments . . . Good Lord, what on earth is Papaterio –?'

They stared as Gualterio made his entrance, scowling.

'What the piss are you all gazing at?'

Pepe volunteered weakly, 'It's a nice beret, Father,' before turning away quickly.

'Looks really natty with your striped jersey,' tittered Alfredo. 'Where are your nets and lobster pots?'

'I know I said we were dressing casually,' Mina smiled, 'but really!' She poured him his habitual cognac.

He looked at the contents of the glass. 'Thank you, *chica*, I assume I get the rest of it in a minute.' He sank into a chair. 'Well? Where is she, this new scrubber of yours?'

Pepe's frown coincided with Alfredo's yelp of mirth.

'May God have mercy on us all,' continued Gualterio, the cognac glistening on his lips, 'Kindly let us know when you decide to stop rutting, Pepe, I'm pissed off with having to learn new languages! English now, God help me. What's the English for "pass me the bloody brandy?"'' and his hand shot towards his daughter-in-law, empty glass wagging.

'It will soon be dinner —'

'Christ in a truss, girl, my stomach and throat aren't bloody clocks! Fill it!'

'We want politeness and courtesy only, this evening,' said Mina firmly, and 'Isabel, do come in! Welcome!'

Ez smiled a little shyly. Pepe hurried to her, draped a possessive arm around her shoulders. Whispered 'You look beautiful, *princesa mía.*'

She whispered back, 'I wasn't sure how to dress for this evening.'

'Is fine,' he smiled, and kissed her forehead, his mouth lingering.

The sound of applause from Alfredo, and Gualterio muttered loudly 'Christ, she hasn't got much to get hold of, has she? I thought Pepe went for big —' before Mina trod on his foot.

'Isabel, you look lovely,' she beamed. 'Where on earth did you get that evening suit? From Paris, perhaps?'

It was flimsy and black, with a shimmering half-visible pattern of purple curling leaves on the low-necked top, plain flared pants, and a casually-tied sash around the waist. No jewellery. Just Pepe's signet ring.

'I got it from Oxfam,' she said, pleased with Mina's appreciation. Pepe snorted.

'I did!' indignantly. 'They have a very good shop in Kensington.'

Alfredo asked, 'What is ossfam?'

'It's a charity shop,' explained Ez to blank faces.

'Met you before, of course!' bellowed Gualterio. 'With that poof Drach! Some bugger get the girl a drink! What would you like, *chica* – Martini, sweet sherry, some of that white Portuguese piss Alfredo buys because the shop assistant flashes her thighs at him?'

She smiled and shook the proffered hand. She didn't recall much about his face from their last meeting, just the bulk and the voice.

'A glass of Amontillado, if I may . . .'

'Jesus Christ, a bloody Londoner! Pepe, get the Amontillado, so sorry there isn't a butler to do it for you. Idle runt!'

'Really, Papaterio!'

He suddenly snatched back Ez's hand, his eyes riveted on the signet ring.

'Pepe!' he roared, making his son jump in the air and create bubbles in the bottle of Amontillado. 'Is this the best you can do, you dim-witted bastard? Great God in His hammock, where are your brains, in your arse?'

'*Papá*, be quiet!' Pepe laughed.

'I'll give you be quiet, you grinning prima donna! Do you know where he got this from, eh, girl?'

She shook her head, trying not to look at Pepe.

'Papaterio!' pleadingly from Mina.

'He got it from a bloody market stall on the dockside in Barça! Old Emilio sold it to you, remember? You bloody well ought to, you were having it off with his daughter at the time, you useless young stag!'

Ez started to giggle, looking at Pepe's horrified face and at Alfredo collapsing against the wall.

Mina decided that the evening was in jeopardy. Ana was already waiting on the terrace, where dinner was to be taken. 'I think we should eat now,' and moved ahead with determination. 'Pepe, if you would give Isabel her drink –?'

Gualterio snapped, 'Instead of mincing around the waterfront looking bloody soulful, get a ring for the girl from a decent place this time! A good ring!' He put his hand beneath her elbow to escort her. 'A ring with fine jewels, eh, girl? What will it be – rubies? Diamonds?'

'Sorry,' she smiled, 'I dislike jewellery of any kind.'

'Jesus, no wonder Pepe likes you, you must suit the stingy sod

146

down to the ground! Anything that costs more than four pesetas, he breaks down and cries!'

Moths, untaught, flew and fluttered as they ate, Ez dreamy and tired and happy, joining in the conversation as more and more Spanish came back to mind, smiling to herself when they thought she wouldn't understand. Gualterio, for example, laying down his fork and solemnly saying to Pepe, 'Do you reckon this *chica*'s fertile? If she is, don't discourage her, we'll keep the buggers and bring them up here. You might have better luck this time!'

She tittered unheard.

There was good black coffee afterwards in the sitting room, and glasses clinked pleasantly on the bar.

Pepe whispered, 'We will only stay for an hour more,' and kissed her. His hand half-moved to the low neckline.

'Did you say fifty minutes?' she murmured.

'Oh – at least half an hour,' tilting her chin.

'Say – ten minutes?' hardly breathing.

'Christ! You're making me –'

Piano music suddenly blasted into the room and they jumped. Alfredo sniggered. 'Thought you might like some Albéniz,' he grinned.

Gualterio took her by the arm. 'Come and make intelligent conversation with me,' and 'Turn that fucking rubbish off!' before leading her to a comfortable armchair and seating himself opposite. 'Now, Isabel, I am very anxious to learn English words. For example –'

Mina smiled at them, then murmured 'Pepe, while he's entertaining Isa, may I tell you about Judit's visit? Only she said she was going to ring you, and –'

\*     \*     \*

'I want to come back,' Judit said, sitting down before she was invited.

Mina stared. 'Come back? To Pepe, you mean? But –'

'Well of course, to Pepe!' Judit laughed, and placed dove grey gloves neatly on her handbag.

Mina looked away, flustered. 'Shouldn't you be saying this to him, rather than to me?'

'Of course! But I happen to know that he is away. And I would like to know, if it isn't too much trouble, when he is coming back. And how long he will have at home before shooting off elsewhere.' She spoke each word separately, clearly, as though to a child trying to memorise its own name.

Judit smiled sarcastically. 'I would like to know, my dear, so that I may judge how long I shall have with him, to put my case.'

The fuzzy-haired maid, Elena, brought them coffee. Mina said cautiously, 'I'm very busy today, Judit, I'm afraid I really don't have the time to −'

'Of course. Well?'

'Well what?' Same Judit, hopping from one branch to another without warning.

'When,' patience exaggerated, 'is he coming home? Today?'

'This evening, I believe. He's bringing a friend with him from London.'

A sharp laugh, refined amusement. 'Bringing a friend? God, Mina, you make him sound like a child coming home for half term!' Abruptly, 'Who? Who's the friend?'

'I've no idea. Look, you really must forgive me, but −'

'So, he'll be here tomorrow, resting. Good. I'll ring him in the afternoon. Mina,' earnestly, hair swinging, 'it's very important. Immensely so.'

'Yes, I'm sure it is.'

'Thanks for the coffee,' smiled Judit as she left.

'My pleasure,' murmured Mina to the closing door.

\*　　\*　　\*

Ez laughing: 'Well, tell me what it's called, then! *Mosca?*'

Shouts of glee from Alfredo and Gualterio. '*Mosca!* Bloody *mosca!*' and Gualterio slapped his leg.

Pepe turned, half-smiling, wondering what the joke was. Then he looked again at Mina, the smile gone.

'God damn it!' he snapped. 'Didn't you tell her that −?'

'I told her exactly what I have just recounted, Pepe.'

148

'Yes. Of course. Sorry.' Brushed a hand over his hair. 'I'll just have to ring her first. Shit! Why now, of all times?'

'She wasn't to know, was she?'

'True, *querida*. Ah well —' shrugging. 'Thanks for telling me, anyway.' Yawned. 'God, I'm tired!' Then saw Mina's laughing eyes, added hastily 'Travelling, hotels —'

'Yes, Pepe.'

He sauntered over to the merry group in the armchairs. Ez, he noticed, was smoking one of his father's cigars. A blue haze hung over their heads, undulating. He perched on the arm of her chair; she looked up and smiled.

'What's the joke?' he asked.

'Oh *hombre*, have you picked yourself a good one!' chortled Alfredo.

'All I said was —' protested Ez.

'All she said was, what is the Spanish for this?' and Alfredo pointed down at his trousers.

'You WHAT?' Aghast, he stared at her.

'No, no, not that,' she said hurriedly, then caught Gualterio's eye and pealed with laughter.

'The fly!' cried Alfredo. 'She asked if the word was *mosca*. But we have explained, a *mosca* is an insect fly, not one of these!' Tittered.

'I merely thought you might use the same word for it, as we do in English,' chuckling as Pepe tickled the back of her neck. Fumbled in her shoulderbag for her notebook.

'So — a fly is *una bragueta*. . . .' and scribbled it down.

Pepe grinned. 'May I ask what led to that topic of conversation?'

'Father wants her to teach him filthy words in English!'

Pepe blustered 'She will do no such thing! Isa, I forbid —'

Gualterio cleared his throat, raised his eyebrow at Ez. At her encouraging nod, he looked at Pepe and said slowly in English, 'Bugger off, you miserable sod!'

'Oh God!' Pepe put his face in his hands, laughing. 'Isa, please!'

'I was asked,' she said primly.

He took her by the arm. 'Is time we went,' firmly.

149

'Bugger off,' murmured Gualterio. Then 'Hey, *chica*, more lessons for me tomorrow?'

She grinned and stubbed out her cigar. 'If Pepe permits.'

'If Pepe permits?' he bellowed. 'Bugger Pepe! Lock the warbling idiot in his music room, and I'll take you for a walk, tell you about this house and its history!'

'I'll try,' as Pepe shouted '*Buenas noches!*' and hauled her away.

Sauntering along the tunnel, arms around each other, Ez tugged him to a halt in front of an alcove and pointed to the illuminated painting. 'I noticed this one before,' she said softly, looking at the lady in the long brown robe and roses that cascaded down to perfect bare feet. 'Who is she? She's got such an infectious smile.'

Pepe smirked. 'That,' he said, 'is Our Lady of Sorrows,' and tugged her away.

*     *     *

Mina had placed orchids on the bedside table the day before, and for some reason had left them in an old kettle. Ez smiled as she slipped out of bed. She liked Mina. Always earnest, doing ten jobs at once.

It was daylight, sunny pieces of it filtered round the edges of the closed shutters. It was cool in the room, and her bare feet seemed to miss every rug and land instead on the cold parquet. She quietly removed a skinny satin nightdress from her bag.

By contrast, the bathroom was filled with sunlight and warm perfumes from the vegetation outside: the kind of warmth, she reflected as she splashed water over herself quickly, that makes you feel already browned by the sun. The fluffy towel didn't dry her skin properly, and she struggled with the cream satin shoulder-straps; puzzled over a biro mark on her collarbone. Rinsed her mouth busily with a lemon-tasting liquid she found on a glass shelf, daubed herself with gentle aftershave from a tall royal blue bottle made of frosted glass with a label, *ARISMO* in thick black italics. It smelt, she decided, of melons.

She tiptoed back to the bed and perched there, gazing at him as he slept. His full lower lip sagged a little. She leaned forward and gently touched it. A strong arm shot out and gripped her wrist.

'Why are you dressed?' he demanded, and pulled her down on top of him. She smiled into the brown eyes.

'*Buenos días*,' she murmured.

'Mmm, if you say so. Closer!' he ordered. She complied, wriggling along his length.

He rubbed his face in her throat. 'You have a new smelling today, *mi princesa*,' and sniffed her skin.

'Your aftershave,' she admitted, placing her mouth on his cheek and teasing the encroaching bristles. 'Your chin looks not only blue, but navy blue in this light.'

'Good, good . . . oh mmmMMMM! Do that again!'

'What?' innocently. Her knee moved again slightly.

'That! . . . Oh Christ!. . .'

She chuckled, enjoying the satin on his nakedness. Suddenly, he tried to sit up. Failed, sank back, smiling. 'Isa?' His hand ran gently down the bumps of her spine. '*Querida*, which aftershave?'

'What? I only saw one.' And, as he slipped the straps over her shoulders and sniffed vigorously at her skin, 'What are you doing, bloodhound?'

Another prod with his nose around her breasts. 'Great Christ!' and the room rang with his laughter.

'They're not that damn funny! . . . Will you shut up, you'll wake the orchids!' as he hooted 'Oh bloody Jesus!' The laughter redoubled as she stared at him, bemused. 'My crazy *cucufato*! – where did you find the aftershave?'

'In a tall bottle,' indignantly, 'a blue one. The label said "*Arismo*".'

A yelp. 'The label must be half,' he said, tittering.

'Half of what?' impatiently.

'The label is. Is not all of it. It should read "*Gargarismo*".' A shout of joy. 'Is my gargling liquid,' and held her fast as she spluttered furiously and tried to climb off his shaking body.

'I can't lie here covered in bloody gargling liquid!'

'Be still! I've never made love to a *gargarismo* before,' and they collapsed laughing. As their noisy merriment began to subside, he said softly 'But there is something you do that is absolutely of right. Exactly, wonderfully so.' He touched her nipples. She melted

151

against him. Another touch. '*Soldados,*' he said helpfully.

'What are?'

'These,' with a gentle squeeze.

'I thought *soldados* were soldiers.'

'Is true,' His fingers delicately circled them. 'Is because they are standing up to attentive.'

'I am very pleased to hear it. I thought the word was "*pezones*". Why do you call them *soldados?*' arching closer.

'I told you! Is because they parading attentive. Like *soldados.*'

'Do you know, I'm really glad I asked!' and suddenly plunged her hand between his thighs.

'OW!'

She tittered faintly. 'Right, professor, what is this called in Spanish?'

Breathing heavily, he stuttered 'Has many names!'

'So tell me one!'

Laughing again, he whispered in her ear.

'What? But that's part of a tree!'

He pulled the sheet over them, muffling her squeaks. The orchids in the kettle continued exploding their beauty.

\*　　\*　　\*

He wrapped the telephone cord around his wrist and stared away from the sound of her voice.

'Judit! I am not arguing with you, I am telling you quite bluntly that the answer is no. The answer is no because I do not want you near me, I do not wish to see you again, and I don't give a damn what your gynaecologist now tells you! Don't interrupt! I don't intend to repeat myself. The answer is, for all time, no! Nor is this house yours to visit whenever you wish. God be with you!'

Isa was on the terrace, reading the Lorca manuscript. He unwound the cord from his wrist, and went to her.

\*　　\*　　\*

On the steps of the clinic near Bologna, Bruno Busoni held up his hand as members of the press and photographers surged forward.   He was pale and longing for sleep, longing for a comb to straighten his hair.

'Ladies, gentlemen! I shall make this statement once and once only!'

'Ssssh!'

'Sssh!'

A camera whirred, another flashed silver in his eyes.

'Ladies and gentlemen. I have to tell you with much sadness that *Signora* Fazzoletto has lost the child she was carrying. *Signor* Pio is with her, and cannot speak to you. His wife is very weak, but the doctors say, please God, that she will make a full recovery in due course. *Signor* Fazzoletto is hoping not to cancel his scheduled performance in *I Due Foscari* in Rome. That is all.'

The shouts came thick and fast as he turned away. A journalist from the *Corriere della Sera* clutched his departing arm – '*Signor* Busoni, did that hoax call have anything to do with this?'

Busoni hesitated, then replied courteously, 'It is very difficult to say whether the hoax was in any way responsible for this unhappy event.'

Feeling suddenly nauseated, he turned on his heel and went back into the clinic.

# 10

Pepe sent flowers.

Modesto and Mimosa sent an affectionate telegram. And Vito Lavagna rang the clinic in Bologna, where the receptionist coldly informed him that no interviews were being given to the press – a statement had already been issued.

'I am not a journalist,' he said, equally coldly. 'I am a friend.'

'I'm sorry, *signor*, but my orders are quite specific.'

'My name,' pausing deliberately to allow the glorious truth to percolate, 'is Vito Lavagna. I am a member of *Signor* Fazzoletto's profession.' Then with malt vinegar in his voice, 'I sing, damn it!'

The receptionist gasped and chirped 'Lavagna! Of course I know your name! So sorry, *Signor* Lavagna, oh gosh, I simply loved your record!'

Which bloody record, he thought. I've made thousands of the damn things. 'Oh, really? That is most kind of you.'

'It got to number one last year, didn't it!'

Her excitement was quite contagious. He beamed, in shock, 'Did it really?' Had his financial advisers told him about this? And which one? He couldn't visualise semi-naked druggies jigging up and down to Bellini or Donizetti.

'Of course it did – all his records do!'

His? Whose?

'You and Azucarero sing brilliantly together! He's ace, I've got most of his albums. Are you going to do any more with him?'

Shit. The one-off single, with that crazy Spanish cretin, Azucarero, lead singer of the rock band El Pedo Negro. Bloody Brahms lullaby. With synthesizer. He suddenly remembered with wincing clarity that they were on the same bill next January, a charity event in Seville.

'Perhaps so,' he said cautiously to the receptionist. 'You never know! So now, *signorina*, perhaps you would be kind enough to put me through to –?'

'Sorry, *Signor* Lavagna,' she cooed, 'No calls are being put through to the Fazzoletto suite. Sorreee!'

He slammed the phone down, and it pinged sharply. Vito went in search of Keta. She was busily folding garments and arranging them neatly in a suitcase on her bed.

'Steady on!' he smiled. 'Berlin's a whole week away!'

'Darling Baby, I shall have to cancel Berlin, I'm so sorry.'

'But you said –'

'After what's happened to poor Adriana? Vee, she's my friend! I'm going over to Bologna to look after things until she's recovered. Those poor kids! And Pio will need to get away for *Foscari*, he's already cancelled one concert and Rome is getting worried. At least he can go knowing that things will be okay in my hands.'

Vito sat weakly on the bed, watched her as she rolled up pairs of tights and put them in a silk bag. 'Don't you think you ought to ask them first?'

She stared at him. 'Do you honestly think I'd go without asking? Really, Vee! I've spoken to Pio twice at the clinic today, and he asked me if I'd help out. He's sending Riccardo over in the car –' Looked at her watch. 'Jesus, he'll be here in less than an hour! Honey, you're sitting on my sweaters – would you pass them, please?'

Bitterly, he did as he was bidden.

\*　　\*　　\*

The surgeon was tall, grey-haired and tired. He briefly placed his hand on the broad shoulders and said 'She will be fine, Pio. A lot of rest, much gentleness, yes. For some weeks to come. But medically and physically, she is doing well. There is no worry. She is a strong woman.'

Dark swimming eyes looked up at him.

'They murdered my son!'

The shoulder was given a rough pat. 'We don't know that for sure. Perhaps –' He bit his tongue before he could say 'if you hadn't bellowed the news to her down the phone and given her a shock, it might not have happened!' Instead, he stooped to pick up a red silk square that had slid to the floor and placed it on Pio's knees, saying 'It could have happened anyway. Given your wife's age, and the frequency of child-bearing, one cannot be sure.'

He turned to go. 'It might have happened anyway,' he repeated.

Pio fell into a brooding silence until a nurse announced that he could now see his wife. He lumbered wearily to the door, saying to the nurse 'They killed my boy!' Then he disappeared into the recovery unit.

\*     \*     \*

'Did you send the telegram to Pio?'

Mimosa nodded silently. Modesto looked at her profile with pessimism.

He had found her wandering through what she joyfully called their secret garden, so small and secret that it extended through a couple of acres and was mostly visible anyway from the upper storeys of the house. Still, compared with the rest of their land, it was wooded and wild, no manicured knee-high shrubs here. Now, the air was still, and the trees silent.

He cleared his throat cautiously. 'I hope Cherri will be fit in time for La Scala.'

Two late butterflies zigzagged near his hip.

She said stiffly, 'She's fine.' And walked on, towards a large wall covered with strong bougainvillaea vines.

He caught her up in three strides. 'How do you know that?'

'She rang a couple of days ago.'

'Oh, thanks for telling me!'

'You were out with Gruñón. Then I forgot.' Bitterly.

He gripped her arm. 'Mimosa, this is bloody ridiculous! I've explained everything, I've been honest with you −'

'Have you?' she flared. 'Have you really!' She looked pointedly at her arm, and he let his hand slide away.

Mimosa walked to the mass of bougainvillaea, combing the flowers with her fingers. 'Cherri was most informative,' she said, her back towards him. 'More photographs, I hear. Cherri's seen them. And read something about an interview.' Her voice cracked.

'Oh for Christ's sake!' Angrily, he kicked at a stone.

'An interview, Moddie,' sarcastically, 'with that woman's understudy! I hadn't realised that you were a part-time bloody chiropodist!'

'What the hell are you talking about? What has Cherri been saying?'

'Oh – something about the understudy telling all to a *Yanqui* newspaper. . . .' She swung round. 'You – kissing that bloody cow's toes!'

Sweet inspiration, where are you! 'Oh, that!' he laughed smoothly.

'Yes. That!'

I will not panic. God. 'Darling precious, we were rehearsing! That little scene . . . er . . . it comes in the wedding ceremony.' His thoughts took wing. 'You remember, *querida*? Where Pinkerton has to . . . er . . . symbolise his love by kissing her feet? Well, it is a Japanese ceremony after all, and they always kiss –'

'In the opera, Modesto, they do not perform the Japanese ceremony of marriage.'

'Ah. No . . . .Yes! You're quite right, of course, but don't forget this was Tim Divine, darling, and you know what he's like, always coming up with little touches of his own. And, well, Lucha kept giggling during rehearsal, said I tickled her feet, so Tim packed us off to the dressing-room to practise, and of course the understudy came too, to watch in case she had to take over . . .'

He took a deep shaking breath, and held it. Mimosa said nothing.

Wildly, he cried 'Dear God, I didn't DO ANYTHING! What do you want me to do? Come on, tell me, I'll do it! Shall I jump off El Escorial? Give all my money to the fucking Romanians? What will convince you, dear God, what?' He was aware that by now he was exhibiting all the distress of a wounded bull and that not even Optrex would restore his twinkle.

'Angel-body, it was all distorted by the sodding media! I love you, I know it's hurt you, I'm sorry sorry SORRY!'

157

In frustration he thumped his fist into the vines and connected with the wall.

'Shit!' he howled.

Somewhere in his head a faint titter registered, and he spun round.

Crushed in his arms, tasting his kiss, she sighed. Perhaps it was all true, what he had said. She of all people should know what the press was like – look at the time Modesto had had a fit of coughing before the Flower Song in *Carmen*; every paper yelping that he was ill, (possibly tuberculosis), too old, it was a hangover. And all it had been was a wine gum lodged in his throat.

'I shall come with you to Milan,' she said firmly.

'For *Otello*?' surprised. 'I thought you hated that opera, *querida*?'

'For other reasons, you stupid brainless idiot!'

Glancing up, hiding a smile of love, she saw that the twinkle had returned.

*     *     *

And then it was Monday afternoon, with Lluís and Pau. Aged eight and five respectively. They had been advised pleasantly by their mother that Aunt Isa would appreciate their company and entertainment while Uncle Pepe was working in his music studio with Uncle León Salvaj. In accordance with Mina's wishes, and not relishing the thought of being deprived of lemonade for the next ten years plus a good smack from their father, they took her to their playroom.

As she admired the yellow tiles and orange plastic furniture, Pau asked eagerly, 'Do you remember our mouse, Isa?'

She smiled. 'Roberto? Of course I do! He was sweet. May I see him again?'

The boys looked at each other in alarm.

Then reluctantly, Lluís said, 'Well . . . if you want to.'

'I'd love to! Would you mind?' Ez looked from one to the other.

Then they shook their heads, of course she could see Roberto if she wanted to, they would go and fetch him immediately.

They left her then, at a run; and smiling she strolled round the room. The windows, wide open, looked out on to a brick path

158

winding through glossy broad-leaved bushes and ferns, stone animals at irregular intervals dominated by a weatherbeaten antelope with a broken hoof, around which trailed a feathery weed.

Mina put her head round the door. 'I thought those *diablillos* were looking after you!'

'They are,' laughed Ez. 'I said I'd like to see their white mouse again, so they've gone to fetch him.'

'Oh no!' and Mina disappeared.

A large clock chimed. It was a replica of the gingerbread house in Hansel and Gretel, birds on the roof. Then a clatter, door banging, feet.

'Here he is, Isa!' That was Lluís, holding a cardboard box, while Pau rubbed dirty hands down his shorts, and beamed.

'That is very kind of you,' giving them a mock bow and taking the box. Gingerly lifted the lid in case the mouse sprang out.

It didn't. Roberto lay yellowing and very stiff, on a small handkerchief with the initial "P" in one corner.

'Erk!' She jumped back, still clutching the box.

'He is dead,' explained Lluís gravely.

'We dug him up for you,' said Pau eagerly. 'He didn't mind.' Then, sadly, 'I don't think he minded.'

And then Mina – rushing in, shouting, apologising, grabbing; and the two boys exited grumpily with the late Roberto.

Still laughing, she strolled back to the kennel, stood for a while in the tunnel looking at her favourite painting. Our Lady of Sorrows. *Nuestra Señora de Dolores.*

I love him, Dolores. Tell God for me.

\*      \*      \*

And it was Tuesday, just as suddenly.

In the morning, in the music room, they had chosen seven more poems to go with *The Gipsy Romance.*

'You will insist to Nathan that I am keenly interested?' spitting on his finger and rubbing at a brown stain on the top D of the keyboard.

'I'll get in touch with him just as soon as I can, *querido*, either from here or from London. Once he knows it's viable, we can arrange for you and he and Tom Patna to meet and plan the album.'

She sat with him on the piano stool and applied her hand-kerchief to the stain. 'Pepe, I've been thinking. Once the album is done, perhaps you'd consider doing the whole thing on television, on the European network? – not just to promote the album itself, but also to announce the Magda Fund at some point during the programme? What do you think?' and 'Oh!' as his kisses de-monstrated his enthusiasm.

She left him then to an hour's close study of the *Carmen* manuscript, and sat for a while on the kennel terrace, trying to remember an idea that had briefly buzzed in her head in the music room. Something he had said. She frowned. What the hell was it? Damn it, she hated losing ideas. He'd said . . . .'I hope that Nathan limits the top C's in the next seven,' and laughed about the number of throats he'd need. And an idea had tugged.

The kennel phone suddenly chirped into life, and the idea fled further. As she picked up the receiver, Pepe came in smiling and pointing dramatically to the bedroom, panting.

Her laughter rose as she said 'Hello?' to the caller.

A familiar voice said 'Do you have to bloody well shout?'

'Bobby!' she laughed. Pepe scowled. 'It isn't Thursday yet, you know!'

'Oh, glad to hear that Spaniards use the same bloody calendar as we do. Not interrupting anything, am I? If I am, sorry, just tell him to pull up his zip for a few mins!'

'Bob, honestly –!'

'Seriously, darling, how are you?

'Great, wonderful, fantastic! It's the most heavenly –'

Acidly, 'I only asked how you were! Look, Ez, apologies for gate-crashing your lovenest, but that VIP meeting in Swansea has been re-scheduled for Thursday afternoon – you sure you'll be back by then?'

'I'll be back,' sighing. 'But Bob, I've got such a lot to do in one week, things into storage, all my books, dealing with my house in Somerset, and Swansea's going to take all afternoon and well into the –'

160

'You ready to take a breath yet? Fine – let Bobby hear you breathing – good girl! Right. The meeting's from one-thirty till three, a car's being sent for us, look you whateffer, and will bring us back. God bless the Prince of fucking Wales, say I. And Bobby will help you sort out your shambolic hutch, okay?'

Laughing, 'Okay. Bless you, Bob,' and Pepe hoisted himself on to the desk, aimed a punch at Ignacio who was sparkling in the sun at the side of the phone.

'Hang up,' he hissed.

Kissed his cheek. 'Sorry, Bob – didn't catch that?'

'Ah well, they say it makes you go deaf in time. I was saying, duckie, that there's a wonderful article in this month's trade mag!' He gave a bark of joy. 'Oh yes, indeedy! I thought of you and Sniffer right away!'

'Go on,' she sighed. Pepe frowned impatiently.

A high-pitched whinny from London. 'Musical condoms!'

'You what?' incredulously. She gestured to Pepe to pick up the extension, a finger on her lips.

'Musical condoms, you deaf bitch! I'll save it for you to read. My God, just think what they'd do for Sniffer's image! I'm not kidding you – the idea is for these condoms to come with different tunes! I've been having visions of bloody Sniffer wasting valuable banging time while he decides whether to have that *Grand March* thing from *Aida* or Beethoven's *Ode to* bloody *Joy!*'

Pepe had a hand over his mouth to hide his laughter.

'Bobby, will you shut –' tittering.

'Don't you think it's brilliant? If you weren't in the mood, just think how up-market you'd be, complaining about the music instead of a headache! Or,' and convulsions rocked the airwaves, 'you could make a whole evening of it, like Desert Island Discs . . . Oh fuck me, I'm wetting my drawers! Ez, why don't you ask Sniffer to record *My Way* for Durex, he'd make a bloody fortune!'

Weak with laughter, she nodded as Pepe signalled to her.

Bobby's voice, plaintively asking 'Are you still there?'

Pepe saying 'Yes, of course I am. How are you, Roberto?'

An appalled silence. Then, 'Oh Lord bloody Jesus! Er . . . Pepe! Hello there!'

Pepe wiped his eyes. 'Roberto, I would have thought that *High Hopes* would sell even better!'

'Christ, you were listening in!'

'I would not have missed it for anything, *amigo!*'

A mutter down the line.

'Bobby?'

'Ezita? Now you're confusing me! Has Sniffer buggered off?'

Pepe said sternly, 'Sniffer speaking.'

'Oh fuck,' whimpered Bobby.

And afterwards, they fell laughing on the sofa, and drank a mirthful toast to Robert Drach.

\*     \*     \*

They walked down the steep slope to Sant Moiseps, just before the afternoon started to die under rainclouds and the squalls began.

The road, dusty and pot-holed and only properly surfaced in a few selected places, plunged steeply through the olive groves and passed the rear of the canning factory which looked so different from the picture it presented from the main Barcelona road. Here, there were huge steel doors and trucks, and warnings stuck to anything stationary, depicting a cigarette with a red wavy line through it and *Prohibido* underneath.

The church, further down the slope, was squat and white with open doors showing deaf darkness inside.

'Is named for Our Lady of Sorrows,' smiled Pepe. 'But no pictures of her inside. Just one of St Peter, is horrified awful, he looks as though he has just received his tax return!'

A few residents of the village sat on benches, even as the rain began and the wind blew ash from their cigars. One old man, in summer shirt sleeves and prodding two dogs along with his walking stick, smiled at Pepe sourly, *"Días, chico!"*

'Is the barber,' he whispered, 'he still calls Alfredo and me *"chico"*. And always looks at us as if we were again going to steal his razorblades!'

'You stole?' Mock-horror.

'Of course! Razorblades we had to have, for cutting words on

162

trees. Magda was forever going to him with money and saying sorry!'

She would have lingered at the *taberna* and the converted barn that was a billiard hall much frequented by Gualterio and his friends; but Pepe suddenly looked distant and his mouth frowned as though angry. He said abruptly 'We will go back now, it will rain very strong soon.'

Surprised, she allowed her hand to be gripped tightly, and they panted in the strengthening wind up the steep slope, dodging into the olive trees to avoid the worst of the potholes.

'Pepe?' breathlessly as they reached the ivy-covered gate that led them on to Contreras land. 'Is there something wrong?'

'For God's sake, Isa,' and he tugged her arm viciously. The rain was getting faster and drops clung to his black hair like transparent buds.

Amazed, she swore and started to speak, then the wind blew the words away and she stared at his stiff profile instead.

The house was quiet. In the tunnel, the votive lights glowed, and the only sound was their fractured breathing and the thud of their trainers.

Suddenly, he tugged her to a halt. Gasped, 'Oh Christ, I didn't think I'd make it!' And smiled.

Almost tearfully, 'What is going on, Pepe? Why are –?'

'Oh *princesa, princesa mía*! I am sorry – but when there is something I must do, nothing is to get in my way.' He held her close. 'Isa *mía*, do you see where we are?'

Slightly dizzy, heartbeats slowing, she raised her eyes and saw the painting of Dolores. She smiled at him reluctantly. 'But why?'

'The first time we were together, you and I,' he said slowly, 'was on the fifteen of September.' Kissed her forehead. 'That, Isa *mía*, is the feast day of Our Lady of Sorrows,' and watched her smile widen with surprise. 'So it had to be here, don't you see? Is so perfect, so right. In the village, all I could see was *Nuestra Señora* looking so sternly at me as if she was to say. . .' He looked at her sheepishly. 'You must think I am ace *cucufato*!'

'I only fall in love with ace *cucufatos*.'

'Would you marry this one, Isa?'

She jerked away. 'What?'

'Please?' gently. He kissed her, not gently. 'Please?' Then, 'I shall keep you here until you bloody well say yes!'

And they clung together with tears and smiles, bodies arched together.

'Perhaps,' softly, 'I could make us a cup of coffee, in our kitchen?'

'In our kennel, *preciosa!*'

They smiled *adiós* to Dolores and the cascading roses.

\* \* \*

Coffee, of course, came much later.

Pepe came into the sitting room, wearing his old knee-length robe.

'I thought you said there was not any coffee?'

'There wasn't. I mean, there isn't. Not in the cupboard, anyway.'

Ez was reclining on the sofa, flushed and bristle-scratched.

From behind his back, he produced a jar which he rattled at her. 'Coffee beans,' he said sternly. 'In the cupboard. Middle shelf.'

'Oh, is that what they are? I thought they were lentils.'

'Isabel, have you never made coffee?'

'Don't be a *cucufato*, of course I have! I drink pints of it!'

'But you failed to recognise these?' Another rattle.

'How could I? That jar doesn't have a Nescafé label – Ouch!' as he cheerfully scattered a handful of beans on her chest.

'Oh well, Contreras,' he said to himself, 'let you and I go and make the coffee. In fact, you know, I think I will marry myself; at least I recognise bloody coffee beans!'

Blissfully, she listened to him singing in the kitchen.

\* \* \*

It was a nice port, as ports go; but Gualterio put his down untasted.

'You are what?' he asked slowly.

'Getting married again.'

164

'Yes. I thought I heard you correctly.' His face suffused. 'What the hell for? Can't you just keep the girl as your resident fuck without all that rigmarole? I will, thou will, until we get pissed off each other; and Isabel pretending she's not after your bloody bulging piggy-bank?'

Angrily, Pepe shouted 'Watch your foul tongue! She is not after my money!'

'What is she after, then?'

'Nothing! She loves me, I love her, that's it!'

Gualterio said scornfully, 'You live in a bloody opera of your own, don't you? First that bitch with the deformed ovaries, and now a bloody English nobody! Why the hell can't you be like your brother, marry a fertile Spanish *chica*?'

'Because I don't happen to be in love with one! I thought you liked Isabel!'

'Oh I do, I do. The fact that she's a tittering idiot has nothing to do with my liking for the girl.' He swung round. 'If it wasn't for her and that bloody *maricón* Drach, you'd still be with –'

He bit his lip as Pepe crowed 'So that's it! We're back to friend Gusano, are we? Well, let me tell you something – Isa and Roberto have already done more for me in two weeks than Gusano did in two bloody years! And that's being kind!'

'How dare you, you –' as the door opened.

'Hello! Family chinwag, is it?' Alfredo grinned.

'Fuck off!' yelled Gualterio.

Alfredo came, in and closed the door with his foot. 'Greetings, all!' and gravitated towards the bottle of port. He looked at it closely. '1989? Couldn't we afford one a little bit more mature?'

'You'll just have to get used to the idea, Father. She is here to stay, and she will be treated WITH RESPECT!'

'Oh sure, sure she'll stay, until that cock of yours starts to fidget again! And then where will we be, eh? We'll still be here, your bloody family, to mop up the damned pieces as we did with Judit when you buggered off to that Italian tart! Put that port down, *coño*, you weren't invited!'

Alfredo looked round, mystified. 'Oh, sorry. Thought I lived here. All the houses round here look alike, that's the trouble.'

'I did not go off leaving you to pick up the bloody pieces!'

165

'No? NO? Where were you, you male whore, when Judit was wandering around at bloody midnight like Lady Macbeth, and getting pissed on my brandy? Eh? I'll tell you where you were – somewhere in Italy with that warbling lump of ravioli! What is it with you, you rutting has-been? If it's not posing for some photo looking tragic and half-bloody-dead, it's some tart –'

'Shut your filthy mouth! I am not a has-been! And don't you dare refer to Isabel as a –'

'Mmmm, not bad, though, for an '89,' mused Alfredo.

'So what the hell is she, then? One of the Untouchables?'

'She is my fiancée!'

Alfredo said, 'Oh, that *is* good news! Good for you, brother – great girl!'

'And don't you bloody well – Oh! Thanks, *amigo*.'

Gualterio rubbed his jowls. 'You are serious.'

'Of course I'm bloody serious!' shrieked Pepe.

'Has something upset you, Father?' Alfredo asked mildly. 'We'd better ask Isa to come and soothe your nasty temper, hadn't we? Where is she, by the way?'

'On the phone to Nathaniel West,' grumpily.

'Isn't he the one who writes all the original music that Schubert thought of first?'

Pepe grinned. 'Be fair! Not all of it's by Schubert.'

'Whoops, sorry, apologies to Chopin!'

'When do you propose going through with this farce?' bellowed Gualterio.

'Thank you for your kind interest, Father. We haven't yet decided on a date.'

'I bet that conniving slut has!'

The glass of port hit the floor and rolled fitfully. 'Take that back!'

Mina's voice, 'What on earth is going on?' She came in, stared at them.

'Nothing,' Alfredo said cheerfully. 'Want some port?'

'No thank you,' picking up Pepe's glass. 'Where's Isabel?'

'They want to get married!' bawled Gualterio, grasping her arm.

Mina smiled broadly. 'Oh Pepe, that's wonderful news! Many

166

congratulations, dear!' and she hugged him. Alfredo thumped his
arm, smiling.

Mina looked at her father-in-law. He shuffled his feet.

'Papaterio?'

'Fucking congratulations,' he muttered.

'Sorry, Papaterio – we didn't quite hear that.'

'Congratulations!' he shouted.

Father and son solemnly shook hands.

*　　*　　*

Of course, she tried again. Because he hadn't meant it; words as
usual, before thought. Dialled the number of his hotel in Zurich,
fingers stiff with impatience.

Sorry, *Herr* Contreras is at the theatre.

Sipped a little vodka, then rang the Opera House she knew so
well.

Sorry – *Monsieur* Contreras left about ten minutes ago.

She held her temper. Is *Madame* Bragas in the theatre?

She is. Putting you through!

Teresa Bragas was in her cold dressing-room being fitted for a
new set of frills when the telephone was wheeled into her presence.
The seamstress was on her knees, measuring the distance between
calf and high-heeled shoe. She had abandoned the fitting of the
bodice halfway through, and hoped that Bragas would be in a
better humour when she resumed pinning it later.

*Madame* Bragas had arrived in Zurich fresh from the despair of
her forty-fifth birthday, only to find that Buzzer Ahmet expected
her to attend first call as though she were a thick child.

She turned slightly, looked down, and frowned. What was that
French cretin doing down there resting when she was supposed to
be fixing?

And as if Buzzer Ahmet wasn't reason enough to hang oneself,
the brainless producer had insisted on new colours for Carmen
herself. Teresa knew that red suited her best, or a chirpy sparking
orange. Now the producer, may his wife give birth to piglets, had
dragged in a French needlewoman from Lucerne, loaded her
arms with rolls of chintz in anaemic pink and sick-bag yellow and

167

demanded that she create a pale Carmen who looked like a cigarette-smoking factory girl instead of a tourist poster for flamenco.

Her eyes, black as her hair in its single plait, slanted to the door which squeaked as the telephone trolley was wheeled in.

'For you, *madame*,' smiled the attendant.

The eyes swivelled down to the dressmaker. 'How much longer?' curtly.

'A few minutes only, *Madame* Bragas. I think I can do the bodice without bothering you further.'

She nodded, picked up the phone. Then a sweet smile. 'Judit, how nice! How are you, my dear?'

'Thank you, never better! And yourself? Pepe tells me that your last recital in London went absolutely wonderfully!'

Teresa stifled a laugh. As her caller spoke at length (Teresa always lost track of what Judit was talking about and had long ago dubbed her "Mrs Smirnoff"), she narrowed her eyes. Went wonderfully? Oh yes, sure. That pompous sod – your ex, dear – first of all confusing my dear Felix so that he played the intro to *Tutti Amori* twice, then manipulating his bloody beak as if it were full of sewage; standing there with his little hands clasped to his little midriff, opening his flabby mouth to sing one of MY lines and then looking like an axed cod when I kicked him to remind him. Oh yes, it all went –

'– if he'll be coming back to the theatre this evening?'

'Oh, sorry, dear – I was distracted for a moment. Pepe, you mean? I doubt it, he and Ahmet are dining *à deux*, probably arranging for him to sing Carmen as well as Don José. By the by, wasn't that news of his absolutely electrifying? We couldn't believe it when he told us – in confidence, of course, since it has to be hush-hush for the moment. And he looked so excited, shaking hands with everyone, as happy as if he were in paradise, bless him!'

Which is where he will be on opening night if he doesn't find a dredger for that nose of his.

Rushed on, 'He's got to be a good boy now, hasn't he, no more wanking between arpeggios as he did with Merdina!'

Judit's voice was gentle. 'Is this the news I think it is?'

168

'His engagement, yes of course! Have you met her? English, he says, he calls her Isabel, but I think her name is something utterly silly, let me think . . . oh yes, Eliza!' She tittered, then poked her tongue out at her caller. 'Eliza Pepper. Doesn't she work for Pepe's new agent in London?'

Drach, Judit thought. Mina had mentioned something about dearest Josep being given his nosebag and Robert Drach taking over. She was rigid as she sipped her drink. Seeing nothing but wild fog, she said 'Well, I won't keep you any longer. Give Pepe my love. Oh – and Teresa? The very best of luck for the first night!'

Teresa Bragas hastily crossed herself and spat down the silent phone. You jealous cow, Mrs Smirnoff! And smiled.

The dressmaker was waiting patiently, her face lively and curious. But all she said was, 'If you will step out of the dress now, *Madame*, I can begin sewing.'

She allowed the woman to assist her. Then said softly in her ear, 'Perhaps the bodice would fit better if you allowed for two tits instead of one!'

*　　*　　*

Sunday morning, cool and damp, a new patch of wet wallpaper in the hall.

'Mum!' Clair Tinker was sitting at the table, wearing one of her divorced father's left-behind jerseys and her leg-warmers, three large rollers on top of her head, long strands of silky hair over her shoulders. 'Have you seen this? Look!'

Eve peered round the packet of Weetabix. 'If you're referring to the Sunday paper, no I haven't because you grabbed it first. Why?'

'Mum, it's about Ezzie! That's why I asked you –'

Eve, startled, snatched the *News of the World*. 'Where? What are you talking about?'

'There, look! By that photo! Oh why haven't you phoned her since she got back?'

'I've had no damned time, that's . . . Oh!' She looked at the photo, a man in uniform. Beneath it, a caption: 'Contreras as Carmen.'

169

Eve chuckled. That should cause a bit of head-scratching in the music world. Her eyes widening, she read the accompanying paragraph.

'From our correspondent in Zurich. Is the singing sensation Pepe "I've got what it takes" Contreras about to bite the love-dust again? After the startling accounts last year of his steamy and acrobatic romance with Italian singer Bionda Merdina, I can reveal that Spanish tenor (that's the high voice) Pepe is secretly engaged to a Brit! My sources tell me that his latest heart's delight is the partner of Robert Drach (London-based agent for stars of the serious music-go-round), Eliza Pepper. For opera and Pepe-lovers everywhere – watch this space!'

Eve read it again, disbelieving. Ez? Ignoring Clair's excited 'Will she be famous now?', she sped to the telephone.

*　　*　　*

Exhausted, Ez lay on the floor and tried to find the Arts pages in the *Sunday Times*. Half-past ten. And a gruelling session with Ada. Tears; old and frightened, life's familiarity suddenly escaping, catching her unprepared in its downdraught. Worried about all the shelves of books in Ez's rooms, would she take them with her, there were so many, suppose I get someone who makes a noise. She had now been collected by a friendly parishioner and was on her way to church.

I wonder if I'm being prayed for, thought Ez, feeling sad, and finally finding the page she sought. Opera review. Zurich. *Carmen*. Headline:

*BEWILDERMENT FOR BIZET.*

Oh dear. Glanced at the photo of a disdainful Teresa Bragas. Tried not to giggle.

'This bewildering production appears to have everything but love, passion, hatred and jealousy.'

Grinning, Ez skipped the next lengthy column, which was devoted to poor scenery, clumsy sound effects, and the question posed as to whether Zubair Ahmet had been very moved or asleep during Act II since his eyes remained closed throughout. Then came 'Contreras gave a rare performance, but of which opera

170

remains a mystery. His acting technique has often puzzled reviewers, myself included, and on this occasion I was glad of the identifying uniform. There were occasional moments of the familiar lyric beauty, but not unfortunately in the unsurpassable aria "*La fleur que tu m'avais jetée*", which he had to emote whilst circling the drab figure of Carmen (Teresa Bragas) who, for some obscure whim of the producer, was standing stiffly on a crate of tomatoes in a weird mist. Contreras seemed unable to override the serious failures of this production, and wandered heavy-footedly around the stage as if begging for directions in a foreign city.'

Ez put her hand over her mouth to prevent the escape of disloyal laughter. Oh my poor *querido*! Still smiling, she got up to answer the phone.

'Oh hi, Eve, sorry I haven't been –'

'Never mind that! Have you seen the *News of the World* today?' and, ignoring protests about never reading that toilet paper, raced on 'It's in here, about you getting engaged! To a Spanish bloke, that singer, Contreras! Is it true, Ez?'

'You WHAT?'

'You heard! Is it true? Because it's down here in black and white, dear. And Clair wants your autograph, please!'

'Fuck Clair! Eve, are you being serious?'

'About Clair?'

A scream. 'No, you idiot! About my name being in that bloody rag!'

Eve read it out slowly and clearly.

'Oh Christ, how did they find out? He'll kill me, he'll think it was me who opened my big mouth!'

'Then it's obviously your fiancé who told them; why the panic?'

'It couldn't have been him, he wanted it kept under wraps until the official announcement to the press at the end of November! Oh God, he'll be furious!'

She hung up and sank on to the settee. Had he really told the press boys without telling her, warning her? When the phone rang again, she lifted it cautiously, but reassured that her number was under Ada's name only.

'Ezita?' The tone of voice was edgy. 'What the fuck is going on? Enlightenment, please!'

171

'I don't know what you –'

'Listen, mop-head, I've had nine bloody phone calls so far this morning, and before you say oh lucky Bobby, they were all from journalists bombarding me with bloody silly questions about you and Sniffer! So tell me, before I cut not only the phone wire but my fucking throat as well!'

After listening to her stumbling panic and bewilderment, he snapped 'Okay, save it! I'll bring some goodies over and a bottle of stomach-stripper, and we'll hole up in that scruffy pad of yours and fathom out what to bloody well do!'

On his way over, he stopped and bought the *News of the World*.

\* \* \*

Ez glanced nervously at the clock. Pepe had told her he would ring as close to two o'clock as he could. In the meantime, she tried to count and pile up her books.

'Has Sniffer said anything about that Charity Gala next January?'

Bobby was stretched out on the settee, an empty plate balanced on his stomach. He had recovered somewhat from the shock of the engagement, and had decided, with her relieved approval, that he would stick to his 'No comment, sorry, Miss Pepper is abroad' line.

God, her mind fluttering, how do I try and explain – 'What?' absently. Then 'Where on earth did I get *Watership Down* from? . . . Oh, the Charity Gala. Yes, he'll do it. One item, he said, no more.'

'One fucking song? Is that all? What's the matter, has his bloody larynx gone on strike?'

The phone made them both jump.

It was raining heavily in Zurich. His catarrh was a bastard, and Bragas had delivered a hundred boxes of Kleenex to his dressing-room. He had tripped over a traffic cone on his way into the theatre for what he considered an unnecessary run-through of the final scene. And the newspapers finally undermined his uncertain temper. Gleefully, Bragas had put them in a neat pile in the Green Room. *News of the World, Le Figaro, Berliner Zeitung, La Stampa, El País*, all with the same item of gossip.

172

Bobby was *en route* tactfully to the kitchen when Ez answered the phone. He heard her shout 'Pepe, please! I did not! . . . Damn you, will you listen . . . I DID NOT!' Bobby also heard tears in her anger, and marched back into the sitting room.

'Don't, Pepe. . .' whispering. And he snatched the phone from her. 'Contreras? Drach here.' Very icy. Very baritone. Listened, then 'Don't be such a bloody idiot! That's why I'm here, she's in such a bloody state! . . . No, she did not, who the hell do you think she is, some bloody tart who couldn't wait to tell the world? . . . Yes, I can understand that . . . It's in one of the tabloids over here – you savvy the word tabloid? . . . good! . . . what do you mean, what's savvy? We used it to all the bloody foreigners during the war! . . . I don't give a cow's cock what other bloody languages they've printed it in, the byline in this one is fucking Zurich! . . Use your bloody brains, Contreras, if the article was written in Zurich, it means there was some loose-mouthed bugger at your end! . . Yes, well, tell her that, not me! . . . All she's had is one chicken sandwich . . . Okay, then, I'll just go and see if I can cut her down from the fucking rope. Oh! – congratulations!'

Smiling again, she took the phone from him. Bobby returned to the kitchen and busied himself with the coffee.

# 11

Having wasted twenty minutes getting his bearings after turning left off Berlin's Wilhelmstrasse, Vito's exaggerated saunter became a brisk walk.

It was, at best, a shabby evening. After a day of intermittent rain, the premature darkness was bringing with it a fine and penetrating mist. Elderly raindrops still clung to parked cars, and condensation spread across lighted shop windows.

He made his way to the rendezvous carefully, dressed casually, his suede jacket half-buttoned. It had been several years since he had visited the cafe, Die Katze. This evening, through the steamed windows, Vito could see two people standing by a display of cream cakes, and only two others sitting in the far corner.

He went in, and made for the corner.

'Hi,' said Louis, smiling.

'Hello there,' Vito murmured, sitting down and arching an eyebrow at the skinny young man with him.

'This is Gianni,' said Louis.

'Good to meet you at last,' said Gianni. His accent was unmistakeable. Naples.

Louis said abruptly, 'Coffee, I suppose, Lavagna? After that, we go to Gianni's hotel. How long do you have?'

Vito stared at him. 'Hotel? I thought this was just —'

'A social call?' interrupted Gianni, looking at Vito's mouth as if he were lip-reading. Louis sniggered, eyes coldly watchful.

Vito made a show of looking at his wristwatch. 'I have about an hour.'

After drinking half of his coffee, he followed them out of Die Katze into the thin mist.

\*     \*     \*

174

'Where the hell is he?' demanded Monda Ballena.

Her smooth face gleamed with heat and indignation. This was the final run-through before the dress rehearsal. Her eyes roved to the wings and out to the darkened auditorium. Aggressively, her turbanned head gestured to the producer.

'Where is the Italian prat?'

'My apologies, *Madame* Ballena, I –'

'You don't know! Of course you don't know – how unreasonable of Monda, expecting a damn producer to know anything!'

Her unexpectedly small feet executed a neat turn, her grey voluminous dress arched its skirt around her calves, and she stormed to the tea-trolley. Other members of the cast grinned at each other. Dear old Wailing Wall, the grin said.

'Ah,' said the producer, swallowing his nerves with a gulp. 'Yes.' He glanced at the theatre clock. 'He's only a little late –'

'A little late?' The scream jolted the partially-erected scenery. 'He should have been here nearly an hour ago! Saints and God above, how much longer do we have to wait for that wrinkled drag artist?' She marched her kilos towards the wings.

'Here he is!' someone called, as a figure emerged from the theatre's gloom and hurried towards the brightness of the foot-lights.

'Vito! We were about to send out tracker dogs!' the producer called heartily.

Lucia di Lammermoor watched as her Edgardo scrambled on to the stage, then gave him a sweet smile of welcome. 'Naughty boy!' and kissed him on both cheeks before drawing back dramatically. 'San Antonio! What has happened to you?'

Vito stood shakily in the glare of the lights. He was damp. Wisps of hair hung over his face; a long red scratch from temple to mouth.

'I fell. Slipped. In the street.' Tried to smile. Surveyed the assembled company. 'Sorry,' he said.

'We were getting anxious,' Monda purred, then wrinkled her nose. 'Are you going to have a wash first, darling?'

'Perhaps . . . yes, yes . . . excuse me . . . five minutes,' and he turned and fled through eighteenth-century Scotland to his dressing-room.

175

*    *    *

They were walking in the gardens, Isa and the two small boys.

Pepe was expected home at seven o'clock. Moncho had set out for the airport forty minutes ago.

She was tired, her heart was not. The journey had been fine. Pepe had insisted that his secretary, Federico Golpe, be despatched to London to escort her safely and above all, privately, to Barcelona. Federico, tall and lean with bifocals sellotaped to the bridge of his nose, made untaxing company. He told her that he had his own rooms in the Contreras house during the season, and an office next to the music room; that he was divorced with a spastic son whom he saw twice a year.

How sad, thought Isa, and wanted to question him further, but he withdrew into his pleasant shell after that, and only seemed interested in hearing the new additions to her vocabulary.

She was tired, for sure. Mercifully no intrusions by the press, who soon got bored with the mechanical 'no bloody comment' from Bobby; her belongings in storage, the Agency, Ada, all dealt with. Recurring indecision about the future of her little house in Somerset, currently rented out to tenants since her father died. Bobby told her not to sell it, it was a roof over her head, just in case – and he looked at her face and shut up.

Now, a feeling of unreality as though her feet weren't actually in this garden.

'My bike was stolen yesterday,' announced Lluís importantly.

'Goodness!' and she smiled at the face turned up to hers, the mouth contorted as he chewed gum.

'Yes,' he nodded, 'from the school playground.'

'What did your *Papi* say?'

'He swore a lot, told me I should've chained it up. Do you think a chain would have stopped them, Isa?'

She pretended to think. Pau tugged her hand, 'Do you, Isa?'

'Well, it might have helped. It would have taken the thief much longer, wouldn't it, and then someone might have seen him.'

'*Papi* won't buy him another one!' chortled Pau. '*Papi* says he can . . .' He turned to his brother. 'What was it *Papi* said?'

Lluís sniggered, removed the chewing-gum and stuck it on the

176

back of his hand. 'He said – I think, cos *Mamá* was trying to shut him up – I think he said I could get used to fucking walking until I learned to take care of my things. Would that be right, Isa?'

She quickly averted her face. 'I'm sure he'll buy you another one soon,' was all she said. They strolled amicably on under sweeping branches, Isa touching the heavy leaves with ageless joy.

'What does fucking-walking mean, Isa?' Pau, leaping from foot to plimsolled foot. Then he gave a sideways jump before she could think of an appropriate answer and cried 'I bet I know! It's something to do with mountains, isn't it, Isa?'

She and Lluís stared at the animated little face, and Lluís gave him a shove. 'You're thinking of mountain bikes, you stupid bugger!'

Oh God, thought Isa, trying not to laugh, Mina would have hysterics if she knew how much they were learning from Alfredo.

'Do you have mountains in England, Isa?' Pau asked, unperturbed.

'A few,' she said cautiously, trying to summon some up in her mind, 'but only small ones. Not like the ones you have here.'

'Or like in Switzerland,' Lluís cried, and hurled the chewing-gum into a clump of cactus. '*Papi* says they have gnomes in Switzerland, all of them sent by God to look after Uncle Pepe's money. Why does Uncle Pepe need gnomes, Isa?'

'Ask your *Papi*!' she laughed. She'd love to hear the answer.

Then Lluís shouted 'Look! There's his car!' pointing through the trees in the direction of the drive. 'Uncle Pepe's here! He's home!'

Pau tugged her hand. 'Uncle Pepe's here! Come on, Isa! He promised to bring us a cuckoo clock from Zurkik!'

They squealed excitedly and raced to the car.

Pepe, on his way through the house to find her, paused at the sound of their voices and peered through an open window.

He saw Isa gazing at the car, her eyes transfixed, her mouth smiling.

He saw Lluís grabbing her sleeve, 'What's the matter, Isa, have you had a vision?'

He saw Pau, 'Of Our Lady?' squeaking, dancing round her, 'Like Saint Bernadette?'

And then Pepe ran, the widest grin, leaping down the steps two at a time, Pau scampering out of the way.

'Pepe!'

'Isa! My Isa!'

and a wild spin through the air in his arms, both of them laughing, eyes shining, 'God, Isa, we made it!'

'We did!' she shouted.

And Lluís and Pau charging round in circles giggling and yelling 'We made it!'

Until the voice of Gualterio bellowed 'Have you no respect for the dead?'

They stopped suddenly, the boys colliding, Isa with a startled 'What?' and Pepe looking at his father with a sudden sharp anger. He said quickly in her ear, 'Josep Gusano. He died suddenly on Sunday night. The funeral was today.'

'Oh God, Mina never said . . .'

Holding each other tightly, Pepe ruffling Pau's hair and winking comfortingly at Lluís, they went towards the elderly man in his dark suit.

His sadness had defeated his growl.

'Welcome home,' he said quietly to Isa. To Pepe, 'Welcome back.' And went slowly up the steps into the house.

'Oh I'm so sorry,' she said distressed.

He kissed her, gently bit her nose. 'How were you to know, *princesa*? When I last phoned you, I did not know, either.' Then sternly, 'Kennel!'

'Kennel,' meekly, and snatched a kiss from his mouth.

'Uncle Pepe! Did you bring a cuckoo clock?'

'What?' and Isa giggled behind her hand.

Lluís cried 'You promised us a cuckoo clock!'

To the chanting of 'Cuckoo! Cuckoo!' from an excited Pau, Pepe pretended to think. The boys gazed at him.

'Well. . . .' They squealed. Pepe relented and grinned. 'Go and ask your *Mamá* if she will open my brown bag in the hall. If there's a parcel inside –' He paused as they turned to run, '– you may have it!'

Skidding on the gravel, they flew into the house, leaving Isa and Pepe laughing.

'The passport to privacy,' murmured Isa. 'A cuckoo clock!'

178

He slammed the nailbrush up and across his fingers, shaking. Just like an old man, he thought, I am trembling and confused.

He had thrown icy water over his head and face, and his pale yellow hair looked thinner than ever, wet strands plastered against his skull.

A trick of the light bouncing on the mirror made him believe that his moustache had gone. He touched it several times.

I'm crying, he thought hysterically. Stripped off his sweater. Armpits stank. He scoured them, sprayed his torso with cologne. Clean shirt, blue and yellow checks, fumbling with new stiff buttons. I'm a whore. Louis, you are assassinating me. Louis, laughing in the shadows, and the shadows were suddenly upon him and he called for mercy and for more. Gianni counting, Louis intoning like an echo, a cleft where his hand lay.

Never again, never, remember it. Remember never again.

Whistling and refreshed, he left the dressing-room.

*　　*　　*

Gualterio had absented himself from dinner, preferring silence and salad in his own rooms on this day of mourning.

By contrast, the family rooms were lively and festive.

There had, of course, been one or two remarks concerning the latest production of *Carmen*. Alfredo had made it his business to remove an *en passant* review from *La Vanguardia*, and this was waved gleefully during the fish course, following Pepe's briefing to the diners about the poor performances and fading vocal powers of Bragas and Lemuel Doe (who, he said, sounded about as *basso* as a goose on guard duty).

'And how about you? Yourself? How did our beloved Golden Throat perform?' asked Alfredo solemnly. Only Isa heard the warning rustle of newspaper.

'Well, in my view,' pompously, 'I was barely extended to my full —'

The rustle of paper and laughter merged triumphantly.

'You were bloody dreadful!' Alfredo sniggered, waving the cutting, '*La Vanguardia*!'

Pepe sniffed. 'Their so-called arts critic listens through his arse.'

'Pepe! Please!' Mina choked on her fish.

Isa whispered, 'Mina, I was so sorry to hear about *Señor* Gusano. Why didn't you tell me?'

'It says here, *coño*,' tapping the paper, 'it says here, and I quote, "Contreras moved so mechanically through his rôle" – get that, *hombre*? Mechanically? – "that one was tempted to look for the key in his back"!'

'If that puerile shit amuses you –'

'Isa, does he have a key in his –'

'Alfredo!'

Then Mina whispered, 'I'm sorry, Isa, I should have mentioned it to you. You never met him, did you? Poor man, to die like that, on his own. I keep –' She broke off. 'Pepe, Alfredo! . . . We'd better adjourn, I think,' and stood up, the men breaking apart and panting heavily.

Leading the way into the sitting room, she continued 'I keep wondering who he was speaking to when he died. What did they think when it all went silent? Or perhaps he hadn't even finished dialling.' She sighed deeply. 'Poor Papaterio, he is so lost and sad. Do you know, he has covered his chess table with a black cloth?'

'Champagne!' called Pepe.

'Was it his heart?' sitting down on the familiar sofa.

'Had a history of it,' nodded Mina. 'But when you consider that he was only –'

'Champagne!' yelled Pepe. Alfredo looked up angrily, the bottle rammed between his knees. 'You'll get it all over your stupid head in a minute!' He struggled with the cork. 'The bloody thing's stuck!'

He suddenly shouted with laughter. 'Hey, *coño* – does it remind you of anyone? Pulling it out with difficulty?'

Pepe's shout, 'Christ, yes! María Sangría!'

The brothers clung together, howling.

'Who is María Sangría?' asked Isa.

Mina's lips tightened. 'Alfredo, will you please –'

'Jesus, once you got it stuck in her narrow –'

180

'ALFREDO! Pepe! Please don't laugh, Isabel, it only encourages them!'

Then she smiled and cheered as the cork popped and bubbles flew. As the glasses were charged, Alfredo called for silence.

'A toast! A toast to the happy pair! *Vaya por* Isa! *Vaya por* Pepe!' and they drank, Pepe kissing Isa, Mina kissing everybody.

'So!' said Alfredo, sitting cross-legged on the floor, 'When are you buying the ring?'

'Tomorrow,' Pepe said, and belched. 'Christ Almighty, this is foul! What the hell is it – Dom Estos?'

'We are not,' Isa said smoothly. 'I don't want a ring, I don't like jewellery. I shall wear this,' and she waved the signet ring at them.

Alfredo stared at it. 'You serious? Jesus, Gualterio will shit bricks!'

'Alfredo!'

Pepe said, 'If you don't have a proper ring with a proper bloody diamond in it, woman, I shan't –' and whispered in her ear.

Her eyes grew round. 'Do you mean that? . . Oh! In that case,' smiling at Alfredo and Mina, 'we shall choose a ring soon.'

A round of applause.

'And have you decided on a date for your wedding?' asked Mina.

'Sometime next June,' Isa replied firmly to her new family.

Pepe scowled. Opened his mouth, and Mina said 'Pepe! Please!'

\*　　\*　　\*

The suite in Milan's Hotel d'Orinatoio was littered with boxes and wrapping-paper. And, as Alfredo Contreras was removing a champagne cork in Barcelona, Cherri de Canasta was gazing at herself in the mirror, amazed and delighted.

You Aussie wonder-girl! The dieting had paid off, oh holy kangaroo dung, it had! God bless muesli trees everywhere – oh look at yourself, mate, look at this sylph, you'd make frogs sing!

'Frankie!' she yelled, 'Come and take a look at this!' She twirled gaily in her new black dress, still glancing at her reflection.

Francesco Giormani emerged from his dressing-room, knotting

his tie, and smiled at his wife's pleasure. 'Not bad, not bad at all,' and whistled.

'Not bad? You gone bloody blind, mate? You know how long it is since I wore a dress this size? Twelve years! Must be, easy, twelve years!' She gave him an exuberant kiss, then dabbed the lipstick off his cheek, spitting on a ball of tissue paper from one of the dress boxes.

'You're crazy, lady!' laughing.

'That is no way to speak to a sylph,' and she thumped his back. 'There – you'll do, clean as a baby's bum! You nearly ready? Moddie and Mimosa will start feeding before we get there!'

He watched her, whistling as she brushed her hair.

Thin. Collarbone like Choctaw Ridge.

'You're as sylphlike as you're gonna get,' he said firmly. 'Tonight, you eat. And you eat good!' He put his arm round her, found her ear and kissed it. 'You'll be a great-looking Desdemona. Now I want my Cherri back, if you don't mind!'

*     *     *

Sasha's Daddy laid down his baton and addressed his front-row violins.

Afterwards the chattering began, chairs scraping back, music stands cleared of their scores. He bent down to his already-bulging case and crammed the last act of *Otello* inside. Then he remained on the podium, hands loosely resting, gazing unseeingly at the bustle on the stage in front of him.    Sasha's Daddy stroked the tip of his baton and murmured the first two lines of a verse by Tasso. This was his superstition. This was his small ceremony whenever electricity burned in his gut and he knew that something was about to happen.

'G'night, *Maestro!*'

'Oh . . . goodnight, Maurizio . . . Guido . . .'

The bass players had laid their instruments carefully on their sides, and saluted cheerily as they shrugged on jackets and clattered their way through the orchestra furniture.

Sasha's Daddy was a recent appointee as chief conductor at La Scala. Recent, in the sense that this was only his fourth opera for

Milan. A successful second and third, a much-hissed first. No-one in the Milanese audience liked drastic change, and they had been noisily defiant when he made his debut in *Il Trovatore* – too soon, they felt, after the premature death of *Maestro* Stronzino. Why not the deputy? Why a new chief so soon? Then came redemption, and now they approved as ardently as they had hated.

Sasha's Daddy came from Parma. Black-haired and hollow-eyed, born Claudio Rosco, he had become known not only for his arm-swaying technique so reminiscent of Rudolf Schwarz, but also because he was the automatic replacement whenever Buzzer Ahmet vacated an orchestra. La Scala was his first appointment without the shadowy cloak of Ahmet behind his dressing-room door.

He had acquired the sobriquet of Sasha's Daddy quite by chance, when a radio interview on the BBC was repeated throughout Europe. Claudio Rosco had once been the passionate lover of a Norwegian pianist; and, according to the interview she gave, was the father of her child Sasha. Gleefully, musicians everywhere immediately re-named him. Even the La Scala management referred to him as S.D.

The sound of scenery scraping, the shouts of laughter and bellowed orders all pierced his dream ceremony; and he became aware, too, of a pair of feet in soft shoes on the stage in front of him at waist level. Looking up, he saw Modesto Martes hunkered down and gazing at him, sweat escaping down his brown sticky face.

'You know what I think, *Maestro*?' and his fingers fiddled with a piece of string caught in the floorboards near the footlights.

'I believe I can guess,' said Sasha's Daddy.

'*Signor* Martes! We're going to have to darken that skin base some more for tomorrow night, the new spot's too bright!'

'Oh, right. Thanks, Andrea,' absently. He picked up the string and wound it round his thumb. 'You can always tell. Just something.'

'Just a little something,' agreed Sasha's Daddy.

They said goodnight and went their separate ways.

\* \* \*

183

'And has he decided in his superior wisdom,' sarcastically, 'which song he'll be blessing mankind with at the Charity Gala? They are pressing me for it, I've had the buggers on the phone twice already. And will I have the nerve to mention his fee?'

A giggle. '*La Mattinata.*'

A prolonged groan. 'Oh God! Are you bloody serious? Please say that Ezita is joking with Bobby!'

'Cross my heart! Anyway, what's wrong with it?'

'I'll tell you what's bloody wrong with it! Everyone – and I include here Greek pensioners and Bantu babies – is pissed off with hearing him sing it!'

Protestingly, 'Other tenors sing it –'

'Point number two: he'll be on the same fucking bill as Lavagna and Martes, not the bloody Andrews Sisters.' He sighed lustily. 'Can't he dream up anything else? Martes and Vito are cramming in a Verdi or two, and a Massenet, plus that Bizet number from the bloody *Pearl Fishers*. And those two cows whom they laughingly refer to as "girls" are going to make us sob our acrylics off with Puccini –'

'So? *Mattinata* will lighten the proceedings. And don't forget that Azucarero and his rock band are also on the bill,' defensively.

'Yes, darling, I'm only too aware of that. Arrogant unwashed lunatic! Rumour has it that he's so vain about that bloody prick of his that he dips it in starch every night.' Ignored the titter, swept on 'Doesn't Sniffer have anything else he could warble?'

'Er . . . *Granada*?'

'Oh shit!'

'Bobby, he's branching out now, he wants to do more –'

'You call *Twattinata* and bloody *Granada* branching out? Christ, I'd hate to see him stuck in a rut! Oh no! . . . for God's sake! . . .' A low whimper. 'Just looking through his documents concerning fees. Bloody hell, he's never asking that much for bloody *Mattinata*, is he? Oh, sympathy for Bobby!'

Cheerful laughter from Barcelona.

'Thanks, Ez, you've made my fucking day! I'm looking forward to telling the impresario all this good news. Have I got time for a quick weep before I ring bloody Seville? Ah well – toodle-pip, darling, and . . . oh, tell the Dynamic Dwarf I may have some good news for him soon – I'll ring later in the week. Take care of yourself, you giggling mare!'

*    *    *

The curtain fell for the last time, and still the yells and calls and the beating of sore hands, thudding of feet, '*Bravo!*'
'Cherri, *bravissima!*' 'More, more!' '*Bravissimo!*'
But the curtain's heavy folds swung slower and slower, trapping a mess of loose flowers and ferns.
No more.
Modesto said in an interview later that the ovation had lasted for one hour and fifty minutes. 'It would,' he said with a twinkle, 'have been almost as quick to do the opera all over again!'
But now, on this night, the auditorium was a pandemonium of loud talk, excited trills of laughter, hundreds upon hundreds of legs moving towards the exits, and hypnotized glances over shoulders at the unmoving curtain, seats thumping up, thunder-struck reviewers and *cognoscenti* racing for phone and typewriter, calling for stenographers and coffee.
Sasha's Daddy wound his way through the chattering musicians and sagged in the gloom of the entrance to the pit. Fumbled for a stool and sank down, his head in his hands.
Otello and Desdemona stayed where they were behind the heavy blue curtain, clinging to each other, make-up running with sweat and mingling with their tears.
'Oh Christ!' Cherri sobbed on his shoulder. 'Oh sweet Jesus!'
Modesto held her tightly, breathing fast through his mouth, gasping, his eyes fixed upwards and nowhere. His hair and beard were soaked, and their costumes stank with perspiration. Iago, alight as a fire with his own enthusiastic reception, ran across to them, arms outstretched, carrying his wig. The three of them, in a tight and shuddering embrace.
Modesto said 'Whew!' shakily wiping his forehead with his sleeve. 'You okay, darling?'
'Shit, yes, just about! Jeee-sus, what a . . .!'
Iago shook his head and sobbed happily. Modesto thumped his shoulder.

'You!' he cried. 'You! God damn it, you brilliant bastard!'

And whooping like schoolchildren, they ran hand in hand off stage, Cherri rubbing her ribs. She giggled even as the pain stabbed. Moddie had arms like bloody boa constrictors when he had to carry her dead body in the final scene. Or perhaps the weeks of inactivity had taken their toll.

Mimosa met them halfway, running headlong with champagne, crying with happiness. And the hugs began again, mouths that came away from kissing sticky with make-up base. And Iago felt himself grow taller, part of this, part of them, his musical milestone family.

And Modesto Martes looked like God to him, even standing there with an idiotic grin and scratching his groin.

*     *     *

Sitting at the piano in the music room, Isa was unaware of the raised voices in the great hall beyond the closed door.

The manuscript was in front of her. Eight poems and their music. Of course, it wasn't the full orchestral transcript, not yet. But after the successful meeting between Pepe and Nathan and Tom Patna, the full arrangement would soon follow. The important thing was, it had all been agreed and charted. Bobby had been given the go-ahead. The City of Barcelona Symphony Orchestra would assemble in London for recording and eventual transmission. The month chosen was February, Byron Larch and Decca alerted. Isa had met and liked the young conductor: young and curly-haired, Simón Estertor was genuinely in favour of musical adventure. His only drawback, she felt, was his habit of picking his ear and wiping his finger clean afterwards on his thigh. He had also been assigned to the Charity Gala in January, which pleased Pepe.

Isa was not a pianist. Her finger stabbed awkwardly as she read the manuscript and mouthed the words. She could vaguely hear Federico in his office, talking to himself as he sorted out drawers and tried to create more space.

The piano drifted suddenly into silence. An intake of breath. The idea she had had. The idea she had lost. Surfacing again, in

186

memory of Pepe running through this new song and laughingly protesting 'Three more top C's in a row? What does Nathan think I am, bloody triplets?'

And she suddenly banged the keys and closed her eyes, muttering. And then a shriek that brought Federico running.

'I've got it!' she yelled, hugging him. 'I've bloody well got it!' and raced for the door. Turned to look at him. 'But don't say a word to him yet!'

Federico shook his head dumbly. 'Not a word,' he said solemnly.

She paused in the hall as the main door banged mightily shut. Waved to Mina.

Mina was standing, hands on hips, regarding a large object wrapped in brown paper and cardboard tubing. Isa crossed the shining tiles and peered at it.

'It looks like a bicycle,' she said helpfully.

Mina said angrily, 'It *is* a bicycle! A mountain bike!' Pointed her toe at a box slung against the front wheel. 'And a helmet! And leather gloves! And a sweater! And –' fishing in her pocket, '– and a ten-year guarantee! My God, Isa, he's only eight years old, not a contender for the Tour de France!'

Isa, bewildered, prodded the handlebars. 'Didn't you buy it, then?'

'No, I did not! That woman, that bloody Judit, she's just delivered it, without a word of may I or do you mind. Said she'd heard that Lluís had had his bike stolen, and so she thought his auntie would make amends! God knows what Alfredo will say!' Then pensively, 'You wouldn't think that Pepe had banned her from the house, would you?'

*     *     *

While Bobby Drach waited for the phone to be answered, he glanced at the painting on the wall of his office, and smiled at it. Ezita had done that, he thought proudly, though why she'd chosen to paint a still life of a tin of John West red salmon and a Union Jack, he still didn't know.

God, he missed her. Crazy mare. Unsophisticated to the point of shambles. He grinned, drummed his fingers. Nearly seven, they should be there by −

Hooray, about bloody time!

Pepe answered.

'Got a few minutes?' asked Bobby, after the preliminaries.

'A few,' conceded Pepe. 'Isa is preparing a . . . sorry, the English of it escapes me. Is a *puchero húngaro*.'

'A whatto?'

'*Puchero húngaro*. Is a sort of stew. Hungarian.'

A burst of laughter. 'A goulash? Ez is cooking a bloody goulash? God, I hope you've got lots of fucking water to drink, she's got ten arms when she uses paprika!'

Pepe laughed. 'The kitchen is filled with things to put in the pot.'

'Yes, I bet it is. Just tell her to go easy on the cement-mix and seaweed!'

'Pardon me?'

'Oh, nothing. Look, Pepe, two more things for you to think about − could be interesting. Just remind me − you're in Paris around the end of November?'

'Is right. *Tosca*, with Cherri de Canasta. I am due back home on the 29th.'

'Good, good, no clashes then. Oh − perhaps Ez ought to hear this as well − could she spare a minute to pick up the extension?'

Isa saw Pepe beckoning, wiped damp hands and mixed herbs on her jeans, and knocked Ignacio over as she reached for the phone. 'Hi, Bob! Just a minute, I didn't stick it in properly,' and she picked up Ignacio's latest ornament, a castanet, and wedged it firmly under the furry arm, setting him upright.

'Christ, I thought you were cooking, not having a bloody quickie! I do beg your −'

'Bloody fool!' from Isa. Pepe sniggered, and put his hand on her bottom.

'Right, you two! This is for you, Pepe, no interruptions from you, Ezita, just wanted you to hear and take note in case a certain person's English isn't quite up to it and he misses something. Two more bookings, Pepe.'

'Makes him sound like a performing dog,' murmured Isa.

'Shut up! Pepe, are you listening, dear? First – football.'

'Pardon me?'

'FOOTBALL! Don't go deaf on me, duckie, not at the start of our bloody partnership. By the way, you're not constipated, are you?'

'Not constip–?'

'Only if you are, her bloody goulash will cure it. A sure laxative. Ask anybody in south-west London. Now – football,' ignoring splutters down the line.

'I do not quite follow this, Roberto. What has it to do with singing?'

'About as much as bloody *Mattin* . . . Never mind.' Throat clearing. 'This is more charity work for you.' Added impatiently as another perplexed 'Football?' was heard, 'You'll be playing the bugger. Klaus Ruwald has been in touch – you know him? Martes' dogsbody, poor bastard – and if you're happy, you and Othello are down for a fifteen-minute appearance on December 5th, Madrid Stadium, beginning of the first half. One of you will present a trophy to the winning team, the other gets to present a cheque to a fund for bloody babies.'

Beaming with delight, 'No joking this, Roberto?'

'Of course I am! I love wasting time and fucking money on long-distance calls just to make jokes!'

'But who is playing, Roberto?'

'You are, dear. You and Martes.'

'No – I mean, which teams?'

'They're both Spanish, so what's the bloody difference? Still, if you're going to be that fussy over details, it's – where are we? – oh yes, it's Barcelona and Real Madrid.'

Then, as Isa intervened, 'Oh bloody hell, I do crave pardon, I meant *Rayarl* Madrid. Now bugger off! Is that okay with you, then, Pepe?'

'Oh sure it is, is *fantástico*! Do you know which position for me?'

'Don't tempt me, dearie!' Impatiently, 'I'm not the bloody team manager, am I? All I know is, you're Barcelona, and Othello is Madrid. Ruwald will give you the details, it's the date I was concerned with. Oh – perhaps you ought to get a sturdy pouch for your pecker, in case of injury –' Gales of laughter. '– you can get

189

them in Liberty's, that I do know. If I remember, I'll send you some.'

'How many do you think he'll need?' hooted Isa.

Pepe sniggered. In the laughter, their hips touched and his eyes grew heavy-lidded, nearly dropped the phone as he tried to cup her breast.

'Fuck it!' he muttered, scrambling to unwrap the cord from his neck. Helpless with laughter, she hastened back to the kitchen, 'Something's burning, tell him!' and yelped as she walked into an open cupboard door.

Pepe doubled over, the phone hanging over his shoulder, waving *adiós* to his premature erection. Heard Roberto squawking 'What the hell's happening over there?' and hastily returned the phone to his ear with painful bang.

'Sorry, Roberto, Isa had to go to the oven quick. You were saying?'

'Oh, there you are! Pepe, this second booking for you – are you listening? It's for next March. The thirtieth, for twelve days. New York is calling you, dear boy!'

'*Dios mío!* – you mean the Met?'

'No, no,' sarcastically, 'the Odeon in fucking Brooklyn! Of course the Met! *Turandot.* You can get your revenge on Fatty Fazzoletto with your own version of *Nessun Dorma!*'

'But this is tremendous, how in the name of God –'

'They've been after you for quite a time, dear, but that silly twat Gusano – oh sorry, may he rest in peace – kept insisting that the terms weren't right. As I told Tim Divine, just think of his fee for bloody *Mattinata*, multiply it by four hundred, and he's yours!' Bobby swept aside the laughing protests and continued, 'That's where the other pecker-pouches come in – your Princess will be Catalina Lucha.'

'God!'

'You'll need Him, pet. Mind you, I must say that Martes' record sales have soared since his much-publicised wanking. You never know, Pepe, you might even get to number one with *Mattinata!* Oh well, I'll leave you both to your goulash. Love to Ezita – oh, I forgot to tell her, I'm looking forward to seeing her in November, pity you won't be with her. *Adiós!*'

'*Adiós, amigo* – and many thanks!'

He swooped into the kitchen as a knife spun to the floor, followed by a left-over carrot.

Punching the air excitedly, he told her about the Met, then swung her off her feet.

'How is the *puchero, carita?*'

'Cooking nicely, *gracias, señor*. What time are Mina and Alfredo coming?'

'At nine. Mmmm-mmmm! Come here!'

'Far too busy, sorry,' with a catch in her voice.

'What is the English for "I love you"?'

'*Te quiero,*' she tittered.

'Okay then, foreign person, *te quiero*. Oh Isa *mía*, I do!' Their lips met, and he whispered 'Is the *puchero* happy to cook alone?'

'Very happy,' as he dragged her from the kitchen. Adding 'You know? Our bedroom will be perfumed with paprika. And onions. And leeks.'

'That is good harem stuff!'

'. . . and courgettes and mushrooms and carrots. . .'

'Anything else?' picking her up fiercely.

'. . . and barley and apple . . . and garlic and. . .'

\*     \*     \*

Still entwined, muscles relaxing, Pepe stroked the wildness of her hair and asked plaintively, 'Is there any meat in it?'

She opened her eyes, reluctant to move an inch from him. 'Meat?'

'Mmm.' He tweaked one of the thick curls, placed the end of it in her ear. 'In the *puchero*.'

'Damn! I knew I'd forgotten something,' and giggled as they rearranged themselves comfortably side by side.

'What did Roberto mean, seeing you in November?'

She turned her head on the pillow, frowning slightly. 'I'm going over to London for a couple of days – I told you! Didn't I? I'm sure I did. You'll be in Paris, so I thought it would be a good opportunity to get this business of my house settled once and for all. You don't mind, do you, *querido?*' At his silence, '*Superquerido?*'

191

He tried not to smile, but failed. Then forcefully, 'Enrique will go with you! I shall take others to Paris.'

'Why on earth should Enrique come with me?'

'Because I say he will! Since that British goon and other European *paparazzi* tracked our engagement down, I want you under wrappings, close! I do not have you hounded. It is to be far bad enough for you when the announcing is officialled on the thirty November. Until then – and especial to London if you say you go – Enrique!'

'Were you speaking in Russian just then?' she tittered. 'I think I understood two words,' and he kissed her into silence.

He said seriously, into her lips, 'You know bloody well what I mean.'

'*Si, señor mío.* Enrique it is.'

She began to stroke him slyly under the sheet.

'Is too soon!' he protested. Then, surprised, 'Oh! It isn't!'

Then her fingers slid away and she yelped with mirth.

'What the –?'

'Sorry,' she snorted, 'it just reminded me – did I put enough courgettes in the *puchero*?'

'I beg your bloody pardon!' he glared. 'Are you comparing this to a courgette? Is an insult to my –'

She giggled and leapt out of bed. 'No comparison,' loftily, as she began to dress, 'My courgettes are much bigger! Come on, our guests will be here soon!'

He looked at her dolefully. 'A courgette?'

She nodded. 'A very small one,' and shrieked as he chased her into the kitchen.

# 12

Standing in the wings, tapping one large glassily-polished shoe to the *Candide* overture, Pio Fazzoletto performed the traditional exercises of nose and throat. (Pepe always referred to them as the unpaid *pasa doble*.) His Adam's apple jerked. After several seconds, his tongue slid out and wiped his lips.

This was his first solo concert since the miscarriage. He had stopped thinking about his dead boy some time ago, arguing with himself that you couldn't love someone you had never met. But Adriana had shouted at him yes you could, oh Christ you could, before lapsing into quiet passivity and veiled eyes. This, and sod-all from the police. But now, most important of all – may there be numberless blessings on all the saints mentioned in his diary – Adriana was well. Keta, they told everyone, had been marvellous: and what were two hundred red roses plus air freight charges, compared to their gratitude? Best of all, Adriana had started to bully him again about his roast chicken intake, to make cooing noises at bedtime.

His motto *Cantare! Mangiare! Fottere!* once more travelled with him.

He waited for the overture to end. Half-past seven, and the weather was closing in. It had been misty most of the day in Barcelona, the lights around the Liceo were shrouded with it when he arrived. Fuck it, if it grew foggier! He was due to fly home again after the concert, and wondered if he could get away with just two encores, preferably of *O Sole Mio*. Then remembered that this was a Barcelona audience, and knew that he couldn't. Sod fog and its Creator.

He shifted his stance, flapped the handkerchief attached to his wrist, heard the overture squall to a close. As the audience applauded, he made a quick sign of the Cross; knew that the Lion would be bowing and making come on get up will you signs to his orchestra. He cleared his throat, the jaw and beard tilted in readiness, and waited for the conductor to come and fetch him.

The Lion was approaching, smiling, beckoning. Whispered in Pio's ear, 'Just heard – Barcelona Airport's closed, fog's very bad down there.'

'Shit!'

A wide grin as he approached his chalked circle on the platform, the orchestra joining in the applause, his arms raised in acknowledgement of the tremendous cheers. Adriana called it his Mount of Olives stance.

Composed his features solemnly as the intro began for *E lucevan le Stelle*. Ludicrous timing, stars brightly shining, and bloody fog outside.

With fluid ease, he began.

*　　*　　*

There was no fog in Paris that evening.

In fact it should have been an evening for angels to sing like Pio, the stars were so bright and the air standing still. The lights of the city suburbs shone without a veil outside the apartment window. The angels, however, had decreed that Bo Lehatz would sing Puccini instead, to her unbridled fury.

The apartment was very nearly circular, white on white, furniture of dark smoky glass. The only touch of rainbow came from a single gold rose in a gold basket, twinkling under a small spotlight in an alcove. Bo Lehatz seemed to mock her own décor, sitting cross-legged on a long sofa and dressed in torn jeans and a vest top, hair in a long tail down her back. She was chewing a slice of pizza, and spitting poison.

Her companion in the dark suit was impervious. He perched equably on the window-seat, Paris at his back, hands resting on his briefcase.

'No way!'

The yell died. She glanced at him, her mouth again busy with the pizza. He said nothing. She swallowed impatiently. 'Are you hearing me, Coqueluche? I said no way!'

'I hear you,' he said. His lips were singularly still as he spoke, like those of a ventriloquist. He added, glancing over his shoulder as a police van screamed in the street below, 'But you will still do it, *ma chère*.'

'Go bake your cock!'

He smiled. 'A poet as well as a singer. Is there no end to your talents, Bo?'

'You ever wanted to be unemployed, Coqueluche?' She slammed the remains of the pizza into a white cushion, and lit a cheroot. 'Why me – why, damn you?'

'You should be rejoicing, happy! *Tosca* on your home ground, Paris at your feet, adored by millions. And a double exorbitant fee for a short-notice engagement! My my!' and he shook his head in wonderment.

'Balls to *Tosca*! Point me where I've never been before, point me to Wagner and I'll go! Christ, for Brunnhilde, I'd even kiss that ox-bodied moron, Fazzoletto!'

'Bo, calm down. De Canasta can't be blamed for being ill.'

'I'm not blaming that silly Australian ratbag! Anyway,' spitting out a shred of tobacco, 'she's not ill, she's afraid of letting herself down after that Desdemona of hers.' Adding generously, 'I know, because we all go through that. But I ask again, why me, when I'm up to my bloody neck in commitments?'

'Cherri has – I quote – a chest infection and has been advised to rest. Why you? Because you're already rehearsed as Tosca, you are popular as Tosca, and your Tosca will be an excellent foil to the Cavaradossi of Contreras.'

'Oh, isn't this just my bloody lucky day? That Spanish pimp, on top of everything else! Coqueluche, he is the only Cavaradossi I've worked with who wears heavy squeaking shoes on stage! And his fucking nose is always dripping!' She screwed the cheroot into a burning heap inside a backless porcelain swan.

'Then I shall ask the director to ensure that Contreras wears sandals and has a hair-dryer inside his nostrils. Anything else?'

She glared at her manager. 'I am not having that olive-skinned twerp lurking round my dressing-room! Any bloody excuse to creep in and start fiddling with his zip! I'm surprised Bionda Merdina ever remembered how to stand up, Jesus, no wonder they call him the Eternal Climax!'

195

Coqueluche unfastened his briefcase and took out two documents. He sat beside her on the sofa, ignoring the pizza behind his back.

'I doubt very much,' he said smoothly, 'that he will trouble you in that way.' He placed the documents firmly on her knees. 'I have heard that he is on the point of getting himself a new wife.'

'What? You mean it's true? There was some tittle-tattle in *Le Figaro*, but –' and, diverted, signed the documents where his finger indicated. 'Who is she, do you know? Poor, poor cow!'

'Some Englishwoman, I gather, and not a singer. I also hear,' patting her shoulder and retrieving the papers, 'that a certain person is out for his blood. And I do not refer to *Mademoiselle Merdina*.'

She glanced at him; then smiled. 'His ex! Of course – that drunken bitch! You know, Coqueluche, I think I'd sooner have an angry Bionda than even a pleasant Judit Contreras . . . Have I just signed that damned contract?'

'You have, my dear. Now Miss de Canasta can rest, relieved.'

'You and Miss Muscles can both go and fry in hell!'

\*     \*     \*

The mist slid around Sant Moiseps, wraithlike compared to its traffic-stopping sister in the city. The kennel was snug and lamp-lit.

Pepe, after several days recording *Don Carlos* in the sonic studios of Hamburg, lay on the sofa engrossed in a ghost that haunted him. The ghost was *Otello*, and the composer was Rossini. An opera that didn't even appear in *Kobbé*. He was reading a résumé of it, a generous footnote to pages of Rossini biography. No-one seemed to know where he could find the libretto and full score, not even the archivists in London. It seemed to have died, years ago, unlamented. Sometimes he swore he dreamed of it at night, his forgotten Rossini. Dreamed of that, and the forthcoming football match.

Isa smiled as she poured wine, watching his mouth move.

'Have you scored yet?' she asked sweetly, bringing him a brimming glass.

'What?' He struggled to sit up, startled. 'Scored?'

'You whispered "Goal, goal" just then!' and laughing, sat on his knee.

He grinned. 'Still no pecker-pouches from Roberto!' and they sniggered.

'I'm glad you got home before the fog settled,' she whispered.

'*Cristo*, yes! I expect the airport is closed by now.'

'Pepe?' and she fiddled with the top button of his shirt. It came off in her hand, and she stuck it neatly into his pocket. 'I've had an idea.'

'Mmm, so have I! Tell me yours first.'

She began working on the second button. 'You said some time ago something about all the top C's Nathan had given you in the song cycle –'

'Is already down on my Christmas list – two extra throats!'

The third button pushed through easily. 'It started me thinking, that's all. You see, *querido*, if more than one –'

'Your fingernails need cutting again! OW!' as she poked the shirt away from one hairy nipple. She examined it, distracted.

'You've got a scar here.'

He squinted down at his chest. 'Oh, that! Is where I was once shot through the heart.'

'Was it fatal?'

'Fairly so. I died very peaceful, though.' And his lips pressed hard, flattened her giggle. 'Incidentally, you insulted me the other day.'

'Oh?' and wriggled suggestively.

'God, your arse is bony! . . . That's better . . . never damage the steering wheel. You said that this –' pointing down '– was a small courgette.'

She tittered feebly. 'So I did!'

'I wish to inform you, Queen of Birdbrains, that I prefer it to be known as *un calabacín*.'

Laughing, she got off his knee and began hunting for her dictionary. 'What did you say? Cabal-what?'

'*Ca-la-ba-cín.*'

He looked smilingly at her, his Isa, wearing one of his sweaters that reached her knees, and his winter socks on her long legs. It was obvious, as she bent over, that she had decided it was irrelevant to wear anything in between.

'*Ca-la*– . . . got it!' Threw back her head with a shout of laughter. 'You big-headed sod!' She returned to his knee and rammed a cushion against his grinning face. 'You impossible conceited sod! A marrow?'

He peered round the cushion, laughing, as she spluttered 'A marrow!' She put her arms round his neck, tears of laughter.

'Old Poached Eggs!' he crowed. Then roughly, 'Come on, *cucufato*, let's go and discuss our wedding. Fancy a visit to my vegetable stall? The marrows are very good today!'

She snorted as he tugged her across the room. 'I hope they're better than the last lot of courgettes I had from you,' and dodged his fist, trying to shut the bedroom door in his face.

He pulled the sweater over her head, laughing.

'And the socks,' sticking out her feet.

'*Cojones* to the socks!' and they collapsed in a tangle on the bed.

They stopped laughing at the same moment.

'What the hell was that?' They struggled to sit up, breathing hard.

A door slammed.

'Hey, Pulgarcito! You at home?'

'Great Gods, it's Sperm Bank!' and fastening his trousers, laughing, Pepe shot out of the room, leaving Isa clutching her breasts in panic.

Tom Thumb? Sperm Bank? And where the hell is my sweater?

She grabbed it from the headboard and struggled to pull it on, one of the sleeves was inside-out, naturally. She could hear loud voices and laughter, Pepe saying 'Don't be a damn fool, *amigo*, of course it's okay!' and 'Isa! Come here!'

'Coming!' racing instead into the bathroom and grabbing Pepe's third-best comb, which wasn't used to tangled snakes of hair and promptly shed teeth into the handbasin.

'Isa!' She tugged up her socks to a matching length just below her knees, then quickly went to the sitting room; and collided with herself in the doorway, staring at Pio Fazzoletto. Her first thought was, how strange to see the familiar giant in full colour and not surrounded by newspaper columns. He looked like a bearded tree, his shoulders weighed down with cashmere scarves.

'Hello,' she said shyly.

His grin was lascivious. He didn't offer her his hand, simply nodded and turned to Pepe, 'And who is this one, my friend?' before grinning at her again and saying 'No autographs, young lady!'

Shyness took one look at her face and fled.

'And who are you, my friend?' she asked icily.

Pepe hooted, punched Pio's arm. 'Your face!'

Isa allowed two disdainful moments to pass, then tossed back her clustered hair and asked frostily, 'Do I get introduced to Mr . . . er . . .?'

Pepe's muted squeaks, Pio's grin fading a little into uncertainty.

Pepe led her forward, enjoying the joke. 'Pio, this is Isabel. *Querida*, this is Pio Fazzoletto,' waiting for her to laugh and say I know that, you idiot.

Her icy politeness did not falter. 'So nice to meet you, Mr . . . er . . . Fattolecho, may we offer you a drink?'

His extended hand fell to his side, untouched. His eyes were suddenly round and doleful. He looked helplessly at his friend. Pepe started to laugh again, slapped Pio on the back, hugged Isa. 'Do please have a drink, *Signor* Fattolecho,' he spluttered, 'the lady insists! Christ, your face, Sperm Bank . . . Isa, go get the wine glasses! Isabel is my fiancée,' he added.

'Holy shit!' roared the Italian in Spanish. 'Why didn't you say so instead of farting around? I thought it was someone giving you a quick *quiqui*!'

'PIO!' yelled Pepe. 'He was only joking, *querida*,' hoping that she hadn't understood anyway.

'I was only joking,' repeated Pio, loyally.

'That's okay,' she said sweetly, 'he doesn't have time these days for a quick screw. Wine, you said, Courgette?' and she sailed across the room, tugging the sweater. As she poured, smiling to herself, Pio materialised at her elbow. Suddenly, his hand shot out.

'Pio,' he said.

'Isa,' she responded, and shook it.

*     *     *

199

'I am fog-tied,' he explained in English. 'Mina ees so good, you know? When she see me, and I explai' about fog-weather, airport dead, she say to Pio with such nonsalanche oh you stay here, much rooms!' Looked at them both anxiously. 'Ees okay?'

'Ees fine!' mimicked Pepe. 'Fat idiot!'

The second bottle of wine had had to breathe first, much to Pio's disgust. Now, as Isa got up and began to pour it, explanations were given about their engagement, the wedding next June, how thrilled Adriana would be, were they invited. Yes, Adriana was fine now, thanks to God and the clinic.

Isa knelt on the floor, lulled by the night-time cosiness of the room and its occupants, listening to the conversation and the sniggers.

'Isa, you may pour some more of this Ardanza!'

'Thank you, Pea-pod,' pleasantly, and obeyed. She realised, sipping her own, that not only did she like Pio, but that he had appeared like a gift from her dream. He would be perfect. After all, they were good friends, he and Pepe. Why not?

Pepe and Pio. In concert, together. And someone else; say, Vito? What a scenario that would be, a battle between top C's, riveting the audience as voices rose purely in unison. The rivalry between them! Orchestras –

'Okay, *querida?*' Pepe touched her shoulder.

'Mmmm, fine,' smiling at them both gleefully.

Pio said, 'Why you staring at Pio, eh? You realise too late that you picked the wrong man?'

'I think,' she said, swamped with excitement, 'that I've picked both the right men!'

Pepe touched his head, said to Pio 'The wine, you know.'

'A good idea!' bellowed his friend and wagged his empty glass. 'By the way, Pepita – have you heard about old Lavagna?'

\*    \*    \*

Upstairs in the main house, a brightly-painted bird shot through its wooden door and uttered one 'Cuckoo'.

In the kennel, the sitting room clock uttered a whirring click only, thanks to energetic winding by Isa when she first moved in.

There were, by now, four empty wine bottles on the floor, and a fifth was attempting to breathe despite Pio's cigar smoke. The trouble with Pio, she sighed, was that he was easily sidetracked, and wished he would get back to the topic of Vito again in case it was something Bobby would enjoy hearing.

She was about to remind him when he suddenly yelled 'Let's drink to what life is all about, my friends! Charge your glasses!'

'Mine's already sharged,' mumbled Pepe.

'And my fucker isn't!' roared Pio. 'Isa – bottle! . . . Right! Ready, Pulgarcito? . . . One – two – three – *Cantare!*' A cheer. '*Mangiare!*' Another cheer. '*Fottere!*' Several cheers. Then they looked anxiously at her bent head.

'Sssssh!' said Pepe belatedly.

She smiled to herself, memories of Aldo at the Colorno, Aldo in a temper. Poker-faced, she raised her glass, said in passable Italian 'I agree with the three toasts, gentlemen. I can't sing, but by God, I love eating and fuc–'

'Isa!'

She sniggered. 'You,' she said to Pio, 'were going to say something about Vito Lavagna two hours ago!'

'Shit, yes, I was!' Looked craftily at his friend. 'You hear about him? Ho! Me, I've heard plenty!' tapping the side of his nose. 'Something nice and juicy from the old grapevine!' He winked.

'Any particular grape?' asked Pepe.

'Monda Ballena. The world's favourite singing group!'

'Oh c'mon, she's not that fucking big!' Schoolboy snorts. 'What does she say, then?'

'She thinks – only her opinion, mark you – that Lavagna's into drugs!'

Pepe stared owlishly. 'That's bloody silly! How does that old balloon know?'

Pio belched formidably, held out his glass. Anxiously, 'Don't bother about it breathing!' Continued, 'This stemmed from the *Lammermoor* they did together in Berlin.'

He leaned forward. 'Vito cocked it up! Rehearsals, first night, you name it! Monda said he could hardly stand up at times, rambled like a half-wit. And he threw up on a couple of occasions by the fusebox backstage! Oh – and on the second night, you know the second scene, Act I, where Lucia meets Edgardo by the bloody fountain?' He hiccupped. 'And his farewell, *Verranno a te sull'amore?*'

Pepe nodded solemnly, and they began to sing softly.

'Thass the one,' nodded Pio. 'Well, instead, the old bugger sang *Ah verme a tue sorelle!*' He cackled.

Isa thought about it. 'Doesn't that mean "worms to your sisters"?'

'Exactly. Now, Ishabel, while Pepita and I try to puzzle out this problem, how about a small coffee and a large cognac, eh?'

'Goodnight,' she said sweetly, and departed.

*　　*　　*

'Come on, fellers, COME ON! . . . Ruck the bugger! . . . RUCK IT! . . . shitteroo, eyes in his friggin' arse! . . . A clue, boys, it's bloody rugger not tennis! Oh Christ, he's lost it . . . That's it − go on, go ON, GO ON! . . . good . . . good . . . NO! What the hell's wrong with the bloody clown? . . . PASS IT! PASS THE BUGGER!. . . not to the bloody Frog, you short-legged half-wit!'

Francesco Giormani winced, deafened, trying to listen to the commentary on TV and realising that his wife was winning. He blamed himself, for noticing that the match between the Wallabies and France was going to be shown live from the Parc des Princes, and then stupidly telling Cherri. He glanced at the irate Mrs Giormani, perched upright in bed, eyes glued to the screen, a gold Wallabies shirt over her pyjamas.

He smiled, his anxiety abating. A chest infection? Or perhaps the onset of pleurisy, the doctors said. No way, pally, not if she can rant and swear like this!

Rest, they said, and antibiotics. She had been in bed for five days now, studying *Rigoletto* for February, apologising long-distance to Contreras for having to cancel *Tosca* in Paris.

Was she sick? The thinner shape of her. But all that goddamned muesli! − hardly a muscle-producer, hardly anything at all, and that's what she had wanted, to be slender for Desdemona. He looked at her again, at the accounts book she used as an en-gagement diary: full of work, as usual, a mass of Rossini recording sessions soon, a concert tour back home in Australia, interviews with her biographer.

He started to say 'Honey, perhaps if we saw a –'

'You bloody jammy Frog! . . . that was a friggin' forward pass, you sneaky bastard! . . . Yes, you fat bugger, that's the ball! Christ, he's looking at it as though it were a bloody bar of chocky! . . . Go on, kick the silly prat in his sperm-bags!'

"Francesco, heartened, smiled."

*     *     *

The football had lodged in a tree. Modesto Martes shaded his eyes and peered up at it. It nestled firmly between two eager thick branches.

His son grinned. 'Good kick, that, Father Dear!'

'So go climb, beloved son!'

Gruñón said, 'Not ethical. You kicked it there, you fetch!'

'Have you two little boys finished playing?' mocked Mimosa from the terrace. She wore an old tracksuit and large sunglasses, legs and feet on a stool, newspaper idly dangling from her hand.

'This is not playing, this is serious!' protested Modesto.

'*Puf!*'

'Oh but it is, *Mamá*,' said Gruñón, strolling across to her. 'I mean, look what he's got to face next month! Not only the entire Barcelona team but the mighty Contreras as well!' They sniggered together. 'I'm off for a shower. Yell, will you, if Dad gets stuck up that thing?' He strode off, whistling, as Modesto tried to gauge the strength of the branches soaring above him.

Then, 'Father Dear!' from the terrace. 'Phone call for you, from Cherri. Says it's urgent, can you ring her back at the Naples number?'

'When I've retrieved this sodding ball!'

An hour later, sticking plaster on his cheek, he replaced the receiver thoughtfully. Mimosa's flower arrangement, spiky and pink, reflected itself in the polished surface of the table. He idly stroked an opening bud.

What, he mused, had all that been about? Urgent my arse! Just Cherri, joking about her antibiotics – useless buggers, Moddie, not worth the bottle they come in – and laughing as they re-hashed the lighter moments in *Otello*. She'd said thank God it's on video, pity the release date isn't until next September. Then a complete non-sequitur about Buzzer Ahmet who was to conduct their *Rigoletto* next February, that he was the best there was, nothing fazed him, he'd know what to do.

Know what to do? Then she'd rushed on, have you seen Buzz lately, he's got problems, mate,whenever you mention the word "photograph", he goes glassy-eyed! – A noisy kiss down the phone, love to Mimsy and the gang, I love you, thanks again for *Otello*, roll on "Riggo", eh?

And finis. No point in it at all. He gave up contemplation, and shrugged. She'd sounded like a battery hen that needed space. His finger slid across the phone.

\*     \*     \*

Two evenings before he was due to fly to Paris, Pepe took her to a restaurant in Barcelona.

It was known simply as La Tasca. The original name still hung lop-sidedly from its rusty screws, but the paint had faded and no-one could be bothered to remember what it was.

That evening, the place was only fairly busy. The *dueño*, an energetic man in his early seventies who always introduced himself by his full name of Alfons Alsina Soler, had known Pepe and Alfredo and their father for many years, and consequently Pepe's arrival caused no particular tremor – although an eyebrow or two were raised when he walked in with an unknown lady and, what is more, holding hands. La Tasca was, quite simply, accustomed to the Contreras family and its presence, and the casual eccentricities of the place suited that family perfectly.

And eccentricities there were, in this dusky old restaurant. Over there, for example, in that corner – a cartoon poster, much loved, of a bullfighter taking a dive with a French horn through his backside. And, nearby, a jazz pianist played an ancient piano which was painted blue; his billowing cigarette smoke and empty packets of Celtas never moved from this corner as he sang Harlem blues songs in Catalan, an untutored baritone. On Mondays, Pepe told Isa, he sang only love songs because then La Tasca became an unofficial *puticlub*.

'A what?' smiled Isa, reaching for her aperitif and knocking her cigarettes to the floor. Her face reappeared, flushed. 'What is a *puticlub*?'

He grinned, relaxed, their first public appearance together. Grinned because she looked so appealing in her tweed trousers and unmatching checked Oxfam jacket.

'A *puticlub* is . . . Is where people go if they are by themselves with love. Alone. You know?'

'Oh, a singles bar!' She smiled happily as he trapped one of her knees between his own. She watched him as he ordered their meal, chatting vehemently to Alfons Alsina Soler. The *dueño* smiled at her and nodded. Fascinated, she listened to their exchanges in Catalan which sounded to her like Hungarian. Loved watching him, the movements of his strong hands, his black hair a mixture of straight and wavy, his eyes smiling when his mouth did. I must tell him now, I must tell him my idea. No, not idea; my plan, she corrected herself. Soon be official engagement time, too. With this signet ring, I, Marrow, take thee, *Cucufato* . . . .She giggled. She had held out against diamonds.

'And what is funny?' he demanded, turning back to her.

'Oh, nothing. Well . . . marrows!' She gave a workmanlike snort.

He muttered across the table, 'The way these jeans are cutting through me, you'll be lucky to get a slice of cucumber!'

The food came, heavily-hot *calamares a la plancha*, *gambas*, salad. She squeezed a slice of lemon over her plate, a pip flew out and juice squirted over her jacket.

'Don't the prawns want any?' he asked sarcastically.

And they raised glasses of a white wine that was called 'House', eyes loving.

*     *     *

With coffee came cognac. No balloon glasses here at La Tasca; you drank from rough-cut tumblers, and the brandy peeped over the top if you moved your glass too sharply.

205

'Pepe,' she said, as he appreciatively sniffed the cognac after several swallows of it, 'I'd like to tell you something. An idea.'

'Another one?' he grinned. 'What's this to be? Singing Shakespeare in French?'

She frowned sternly. 'And without interruptions!'

'Yes, mother.'

Plunging in, 'What would you think about doing a concert with Pio? And perhaps either Vito or Martes? Just the three of you, three tenors, arias, perhaps some popular songs too?'

'What in the name of the Holy Masturbator are you talking about?' and he choked on his cognac.

She wiped his chin patiently. 'I, *cucufato*, am talking about a spectacular. A huge concert. The spin-offs would be enormous. I'm talking about world satellite coverage, live transmission. I'm talking about –', pausing dramatically, '– Luciano Bardi!'

He stared at her, brown eyes shocked. 'Bardi? The Vatican gun-runner? That Bardi?'

A brisk nod. 'Roberto knows him well. Bardi could fix anything.'

Luciano Bardi could. Impresario, TV supremo, a notable banker, friend of the Pope, Venerable Grand Master of the P2 Lodge and several others of his own devising; and an old comrade of Robert Drach.

'And where,' recovering his sarcasm, 'would this take place? Inside the Vatican?'

'I have the venue in mind, beloved. Italy, yes. The Arena della Doccia.'

'But that's outdoors!' appalled. 'Rain! Wind! Bloody pigeons with white diarrhoea! Jesus. How much brandy have you had?'

'The weather in Italy in summer is usually pretty good, so I understand,' smiling, 'and the della Doccia already caters for big events. The wiring, sound stuff, and the lighting are already there. I'll get nappies for the pigeons, and even hire a moon for the evening! Oh – and I'd thought of two orchestras –'

'Logical, yes. And how many conductors? Seven?' He sniggered, eyes thoughtful.

A hearty gulp of her cognac; continued benignly 'Just the one; with perhaps another to co-ordinate the musicians in rehearsal.

Pepe, Roberto could fix it with Bardi! Please – don't turn it down without thinking about it first, don't just laugh and say that I've lost my –'

'Martes,' he interrupted firmly. 'Not Vito. Modesto, with myself and Pio, I reckon; is good, feels good.' He slapped the table. 'Bloody hell! You're crazy, Contreras, you're as equal crazy as this . . . this wonderful, brilliant beloved girl!'

And La Tasca shattered its dusky calm under his sudden yell, 'Yaaaa-HOOOO!'

# 13

'. . . And so you see, my dearest Ellie,' she wrote to her lover in Washington, 'the complexity of it all! I just couldn't believe it, the sound of his sobbing through the open door – wide open, anyone could've heard! – the door by the palm tree you like so much, the one in the bronze tub. If any of the staff had passed by, God, my mind freezes over! He was pleading, on the telephone, begging with that whine in his voice and saying "Louis, it would be impossible, no no, I said I couldn't, not that I wouldn't." Then he spoke to someone else, and began to cry all over again. And not once has he looked at *Il Trovatore* for Vienna: only a little while back he was eager for it, couldn't wait to get to the Staatsoper again. And thin! – my God, Ellie, he is haggard, even the pouches under his eyes are fatless. What he eats now, I don't know. I just don't know. But this phone call – as I went in, pretending not to have heard, all bright and chirpy to say to him "Lunchtime, Baby!", he said the oddest thing, to this Louis of his. "So not only on my doorstep, you also get to choose the music, do you?"

And now he tells me that on Friday I have to go out, and he's given me tickets for a ballet feast in Turin for that evening! Jesus, I don't know what's happening. . . .'

*　　*　　*

Isa gleefully unpacked the last of her worldly goods, which had finally arrived after much telephoning and swearing. Each familiar book had been greeted, a few family photographs laughed over, an eager pounce on her sketch block and paints.

That had been the vexing question lately: what to give Pepe for Christmas. So what if it was still a few weeks away? Her thoughts about it were not. No use asking Mina, she was in another time warp when it came to gifts, filled with Gucci and unusable things

208

made of crystal. She had, unwisely, mentioned her dilemma to Eve on the phone one evening, and had had to contend with a sarcastic 'Hankies with his initials?' Gritted her teeth at 'How about socks, they do packets of three pairs in Marks.'

And then the answer came. On the Sunday morning before he left for Paris, Pepe had donned a dark suit and gone to Mass with Gualterio and Alfredo, and from there to Magda's grave to commemorate her death three months earlier.

Isa had asked Mina, 'Why are there no photographs or portraits of Magda in the house?'

They were in the laundry room together, Mina showing her how to operate one of the large built-in washing machines, Isa peering at it blankly.

'Oh, there are some photographs,' Mina assured her. 'But definitely no portraits! Magda hated the camera, she would have gone mad at the thought of sitting for an artist! Even when we took family photographs, it was very rare for her to join in. Why? Have you never seen what she looked like?'

'Only a little creased photo that Pepe keeps in his wallet.'

Mina smiled. 'His mascotograph, he calls that. Look, Papaterio has some in an album; one I think you would like, taken years ago, when she was about thirty, I think. It's a lovely likeness, she's actually smiling! Probably for Pepe. She always smiled for him. I'll get it for you later. Now – did you see which buttons I pressed here?'

'Yes, thanks,' lied Isa.

So now she had the photograph and her sketch pad. Pepe was in Paris, and she had time to kill before she and Enrique flew to London. To get her eye in tune, she decided first of all to do a sketch and colour-up of the house from the east side. Armed herself with stiff smooth paper, the paints, and a handful of sable brushes.

Alfredo bumped into her on her way to the gardens, raised his eyebrows at the burden.

'I'm going to paint the house,' she explained.

'Good idea, it certainly needs doing. But won't you need bigger brushes?' Chortled as she thumped him and went on her way.

*    *    *

Several times, surreptitiously, Enrique glanced at her still pale face during the flight to Heathrow. Her hands and pen were motionless, the notebook unopened. When he spoke, she either answered softly, or didn't seem to have heard him. She looked, he thought, extremely tired. Knew for a fact that Pepe would have forbidden the trip had he but seen her.

Her eyes ached, and she rubbed them slowly. The pain was still there, but muted. How she had hated leaving the kennel; even with the photograph still there, the one that had fallen out of a book. Her mother. Sitting on a sea wall, seagulls plummeting as she held out bread for them. The shadow of the photographer, her father, lying across her ankles.

Her mother. A distant speck in her mind, pushed there in case the same thing ever happened to herself. It must be your bloody vivid imagination, she told herself sternly, trying to ignore the pains, smiling determinedly at Enrique.

Glad of a communication, he said 'Have you remembered what I told you, *Señorita* Isa?'

'*Sí, señor!* When we land I'm to walk two paces in front of you, wearing a black sack over my head, eyeholes supplied, and I'm to scream if someone shoots me dead.'

He snapped, 'This is not a joke! Not fun and games! Don Pepe made it quite clear that −'

'To me, too. Sorry,' smiling apologetically. And wished that the wheels would stop their incessant turning in her head. Sleep had been hard to come by, with sparking visions and sounds and awful noises from her mother. And she ought to have told Pepe about Uncle Don, too. Ought to have. Didn't. Their phone conversations began and ended with love, the middles filled with it.

Enrique lit a cigarette just as the 'No Smoking' sign flashed on; his alarm grew even more because she didn't even giggle.

*    *    *

Pepe knew that it had been a mistake to eat a garlic-flavoured lunch. Two hours later, he was still burping the bloody stuff. And

210

the Paris-Opéra management still hadn't fixed the squeaking floorboards at the left of the stage.

He waited for the phone to ring at the other end, scowling at the itch under his new beard. A luxury at first, not having to shave at frequent intervals, until the itch began. Apply the cream five times a day, the House doctor had said, and what Pepe angrily wanted to know was how the hell you applied fucking cream to a chin buried under three-inch bristles. He scratched at it vigorously. What made it even worse was that, for the first time in its sporadic career, the beard had grown not only fast but iron grey.

He laughed suddenly as the phone in London began to ring: Isa, disappearing under the sheets with a torch to see if the marrow's nest was similarly afflicted by signs of age. His *cucufato*!

'Hello?' Breathless voice.

He relaxed, smiling. '*Hola, princesa*! Have you been running from somewhere?'

'No, *querido*, I was just getting Khan out of the suite, he's the hotel dog. Oh Pepe, I'm missing you!'

'Is only until tomorrow night –'

'*Querido*, I must tell you before I forget, tomorrow I'm going to visit my Uncle Don after I've sorted out the business of my house, he's an old family friend, not really my –'

'Steady on, *carita*,' he laughed. 'Is okay, providing that Enrique goes with you. Isa, I must tell this! – guess who I ran into this morning? – Pio! He is doing a show for French TV, and I told him about our idea –'

'My idea!'

'– Our idea, and he is so keen, he was like a kid with many toys, he says to count him in there! But please, not a word yet to Roberto when you see him, I wish a talk with Modesto first, okay?'

'Okay! Oh that is terrific news, Pepe!'

'– But now for some news that is not! On my way to the theatre today, I saw . . .' He gulped, and grinned down the phone. '. . . a stall in the market. They were selling marrows. At half-price!'

Afterwards, she took more aspirins and determinedly thought of half-price marrows and Pio and her idea.

Oh alright then. Our idea. And she smiled.

*     *     *

Sitting by the café window, Enrique watched her cross the road and hesitate by the flight of steps leading up to the front door. A neat three-storeyed house with sash windows. She touched the iron railings, then climbed the steps, opened the yellow door, and disappeared from his sight.

'I should only be half an hour,' she'd said. 'Uncle Don is an old friend.'

It was a windy day, blue sky and fast clouds over the Georgian terrace. Enrique ordered more coffee, never taking his eyes off the yellow door across the road. In his last stern briefing, Don Pepe had never mentioned anything about side streets in Holland Park, nothing about a lady whose eyes had pain and distance.

The racing clouds made him restless. After the coffee, he went out to the waiting car and stood there in the wind, chatting intermittently with the driver.

*     *     *

Monda Ballena emerged on to the blank echoing stage of the Gran Teatro in Seville and peered round. There seemed to be a certain reluctance to attend this preliminary briefing on the Charity Gala. The conductor, Simón Estertor, greeted her casually and examined his finger before wiping it clean on his trousers.

'Lavagna isn't coming,' he said laconically. 'Unwell.'

Monda eyed him, her face pink from the cold wind, long and dancing earrings emerging from her turban. 'Oh surprise, surprise! What is it this time? An overdose of LSD?'

Estertor looked at her sharply, and aimed a swipe at a chair seat with his handkerchief before shoving the chair towards her. 'A sore throat, I think he said.'

'HAH! You hear that, Teresa?' as Bragas climbed on to the stage from the auditorium, hampered by her tight skirt and two handbags.

'Hear what?'

'Lavagna's got a sore throat.' Monda laughed sarcastically.

212

A shrug, fastidiously placing a headscarf on a chair before sitting on it and nodding curtly to Estertor. She lit a Sobranie, said 'The way he sings these days, I thought he'd always got a sore throat.'

Monda laughed approvingly. Then demanded 'Where's Pepe?'

'Still poncing around on-stage with that French whore Lehatz,' sniffed Teresa. 'I've heard that she's having a thoroughly good time knifing Scarpia!'

'Who's singing Scarpia this time?'

'That ex of hers, the castrated bass. Got as much sense of drama as a bloody voucher on a packet of butter.' Looked at Monda keenly. 'Why the sparkling danglers, dear? Were you all dressed up for the Mighty Crotchet?'

Monda stared at her frigidly. 'Are you referring to Pepe?'

Teresa barked with amusement. 'Not still yearning for him, are we? Christ, what a perfect match, a huge cake and a bloody mint imperial! Anyway,' crossing her ankles, 'you no longer stand a chance. The lovesick little turd's thinking of getting wed. Again. Hadn't you heard?'

Monda looked hurt. Pepe was her pet, maternal affection given in large doses. It was said that she carried a jewelled collar and lead for him in her bag.

Her look grew anxious. 'God, it isn't Bionda Merdina, is it?'

Teresa sniggered. 'No, some English maiden, God rest her soul. Name of Eliza. Don Juan calls her Isabel, presumably because he can't pronounce "Eliza" . . . . Jesus, the producer's arrived! Wonder who disinterred him?'

'I ask myself, does dear Judit know?' eyes gleaming.

'Sure she does. I told her myself,' and they smiled at each other blissfully.

The producer called out, 'Anyone seen Martes?'

'Probably still in bed shagging his wife,' drawled Teresa. 'Christ, what a price to pay for giving Lucha a quick feel! You seen Mimosa lately, Monda? One podgy little heap of freckles. Last time I saw her, I expected her to hop. . . . Oh Jesus! – take a look at this!' and the ladies hooted.

The producer was smiling, and greeting a young man with corkscrew curls. The parts of his skin that could be seen were

213

plastered with red stick-on circles. These Azucarero wore at all times to remind himself (he said) of the perpetual acne of adolescence that lurks within us all.

'What is he doing? – advertising redcurrants?' tittered Monda.

El Pedo Negro, five members in all, drifted after their leader, jostling and scraping chairs, abusing each other loudly. They glanced at Monda and sniggered.

Teresa said loudly, 'What a load of shit!' as the producer called for attention.

'Ladies, menfolk, this is just a prelim to let you know rehearsal details for the recording sessions. While we wait for the shag-weary Mr Martes –'

'What recording sessions?' interrupted Teresa. 'We're going out live!'

'We shall be appearing live, Madame Bragas, but the sound will be pre-recorded.'

'You mean we've got to bloody mime on the night?'

Azucarero and his team guffawed.

'Correct, Bragas,' wearily. 'It's in your contract so don't start an argument, it's quite simple, all you have to do is open your ruddy mouth and pretend. Right!' snapping his lighter and billowing forth smoke, 'The recording will come first, preceded by the usual run-through. Then we'll have the stage try-outs, movements, and so on. I anticipate that the latter will be around the beginning of January. Now, may we co-ordinate the programme? I have already allowed for Mr Lavagna's *Una Furtiva Lagrima* and his duet with Martes and that bloody thing from *Werther*.' Rustled his papers. 'Los Quince have just one choral, first half, no probs. Ah yes . . . and I've got Mr Contreras down for *Mattinata*.'

El Pedo Negro made puking noises. Even Monda tittered.

'Holy bloody Mary!' from Teresa. 'Is it beyond him to think of something else? Mindless twerp!'

'I'm getting quite excited about this show, aren't you,' murmured Monda.

\*     \*     \*

214

The kennel was neat and polished, fresh flowers in the sitting room and bedroom. There was a new potted plant, silvery-green, on the desk. And Ignacio gleamed suddenly as she switched on the lights.

'*Hola*, Iggy,' and dropped her bag and briefcase on the floor. She heard the clock whirring. It whirred ten times. Two hours or more before Pepe arrived.

She was tired beyond imagining. Hunger still passed her by, only a craving for coffee, and an occasional cigarette. The pains still made her catch her breath, but their intensity had lessened. Thank God she had managed to avoid Mina's eagle eye before she left. Her relief at being home made her eyes fill with tears. Wiped them away angrily with the back of her hand and went into the kitchen. A new jar of Nescafé stood ready, with a mug and a spoon. She smiled. Either Mina or Ana. She filled the kettle in readiness, then went for a quick shower.

Before he had left her in the pool of anxiety, Bobby had shoved a parcel at her, wrapped in tempting silver and raspberry-coloured paper. 'Wear these,' he had intoned sepulchrally, making a sign of the Cross, 'in remembrance of me!' Then added, encouraged by her faint giggle, 'Something to seduce old Parrot Beak with, darling! A nice pair of sexy pyjjies!'

She shampooed her hair, then eyed the parcel. Unopened. Her hair, wet and springy, curled and dripped around her head and shoulders as she unwrapped the de luxe paper.

She could almost hear Bobby cackling in her ear.

Teddy bears. A mass of pink and yellow teddy bears on pyjamas of the thickest flannelette she had ever seen. They capered from high roll-collar to the trouser hems, grinning, waving, dancing. She sank to her knees, gasping not with pain but with laughter. Had visions of wearing them at the engagement press conference tomorrow, perched on Pepe's knee with a dummy in her mouth.

Still laughing, and wearing them, she sank on to the sofa with her coffee. When Mina arrived suddenly, she didn't even appear to notice them; bustled in, 'My God, Isa, are you alright? You look terrible, you should be in bed with hot milk, oh dear, what is

215

wrong?' and for an hour she fussed and fetched hot milk and aspirins and wanted to send for the doctor.

Too exhausted to protest at the fussing, Isa felt nothing but relief when Mina eventually left her with 'If you're no better tomorrow, we really do get the doctor. Now, try and sleep!'

Sleep? Not in a thousand years. Pepe would soon be home.

*     *     *

It was just after two in the morning when he arrived. The flight from Orly had been delayed due to a missing pilot, who was dragged from his hotel bed and too-hastily sobered up with thick black coffee.

Pepe spent part of the journey shaving off his Cavaradossi beard and frowning at the revealed rash on his chin and jaw. The audible wild laughter from the cockpit scarcely registered. He gazed at himself as he shaved, and thought that, all in all, it had been a successful few days. The presentation of the opera had been first class. He and Lehatz had established an easy rapport, though her sometimes open-mouthed admiration of him had been a little embarrassing.

He could only assume that her mind had been elsewhere when she had suddenly snapped 'Oh for shit's sake, hurry up and die, Shorty', during his firing-squad scene on the battlements.

He suddenly fumbled in his pocket. Christ, where was it? The packet? It should be . . . oh bless the Holy Erection, there it was!

The airport was almost deserted when he arrived; and Moncho was waiting, a welcoming sight indeed. Yes, he hastened to assure Don Pepe, *Señorita* Isabel had arrived safely. He didn't add anything more; gave him a sympathetic smile instead.

Isa! And later today – official! He no longer felt tired, and was out of the car as soon as it pulled up, running up the steps into the hall and

'Pepe! Wait!'

Mina's sleepy voice, echoing. He looked round, startled, she was sitting on the broad stairs waiting for him. 'Just a word, Pepe – I don't know what's wrong with Isa, but –'

'What? Where is she?' he shouted.

'Sssh! She's in the kennel, but she's got some kind of pain, I didn't know whether to send for Don Salvador, she's terribly −'

He ran down the tunnel, overcoat flapping, past Dolores who smiled in vain.

Shouted her name, and she raced into his arms, laughing and crying and clinging, and they rocked together tightly whispering 'Isa' and 'Pepe' over and over again.

Then he held her at arms' length and saw her face and eyes, cried 'What's been happening to you? Tell me!'

'Pepe, it's nothing, it's all over, it was just −'

'Tell me, dammit!' He picked her up and carried her into the bedroom, sat on the bed and arranged her gently on his knee.

'Er . . . sherry?' she asked feebly.

'For God's sake, will you tell me what has happened to you?'

She twisted round in the circle of his arms, kissed his mouth, the quivering lower lip, the newly-shaven jaw. Feeling foolish, she muttered 'I thought I had cancer.'

His grip tightened painfully. He shuddered. 'You − thought − what?' The whisper was a shout.

She kissed him softly again. 'So stupid of me. But I had pains, you see. I couldn't eat, didn't want to after a while. My mother −' a tear slithered, '− she died of stomach cancer. So did her sister, my Aunt Joan. And I thought, well . . . family, you know? I've never been sick in my life, Pepe. Just like my mother. She was tough, too. Then just the one time she was ill, it was, well . . . Cancer.'

He held her as tightly as he could, she felt his heart thudding. 'That's why I went to see Uncle Don when I was in London. I mentioned him on the phone −' He nodded. '− I thought, he's my doctor, he's like my family, he'll know what to do, it won't be so bad coming from . . . I panicked, Pepe. Like a stupid kid, I bloody panicked. I −'

'Isa, what the fuck did he SAY? For Christ's sake −'

A smile glinted through her tears. 'He examined me, of course. *Querido*, do you know what it was? Bloody gastric flu! Can you believe it, all my stupid terror just for gastric flu?'

He whispered, his eyes wet, 'You are the most idiot, the most brain-dead, the most crazy fiancée a man could possibly have! *Oh*

217

*mi preciosa, mi vida!*' His mouth buried itself in the nape of her neck. Muffled, 'Why oh why didn't you say before you went all that way? Don Salvador would have −'

'I told you, I panicked. I was a child again, wanting to be with family. I'm sorry.' She sniffed, then smiled at him. 'I upset poor Roberto as well. And he'd bought me these!'

'Jesus Christ! Teddy bears!' seeing them for the first time, laughing.

She said slyly, 'He said I could use them − and I quote − to seduce old Parrot Beak.'

She touched his nose and giggled.

He also touched his nose, and didn't. 'Bloody *maricón!*' Then he kissed her. 'Come on, let's put the bears to bed and have a very bloody stiff drink!'

Lying together, close and warm, it was as if her mother had never been back to visit her. And she smiled as he blew a strand of her hair under a closing eyelid saying 'We wake up early. The marrow has not yet said hello.'

A chuckle. 'It has, you know.'

'Has not! I should know, I'm attached to the bloody thing!'

She giggled. 'A clever invention, marrows. Uncle Don says that I'm pregnant.'

'Shut up about Uncle Don! Tell me, before I fall asleep, how was Roberto?'

'He's fine, sends a big kiss. Oh, and another thing − I'm having −'

'Is it too much hoping that you kept your lovely big lip shut about my idea, the concert?'

'My idea, poltroon! No, I didn't say a word − promise. What shall we call him?'

'We will call him when I have seen Modesto on the 5th; if he agrees to this concert, we ring Roberto and invite him here before Christmas. Now, will you please kiss me to sleep?'

'Pepe,' she said in Spanish, pushing some of her hair into his mouth, 'I will kiss you to sleep when you have said hello TO OUR BLOODY BABY!'

\*      \*      \*

And so sleep had to wait until dawn came and fuzzy-haired Elena clattered in the tunnel with her industrial hoover. Even then it was fitful and kissed away.

'Beloved Isa *mía*,' he said after they had dozed and she awoke yearning for food and coffee and wondering why the pink and yellow teddy bears were draped over the bedside lamp. 'You will now must, essential, go to see Salvador. Don Salvador is our physician and – what is the long word – gyno? . . . the baby person – he will confirm –'

'It's been confirmed, you thick –' Tittered. 'Yes, dear, I will, dear.' She sighed happily. 'If Uncle Don was right, that June 15th is a likely provisional date, that means it would be exactly nine months since we first –'

'Exactly nine!' he crowed happily. 'My son could not wait!' He nuzzled her with vigour.

'We shan't have any difficulty with names for him then, shall we?' chirpily.

He said promptly, 'Of course not. No questions of it. Pepe, after me. Gualterio for my father. Sounds okay! – Josep Gualterio. . . .' His voice faltered. 'Shit! He will have your surname as well – how the hell will that look, Josep Gualterio Contreras Pepper!'

Marooned in laughter, she said 'Bollocks! Our son's name was already chosen before you thought of those. Easy!'

'Is nothing easy about a son whose last names are Contreras Pepper!'

'No, no, I'm talking about where and when he was conceived. The hotel and the feast day.' She folded her arms behind her head as he looked at her blankly. 'Grosvenor Dolores. Simple.' Chortled as he began to howl, 'And if he's a girl, Parrot Beak, simple again. Dolores Grosvenor.'

He snatched her to him.

Much later, he said 'I go and make coffee before my marrow falls off. You will stay here in the bed and rest. Is an order!'

'Eet weel be o-byed,' she mimicked, and giggled as he climbed wearily out of the sheets and sat for a moment with his head sagging and his hair in tufts.

'Jesus Christ,' he muttered, 'I must be getting old!' Then leapt up as though stung. 'Oh bloody hell! Is today we tell our en-

219

gagement to the press! What do we tell them, come on, think quick! We cannot wait until June month now for our wedding!'

'That had crossed my mind, *querido*! What about next February? After the Charity Gala, after the Lorca? You'll already be in London –'

'A London wedding?' doubtfully.

'It will have to be, I shan't qualify here as a resident for months, whereas you will only need to stay for three weeks over there.'

He nodded slowly, exhausted. 'But we say nothing about our baby yet to the press.' He ambled off to the kitchen.

He came back, skidding on the rugs. 'The ring!'

'Ring?' buttoning teddy bears with modesty.

'Is here! Was there!' He flew from garment to discarded garment frantically. 'Oh fucking Christ, where is it? RING! Come to Pepe! Where are you?'

Helpless with laughter, she watched the dizzy speed of him.

'Where is my topcoat?' he shrieked.

'At the dry cleaner's?'

'I was inside it when I got home! Is dark brown with a bloody tan collar! Is easy to see!'

'Then why can't you see it?' her eyes streaming.

'Oh bloody bloody fuck!' and he raced into the sitting room.

He returned, out of breath and smiling, running a hand through his distraught hair.

Sat on the bed, placed a small package in her hand.

'Your ring, *querida mía*. And take off the signet, I wish it back!'

'But I told you I didn't –' The ring lay in velvet. 'Oh God,' she whispered, and gazed at it. A replica of the signet ring. But this jet stone was surrounded by tiny diamonds that threw sparks of blue into the sunny bedroom. 'Oh *superquerido*!'

They kissed for quite a while after that.

'I told you I wanted you to have some diamond,' he murmured smugly.

*     *     *

He stared, frozen and appalled.

A long cold drive home, the stirrings of flu in his head, throat

220

raw from undiluted gin of the previous night. Utterly sober as he sat on the sofa while Keta prowled round the music room.

'I'm sorry,' he said helplessly, gesturing at nothing, letting his hands fall.

'You are what? Sorry?' she screamed. 'Sorry, for this?'

She ran to the piano. 'For this? For all this filth?'

'I . . . .'

'Perhaps your friends the musicians would like to get their dirty asses over here and do a spring-clean?' throwing a pile of manuscripts on the floor.

'I . . . They've gone, Keta.'

'Gone, have they? Just left you, did they, after their nice little concert? Which ballet was it, Vito? Me and my friends, we saw *Swan Lake* in Turin! Which one did you have, you scum? How many of them, Vee? A nice little trio going down on you at the same time?'

He looked at her stretched face, restrained a sneeze. 'I . . .'

'Something gotten your tongue, Baby? Worn out, is it, from poking around so many asses? You perverted whore!'

Ran to the shelves, to the rows of books and trophies. 'See these, prick-head? Do you see them? These are forty years, Vee, forty goddamned years of YOU! Remember that critic, Vee, the one who said that Gigli himself would have wept jealous tears had he but heard your Werther? You WERE Werther, you pathetic bastard, like you were Nemorino and Don Alvaro!' A volume was thrown to the floor. 'Just one of your biographies! You want they should all have a bloody final chapter, Vee? One last damned chapter to describe all this − this −'

Her mouth was ragged. 'So now you can clear up this mess. Every turd, every last trace of your ejaculations, you hear me? You −!' and she turned and spat into his faded face.

# 14

The lunchtime celebrations had been marred only when Lluís and Pau demanded Coke and the ring-pull had sliced the palm of Alfredo's hand, necessitating emergency stitches at the hospital. For the rest, it had been silky champagne and family voices all talking happily at once.

Gualterio had syphoned brandy into his glass of bubbles, proclaiming that at last his youngest son had stopped frittering away valuable sperm around the opera-houses, and was now getting down to serious channelled breeding. Mina nearly fainted, though whether it was because of the bellowed remark or the sight of blood racing from her husband's hand, no-one could be sure.

Afterwards, sobered and tentative, Isa sat at Pepe's side in the formal sitting room for the press statements, conscious of the selected Mendelssohn chamber music in the background, and the extra flowers. She nervously stroked one of the stems, until Pepe nudged her and pointed out the crust of blackfly near the top.

Pepe wore his best public smile for the occasion, glancing at her frequently, and dealing audibly with more catarrh.

Federico Golpe cleared his thin throat, offered sherry to the three journalists and two photographers and read out the official announcement. He then handed out copies, with appended biographies, to each of the correspondents. Isa liked hers: two years off her age and her surname spelt Peeper.

Federico said 'Five minutes for your questions, please,' and sat down to join the sherry party.

After the questions, Pepe frogmarched her back to the kennel.

'You bloody stupid *cucufato!*'

'Why?' dodging into the bedroom to change.

'Why did you tell them that we enjoy growing marrows?' He followed her, his face and skin rash flushed.

Grinning, 'Well, we do! They asked what else we had in common besides music −'

'You could have said reading! Sport! Collecting bloody currant buns! Anything!'

She had to giggle quickly before his hand went round her throat. 'They wanted to know what type of marrow!' he hissed.

'Yes, that was a difficult one. That's why I said little pink ones,' and she fell on the bed hooting.

'Is not little and pink!' he fretted.

'What is it, then − little and blue?' gasping with laughter.

He watched as she buried her face in the pillow. 'At least,' he said sarcastically, 'you didn't mention our baby!' Then yelled 'But did you have to point at your belly and wink at that guy from Reuter's?'

That evening, Modesto Martes rang with his congratulations, followed by a reminder about the football confrontation. Isa watched Pepe as he grinned and gesticulated by the telephone. She tittered. She and Alfredo had added a small surprise to his football gear which was now packed and ready. Pity she hadn't reminded Bobby about the pecker-pouches from Liberty's.

He would be away for four days, going on to Seville from Madrid, for the Gala recording.

Four days to get on with Magda's portrait and to come to grips with the plain smiling face in the photograph.

*     *     *

Gualterio was assisted to his feet, pale and shaking. His concern was for the boy.

Pau was standing, shocked, in the circle of a woman's arms, his eyes screwed shut, taking great gulps of breath, tears in his throat.

'*Abueli*!' he sobbed. 'There there,' soothed the lady.

'I'm here, Pau, I'm here,' and the big solid arm of *Abueli* dislodged the kind lady and wrapped itself around the terrified boy.

Night was closing in, almost frosty. Overhead sky black, the horizon golden-grey. The streetlamps had been glowing for over an hour. And despite the shoppers, the traffic noise, the music blasting out from rival record stores, he knew that the car had been driven at him. His soul said so. At him. Pau had been behind him, he thought, reluctant to leave the shop, no-one else near them.

The voices of the onlookers rising and screaming; and the car had deftly reversed and screeched away up the broad street, a shrill yell of gears as it nearly missed its left turn.

No-one had seen the driver, only the reflection of shop windows in the windscreen, and his hands on the wheel. Gualterio, they said, had been most fortunate. Dazed, he still saw the headlamps, oblong eyes, pinpointing him and mounting the pavement, shopping baskets falling, people shoving, a frozen turkey in its carrier bag sliding under a stalled bus. And Grandfather, *Abueli*, knocking Pau brutally out of the way and into the arms of the kind lady.

Gualterio sagged a little, the police officer steadied him.

'Want *Mamá*!' sobbed Pau. 'Want my *Papi*!'

*　　*　　*

Isa stood back from the easel and frowned, eyes critical. Her hair was bunched on top of her head, tied with a piece of string, one end of which dangled into her mouth and was chewed reflectively.

María Magdalena Contreras. A half-smile, eyes already turning to face the way she would go after the photograph had been taken. There was love in the smile, mixed with patience. A face so oval and plain which, without her hair, would have been simply an egg. Her dress was brown, honey brown. The top button unfastened, and a Toledo brooch on the collar. Mina said that the brooch had been a birthday present years before the photograph was taken, given to her by her small brothers.

Having studied all the details diligently, Isa had decided to paint her as she was: unextraordinary, ungifted, plain, and very much loved. No hints of anything more, she thought firmly, no Mona Lisa, not even a sparkle in the eye.

None of the family knew about the portrait. Isa's silence had ensured peace, and best of all, no advice, no 'oh her hair was a bit darker than that, really'. She was one to one with Magda,

224

two strangers eyeing each other.

Smeared with paint, she went into the kitchen to make coffee. Hesitated between the Nescafé and the jar of beans. Pepe had said he would invent divorce before marriage if she didn't start making real coffee that smelt warm and rich.

'I bet you'd soon sing for Nescafé's adverts if they offered you enough pesetas,' she'd said nastily.

She balanced the beans in her hand, suddenly thought of Beethoven. Smiling, recalled that he had scrupulously placed sixty beans in each cup at dinner parties, added the boiling water, and there it was. Simple! She punched the air. Hooray the boy from Bonn! The punch reminded her of the football, and she giggled as she stirred. The match had been televised live ('I thought the stupid runt was supposed to be on Barcelona's side!' and 'Christ, look at Pretty-boy Martes rubbing his privates! Was that a football injury or memories?'); and Pepe had telephone her afterwards, jubilant.

'Isa, ring Roberto! Get him here as soon as you can, Modesto wants to come in with our concert! Don't tell him what it is about, just say we have something unusual to discuss with him – offer him enticements! Oh – and Isa *mía*, thank you for the surprise . . . you crazy *cucufato*! Lucky for me that I was all alone in the changing-room – and stop laughing, *bruja*, footballers do not have their photographs glued to the front of their jockstraps!'

\*     \*     \*

Vito edged his way carefully through the mess of cables and sound equipment. The sudden piercing whine of a sound mike on stage, the raucous laughter from El Pedo Negro, the strident yells of the producer, all jangled unbearably between his ears.

And Azucarero, greeting him with a kidney-bursting slap, 'Long time no see, Ancient Mariner! Time we made another chart-topper, right? How about an *Ave Maria* next time, lots of bass guitar and rhythm?'

He halted, breathing raggedly. He could hear the choral group, Los Quince, a few bars then a shout of 'From the top! Take it from the top, that G was over-pitched again!'

225

Vito reached his dressing-room and shakily poured himself a glass of Perrier.

Pepe poked his head round the door. 'Okay?' he grinned.

'No, everything's not okay! How the hell can I concentrate with this bloody racket going on?'

'We're all on board the same ship, *amigo*,' coming into the room and suddenly seeing Vito's silvery-white face in the daylight from the window. 'Christ, you look rotten! Are you sick?'

'Lousy head cold,' he mumbled. Then dragged out a smile. 'Didn't get the chance before – all my congratulations, Pepe, Keta sends her love. Seems a long long time ago, that I met Miss Pepper.'

He lifted a limp hand, shook the strong one. He waited for Pepe to go so that he could sink into a chair and rest. Oh, but sleep would be better.

Loud voice, 'Order of appearance, please! Ten minutes! Cue Miss Bragas, Los Quince –'

Monda Ballena heard the stentorian voice approaching down the corridor, swiftly screwed in her earrings, patted the smooth black hair, waggled her mouth from side to side, emitted a ringing F sharp 'AAAAAH!' and picked up her handbag. She could hear El Pedo Negro somewhere, guitars wailing, different keys. She sniffed. Amplified crap. Pepe caught up with her, linked his arm through hers.

'You really are perky today,' she observed, her eyes slanting at him.

'Shouldn't I be, my darling?' he grinned as they passed an overflowing litterbin and an abandoned sweeping brush. 'All this excitement and glamour? Enough to turn anyone's head!' and they cackled as someone hollered 'Who the fuck's left this packet of condoms on my sandwiches?'

'The glamour and excitement!' agreed Monda, squeezed his arm.

'Monda-girl, I can't wait for you to meet Isa, you'll adore her, she's straight out of the zaniest movie! She's –'

'Pregnant? Is that why you're marrying her?'

He stopped with a jerk, smile snapping in half. Hoods down over his eyes.

'Thank you, my friend. If you'll excuse me –?' and he walked away.

That means she is, thought Monda. How many times had she seen him like this when Judit was trying to have babies?

Teresa Bragas marched full tilt into the musing corpulent figure. 'I hope bloody Azucarero electrocutes himself!' They walked on together. 'Monda, do you reckon Lavagna needs a life-support machine? He reminds one of a hedgehog under a truck.'

Monda smiled absently. Pepe shouldn't have snapped at her. She hadn't really meant it nastily. Then she tilted her chin as they walked on stage. The place was a giant beehive.

The producer juggled cue cards and clipboards, bellowed a stream of orders and comments. 'Where's bloody Martes?' 'Recording engineer, left ridge, move it!' 'BraGAS!' 'Estertor, position pleeease!' And again 'Bloody BRAGAS!'

'Here, sweetie,' acidly in his ear. 'Oh wouldn't you know it, I need a piss,' and ran blithely off-stage.

Vito Lavagna sagged over the handbasin in his dressing-room. Nothing left to bring up. Just memories. His head felt hollow, a waste land.

No word from Louis. Nothing. His hand thumped the basin feebly. Not a single bloody word. As if he had never been, never hypnotized, never held him and filled him.

Louis, wherever you are, come back, for the love of Christ, come back.

'Mr Lavagna! Cue call, please!'

'Fuck off!' but the young man had already gone on his way.

\*　　\*　　\*

On stage, scattered applause greeted Modesto Martes from the Real Madrid supporters in the orchestra. He waved, grinned, grabbed Pepe by the sleeve.

'What about Buzzer Ahmet?' he hissed.

'What about him?'

'For our concert, thickhead! . . . The Big One!' as Pepe looked blank. 'The one you dreamed up!' Pepe beamed. 'I'll give him a ring next week, shall I, he'll be taking his usual break in England then.'

'Excellent idea, he's –' The remainder of his reply was drowned as the producer bellowed 'Oi, you! – Spiderman! Sound boom lower, this is a recording session, not a fucking aerial ballet!'

Modesto strode off, waving in all directions, a brisk '*Hola!*' and embrace for Azucarero, disappeared. Pepe stood, savouring the idea.

Teresa Bragas watched him, the manipulations to his nose, finger pressing the bridge then a vigorous rub of each nostril. She nudged Monda. 'Imagine that in bed with you! If he goes through all this just for bloody *Mattinata*, what the hell's he like before a shag?'

Monda's earrings shook. Teresa crept up behind him.

'Boo, Dwarf Balls!' making him jump.

'Middle-aged cunt!' he hissed with a pleasant smile.

The director of Los Quince, one Enrique Cristobales, accosted the producer.

'Just a quick run-through of the Pachelbel, if you don't mind?'

A frown. 'What Pachelbel?'

'Aria and variations, it comes after the interval.'

'No Pachelbel down here, mate,' consulting his notes.

'What do you mean, no Pachelbel down there?' impatiently. 'We open the second bloody half with it!'

'*Panis Angelicus* first half is all, Mr Cristobales.'

'Is not bloody all! Pachelbel comes after –'

'Pachelbel doesn't, you babbling fart!' losing his temper. 'Where's that fucking sound engineer? – Hey, Alice in Wonderland, you're too close to the acoustic guitars, don't encourage the buggers! Right, Cristobales, choose your poison fast, it's either lucky César Franck or lucky Pachy, take your pick but get your mob over stage left! Okay, EVERYBODY! All lavatories locked from now until I call a break! Where's Fairy Lavagna? Somebody go resurrect him!'

'I think I'm going to feel sorry for Modesto in the duet with Vito,' whispered Ballena.

'Don't waste your sympathy on that conceited half-wit, he'd sing a duet on his own every time, given the chance . . . . Oh God, here it comes, the ghost of Lavagna! If you look closely, you can see where he's started to decompose.'

'Shut up, Bragas,' tittered Monda, looking venomously at Vito.

He smiled vaguely at nothing, shirt half-buttoned, watch sliding loosely round his wrist. Not a word. No answer on the phone. His vision blurred with tears.

'ORCHESTRA AND OVERTURE PLEEEASE!'

Simón Estertor rapped for silence. The oboe sounded its dutiful A.

Sporadic tuning of instruments; then silence as Estertor raised his stick.

Vito fainted.

\*     \*     \*

The recording had been wrapped up to her satisfaction, and Cherri sank gratefully on to a stool, nibbling a fig.

Not bad, old girl. Rossini was a bugger, notes spread and scattered like fly shit, you could almost hear him wickedly laughing as quavers and semiquavers shot way up in the air and then down without warning or breathing space. Rubbing his hands with glee. Good on yer, you scurrilous ratbag!

She glanced at the studio clock. The specialist would be waiting.

Cherri abandoned her stool and headed off to her waiting car.

\*     \*     \*

Gualterio startled her. She hadn't hear the door opening or closing in her absorption.

Isa left the easel hastily, covering it with an old towel that Ana had given her.

Gualterio said, 'Thought I'd see how you were this morning!'

It was a fine day. Winter birds clawed dead leaves and fidgeted on the lawns in the sun. And Pepe was coming home.

The portrait was nearly finished, just a few more hints of the clematis and the stone wall in the background. She had visited the wall, studied it with care.

Gualterio asked pointedly, 'Hope I'm not interrupting anything?' and glanced at the easel.

'Not at all. Would you like some coffee?'

'Real coffee, or your usual shit-dust?' and she laughingly went into the kitchen, 'Oh, absolutely real!' and murmured 'Hello, Ludwig,' as she counted the coffee beans into the cups. 'How is Pau?' she called.

'Still very shocked, poor child. And the police haven't come up with anything, either. Hah! Police? They couldn't spot a bulldozer in a bloody cupboard!' He watched her from the doorway. 'What's the matter? Your blender broken down?'

'Nope. I like doing it this way.' She reached for a spoon. 'Surely someone saw something, Gualterio? Numberplate, make of car?'

'One stupid old fart swore on her mother's grave that it was a Peugeot. Another swore on his father's that it was a BMW.' He looked over his shoulder into the den. 'So what are you painting, then, girl? Alfredo said you were sketching the house!' and he crossed to the easel and removed the towel.

Double shit. She gripped the spoon, wanting to hit him with it. Then watched his face carefully as the kettle steamed. Gualterio stared at the portrait, eyes narrowed in concentration. He put on his reading-glasses and peered closely at his daughter. Without looking round, he said 'I recognise the photograph you have used. It was taken in 1977, September. We were all celebrating Pepe's first appearance at La Scala. *La Bohème.* His best bloody Rodolfo ever.' He turned and glanced at Isa. 'That's the only reason Magda would pose for this, standing by herself. Because it was for Pepe.'

'Gualterio – I don't want anyone to know about it. Not yet. It's to be a surprise for Pepe. For Christmas. If you think it's any good . . . .'

He reflected carefully, then looked at her. 'This is my daughter,' he said, lowering his head. Said something in a low voice, and she saw his hands tighten. Then he smiled very quickly. 'Here, yes, is Magda. Smiling at us again.'

He took the coffee, and their hands touched. His eyes were damp. Said briskly, 'It will need a frame. A good one. Not one of those fancy gold buggers – a simple one. Oak, perhaps. We'll go out one morning next week; I have a friend, he has an antique shop near the docks. He will help us.'

He sipped his coffee. Growled 'It still tastes like shit-dust!'

* * *

Dr Salvador Meados de Hurón came from a long line of family vintners. Their classically-labelled black bottles of Meados Espumosos were renowned throughout Europe and Latin America. And no-one knew what had propelled this male child and future heir into medicine instead of wine. Yet here he was, permanently swaying as he talked, tall and often flatulent, a teetotaller, esteemed physician and gynaecologist, as though he had never seen a vineyard or a corkscrew in his life.

Isa had been examined, and now sat in an elaborate chair looking at him across the desk. He had confirmed what she already knew – *viva* Uncle Don! – and still smiling, he said 'Now! – diet. Very important. Lots of skimmed milk.'

Hate it, she thought, nodding enthusiastically.

'And fish. Herrings, in particular.'

Christ!

'Fruit, naturally.'

Funny – can't stand that, either.

'Vitamins, with iron. Essential.'

Hooray, got some from Boots a couple of years ago, I think I've still got them.

'Do you smoke?' he asked suddenly, watching her jot down his instructions.

'No, I gave that up.'

'Good, good. Before you conceived?'

'Yesterday morning.'

He looked at her long and hard; handed her a shiny leaflet '*Care in Pregnancy*.' Asked 'Do you drink?'

'A glass of wine, with meals.'

'Very good. One glass per day is acceptable in these circ–'

'And the occasional Amontillado. Or dry fino. Oh, and I usually have a cognac with my coffee, after dinner.'

'No liqueurs?' sarcastically.

231

'Yes, Tía María, and apricot brandy.'

He stood up, swayed over her. 'Exercise,' he said firmly. 'Do you take much exercise?'

'No,' she said cheerfully.

'Then I suggest you do. Gentle exercise,' he added, as though this wild-haired person would immediately leap frantically into aerobics.

'What would you call gentle?' her pen poised.

'Well . . . er . . . gentle. You know?'

She wrote down 'gentle', and waited. The Venetian blinds in his office rose suddenly as a gust of wind and traffic sound hit them.

He said sternly, 'At your age, *Señora* Pepper, a first child is a delicate matter, and therefore –'

'What do you mean, my child will be delicate? How can you tell –?'

'No, no! Let me explain to you in English.' Chewed his lip as he considered vocabulary. 'I do not mean to say, not imply, that the baby is to be delicate of health. What I try to tell is that you are late of life for a beginning to child. Therefore, we must insure it –'

'Insure it? Against what? Fire?'

'No, no, is not going on the fire,' he said, puzzled, thanking God that his next patient was called Felicidad García Moreno and on her eighth child. 'You have to insure it safely in all manners in particular to your age, more so than for a young lady girl. Is natural, yes? Is difficult, but your body has an age now of thirties, you see. Is clear?'

'You may revert to Spanish,' she murmured, and put her notebook away.

'*Gracias*,' with an ironic light in his eye. Then added impulsively, 'I wonder – perhaps you and Don Pepe would do me the great honour of giving your child my name as one of his, if it is a boy?'

She nodded sweetly. More bloody complications, she thought with a titter as she climbed into the car. Grosvenor Dolores was now officially to be Sebastián Josep. Plus promises to Gualterio, Alfredo, Lluís and Pau. Then Enrique and Federico had ahemmed and murmured what an honour it would be if Don Pepe . . .

And now Salvador. Moncho glanced over his shoulder as he turned the key in the ignition. 'Everything okay with the doctor, *Señora* Isa?'

'Fine, thanks,' she beamed. 'He would like the baby to have his name. Wasn't that nice of him?'

'Oh?' Moncho said reflectively. 'You know, I've been thinking. Ramón is also a very good name, a very handsome name.'

'Yes,' she said, straight-faced. 'Ramón . . . .Why not?'

*     *     *

At half-past three that afternoon, storm force hit the tunnel.

Isa heard Mina's laughter echoing past the paintings and votive candles, and she ran to the door of the kennel smiling with delight. 'Roberto!'

He swung her round, kissing her heartily. 'Let's have a look at you, you foreign mare!' Held her at arms' length, his face pale and pouched, grey eyes shining. 'You look a bloody sight better than the last time I saw you!' and gave her a hug of relief.

'I feel great, thanks! Come in, come in, welcome to the kennel!'

He was carrying an enormous striped carrier bag, which he dumped on the sofa before glancing round the sitting room. His eye was immediately caught by the view of the terrace and he stalked possessively outside, peered around.

'Where are they, then?'

'Where are what?' she laughed, pouring wine for them both.

'Sniffer's little swing and play-pen.'

Giggling, 'Shut up!' He said 'Those roses need bloody pruning!'

'It's clematis, you idiot!'

'Oh fuck me, how the rich live! Solid jade weeds, as well!'

As they sipped, she took him on a tour of the kennel. He scowled at Ignacio.

'You mean that bloody thing is glittering by the phone whenever I talk to you? God Almighty! Oh, that reminds me, I've brought your little friend from the office,' and he swooped back to the sitting room, picked up the carrier bag.

'That looks heavy – what's in it?' curiously.

He swung it away. 'Paws off! These are Christmas pressies for

233

you and little Sniffer. Plus – this,' and he tossed her a paper bag.

'Oh Bobby, my magpie! Hello, Giacomo,' and like a contented child, held the wooden bird in her hands.

Bobby sat down. 'Isn't it a fucking shame?' he asked the room. 'Poor cow! Why don't you kiss it, Ezita? Show it where its bloody bed is?'

Laughing, she placed the magpie on the cocktail bar, and resumed the guided tour. He sniffed at the kitchen ('Very handy, you can reach everything without having to move.'), said 'God!' at the bedroom, and finally remarked 'What an enormous palace! What does Sniffer do with all his bloody money, recycle it? Oh, by the way, Mrs Mina's put me in the same room I had before. Just like coming home!'

He slapped her hand as it hovered over the carrier bag. 'I told you – Christmas, not December the bloody 9th! Oh – one of them is the you-know-what for Pepe,' and she flung herself at him with delight. 'And this is for him, as well,' half removing a squat parcel tantalisingly.

She prodded it, mystified. 'What is it? It's heavy.'

'A bag of Gro-more,' he said solemnly, and permitted her to hit him. 'Where is he, anyway?'

'At the TV studios. He was later then expected coming back from Seville, Vito collapsed during the recording take – a nasty case of flu – and they had him flown home. So, Pepe had to step in and do the duet with Martes, plus Vito's other aria, and that delayed things while they did more rehearsing.'

'Poor old Vito, must ring him when I get back. Shit! – will Sniffer be claiming a triple fee for all this deputizing? I'd better warn Europe to tighten its fucking belt if he is.'

Pepe heard the laughter as he came down the tunnel, was already grinning as he opened the door and cried '*Hola*, Roberto! *Bienvenido!*'

'Yes, thank you – and you?' while Isa tittered. 'Good to see you again, Pepe. Ez is looking very well, I'm glad to see! Nice big place you've got here, all this space is likely to bring on my agoraphobia.' Watched as they embraced, eyes and mouths close together; heard Pepe say softly, 'Did you see Salvador?' and her reply, '*Sí, querido*. Everything confirmed!'

Bobby turned away suddenly, pretended to finish off the wine in his empty glass. A tug, then, on his sleeve.

'We've got something to tell you,' Isa said gently.

'Don't tell me – you've fixed a date for the wedding!'

'Yes, we have. And we're having a baby as well.'

He gaped. Then 'Bloody hell!' and his eyes watered. 'Bloody hell!' and 'That's great news!' and ignoring Isa, he went to Pepe and kissed him on the cheek. 'You know, as soon as you walked through that door, I thought to myself, Pepe's putting on weight!' and as they snorted 'You idiot!' he embraced them both, muttering something about an English godparent and that he hoped it would be a little girl.

'A girl?' queried Pepe, still sniggering after the kiss.

'You know the sort of thing – a bit like Ez, but with tits.'

With laughter, they drank a toast to the baby. Eagle-eyed, Bobby said 'That was bloody quick, wasn't it? When is she due?'

'He is due in the middle of June,' and they watched him as he counted backwards.

'Christ, you ever thought of going in for the land-speed record, Contreras? So – when are you getting married?'

'We think February 21st, in London. And you're our guest of honour.'

'Of course. Thank you.' Then, 'Don't suppose you've had time to pick a name for the little one yet? May Bobby suggest Roberto if it's a boy, Roberta if it's a girl?' and wondered why they fell hysterically on to the sofa and Isa whispered 'We've got two more now, besides this. Moncho and Salvador want in!'

Later they announced that they were taking him out to dinner that evening.

'Tell him about it, *querido*!' called Isa from the kitchen, busily counting coffee beans.

Bobby's eyes glittered with interest as Pepe described La Tasca. 'Is an odd place, eccentrical, but friendly and food good. On Mondays, is a *puticlub*, a single . . . er . . .'

'Singles bar,' called Isa. 'Damn, where was I? How can this cup be full of beans and that one hardly any? Start again!'

'And tonight,' continued Pepe, 'is the turn of *El Rincón*.'

'Who the fuck's that?'

'Bobby!' warningly from the kitchen. 'Thirty-two, thirty-three . . .'

'Casting on or casting off, dear? Funny place to knit baby clothes. Anyway, Pepe, you were saying –?'

'*El Rincón* is a poets' corner. We have many young poets in Barcelona, and this is a favourite place for them to do their versings.'

'Poets!' and Bobby's eyes gleamed.

*　　*　　*

Bobby was watching a long-haired waiter pouring wine at the next table.

'Nice girl,' he commented as the waiter winked at him before disappearing into the murky haze of a very crowded La Tasca. He turned back to his companions, and topped up the three wine glasses. 'You say the poets come on later?'

'Yes. Look, Roberto, we have something to discuss with you – Isa, are you permitted wine now?'

'Don Salvador said I could have one glass a day. The ones I had this afternoon won't count.'

'And please explain, why they will not count?'

'Well, if I hadn't gone to see him today, I wouldn't have known, would I?' She beamed at him.

He scratched his head thoughtfully, then said weakly, 'Oh. Then is okay. Roberto, there is an idea we wish to –'

Bobby sliced his steak with gusto, thin trickles of blood running into his pile of salad. He waved his fork. 'Before you go on, Pepe – I nearly forgot with this windbag jabbering nonstop – I've been besieged for your services by the Royal Operating Theatre in London, they want you in that Saint-Saëns thing, *Samson and Delilah*, next Feb, 8th–11th. Won't clash with Lorker or your nuptials. Pass the bread, Ezita – Christ, these radishes are strong, pardon Bobby if he –' He lifted one buttock. 'God, that's better out than in! Yes, Pepe, as I was saying –'

'*Samson et Dalila*? I've only sung that rôle twice before. I take it that I would be Samson?' sarcastically.

'That's the difficult bit, you having to push over the bloody temple and look muscular and convincing. I'll have to make sure it's in your contract that you have three good meals of Winalot every day.'

After a lengthy discussion, Pepe said that he would be happy to do it but without dog-food.

Isa tapped his hand during dessert. 'Shall we try again, *querido*?'

Pepe smiled winningly. 'Roberto, we have something to say to you, to discuss —'

*　　*　　*

Bobby leaned back in his chair and looked at them both.

The Good Appetite place mats had been turned over to provide him with writing space. Now he had finished scribbling, a forgotten crumb of bread clinging to his lip.

'So. Luciano Bardi, is it. I can contact him, no probbies there.' Sighed. 'Poor sod's got nothing to do all day except run the government, the Italian broadcasting network, the Vatican, and the Mafia, not to mention collecting subscriptions from bloody freemasons. Time hangs heavily on his hands. He'd be glad of a few extra quid to rattle in his beaded purse —'

'Bobby!'

He grinned wolfishly. 'Ezita, I'll do it like a shot, it's a brilliant idea and I bet it's yours, so stop letting that birdbrain take all the credit!'

'We both thought of it!' she snapped loyally. Then smiled 'Okay,' quickly, hoping that Pepe was still struggling with the word 'freemasons.'

Bobby patted her hand, then squeezed it. 'Christ, if Bardi's as excited as I am about the potential involved here, he'll go wild! Excited, did I say? I've got such a feeling about this, I could piss in Sniffer's coffee! . . . Is he still with us, darling? He looks perplexed.'

Isa choked. Pepe asked, 'Did you say Bardi was a freemason?'

Bobby patted his hand. 'We've moved on from there, dear. I was just saying, I'll contact Luciano as soon as I get back. You say you've got the other two nightingales to agree? Good . . . Any thought about the conductor?'

'Martes suggests Zubair Ahmet, and I would go along with that.'

'Ahmet? That fellow with the staring eyes?' His eyes were suddenly riveted by movement on the small ramshackle stage, someone trying to fix a mike which sagged in a nest of wires. 'The poets! Come on, let's get more brandies before they start, not you Ezita, think of little Roberta – right, so I can tell Bardi that you'd like to fix it up with Ahmet as ringmaster, okay?' He raised his cup of coffee to them. 'Cheers, my children! Consider it done!'

Two hands met and clasped beneath the table, and squeezed hard.

*    *    *

A new kind of Tuesday had come into being some three weeks ago, one that Judit had noted in her diary with interest; a brand-new ritual, neatly performed in Los Culitos.

This was the nickname given to Las Galerías Galantas, an indoor shopping precinct with a grandeur akin to the Sagrada Familia which was close by. The nickname itself had been bestowed by the first shoppers after the inaugural ceremony, when they discovered that the toilets were scarcely large enough to sit on.

Los Culitos was a feast of pale grey and even paler blue marble, discreet mosaics, and, on each level, clusters of tables and chairs of white wood where one could sit and view the elegant escalators humming quietly up and down in the very centre of the complex. Tall plants in terracotta tubs moved their branches in the flow of air-conditioning; and from the tables on the top level, one could see the giant fountains three floors below, sparkling in the lights from the shop façades.

The ritual, Judit was pleased to see, was being continued today. Pau was there this time, but he was only a small boy and therefore not to be counted. She watched as they sat down in a welter of parcels; watched as Mina fussed over a chair, pulled it out, pushed it back, chose another. Vaguely saw Pau lean on the ornate white rail and peer down the miles to his favourite toy shop.

She watched Isa. Yes, it was happening again. No sooner had

238

she sat down and spilled the contents of one bag or another, than she was off again to the toilets inside the colonnade of square blue pillars.

Isa returned, said something to Mina, and they both giggled. She heard Pau say 'Can we get a birthday card for Jesus?'

Their coffee was served; no *bizcochos* this time, she noticed, just a large iced bun for Pau. She waited for Isa to empty most of the brown sugar into her cup, then, picking up her own bags, emerged from the flower shop and walked over, smiling broadly with surprise.

'Good heavens – how lovely! Mina, dear, how are you?'

Mina looked alarmed. A rapid glance at Isa, then she blinked at the slim figure with the pearl necklace and pleasant smile. 'Judit! What –'

Isa stared, but not too hard, her heart diving in a silly way as though escaping. A stab of jealousy, oh most definitely. This woman and Pepe, together. Her hand patted the slight shape that was Grosvenor Dolores, and stayed there.

There were courteous introductions, of course, and Judit sat with them and exchanged pleasantries, ruffled Pau's hair before he returned to the rail with his bun to watch the escalators. Then Judit turned to Mina with a laugh. 'I suppose you'll be getting the Sunday editions of *El País* soon!'

Mina looked at her blankly. '*El País*? What on earth for?'

Eagerly, 'Oh it should be an absolute riot, my dear! Didn't you know? Dear Bionda Merdina's writing her autobiography, and they've bought the serial rights! Surely Pepe has mentioned it?'

'Bionda Merdina? The soprano?' Isa was interested. Merdina had once almost signed for the Drach Agency, some time before her much-publicized affair with Pepe. Oddly, she thought suddenly, I don't feel jealous of that. Only of this woman.

A laugh. 'Well – if you put it like that, yes, the soprano!' She pulled a comical face. 'You mean he hasn't told you? God, it will keep his lawyers busy, that's for sure, when it's published!'

'Judit, did you hear about Papaterio's accident?' Mina intervened quickly, but in a low voice as she glanced at Pau.

'What? Oh, that. Of course I did, *La Vanguardia* was full of it. So you know about Bionda Merdina, do you, Isabel? – may I call you that? – Oh good, here's my coffee. Very nice brew they make here, don't you think? It reminds me of the wonderful stuff we used to have in . . . in . . .' She straightened her back, laughing. 'This is nice!'

Isa tried not to look puzzled.

'Mina, I'm surprised you haven't heard about her book, it's causing such a storm of anticipation!' She winked at Isa. 'One of those dreadful kiss-and-tell sagas, you know? I really didn't believe that my husband could do such inventive things!' Green eyes sparkled.

'I thought you said she was still writing it?' from Mina.

'Well, yes, but her agent – you remember Piselli? – he quoted me some of the passages. I think he said –' Her voice drifted away. Then brightly, 'I understand that you come from London, Isabel? I used to adore going to –'

'No, I'm from Somerset, actually. A small town – Little Jollytwits. On Sea,' she added smoothly. She turned to Mina, smiling. 'What a pity this book won't be out in time for Christmas! It looks as though I shall have to buy Pepe the new *Rupert Bear Annual* after all.'

Mina snorted, and called to Pau. Said politely, 'You'll have to excuse us, Judit – Isa, we'd better get him to that toyshop, he's gone crazy about something he's seen in there and he won't tell me what it is. Pau! Toyshop!' Pau swallowed the rest of his bun and danced behind a frozen-mouthed Judit. '*Tía* Judit, we're going to the toyshop! And we're going to get a birthday card for Jesus, and an hello card for Isa's baby, aren't we, Isa?'

'Not until June,' murmured Mina, hardly daring to glance at her former sister-in-law.

She didn't appear to have been listening to Pau. She gave a careless laugh, 'Well I'd better love you and leave you, lots to do today! Nice to have met you, Isabel! Will you be here again next week? Perhaps we could meet up again. If not, have a lovely Christmas, all of you!'

She waved, and strode away towards the blue colonnade.

'Bloody hell!' said Isa. 'Exactly,' said Mina.

*     *     *

240

The black cat with glossy nylon fur lolled on a shelf, eyes lively yellow, staring at them. The front paws were stretched out to them, hind legs tucked relaxed. A shiny bushy tail was flung carelessly along the considerable length of its body. It wore a red ribbon, and seemed ready to speak.

'*Mamá, Mamá,* Isa, he's waited for me! Please, please, *Mamá!*'

'A cat?' frowned Mina. 'But you don't like cats, *querido!*'

'Yes I do, oh please, I've already given him a name, every time I see him I say "*Buenos días,* Bufido," and he looks at me and says "*Hola,* Pau, are you taking me home with you today?" '

'Bufido?' queried Isa.

Before Mina could translate, Pau was doing alarming things to his nose, tugging it, snuffling, moving it from side to side. Then he and Mina laughed and looked at Isa.

'He's named for Uncle Pepe!' giggled Pau.

'*Bufido* means snort!' explained Mina.

'That is not only unkind, but it's also a bloody good impersonation,' sniggered Isa, and pulled Bufido down from the shelf.

# 15

The day stretched far over the fields. Frost, that hadn't disappeared all morning. A sky grey and pink and still. A misty haze hung over the surprised sheep.

'I wish to make an announcement,' Buzzer said. He raised his brown eyes to the sky. 'I, Zubair Ahmet, wish to thank Allah-God and Decca for giving me the chance to manifest myself as a complete twat!'

His wife smiled benignly, glancing up from her viewfinder.

'More than that,' he continued, addressing the young sheep around him, 'I have an uncanny feeling that you should not be out at this time of year, and that I shall be arrested and charged with attempted ovicide. Either that, or,' his breath white and puffy, 'they will come for me quietly, the Surrey medics, and try to coax me into a nasty jacket.'

'Buzz, stop fidgeting, darling. And your bow tie is crooked.'

He bowed to the camera. 'Then one will endeavour to make the crooked straight,' and he adjusted the white bow deftly. He waved his baton in the air. 'Are you ready, sheep? Decca brought you here, so they must have told you that we shall begin with Dvořák's *Carnaval* overture. I shall start on a down beat, after a count of three, like so –' He swiftly jabbed his stick to the left, 'and then you come in IN UNISON, like SO!' with another lunge.

Several sheep skipped adroitly out of the way, then stopped and looked at him.

'Will you shut up?' laughed Fancy. 'And stop prancing around while I'm trying to focus this damned thing.'

He stood still, baton dangling. 'Why me?' he moaned. 'Why, Allah-God? Of all the conductors in the world who are used to handling sheep on a daily basis, why me?'

Fancy looked up. 'Does Allah live in Virginia Water with God, then?'

'Why not? They can both afford it. Will you get a bloody move on, woman? I'm iced up!' and he jumped, feet together, from side to side.

'Darling, have another sip of antifreeze, then you'll be fine. And get closer to the sheep!'

'How, please? When I move, they move.'

'Then get the woolly dears interested, baa at them or something. Right – I think this will be okay . . . Ready?'

He bowed to the sheep. 'Zubair Ahmet and bloody Decca proudly present the Royal Mutton Philharmonic Orchestra, leader Sandra Smith –'

'Sandra Smith?'

'The big ewe over there. Definitely a Sandra Smith. Oh no! – Dave's coming, he's heading this way! He can't see me like this!'

'Stand still, dammit! Never mind about Dave. Decca are going to love this!'

'A thousand farts up the noses of Decca! . . . .Hi, David!'

'Good afternoon, Mrs Ahmet, *Maestro*,' and Buzzer's secretary paused for breath after his frosty sprint across the fields. He affected not to stare.

'You ever conducted sheep, Dave?'

'Er . . . no, *Maestro*.'

'Pity. I'm looking for a bloody deputy! Anyway, what brings you here?'

A nervous laugh as the sheep stared at him. 'An urgent phone call for you, from Modesto Martes. Could you get in touch as soon as possible? I told him that you were a . . . er . . . little busy right now.'

'Modesto?' Frowned, shrugged. 'Right, Dave, thanks. Now, darling, are we ready for action, please? I and my orchestra are nicely tuned up and ready!'

\*     \*     \*

After the conversation with Martes, Buzzer joined his wife in the lounge. He poured himself a glass of ginger wine and sat beside her, braces hanging.

'Is Modesto okay?'

'What? . . . Oh. I'm not sure.' He sipped reflectively. 'You know, he's had quite the most remarkable idea I've ever heard. At least, I think it was his. Whatever! – haven't heard anything like it since the time someone tried to castrate von Karajan without anaesthetic.'

Fancy smiled. 'He's not still chirping about being a part-time conductor, is he?'

'Not this time, no. Anyway, I've already told him that if he wants to mount a podium and view the stage from a different angle, he'll have to learn how to read music first and then the names of the instruments.' He sniggered unkindly. 'No – this is new, I can only assume that he has recently hit his head against something very hard.'

He glanced at her, then got up and slowly walked across the carpet, eyes fixed on the pattern.

Lifted his head. 'He thinks –' The head was shaken sadly. 'He thinks that we could do a concert together.'

Fancy laughed, puzzled. 'What's so remarkable about that?'

'Hear me out, darling. Martes says not just a concert. Martes says a very big concert. Martes says a concert with himself, AND Fazzoletto, AND Contreras. Me, conducting. A gigantic concert, Fancy, in the open air. Martes says that it would be grand if we did it in Italy. In that big arena near Rome, the della Doccia.' He uttered a bark. 'Arena della Doccia! Looming bloody great stones and a draught round every crumbling corner!'

She watched him as he paced. 'It is just so damned ridiculous! No-one in their right mind would – that's it! He isn't in his right mind! He has – how did Shakespeare put it? – he's bloody well flipped! The man must be suffering from post-coital dementia. And you know what else he said? Two bloody orchestras! Just me and about . . . what? . . two hundred musicians? The complexity of it, can you imagine? And,' he laughed, 'he wants me to go to Barcelona to discuss it with them! Oh Fancy, what a sad end for such a wonderful tenor – now utterly witless! . . . .Da-VID!'

Fancy smiled to herself.

'Yes, *Maestro*?'

'Diary for next January, Dave. Look up dates 8th to the 11th.'

His secretary reappeared before the second ginger wine had

been poured. He opened a large book, skimming through the first pages. 'Here we are, *Maestro*. You're still in Austria on the 8th, you are free 9th and 10th, then you fly to Hong Kong on the 11th.'

'Hong Kong?' sharply.

'Yes, *Maestro*. Two concerts with the Hong Kong Yang Tung Weng Philharmonia.'

Fancy giggled. 'The what?'

Buzzer grinned. 'I must try saying that after four whiskies! Right, Dave, contact Martes *pronto*, tell him I can fit in a meeting on the 9th, in Barcelona, preferably evening.'

Fancy said, 'That's a long way to go for an idea that's crazy!'

He glowered. 'I prefer to tell them that face to face, thank you!'

\*     \*     \*

Christmas Eve, and Bobby was knotting his tie.

Lunch at Il Finocchio. This time last year, he and Ez had been holed up in his flat for the day, with streaming colds and trying to invent musical Scrabble, Italian words only and no proper names. As far as he could recall, she had managed two words, and his own had been disallowed on the grounds that 'Fukko' did not exist in any language.

He smiled into the mirror. One year later, and the silly mare was not only arse over tip in love with a canary, but also preggy. Ezita – with a kid! It was like asking a lunatic to take care of a basket of unweaned kittens.

As always on this day, he distinctly heard the voice of his mother. It came with a vague memory of an open back door and an umbrella: 'It may be Christmas Eve to some buggers, but it ain't for me!' He'd often puzzled over that. Now, having dutifully remembered his only known parent, he went into the lounge and, for the twentieth time that day, stared out of the window at the street three floors below.

There it stood, his own baby.

A new Mercedes, fire-red, rain-spotted. His old Ford Granada, code name Willie, had been towed away, unfortunately with his best suède gloves on the passenger seat, but that was a small price to pay. His lovely new baby. He beamed and rubbed his hands.

245

Pepe's Christmas present to Robert Drach: and Ezita had embroidered a fat cushion shaped like two entwined hearts with the slogan 'I'm Robert. Lay me,' for the back seat.

He scowled at the inclement weather that was spoiling the showroom glow of the car. Why did God have to blow all His fucking dead leaves down this particular street?

Not quite time for his luncheon engagement yet. Time, perhaps, for a dinkies? Scotch and soda? Instead, he picked up Vito's Christmas card again. It didn't even look like one. Plain cream and a small blue *Buon Natale* in the corner. Inside was a scribbled message, 'Ring me, old friend, soon'.

The announcement of his immediate retirement had come as a shock to everyone associated with his world. Bobby had read about it in *The Times*, and it had stunned him. No more Donizetti *alla* Lavagna. It was sad, terrifyingly sad. So what, he'd collapsed in Seville with flu. Why retire because of flu? If I'd retired because of bloody flu, I would have been a pensioner when I was thirteen.

On an impulse, and because it was Christmas, Bobby picked up the phone. Of course, he groused to himself, every homesick Italian in the UK will be hogging the lines from here to bloody *Mamma*. He drummed his fingers, waiting for the connection, wondering if Pepe and Ez would like the gifts he had left in the kennel. He'd made her swear not to open them before Christmas Day. '*Signor* Lavagna, please . . . Robert Drach . . . D . . . R . . . A . . . C . . . H.' Fucking faint-voiced twat.

Much to his surprise, Vito sounded clear and lively. He complained about a lingering weakness; dismissed his retirement as 'old age, dear boy, glad of a rest', and eagerly begged him to come out to the villa before the end of the year.

'Look,' said Bobby, thinking swiftly, 'I'm in Italy from the 27th, some business I've got with Luciano Bardi – how about if I come to you from Rome? I'll give you a ring from there and let you know more precisely. No idea how long these talks will last.'

'Great!' enthusiastically, 'We'll have a marathon get-together, examine our youth in loving detail! Tell you what – I'll meet you at the airport myself! God, Bob, I feel better already!'

Bobby smiled as he hung up, and patted the phone. Nice

Christmas pressie, a holiday with Lavagna. Picked up his new keys. Time to take his baby to lunch.

*     *     *

On Christmas morning, Pio was cooking.

He was cooking amidst much steam and fragrance, his large apron patterned with new streaks of tomato sauce and also with cameras: a free gift from Kodak for allowing them to use his initials in an advert. The kitchen staff had been awarded the day off, departing at dawn, leaving the ovens timed in readiness and sheets of instructions sellotaped to walls and doors.

As he stirred and peered under saucepan lids, he sang. And as he sang, he thought of Pepe's brainwave, the concert; gleefully decided that he would make a list of all Modesto's favourite arias and grab them first. Upstage the cocky sod.

Pio accompanied both thoughts and stirring with fast sips from the king-size bottle of red wine which was intended for the rich sauce.

Adriana poked her head round the door, sniffing the air.

'I can't smell the ducklings,' she said.

'Eh?' He turned round, grinning greedily.

'The ducklings. Have you scored their skins? Salted them? Why can't I smell them?'

A herb-stained hand reached out for her, and he pulled her to his side.

'What ducklings, little one?'

'What do you mean, what ducklings? There are fifteen of them!'

'Where?' He stirred the contents of the largest saucepan vigorously, and threw in a pile of bay leaves. Looked at it thoughtfully, then added another pile and paddled his wooden spoon happily around the newly-created forest.

'In the cold store! Trussed! Waiting!' and she ran to the large ovens.

They were briskly warm, automatic timers functioning perfectly. They were also empty. She rushed back to the busy hobs around which he worked and sang. Lifted a lid, was obscured by a cloud of steam.

247

'Spaghetti?' she screamed. 'Bloody spaghetti on Christmas Day?'

'A–ha! The *bambini* love it. I love it. We all love it!'

'Not on Christmas Day, you fat idiot! What about my ducklings?'

She sped to the cold store. Emerged slowly, a duckling in each hand. Thrust them under his nose. 'These are ducklings!' she screeched. 'There are thirteen more of them in there! These are for our Christmas meal!'

'Jolly good,' brushing them aside as he bent over the hob, 'we can have them for supper. The kids will enjoy that!'

'The kids are going out for supper!'

A happy beam. 'Good. More for us then, little one. Pass the black pepper, will you? . . . how many, did you say? Fifteen? A pleasant little snack –' and grinning, dodged a duckling that sped towards him.

She began to giggle through the steam.

\*     \*     \*

Pepe stared at his gifts from Roberto.

Isa lay on the floor, helpless with laughter. Her royal blue t-shirt had been embroidered with the slogan 'Merry Christmas, marrows.' The sound system was playing *In Dulce Jubilo*; decorations of silvered twigs and gold-sprayed foliage separated the sitting room from the rest of the kennel. Ignacio had been brought in from the study, and looked benign in his paper hat. Lluís and Pau had stuck mistletoe down the front of his trousers at Alfredo's sniggering insistence.

There were no cooking smells coming from the little kitchen. The main meal was to be a family occasion, with everyone nicely mellowed with sherry. Isa had promised herself one glass of the cream variety, arguing that because she hated it, it would do her less harm than fino.

Pepe glanced at her acidly, and weighed the bag of Gro-more in his hand.

'Have you ever heard of murder by thought-transferring?' he enquired, tight-lipped. His new trowel lay on the sofa.

248

'Oh God!' she gasped. 'And I thought he was joking!'

'What am I supposed to do with it? Eh? Standing in a fucking pot and let you water me twice a day?'

'Oh please, stop it, if I laugh any more I'll turn Grosvenor Dolores upside down!'

Her eyes were streaming as she looked at his face. He had washed his hair that morning, and the sleek black looked fuzzy as though it had been soaked first in fabric conditioner. Impulsively, she got to her feet and touched it.

He moved his head slightly, not to be distracted. 'I'll hide it!' he shouted, glancing wildly at the soft heavy bag. 'Christ, suppose Alfredo sees it!'

She exploded again, took it from him. 'I'll put it on the terrace. We can pretend one of the garden staff left it there!'

'I'll kill him!'

'Open your other parcel,' she pleaded.

'Why? Shall I find fertilizer? Potting-on instructions?' He touched the flat parcel from Bobby gingerly. 'It feels like a book! I bet it's potting-on instructions!'

Fresh laughter bubbled in her as he looked at the card sellotaped to the front of the package. It read 'Greetings from Ross-on-Wye.'

'What,' he snarled, 'is Ross-on-Wye?'

She hid a grin, said placidly 'It's a town near Hereford. Not far from the Welsh border.'

'Oh bloody *fantástico*! Now he wants me to be a border plant!' and slit the wrappings with angry caution. Silence as he looked at the book in his hands. Then

'Oh my God!'

Isa hugged herself with joy. He turned the book over and over, opened it reverently.

'Christ!'

Held it to his face, sniffed the old leather. 'Jesus bloody God!' he shouted. 'Where on earth did he find this, Isa? How did he manage it?' He kissed the title page, eyes softly brown and damp. 'The man's a bloody genius! Oh dear God, I never thought I would see this, ever!'

She kissed the top of his head. Bless you, Bobby. She had

known, of course. If anyone could find the libretto and full score of the seemingly defunct Rossini *Otello*, Bobby Drach was the man.

Pepe grabbed her fingers. 'Did he get it from this town near Wales?'

'No,' she giggled, 'that's what he always calls Rossini,' and watched him as he got up and did a little jig. 'It's mine! Mine!'

And there is something else for you, my beloved Pepe, later. Magda's portrait, now properly framed, was wrapped and hidden in the cupboard of the family sitting room. She and Gualterio had chosen the frame together; and between them had decided on a grand presentation after the Christmas meal. After all, she argued, Magda belonged to the family and her gift to Pepe should be enjoyed by them all.

She dumped the bag of Gro-more on the terrace and put the trowel in a kitchen drawer, smiling happily.

*     *     *

It wasn't yet time to present the gift of Magda. Besides, Alfredo had just remarked 'Good thing you girls didn't go shopping on Tuesday!'

The meal was over. They had spread themselves, over-full, in the sitting room, smug against the drizzling gloom of the afternoon. Pau and Lluís had disappeared, under firm instructions to rest. Bufido had obediently gone with them.

As the resting boys shouted and banged overhead, Gualterio said 'Brandy time! Come on, you idle runt, help me to pour,' and he poked Pepe hard in the back. Pepe whispered to Isa, 'You shall have a sip of mine, *princesa*!'

'What did you say, Alfredo?' asked Mina. 'Oh, thanks, Papa-terio – a happy Christmas, everybody!'

Glasses swiftly raised, slowly lowered. 'That was a gulp!' accused Pepe.

'Then I've still got my sip to come, haven't I!'

'I said,' and Alfredo raised his voice as a screech from Pau rang through the house, 'I said it's just as well that you two didn't go to Los Culitos on Tuesday. Jesus Christ, what is that child doing? I'll screw the little bugger into the ground!'

As Mina and Isa looked at him blankly, he went on 'I'm surprised Ana didn't say anything, it was on local radio. Bloody
bomb scare at Los Culitos, day before yesterday. They thought it
was ETA at first, but it turned out to be a hoax.' Snorted. 'Some
hoax! One poor girl started going into labour because of the panic.
Lost her baby.'

'Oh God!' shivered Isa, touched Pepe's hand.

Mina paled. 'We nearly did go, too, with the boys.' She took a
sip of cognac rather more hastily than was her custom. 'Then we
thought that . . . er . . . Judit might be there again, so we –'

Pepe said quietly, 'You have met her there? You did not
mention this, *querida*?'

'Oh. Well, it didn't seem important, you were away, and then I
forgot all about it,' as Alfredo chortled 'What was it she told you,
Mina? Something about a book?' He thumped Pepe's
shoulder. 'Hey, *hombre*, Judit says that a friend of yours is writing
her autobiography!'

He tittered, looking at his brother's uncomprehending face.
'Bonker, *coño* – Bonker Merdina! Going to be serialised every week
in *El País*. Wonder what it's called . . . *My Adventures with Mr
Miracle Prick*?'

Pepe leapt to his feet. 'I'll break your bloody neck in a minute!'

Alfredo skipped out of reach. 'Imagine! Every Sunday, a new
insight into the secret world of the warbling wizard – page after
page about that playful little cock of yours – sheee-it! Wonder if
she mentions anything about singing?'

'You've asked for it, you –!'

'Alfredo! Pepe!'

Isa giggled fascinated, as they disappeared with a crash behind
the sofa, and grunts and thuds merged rhythmically with the
Christmas music on the stereo player.

Gualterio went to the bar and picked up two bottles of Grand
Marnier, solemnly removing the stoppers.

Mina nudged Isa. 'Watch this!'

Passing her with the bottles, he snapped 'Isa, get that bloody
parcel out of the cupboard instead of sitting there like a grinning
pole-axed cow!'

'Papaterio!' as Isa giggled again and got up. There were yells from behind the sofa, 'You filthy cowardly bastard!' and 'Don't hit me there, for Christ's sake!'

Gualterio climbed on to a chair with the Grand Marnier. Mina gave a chuckle as he whistled shrilly. The sounds of scuffling ceased. Two flushed faces peered over the top of the sofa. He tipped the bottles slightly.

'No, Father, don't!'

'Father! In the name of the Holy Bobbit!'

Isa thought, God must feel this way at times, as she watched the triumph shine on Gualterio's face.

'Right!' he thundered. 'Now shut up! And one of you bastards, pour this for us all! Isa and I have a surprise for you!'

Meekly, the brothers straightened their clothing, fetched and carried, and sat down.

'It's better than hot milk and a lullaby, isn't it,' tittered Mina.

Isa went to the cupboard and removed the large package that was Magda in brown paper. She smiled nervously as they watched her, then took it to where they sat. Placed it in Pepe's hands.

'For you,' quietly. 'For all of you. But especially for you.'

Pepe slowly removed sheet after sheet of paper, Gualterio hovering over him impatiently. Of course, thought Isa, he has to unwrap the bloody thing upside down and back to front. Gualterio snatched it from him, sarcastically handed it back the right way up.

Silence. Isa thought, I wish something would come and eat me up.

Then Mina was peering at it, crying 'Lord above, it's Magda! Oh, how beautiful!'

Alfredo touched the canvas, murmuring, 'I suppose she always looked as loving as this, and we never even noticed.'

'See the brooch? See the brooch?' Gualterio jabbed at it. 'You two buggers still owe me for that!'

Isa looked at Pepe. His eyes roamed up and down the portrait, blinking rapidly. At last he silently handed it to his brother, and went to her. Held out his hands with such love on his face that she no longer wanted to be eaten.

'Beautiful. Beautiful, *querida*. I don't know what to say.' And he held her close and the room was empty for them.

She whispered, 'I ran out of brown ochre towards the end.'

He began to chuckle. 'You did what?'

'Can you tell?' anxiously.

'My dearest craziest *cucufato*, I love you, God how I love you!' A fierce kiss.

'I shan't tell you again!' snapped Mina as Alfredo started applauding.

\*　　\*　　\*

Vito moved his aching limbs miserably. Santa Maria, it hurt.

Stretched out on his bed, he looked again at the Christmas card from Louis. A vase of irises on the front. Inside a florid curly 'L' and 'We do miss you' with enough exclamation marks to build a fence. God rot you, Louis. And he choked on his own breath.

Keta came in quietly with a glass of steaming lemon juice. Under his fretful gaze she added a measure of Scotch.

'Thanks, darling,' and sipped, savouring the hot bite in his mouth.

'Any better, Baby?' She arranged her skirt neatly as she sat on the bed.

'Worse. God, I feel half dead!'

'Then I shall ring Bobby Drach and tell him –'

'You will not!' fiercely.

She smiled, touched his hand. 'The physician will be here at three-thirty, don't forget.'

'What the hell for? It's only bloody flu!'

'And you are very low, Vee. Whatever you may say, the decision to retire has hit you real hard, harder than you think. Anyway, he'll give you a good check-over, and perhaps a tonic to help you. You know how thorough he is!'

He groaned in memory of the thoroughness. 'Happy Christmas!'

'But think of a happy new year afterwards,' kissing him. She tried not to see his proud moustache, untinted and dull.

\*　　\*　　\*

253

They walked up the hill from Sant Moiseps, leaving the lights behind them. Pepe had tucked her hand inside his pocket for warmth.

'It was good of Roberto to offer us his flat for February,' he said.

'And it's a pity we can't stay there,' she grumbled. 'Yes, I know – hotels afford better protection! But why it has to be the Dorchester, I don't know! Why not our Grosvenor?'

'Our first home,' he teased. She joined in his chuckle, said 'Just think, our first child could have been Dorchester Dolores!'

She skipped a little to keep up with his stride.

'Or even,' he added, 'Inn on the Park Dolores!'

They both snorted as she continued 'Things are bad enough as it is, with Sebastián Josep Grosvenor Dolores Gualterio Alfredo Enrique –'

'– Lluís Pau Ramón Federico Salvador Roberto Contreras Pepper!' and laughing, he swung her into the air, she spluttering.

Smiling, kissing his cold cheek, 'So, the Dorchester it is, Samson!'

'God, I wish I was about to start preparationing for Rossini and *Otello* instead of *Samson!*'

'Perhaps one day, *querido*.' Then, 'Why can't we see any stars tonight?'

He pretended to stagger back, dragging her with him. 'God! No stars!' and began to sing *E lucevan le Stelle*, but the climb up the hill had affected his breathing, and he rounded off with a squawk.

Laughing, 'Will you sing that at Our Concert?'

'Could do, I suppose. We'll have to sort all that out – the programme. Oh God, I'm excited!' His teeth gleamed faintly. 'By the way, Ahmet's agreed to come over to Barcelona for the meeting. Oh Isa *mía*, *viva* you! *Vivan* Bardi and Roberto!'

The crunch of feet on frosted ruts, she humming under her breath. Then he said, 'Are you looking forward to meeting Martes, *princesa*?'

'Marmite.'

He stared at her as they emerged from blackness into a puddle of light by their entrance gate. 'Pardon me? Marmite?'

254

'Just what I was thinking! Come on, I'll make some, it will warm us up!'

He pulled her back. 'Hang on, hang on, *cucufato!* What is Marmite to do with Modesto?'

'His voice is rich and dark brown and full of warmth . . .'

'Hah! I won't ask you what drink comes to your mind when you think of your poor old Pepe!'

'Cooking sherry,' and he chased her down the drive, hooting like an owl.

Gualterio, returning from his evening stroll, watched them. Then gazed up at the starless sky. 'Dolores,' he said, addressing his late wife, 'Magda and I did our best with the boys. Honestly, *querida*, we really did try!'

*　　　*　　　*

The car had met him at the airport, but Vito himself was not in attendance and had sent apologies with his driver, Gaetano. Moreover, Bobby's arrival at the villa near Turin coincided with the onset of a bad cold. Keta's first sight of her husband's old friend was a tall figure in a tweed overcoat with a scarf around much of his face.

'I'm so sorry,' he apologised, removing the scarf and revealing a chronically-running nose. 'Perhaps it was foolish of me to come. Germs and all that, when Vito's just had flu,' but she smiled and led him into the hall, 'Don't you worry about it, Bob, you can wear one of those surgical masks. Vee is so anxious to see you!'

Compared to the magnum opus that was the vestibule of the Bardi household, this hall was small and cluttered, only enough space for about a hundred statues. A good second home though for Chelsea, if they ever had to close down Stamford Bridge.

Once divested of his overcoat by a blankly goodlooking man called Massimo, Keta escorted him into a drawing-room and suggested a drink before taking him to Vito.

'Scotch, please, er . . . Kate. Thank you.' He sat down and quietly appreciated his new surroundings; the bright gold of the upholstery defeated the sunlight, and it was serene and pleasantly warm.

'So – how is Vito?' smirking at the generously-brimming tumbler. 'He sounded rather low when I rang him from Rome. I thought his flu was on the mend? He said it was, when we spoke at Christmas.'

She sat opposite him, her Scotch matching his own. 'Cheers,' she said, and smiled at him briefly. 'Vee is . . .'

He glanced at her.

'Vee isn't well at all, Bob.'

'Flu germs can be buggers, can't they? But then, I don't suppose his decision to give up his career helped, either. Vito without singing? Must have shaken him up. Am I right?'

Keta smiled, as if in acknowledgement. 'You and Vito go way back, don't you?' And at his emphatic nod, 'He speaks of you constantly. Very constantly.' She twitched her skirt. 'That is why I agreed to this meeting, Bobby. Because Vee isn't simply unwell. He is very sick. The physician came to see him on Christmas Day –'

Alarmed, 'And I march in here with fucking – beg your pardon – germs of my own! Look, I'd better go, Kate, and – yes, I'll come back in a week or two, when he's kicked off this bug!'

'Bob, sit down, honey. The physician . . . well, he had him taken to the clinic, for tests. They kept him there for three days, until yesterday evening. Then they allowed him to come home. He has a nurse with him.'

'Christ, it isn't pneumonia, is it?'

'Pneumonia that won't go away, Bobby.' Her eyes were steady. 'He knows I will tell you before you see him.' She dropped her gaze for a second. 'He won't be getting out of bed again, Bob. He has Aids.'

Bobby's glass swerved. 'He's got fucking what?'

'HIV positive,' steadily. 'Very, very positive.' She began to weep without a sound, eyelids and green shadow pressed tightly.

He automatically went to her, arms comforting while his disbelieving voice cried 'They must be wrong! Bloody quacks! It can't –'

'The tests, Bobby, the tests. They were positive. And his skin – dreadful little brown . . .' She choked into the stranger's shoulder. 'He's so thin, so bloody thin . . .' As she sobbed, he muttered 'Not Vito. Jesus Christ, not Vito!'

Then she drew back with a shaky smile and comforted him, this friend.

The stunned face stared straight ahead. She refilled his glass. And stroked his hand. 'Bob, you will go see him, won't you?'

'Oh fuck it, oh Christ!' His eyes glimmered. He nodded, yes.

He was standing, nervously balancing on the balls of his feet. 'How long? For Vito?'

She touched his elbow. 'Three months, they said. Until March.' Then, 'Come on. I'll take you to him. You feel okay?'

He nodded, wanted to shake his head. 'For once,' he said slowly and with pain, 'I shall be at a loss for words. Imagine that.'

\*       \*       \*

Monda Ballena compressed her lips on the fresh lipstick, adjusted her blue turban, put on her matching gloves. She was satisfied. The recording had gone smoothly. She hoped that her next engagement would be equally smooth.

The car from the BBC would be waiting for her downstairs. She looked at her watch, and impatiently tugged the strap. It had been chafing her wrist all the way through the final session, and had left an itching sore.

She walked through the studio, waving to the producer and the crew. The future cover of the new album hung there, blown up to giant proportions. She liked what she saw. One half black with her silhouette in white. The other half in reverse with the silhouette of the recently-discovered Russian tenor. The title was *Concerto*. Pity about his name, she frowned. 'Monda Ballena' looked neat and decipherable even when walking past at speed. His name did not. And he refused to change or even shorten it, despite severe pressure. So there it was, a challenge to the sleeve-designers: Anatoly Sergei Medvetseivich. Everyone called him 'Toly', except the album cover.

She was escorted to the waiting car with the usual deference. Still raining; sneaky powerful drops that felt like melted ice. She was happy to sink into the upholstery and warmth, and gradually eased off her shoes until they merely clung to her toes.

Twenty minutes to get to the BBC. Damned interviews. She

certainly wasn't mad about this one. The BBC were now very keen to hear all about the Charity Gala in Seville. From being an obscure event of merely Italo-Iberian interest, it had suddenly escalated into British prime-time, thanks to the collapse of Vito Lavagna and his puzzlingly sudden retirement.

They would, of course, try to pump her about the drugged-up old fart, no two ways about that. She sniffed. Just let them try. What the bloody poof did with his own body was his business, certainly not that of the BBC.

Loyalty to one's profession, she thought. Monda says nothing.

*  *  *

'This is BBC Radio 3 FM. Good evening; I am Tarquin Tillerton Tisker, and this is "Change of Air". After the news summary, I shall be welcoming my first guest, the renowned Spanish soprano, Monda Ballena, who is currently . . .'

He glanced over his shoulder, saw the familiar turban bobbing behind the glass panel, and waved in greeting and relief.

Monda allowed herself to be conducted to the transmission studio; sat through an incomprehensible news bulletin, then an elaborate introduction, and subsequently had to listen to herself singing *The Willow Song* to which she listened critically.

Afterwards, she was polite and sweet and answered a few generalities, glad that her English was so poor. It gave her time to consider her answers: and she knew that it wouldn't be long before this waistcoated young know-all got on to the subject of Vito.

Poor dear Vito.

'*Madame* Ballena, we are hearing a great deal about a Gala concert to be held later this month, in Seville . . . .' A warm trustworthy tone.

Cautiously, 'Ah yes, is so. Is for charities, variouses.'

'Quite so. I understand that rehearsals are well under way, despite the sad collapse of Vito Lavagna . . .?'

I'll defend the turd if it kills me.

'*Madame*, we have heard a rumour at the BBC that is worrying many people . . .'

258

Watch his face when I confirm that silly flu story! Drugs, indeed!

'. . . that in fact, although the concert will be televised live, you and the other soloists will be miming to a recording made earlier.'

Unprepared, Monda turned scarlet. 'Ees not! Ees live to be! We do not never of the mime, ees live, *el concierto*, we sing as from minute of broadcast start!'

'But we have heard –'

'Eet would be dishonestly, for to mime!'

The matter was politely dropped.

Monda returned thoughtfully to her hotel. Tomorrow, she would try to ensure that the producer of the Gala was quietly squashed by a truck.

# 16

His striped shirt had bulged, fingers steepling; and Chianti gurgled at ten-minute intervals from carafe to glass as Luciano Bardi had considered the idea.

It all depended, of course, on the complete agreement of the four.

Don't let them bullshit you, Roberto, he said. No maybe's, no call me again in a year's time, no crap. Just yes or no, one definite commitment.

He had scribbled and talked into a machine and blew dust off a calculator.

Fazzoletto? He's okay, he's a showman, they'd love the fat bastard if he sang the Bible backwards off-key. Only for Christ's sake, don't let him appear draped in those bloody shawls, he looks like a crowd of hairy gipsies. And try to dissuade him from singing the orgasm song . . . . . . *Nessun Dorma*, Roberto, *Nessun Dorma*. Apart from everyone being pissed off with it, it is not an educational nor pleasant sight, all that gasping and licking his top lip at the end of it. We want this on family TV, Drach.

Right! – next guy on the list. Martes. Another bloody good showman, looks ready for a hearty screw even in a death scene. Suggest cameras off him when he starts leering. You'll know when that's about to happen, he only raises one eyebrow and leaves it there. Memo that, Umberto, if you please.

Now. The other baby. Ah yes, of course. The *Mattinata* Mudlark. Up there with the best even if he does stand on tiptoe to reach the high notes. From what I hear, Roberto, we'll – Armando, make a note of this – need to get him special evening trousers with a glued zip. Bionda Merdina's my wife's niece.

So – now we come to Zubair Ahmet. Yes, indeed, excellent choice, know him quite well. Wields a mean stick; he'll treat two orchestras with the contempt they deserve, especially if he agrees to the Italian pair I've got in mind. Apart from the wind section in the Magia Armonica – all would-be priests, celebrate Communion before they blow a fucking note – they'd have him on fried bread with garlic if he wasn't the decisive bastard he is.

So there we have it, Roberto. I'm on if they are, if God is. Wait for this meeting of theirs, then call me. I shall have my engine running in pole position, with an extra phone in each hand. So go, *ragazzo*, God speed!

\* \* \*

This, in part, Bobby had relayed to Isa as she listened carefully to his voice down the line from London. He had puzzled her. Only called her a silly mare once, and even that was half-hearted. When she asked why he sounded so subdued, he merely said that his cold had made him feel a bit low. Added that he had been to see Vito and he wasn't as well as he should be, so they'd had a really cheerful time.

Now, on a blowy evening, dressed in a brown silk blouse and matching ankle-length velvet skirt, she paused on the terrace and peered through the vines into the kennel sitting room. Martes had not yet arrived.

The evening meal would be served with total informality, plates and fingers, while they talked. All were due to leave before midnight.

Mina had evinced interest in the planned menu, and then distress. As Ana and Elena tried to cope with a stream of instructions from Isa, she ventured to suggest that toast with meat paste was hardly suitable either as an entrée or side dish, especially not thirty slices of it with a token garnish of watercress.

'Toast fingers, perhaps, with anchovies?' hopefully.

Firmly, 'These are men, Mina, not ladies at a church social.' And Mina shuddered as onion after big Spanish onion was chopped, and the vast result tipped on to chunks of lettuce lining a ceramic tray normally used for a sixteen-pound turkey.

'Right!' briskly. 'That's the salad, and if they want tomatoes, they can whistle.'

'It won't do,' murmured Mina, distraught. 'Pio will need more than that!'

'I am aware of that – Ana is going to cook him a goose, aren't you, Ana? No problem. Now, where did I put the sausages? Those big beef ones – can you see them, Mina?'

Mina said that you could hardly lose sight of eight kilos of sausages from the English delicatessen in Los Culitos, especially when they were in a massive Union Jack-patterned carrier bag.

'Is the bread baking?'

'It is baking. Did you really need four ovens?'

'Five would have been better, but if Pio is to have his goose . . . Damn, nearly forgot the cheese – Elena, pass me that big block, will you?'

'I've got a nice box of Boussaint in my store room,' wistfully.

'Cheddar, Mina, Cheddar! Big gutsy chunks, great with chutney!'

Mina had retired, baffled and beaten.

And now, on the terrace, Isa checked her wide skirt pocket for notebook and pen, and breezed into the sitting room where Buzzer and Pio were conversing about sheep. Pepe had gone into the study to answer the phone. She was feeling pleased and anxious, since she had been elected chairwoman of the forth-coming proceedings.

Pepe returned, grinning. She frowned slightly. Why had he decided to wear that awful cardigan? He looked like a lawyer trying to be informal.

'Martes,' he announced solemnly, 'sends his apologies – he can't join us. He's had an accident.' He tried not to snigger as his guests looked anxious.

Modesto, it transpired, had been giving his daughter Sara a driving lesson when the car phone suddenly chirped, making Sara jump and take her hands off the wheel. She was unhurt; Modesto had a bruised collarbone. The doctors had told him he must rest, if he was to be fully operational for his flight to New York and *Rigoletto*.

'He says,' concluded Pepe, 'that whatever date we decide, we're to ring him immediately – he'll rearrange anything that happens to stand in the way.'

'Well, then,' said Isa, disappointed, 'we'd better begin. Drinks, anyone?'

Pio and Buzzer were back at the bar before she had finished. Pepe gave her the familiar secret look that sent light bulbs buzzing on her skin. She went to him while the others squabbled over the wine selection and Buzzer told Pio to shut up about bloody sheep and photographs.

'You look eatable,' he whispered, casting a quick glance at the bar and running his fingers across her breasts.

'Stop it, you idiot', she hissed doubtfully. Then 'So do you,' forgetting the cardigan.

'Christ in socks, I could −'

'Will you stop?' giggling softly, holding his hand as it teased.

Smiling into her eyes, 'Look, the soldiers are standing at attentive!'

She moved away quickly as Pio roared 'Hey, Pulgarcito! You got a trumpet stuck down your pants? When do we get down to business, eh?'

'I suggest, gentlemen,' said Isa, dismissing buzzing bulbs for brisk efficiency, 'that we start right now,' and Pio hoisted her on to the table, where she laughingly arranged her skirt and took out the notebook and pen. 'Alright, *querido*?' she grinned, as Pepe sat down and crossed his legs experimentally, his face red.

'Let us open the meeting,' he said pompously.

Pio said plaintively, 'I'm hungry.'

Isa banged a bottle of Rioja three times. 'Gentlemen, I call you to order!'

Three faces looked at her attentively.

'Gentlemen, I declare this meeting open. The one item on the Agenda is −' She paused with a beatific smile. '− the Arena della Doccia!'

'Good,' said Pio, rubbing his hands. 'Now we've sorted that out, I declare the meeting closed. Isabel, where's my goose?'

\*     \*     \*

August 6th.

During her telephone conversation with Bobby, she wondered

how many times she had scrawled and doodled that date in her notebook since the meeting.

'It's agreed!' she said happily. 'Everyone agreed! We rang Martes, he's happy with it: so, Bob, you can tell *Signor* Bardi that it's official! Oh – and the four of them are meeting in Milan on the 30th, to start planning the programme! By the way, how's your cold?'

'Thanks for bloody asking! It's so-so.'

Isa sniggered. '*Soso* means half-baked in Spanish!'

'Oh piss off, you silly mare, let me get on with my call to Luciano!'

'Right! Oh, one more thing before you go – Buzzer wants his orchestras fixed and confirmed before anything else, tell Bardi. He'd like to know before the 30th.'

'Sure it's orchestras, not sheep?'

'What? Oh, the sheep! Have you seen the photograph? It was on the back page of *La Vanguardia* this morning!' Or rather, it had been, until Lluís had claimed it for the door of his toy cupboard. The photo was, in fact, becoming something of a cult item in Europe. Sales of sellotape and drawing pins had soared, thereby boosting the economy of several countries in the Community.

August 6th. As she dialled Eve's number, Isa found it hard to believe that Grosvenor Dolores would be reality in a pram by then, nearly two months old.

'Did you get my Christmas card?' demanded Eve.

Isa thought rapidly. 'Oh yes, thanks, it was beautiful!'

An audible sniff. 'Don't know why you say that, it came from a box of thirty from Tesco's. Where was yours, or don't they sell them in Spain?'

'Oh Lord, I'm sorry, things were so hectic here . . . I'll make it up to you and Clair when we next meet up –'

'And when will that be, do you think? Soon?'

'We're coming over to London next month! Pepe has to get the Charity Gala out of the way, and –'

'The what?'

'A concert. In Seville.'

'And what will *you* be doing – selling oranges?'

'Very funny. Look, will you listen? We'll be in London for most of February. Eve, we're getting married there, on the 21st!'

'Oh, that's nice – congratulations! Are we invited?'

'Don't be so silly, of course you are! Anyway, I'll see you before then; Pepe will be busy with recording, and at the Royal Opera House, so I'll have some free time. . . . Eve? I've got some more news for you, you'll never believe it, but we're –'

'Look, I've got to go, the window-cleaner's arrived for his money. Ring me when you get here, okay? Bye!'

'– having a baby,' finished Isa to the silent phone.

\*     \*     \*

In Hamburg, Pio was brushing most of his beard to a point and glancing in the mirror. His stomach bulged beneath the grey velvet jacket and he stroked it fondly as if it were purring.

The orchestra was deafening over the sound system in his dressing-room, but it didn't bother him. He hummed with the trumpets. He certainly didn't think of it as rivalry, he and Martes both doing *Rigoletto* at virtually the same point in the season. No reason to. His was first, and his was going to be the best. He was going to do more with *La Donna è Mobile* than Martes would ever believe possible. It would become exclusively his. Like *Nessun Dorma*.

His eyes rested on the envelope on his dressing-table. The back of it was covered with smudged scrawl from a blunt pencil: the vague ideas for his concert selection in August. The whole concept was getting to him, bugger Pulgarcito if he wanted *Torna a Surriento*, that one was his! Martes hadn't yet uttered a word as to his own choices.

A knock on the door. '*Herr* Fazzoletto! Six minutes, please!'

'*Danke*whatever,' he called, and dabbed the thick grey make-up on his eyelids. Checked his teeth, ran his tongue over them. Ready for Act III. This was where he liked to picture Verdi somewhere in the ether slapping his forehead and saying 'Sod it, whenever Fazzoletto sings the Duke of Mantua, I know I should have called it that instead of *Rigoletto*!' Especially, Pio thought as he tested his bladder, when I am in such good voice.

Also in good voice was his Gilda. Pity her face didn't match it, he mused. The shape of it belonged in a toolshed. On the other hand, his current Maddalena was of mixed blood and flamboyantly seductive. Balloon Boobs! Boobs that quarrelled with her blouse and nearly gave him a black eye if he approached from the wrong angle.

What nipples! He smacked his lips. Brown ping-pong balls. He already had a glossy signed photograph of her, with a tantalising glimpse of each. He intended to present it to Adriana when he got home. So what, that Martes had got Cherri as his Gilda? Pio had his Balloon Boobs!

'Three minutes, *Herr* Fazzoletto!'

He burped up the last of his Coke, and glanced again at the envelope. 'Check with Pulgarcito,' it said.

He opened the door. On with the nipples, and fuck Pulgarcito!

*       *       *

'Cherri, you can't do this to me! Not again, for Christ's sake! What the hell is it with you? Have you got a hang-up about New York, or what?'

He tilted his chair, leaned back, winding the telephone cord round his fingers. His collarbone was still painful, his temper none too good. Listened for a few impatient moments.

Angrily, 'Never mind about oh Moddie dear, listen to me . . . No, you listen to ME, dammit! This *Rigoletto* could be a stunner, a fantastic follow to our *Otello*, another classic! You'll make Fazzoletto's Gilda sound like the elderly shit she is, and yet you want to toss it all away? . . . Yes . . . .Yes, I . . . Cherri, if you dare . . .'

He listened to the tinny echoing voice from Naples, and his frown stayed where it was. 'Yes, I understand that, darling, but surely if you crammed in a few pain-killers . . . . Well, didn't they give you a cough bottle? That balsam stuff I take is damn good.'

He laughed, swung the chair upright. 'Thanks, kind lady! . . . well, what does the bloody doctor say? You haven't convinced me yet, darling, and . . . WHAT? REPEAT THAT!'

The tinny voice rang in his ear. Modesto Martes sagged.

'I'm going to be sick,' he said when the voice stopped. 'They've got WHO?'

He walked to the bar with the phone, and one-handedly fumbled with the cork of the whisky bottle. A few more squawks down the line.

'I will not!' he thundered. 'You hear me, Cherri? You will get your backside out of that bed, as of now! I will not sing with La fucking Lucha! . . . Cherri, please, darling! Surely by next month . . .'

He could see the second hand sweeping round the face of the clock as the tinny voice spoke uninterrupted for several minutes. He stared at it. How many times had it gone round. How many. The voice in his ear was only punctuated by eyes that widened and a jaw that grew stiff. His hand had fallen away from the bottle.

Eventually he murmured something. Replaced the receiver as Mimosa breezed in, 'Just had an idea, for your concert! Why don't you upstage Fazzoletto and do *La Donna è Mobile*, after all it will be fresh in everyone's . . . Desto? What is it, darling?' And 'Here, *querido*, drink this,' pouring him a tot of whisky.

He took it, drank it, coughed. 'Cherri!' he said, his voice slurred as if he had been drinking all morning. 'She won't be coming to New York with me! She won't be . . . Mimosa!'

The anguish tore from him, and he sat down at the bar, the stool rocking.

'What is it, my love?' Alarmed, she hugged him, kissed the top of his head.

He clung to her. 'Cherri! Oh my poor Cherri! She's just told me . . . Mimosa! . . . lung cancer . . .'

He broke down and wept.

\*　　\*　　\*

Pau said plaintively, 'Uncle Pepe, he won't!' He shook the string attached to Bufido's neck. The red ribbon had disappeared shortly after Christmas. The cat stared.

'Mmmm?' Pepe and Alfredo were bent over the household accounts. There were two ashtrays on the table, one full of paperclips, one acting as a saucer for a cup of coffee.

'He won't sing!'

Without lifting his eyes from the meaningless figures, Pepe murmured 'Who won't? . . . *Un huevo!*' he swore, trying to follow Alfredo's gliding pen. 'Why do I get dragged into this? You're the bloody scientist, brother, not me!'

'Chemist, not a frigging mathematician,' and the tip of the biro halted and dug into the paper. 'Look at this! Nearly a hundred thousand fucking pesetas for wine in October? What do we do here, bathe in the bloody stuff?'

'Bufido won't!' and Pau tugged at his uncle's pullover.

Pepe glanced down with a smile. 'Bufido won't what?''

'I told you – he won't sing!'

'Don't be so stupid!' snapped Alfredo. 'He doesn't sing because he's a bloody cat and he's bloody stuffed!'

'He purrs, so why can't he sing!' the child snapped back.

Pepe's smile widened. 'He . . . er . . . purrs?'

'Oh yes! When we're in bed at nighttime, he purrs extra loud to keep *el coco* away!'

Pepe swung the boy and Bufido on to the table. 'And does he miaow, too?'

'Get him off there! I'm trying to sort this bloody mess out!' and Alfredo jerked a ring-binder from beneath his son's bottom. He suddenly grinned at Pau. 'If you want to hear real miaowing, listen to Uncle Pepe singing!'

Pepe nudged his brother's arm, and a wavy line of red ink extinguished part of the debit column. 'You clumsy bastard!'

'Pau,' thoughtfully, 'which is your favourite song? If you had to listen to just one song, all the way through – what would it be? Do you know?'

'Oh!' No-one had asked him that before. He wriggled. 'With words and everything?'

'Christ, you're not going to warble for us, are you? I don't think my bloody stomach could stand it!'

'Yes, Pau, with proper words.' Groundwork, he told himself. For the concert.

Alfredo yelped. 'Who the fuck's been buying sausages? Look at this, enough here to feed bloody Ethiopia! And cheese! Jesus Christ, is there a famine coming that I don't know about?'

268

'I think that was probably Isa, when the boys came over,' grinning.

'Uncle Pepe, I like the one you sing in France-language!'

Pepe smiled. 'Which one is this, *precioso*? I sing quite a lot of French songs.'

Alfredo tittered.

Pau said, '*Papi* says you always sing this one when you've had a skinful. What's a skinful?'

'Oh he does, does he,' grimly, as Alfredo suddenly laughed. 'I think I know the one he means, *hombre*!' and clasped his hands, raising himself on tiptoe and gazing owlishly. ('Look, *Papi*'s being you!') Sniffed twice, then began to sing in a shrill falsetto.

Pau applauded, giggling, 'That's it, Uncle Pepe!'

Uncle Pepe jabbed open stiff fingers into his brother's solar plexus, then looked at Pau. 'Don't worry about *Papi*, he's only pretending to be dead.' Thoughtfully, '*La Vie en Rose*, mmm? Perhaps it would fit somewhere. I'll keep it in mind.'

Belatedly, 'Good boy, Pau!'

\*     \*     \*

'Vroom vroom, Luciano!' And Bardi grinned, in pole position as he had promised.

The Vatican, no problem. No need even to hint that four of the cardinals had been seen with their soutanes at miniskirt level and doing strange things behind a stack of linen baskets during Solemn Mass; just a steady look and the casual mention of names.

The Vatican nodded pompously, of course you may use the della Doccia, you only have to ask, Luciano!

Next, the orchestras. The two he had had in mind since Roberto Drach first mentioned the whole idea: the Magia Armonica of Florence, and the Teatro dell' Orfeo of Rome. Could be a few fist-fights along the Appian Way, but Ahmet was just the man to deal with them.

Bardi had now assigned a deputy conductor to assist in rehearsals, and Ahmet had arranged for a Spanish accompanist to attend the early vocal get-togethers.

Byron Larch and Decca had been notified.

269

The small fry having been dealt with, he could now turn his energies to sorting out the world-wide network and live coverage in sound and vision. Bardi smiled. How very interesting life could be!

*     *     *

Sadly, it seemed that there was no such thing as respect in Seville.

So brooded Pepe Contreras as he sat, arms folded, while the girl applied his make-up and dabbed occasionally at the eye-shadow, frowning professionally. Her towel was smudged with patches of brown and blue.

No respect. Take the stagehands, for example. An odd mix, as usual, from the ever-present British fed up with job centres and incentive schemes, who usually greeted him with 'Shift your arse, Thingy,' to the few Spaniards who regarded each backdrop as though it had come from outer space and had to be prodded and discussed at length over a game of cards. One of them, a girl, had made a point of whispering '*Buenos días, señor,*' in a shy manner every time he passed by. He had afforded her a number of glances in appreciation of her fresh blonde hair, until she had heard a colleague shout, 'Oi, Mickey Mouse, piss off!' when he was busily appreciating and caught his foot in a moving cable. After that, she giggled whenever she saw him.

God in lace pyjamas, this was going to be a farce! As well as the lack of respect, there were also the chalk marks. No-one seemed to know now which belonged to whom. Monda Ballena had insisted that hers were to be bright red. However, these and most of the others had been scrubbed away by ladies with buckets during the night, and the producer snapped that they'd have to rely on hasty white ones and their bloody memories.

And Martes. There was a puzzle for you. Same swagger, same crunching slap of bonhomie that made your lungs bounce, same twinkle. Yet for all that, a look that saw nothing except thoughts too painful to bear. Odd, thought Pepe, Martes has usually got as much deep thought as a dead ant.

And everyone, of course, was talking about Vito Lavagna. Some said he should have retired forty years ago. Others like

Monda said well, there you are – drugs! Bragas said that that was rubbish, he was just a pathetic old shit with no backbone.

All that Pepe really wanted to do was think about Lorca and the song-cycle, which would officially launch the Magda Fund on the world. If possible, he would like the televised recording to coincide with the birth of his child, rather than with the anniversary of her death.

Pepe exercised his mouth and throat as the make-up girl continued. Her hands were light: reminded him of Isa, thought of her sitting at home with the family, ready to switch on the TV for the Gala. He thought of her hand resting automatically on Grosvenor Dolores, and smiled gently.

The door of the dressing-room squeaked open, and Modesto came in, his make-up finished. 'Can I interrupt?' smiling at the girl.

She simpered back, whipped the towel away, then frowned. 'Your hair,' she said.

'Come in, Modesto . . . What's wrong with it?'

'It looks like fur,' she said accusingly. 'Have you just washed it?'

'Well, about an hour or so ago. What do you mean – like fur?' He gazed into the mirror.

'What I say. You look like an ad for Animal Rights,' and she uncapped a tube of gel, smeared some between her palms and briskly rubbed his head.

'Hang on!' came the muffled protest as his head was buffeted up and down, 'What do you think you're doing, your bloody laundry?'

Modesto cackled quietly and sat down. Crossed his legs. 'I'm worried,' he announced.

The girl proceeded to brush vigorously. 'Nasty boil coming up on your neck,' she said conversationally. 'Want me to put something on it?'

He moaned slightly as she found another tube, cream that smelt of perfume and sour milk, and daubed the back of his neck energetically.

'You'll need a sticking-plaster on that soon,' she said cheerily, 'It's going to be a real mess. Painful, too. Good job your hair covers it!'

271

She smiled at them both, gathered her things, and departed.

'So, what are you worried about?' Pepe asked, touching the back of his neck warily.

'Bloody *Pearl Fishers* duet,' moodily.

'Why? All you've got to do now is mime to the bloody thing!'

'That is just the point, *amigo mío*. In the recording, I put in three extra notes, trying to be damn clever. Suppose I forget when we're miming? My voice will be heard singing them, but my mouth will be shut!'

Pepe grinned. 'Shouldn't worry, if I were you. All eyes will be on me as usual, they won't notice if you sit down and start juggling bananas!'

'Bastard! Uncaring furry-headed bastard!' He walked off, sighing.

'FIFTEEN MINUTES PLEASE!'

He checked his cufflinks, sipped his mineral water. The collar of his dress-shirt rubbed suddenly against the nape of his neck. The growing boil was getting quite sore under the sticky cream and the heat of the lights. Sighed, and thought wistfully once more of Isa and Grosvenor Dolores.

\* \* \*

'You feel up to watching it, Baby?' asked Keta gently.

The nurse, Antonia, had finished her ministrations for the evening. The last injection had been given. She stood to one side, allowing Keta to smooth the pillows behind his neck. Poor old thing, she thought, and took off her mask and rubber gloves, smiling at him as she did so.

'I'm okay,' Vito murmured, and shifted himself, trying to get comfortable on his bones. Keta manoeuvred the table to the bottom of the bed, looked at her watch, and switched on the portable set.

'I should have been there.' The voice was dull.

'Just thank your lucky moons and stars that you aren't,' Keta said firmly, adjusting the sound. 'You can relax and watch those poor idiots. Judit was telling me that the whole Gala is going to be mimed by the solos! Did you know about that?'

He nodded, aching inside, wishing.

Antonia bade them goodnight. Keta squeezed his hand.

*     *     *

Bobby Drach frowned at the screen.

Too late to call in an engineer. Why was it bloody flashing like that, lines going up and down? Perhaps it was the Spanish relay. Years behind in technology, must be their fault. Bloody Spaniards. Why didn't they stick to their paella and fucking bullfights?

He went to the set, glowering. Then made a sign of the Cross over it, intoning 'Spectacles–testicles–bollocks–and crotch,' before bashing it with his fist.

The lines hesitated, then disappeared. Smugly, he settled down to watch the Gala.

*     *     *

Alfredo patted the kennel's new television set, told Lluís to sit down and shut up, and accepted a glass of wine from Isa. Gualterio was not there; he had elected instead to go down to Sant Moiseps for a game of billiards – a needle match, he said, between himself and that Andaluz twit, Rodríguez. The Andaluz twit was the village priest.

Isa waited impatiently. Mina smiled, 'Wish you were in Seville with him?'

'Yes,' she replied simply, before Alfredo pointed out that she'd got enough to do without trailing after him all that way.

'Oh I know, I know. Mina, please say you'll come to London a couple of days before the wedding!'

'Mmmm. Well, I suppose we could, and make it a little holiday. Any particular reason?' bending forward to pull up one of Pau's socks.

'My hair, Mina, my hair! Could you do something with it?'

'What?' Mina stared, appalled. 'Me?' and Alfredo sniggered, planted his feet on Bufido.

'Why not you? I'm not going to one of those salons, you come out looking a damned lacquered golliwog. No thank you!' She

273

couldn't remember if she had had her wine allowance: the eggcup she had started using guaranteed her at least three token drinks on social occasions.

'Oh dear God!' said Mina, looking at the jungle of curls and loops, at the uneven lengths of it. Touched it tentatively. 'Isa, I –'

'What you need,' grinned Alfredo, 'is a lawnmower and a pavement artist! Why don't you chop it all off and carry it?'

'Oh *muchas* bloody *gracias*! Pau, that's my foot, not the floor. Mina –?'

'What would you want me to do with it?' warily.

'I don't know, that's just the point! I thought you might have some ideas!'

Pau and Lluís giggled as Alfredo said 'How about wearing a Mexican sombrero?'

'Shut up, Alfredo!'

'Yes, shut up!'

*     *     *

Simón Estertor bowed, motioned the orchestra to rise.

The audience reaction was hardly fevered, thought Monda. Fancy choosing the *Barber of Seville* overture! Of all the predictable – Then she giggled faintly, her thoughts diving elsewhere.

'What's so funny?' asked Teresa Bragas, removing a safety-pin from the neckline of her orange and pink dress. Let the buggers pop out, see if she cared.

Monda tittered. 'Have you heard about darling Fazzoletto?'

'What about the tuneless fat twerp?' dropping the pin on the floor.

'He's making a film!'

Large incredulous eyes. 'A film? Him?'

'It's true, Adriana told me yesterday. He plays the part of a spaghetti salesman –'

'Which he should have been, anyway!' Guffaws, and a frown from the producer.

'A spaghetti salesman,' Monda continued, 'who, they discover, has the most beautiful and heart-stopping tenor voice . . .'

'So why cast him in the part, then?'

274

'Let's not be catty, dear.' Her freshly-spiked eyelashes were beginning to soften stickily in the heat backstage. She nudged Teresa, 'Guess what it's called?'

'*The Fat Zombie?*' cackling.

'Oh, much better than that – *Scusi, Luigi!*'

A shriek of laughter from Bragas, which disturbed Los Quince as they filed past en route for the stage. 'It's called what? *Scusi* bloody *Luigi?*' and her shoulders shook.

The last trailing members of Los Quince glared at the hilarity, then composed their faces into sanctity as they lined up on front of Enrique Cristobales. César Franck had won the battle against Pachelbel, and what was known in the trade as *Penis Angelicus* rang through the air.

'Mealy-mouthed shower,' sniffed Teresa. 'Most of them are half-stoned!'

'Getting nervous, girls?'

'Shove off, Contreras!'

Monda said sedately 'Are you alright, Pepe? You're holding your head on one side.'

'Stiff neck,' he muttered, and went to have a word with the producer.

'Christ, that makes a change, him being stiff up there,' tittered Bragas.

*       *       *

'Yes, Massimo – what is it?'

'There's someone asking to see *Signor* Vito, madam.'

Keta frowned. 'Well, I'm afraid you'll have to tell them that –'

'Who is it?' asked Vito, staring at the screen.

'He wouldn't really say, *signor*. Just that he was called Gianni.'

'Gianni?' A spark of what may have been hope.

'Yes, sir. He said you would remember him.'

'I do. Please show him up.'

'Vito! You aren't well enough!'

'Massimo, please.' His cheeks were flushed. 'Darling, be patient with me. This man I must see.'

'Is it important, Baby?'

275

'Yes, darling. Very.'

'Okay,' she sighed. 'For a few minutes. I'll leave you while you see him. If you need anything, just press the bell. And only a few minutes, you hear?'

'I hear.' He patted his wife's hand. 'Oh – and turn the sound down on that damn thing, will you?'

*     *     *

Wild turbulent applause had greeted Azucarero and El Pedo Negro as they appeared, and now the auditorium glowed ginger and strobe lights flashed. The recorded noise flattened the ears. Jesus Christ, thought Modesto, savagely chewing his thumb nail. Wish I wore a deaf aid, then I could turn it off.

She was going back to Australia. To a clinic. Francesco was going to announce her retirement once they were safely there and away from the media.

She was going back to Australia, she who never cried unless it was from exhaustion after a great performance and her strength had gone. She had once told him that her tears were so rare that they were remembered long afterwards; that when she was thirteen, she had found a bird dead upon its nest, still protecting its stone-cold eggs. 'I cried like a bloody thunderstorm then, Moddie.'

Back to Australia. His chewed thumb touched the corners of his eyes.

Teresa Bragas hissed in his ear, 'Is it true,' jerking her head to where Pepe stood waiting for his entrance cue and massaging his neck, 'that you're planning a big thrash with him and Fazzoletto?'

'I – How the hell do you know about that?'

She winked. Asked sweetly, 'Got your programme worked out yet?'

Warily, 'No. Not yet.'

'Well, do us all a favour and sellotape Contreras' mouth if he wants *Mattinata*! The very title of the – oh no! talk of the bloody devil . . .'

The first bars of *La Mattinata* soared in intro. Pepe walked out of the wings, smile already in place.

276

'Bless him, there he goes, Spain's answer to cot deaths! Go on, Pinocchio, get their blood racing!'

And Modesto snorted with laughter, his dark thoughts abandoned.

*   *   *

'He's on! Uncle Pepe's on! Uncle Pepe, can you see me?'

Alfredo shouted 'Stop waving like a bloody idiot at the screen!'

'Can he see me, *Papi*?'

'Of course he fucking well can't!'

'Alfredo!'

'Why can't he see me? I can see him, so why can't −?'

'Shut up! Isa wants to see him, and she can't while you're jumping up and down like a sodding lunatic!'

'Alfredo! I shan't tell −'

'Sorry, *querida* . . . SIT BLOODY DOWN! . . . Right. Isa, can you see okay?'

Her gaze was lovingly riveted. Like a child, she leaned forward eagerly.

Close-up of Contreras. '*Naufragio de Cristo*!' from Alfredo in disbelief. Then 'Bloody hell, he kept this to himself, little bugger!'

Mina was staring in comical awe. And Isa was puzzled; it didn't look like him at all.

'Why isn't he snarling with his mouth, *Papi*?'

'He isn't sniffing, either,' giggled Lluís. 'He looks like *un maniquí*!'

Tailor's dummy, thought Isa. Lluís is right. Why is he so expressionless? Another close-up. Profile of. No frown of concentration, no snarls, as Pau called them. Just a smooth set face.

'Oh well done, *coño*!' bawled Alfredo. 'Did you see that? An actual facial movement! He blinked! Encore, encore!'

'I missed that,' giggled Mina. She looked at Isa and giggled again.

'Jesus Christ, look! His mouth is moving but there's no singing!'

The camera hastily panned to Estertor jabbing his baton at the cellos.

'But what −?' from Isa. Mina said, 'He's miming, dear.'

'He's −?' staring.

Alfredo exploded with mirth. 'Shit on a tree stump, did you see that? The words were heard but his mouth stayed shut this time! Boy, am I going to change my name!'

Oh dear, *superquerido*. Isa tried loyally not to laugh, but failed.

\*　　\*　　\*

Bobby stared, appalled and fascinated. The chirping of the phone made him jump, and he snatched it up, still staring at Sniffer acknowledging applause.

'Drach? Byron Larch here. Are you by any chance watching the Gala Concert from Seville?'

'No, from Kensington,' he nearly said. But instead, 'I am,' cautiously.

'You'll be seeing Contreras before I do. Kindly tell him that the Arena della Doccia will be run on very different lines – very very different. I am gritting my teeth and waiting for Martes to come on and make an equal prat of himself!'

'Byron, look here, I don't think they had much say –'

'Drach, I am telling, not asking. I am not having three immobile shop-window dummies on MY show! Warn him – and warn him good!'

\*　　\*　　\*

Gianni had kissed him before he left, a sticky patch of Cointreau impaled on his forehead.

Vito left it where it was, feeling the lips on his skin.

Louis, his visitor said, was in Baden Baden. Did Vito know that Louis, too, was not well?

No, Vito replied. What is wrong? And his anxiety stirred.

Gianni had smiled, a warm smile as he drank his Cointreau. 'Can't you guess? Only he is stronger than you, Vito. It will take longer. But he wanted you to have this gift of love. That's what friends are for. And he wanted to see you embracing it.'

The door was closing on the thin figure when the tears began.

\*　　\*　　\*

278

Even Mina was laughing uncontrollably. Isa gave intermittent squeaks.

The boys, bored, had disappeared. Bufido had been left behind, and sat on Alfredo's knee. He wiped his eyes on the cat's tail and gasped 'Oh Christ, it's *Brindisi*!'

– *Brindisi*, the favourite ending to many a fun concert, bouncy rhythm and popular tune, Verdi triumphant as the audience were encouraged to clap along, soloists with champagne.

'What's it like, planning a wedding to a waxwork?' Mina chuckled, then grabbed Isa's arm. 'Oh Lord help us, look at Monda! Is she on castors?'

Alfredo choked on his wine. 'I'm waiting to see Martes gliding like that . . . Oh look, there he goes! . . . whoops! . . . It's a wonder Teresa doesn't shove her champagne glass up –'

'Alfredo!'

Isa said, 'What is Pepe doing, do you think?' They watched, bemused, as the singers endeavoured to form a line in front of the stage and Pepe jumped sideways as if attached to elastic, and disappeared from view.

Roars of laughter. 'Where the hell's he gone?'

'I'm definitely going to change my bloody name! As of now!'

'What about me?' giggled Isa. 'I haven't even changed mine yet!'

'Oh God,' moaned Mina, holding her sides, 'what's that English name people use if they want to be unknown? 'Smeeth?' That's what I'll be, *Señora* Smeeth . . . Oh look, Pepe's back! What's happened to his champagne glass? He had one a moment ago!'

The glare from Bragas was not mimed, nor was the horror on Modesto's face as his chalk marks appeared to go halfway up the curtain and he was left waving his glass aloft while the others huddled in confusion at the other side of the stage. He pretended not to be running as he joined them.

'I'm glad the kids have gone,' said Alfredo solemnly. 'It simply is not suitable for – Christ, what's Pepe got in his hand?'

More shouts of laughter. 'It can't be!'

'It bloody is, you know!'

Isa doubled over.

'It was that bitch Bragas,' gasped Mina. 'She put something in his hand when she did that twirl . . . It looks like a. . .' Helplessly, she sagged against Isa's shoulder.

Alfredo shouted 'It's a bloody feeding-bottle! Look, it's a baby's feeding-bottle, and the silly sod hasn't even realised! Shit, he's raising it to the audience!'

Afterwards, as they mopped their eyes, Alfredo grinned evilly. 'I'm glad I thought of recording that!'

'Alfredo, you didn't!'

He got up and switched off the video recorder, and pressed rewind. 'We could blackmail him with this,' solemnly.

'We mustn't laugh when he comes home,' laughed Isa.

'Of course not,' tittered Mina.

'Wouldn't dream of it!' cackled Alfredo.

*　　*　　*

Later, Vito lay back on his pillows, holding Keta's hand. She smoothed his hair gently, then gave his moustache a little loving tweak.

'Poor old moustache,' she murmured. 'It doesn't look very golden at the moment, does it? Never mind, Baby, we'll soon have you as good as new, and twice as . . .'

A smile came and went, he touched the moustache and then the teardrop on her face.

'Keta?'

'My Baby?'

'You know what I'm going to ask you, don't you?'

She looked at him steadily, watching his eyes.

'Don't you!'

She nodded. The room was warm and quiet. He smiled at her. 'I never have to spell things out to you, do I?'

She shook her head. Opened her mouth to speak, but he forestalled her.

'I want this to be a heart attack,' he said. 'Aggravated by pneumonia. You understand? I want it reported as that, and no more.' His thumb stroked her hand. He continued slowly 'It's the only thing I can leave you that means anything, Keta. My dignity.. And yours.'

They were silent. Two clocks ticked in syncopation.

'No-one to know about this illness but you and I and Bobby. Trust him; he's kept secrets of mine for years, even after we parted bitterly.' His voice drooped a little. 'The doctors may suspect such an end but they will suspect privately. Even Bobby will not know how the end was.'

'No-one will know,' she whispered quietly, as though the clocks were listening.

'No-one,' she repeated firmly.

She impulsively lay beside him and stroked his face. 'When, Baby?'

'When we say goodnight,' gently. 'Put them in my Scotch. There's my darling – my Keta.'

For the first time, they faced each other on a bed.

'Don't forget, my precious Keta. Heart. Pneumonia.'

She nodded, eyes tightly closed, terrified.

'No crying,' he murmured.

'Stars and stripes forever,' she choked.

'Good girl, my love. Our secret, mmm?'

'Our secret, Baby . . . Oh Vee!' and she buried her face in his chest. His arm went around her.

Clocks ticking peacefully.

# 17

The news was released by the secretary at half-past two on the following afternoon. An eulogy followed the end of the five o'clock news bulletin, and longer tributes were broadcast on both radio and television during the evening. Spain was quick to follow the Italian lead, and rival channels hastily re-scheduled their programmes to run clips of his performances and the first of many tributes from the opera fraternity.

The press was seething. Too late for the evening editions, old news by tomorrow, just an extra-long obit in the culture pages. But then frustration turned and chewed its way out of the bag held by the broadcasters: a tip-off. Anonymous.

The press exulted. Headlines on the following day throughout Europe were unanimous and unactionably clear – Lavagna had died of Aids. (Or, as the Daily Mirror put it, 'Aids, not *Aida*', plus a column explaining to its readers what *Aida* was.)

Stunned and hating – who? who? One of his lovers? – Keta unplugged her phone, shut herself in their drawing-room, spoke to no-one except Massimo and the photograph on the grand piano, squeezing his gold lighter in her hand, pacing.

In London, Bobby Drach cried and wondered.

In Barcelona, the happy laughing house that had greeted Pepe on his return was subdued and grey in sound. He tried to reach Keta by phone but failed. He rang Bobby, who cried.

Modesto thought of Cherri and the stone-cold eggs in the nest; and Mimosa quietly got on with ordering flowers and writing an affectionate letter.

Turin witnessed the arrival of Pio Fazzoletto and his wife, he grim-faced and saying nothing, she in dark glasses and a camel hair coat, silent.

Ballena spoke on the telephone to Bragas, horrified by the

truth. They sobbed together, 'The poor poor old thing, dearest Vito.'

And Bobby cried, his fingers curled into a fist.

*       *       *

A memorial service would be held in Rome at a later date, when the scandal was as dead as February's snowdrops. The funeral itself took place on a mild damp day, a quiet and semi-private affair. A senior reporter and a photographer from *La Stampa* were permitted to attend, and Turin police were drafted near the place of interment and around the villa.

As it happened, they needn't have bothered since there was a live televised football match that afternoon and dead tenors provided no competition.

Pio and Adriana Fazzoletto were there in their capacity as old friends, and Bobby arrived from London carrying a cellophane package of three white roses. He asked Keta if he should lay them by the grave, but she smiled and shook her head, and said that she would put them by the photograph on the grand piano so that Vito could see and enjoy them.

She allowed members of his biggest fan club to attend the ceremony, and she was touched to see that each one brought his or her own bunch of flowers, each heart with its personal tribute. They all cried.

Pepe was unable to travel to Turin. He was having medical treatment. The boil had evolved into an abscess, and he brooded around the house and kennel with a large wad of gauze and padding held in place by transparent sticky tapes which stuck to the hairs on his neck and tugged painfully if he turned his head. The four-a-day antibiotics came with a no-alcohol warning, which did nothing to sweeten his mood. He went instead with Gualterio to the church in Sant Moiseps at the very hour of the funeral, where they knelt for quarter of an hour, while the priest droned to himself at the far end of the nave wondering how he had acquired a congregation of two for the private prayers about his arthritis.

On the day of the funeral, Vito Lavagna's last album, *Canzone d'Amore*, became a best-seller and so outstripped the current contender for the coveted Gigli Medallion, Fazzoletto himself. From the limousine, riding back to the villa, Keta saw record shops ablaze with her husband's face.

*　　*　　*

The sadness of Vito and the despairing shock of Cherri de Canasta were talked of at length at the start of the meeting in Milan; but after the sadness came the business, and Buzzer wasted no time in settling his three tenors in his hotel suite, supplying them with a selection of soft drinks.

He ignored their fretful expressions as they stared at the cans of fizzy orange and glittering limeade; feet astride, smoothing down his pullover of maroon and grey, he scanned a sheet of paper in front of him.

'Right!' briskly. 'Ideas, please, gentlemen. Pio?'

Pio produced a creased envelope. It was covered with scribble and a few doodles. 'My thoughts so far,' he grinned.

Buzzer stared at it, horrified. 'Is that all?' and 'May I?', stretching out his hand and scanning it quickly. He looked up, and waved the envelope.

'Gentlemen, this contains Mr Fazzoletto's considered gems. I am almost too moved to read it. He says here, "Ch.with P.,TAS." There are four minims, what could be a semibreve or an egg, an attempt to draw a three-legged horse, and the initial "N".' To general titters, 'Would you care to clarify, please? This could, like Genesis, be the start of something big.'

Pio smirked. 'Certainly, *Maestro*. It means I am to check with Pulgarcito here about *Torna a Surriento*, because that I would like, I would wish.'

Pepe laughed and shook his head, the neck healing well.

'And the letter "N"?'

'*Nessun Dorma*,' to an outcry of 'Oh Christ, how bloody splendid!' and 'Can't you do anything else, you fat moron?'

Buzzer rapped his can of orangeade on the table. 'Any other takers for *Surriento* and *Nessun Dorma*?'

'Going – going – gone,' whispered Pepe.

'Yes!' Modesto raised a hand. '*Nessun Dorma*; let them see a

284

different and handsome face for a change!'

'Mr Martes, this is not a bloody beauty contest! Right, I'll put Pio down for –'

'Hey, Pio, what does the three-legged horse mean?'

'That,' leered Pio, 'is meant to be me!'

Laughter, as Buzzer frowned. 'That is excellent. Two hours to fill, and we've already got two provisional items. May I remind you that I am due to leave Milan this afternoon?'

'Perhaps we could have a juggling act between each number, or circus ponies!'

'Nudes! Nipples! Bare fannies!'

'Gentlemen, please! Modesto, you must have a few thoughts?'

'I have, sir. Why don't we include songs from different countries?'

'Bags me the bloody *Marseillaise!*'

'Shut up, you fat bastard. I meant a song or two in German, and French and so on. Or even English.'

'With you, they won't know the difference,' sniggered Pepe.

Modesto ignored him. 'I was thinking, Buzz – when you had your first meeting at the Little Cretin's place, wasn't there some suggestion of us doing a few lighter numbers with the heavies?'

'Don't you call Isabel a cretin!'

'I wasn't, you bloody stupid –'

Buzzer rapped his can. 'That is so, Modesto.'

'Well, thinking along those lines, why don't we come on in turn, one heavy, one lighter vein, so that we all do two each?'

'That makes six items in all, Modesto. Six items do not a two-hour concert make.'

'Okay, then – four items each,' plaintively.

'With encores!'

'How many times do you intend encoring *Nessun* bloody *Dorma*, you fat fool?'

'We could all join in and encore that right at the end,' grinned Pepe. 'Just after we've done a pop selection. *Rock around the Clock*, and Buddy Holly's –'

'Go fry your testicles, Contreras! Be serious!'

'Wait a second,' murmured Buzzer.

'He's thinking,' whispered Pio.

'What Pepe just said,' slowly, 'about a popular selection. Oh shut up, Modesto,' as Martes began to whistle *As time goes by*. 'Suppose you did all join forces, towards the end, say for the last half hour? After all, they'll want to see you all together, not just in solo.'

'You mean a kind of medley?' asked Pio, twisting a shawl thoughtfully.

'Just so,' Buzzer nodded. 'Well-known songs, folk songs . . . Modesto, did I hear you say something about *West Side Story*? Pepe, you've done that with Cherri – what do you think?'

'Worth considering . . . not a bad idea, actually, to do a couple from that. And what about *Mattinata*?'

'Oh for fuck's sake!'

'At least you know all the bloody words, Shorty!'

'And I know all the words of *La Vie en Rose*,' called Modesto. Pepe grinned. Pau's song. 'So do I!'

'That is not the point of this exercise, gentlemen! You will, in any case, have phonetically-printed libretti in front of you.'

'Will we? Who says so?'

'I do. I've just thought of it. Yes, Pio?'

'What about that German thing, about Vienna?'

'Could you narrow it down, Tubby, there are thousands of songs about bloody Vienna!'

Pio hummed a few bars, and Modesto cried 'Yes, *Wien Wien*! Good one – we can sing that in German!'

'Trying to start World War III, Martes?'

'Not the way he sings German,' tittered Pepe. 'They'll think it's in Japanese,' and ducked as an empty can sped towards him.

Buzzer looked them all reflectively. Said softly, 'How about a drink to assist us, gentlemen? A real drink?'

It was quite surprising what Scotch and soda could do.

*     *     *

The bed in the Dorchester suite nearly ruined their first night in London.

Pepe sat on it. Lay on it. Attempted to bounce up and down on

286

it. He massaged his backside. 'It's like a motorway,' he said angrily..

'So pretend you're a car,' grinned Isa, investigating wardrobe space.

'I need servicing,' he said, looking at her thoughtfully.

'General or specific?'

'Both. My clutch is definitely dodgy.'

'So's your accelerator!' she giggled, and hung three blouses on one coathanger.

'A maid should be doing that,' he frowned. Then, leering, 'There is nothing wrong with my accelerator – like to test it?' and thumped the bed again.

'Just lately,' she said smoothly, draping a pair of his jeans over the blouses, 'your entire engine seems slow to tick over. Aren't you coming up for your MOT soon?' Giggled wildly. Then suddenly remembered, 'Pepe, what's your schedule for tomorrow? Only I'd like to ask Eve and Clair round here – I wanted you to meet them before the wedding . . .'

'I will try to be here if I can, but! Half-past nine, first music call with Nathan West. Afternoon, Royal Opera House, *Samson* talk-through, meet new mezzo Inés Baltasar. But I will do my best. Now come here and overhaul my engine, woman!'

She slammed the wardrobe door, beamed 'But it's only seven o'clock!'

'*Dios mío*, so it is! Time for Grosvenor Dolores to go to bed!'

He flung himself at the bed again, and winced. 'Don't lie on your stomach, you will give our son concussion!'

'Jesus,' she said, 'is this a mattress or cobblestones?' Nuzzled him. 'Don't forget, *superquerido*, Roberto's invited us to his place tomorrow evening.'

'I swear that's the only thing on my mind,' he whispered. 'You getting comfortable, *princesa*?'

'Oh, very! My bones are loving this!'

'Just lie back – pretend you are a service station . . . .Shit!' He suddenly sprang up.

'There's a bloody spring sticking in my arse!' And they began to laugh.

287

'What do you mean, he isn't here?' A raincoated Eve peered round the suite, dripping and indignant. Clair sneezed twice.

'I'm sorry,' said Isa again, 'He's at music call.'

'Music hall? I thought he only sang serious stuff?'

'It's a rehearsal prelim.'

'Oh of course it is, how silly of me! Now that you've explained . . . Clair, put that figurine down, we can't afford to get the damn thing mended!'

'Would you like a drink?'

'Any tea on the hob?'

'Well, if you'd like tea, I can ring for –'

'No, no, bitter lemon will do. Clair, where are you going?'

'Where's the lavatory, Ezzie?'

Isa tittered. 'Through that door, across the pale blue room, down the white steps, through the drawing-room, along the hall, and it's behind the door with a silver knob!'

'I hope you're not desperate,' murmured Eve, and they giggled as they watched her go.

'So,' said Eve, 'what are you wearing for the wedding? Which reminds me, I saw a most marvellous dress in the Oxfam shop the other day, it really would suit you.'

'I don't somehow think Pepe would appreciate it if I went there,' and she smiled wistfully, adding 'Go on, what was it like, what colour?'

'Well, it wasn't white, though I would say,' looking slyly at her friend in the loose shirt, 'that it doesn't matter! Are you?'

'Am I what?'

'Lambing.'

Isa gave a shout of laughter, and they hugged noisily. And she laughed even louder when Eve said 'If you're stuck for a name for it, I've got a good book of Christian names in the shop that you could borrow!'

*     *     *

Bobby Drach had been determined to do his best with the evening. Although still shaken and in mourning (wearing a black armband with his frilly shirt), he bustled from lounge to kitchen, offered drinks and carried in green oval dishes of what he called 'nice nibblies', and generally fussed over his guests. He selected a long-playing record and turned up the sound.

'Bobby's Weeping Music,' he explained to Pepe; who, after a few blank seconds, said

'Is not! Is Rachmaninov, his second piano concerto!'

'— Which makes Bobby weep with emotion, that's why it's known as my bloody weeping music!' and disappeared into the kitchen again, only to poke his head round the door to enquire if the wine was to their liking.

'Is a young wine,' Pepe began, as Isa fumbled in her shoulderbag for her eggcup, 'but is very pleasing in —'

'I know it's a young wine, I chose it because it had a bloody dummy instead of a cork . . . Ez, what the fuck have you got there? . . . Pepe, don't start on the cake yet, dear, did no-one ever tell you, savouries first?'

'Is looking nice,' said Pepe, eyeing the cake with greed.

'So it should be, at nearly a quid per fucking slice! Ezita, if my wine glasses aren't good enough . . .' He looked round, nodded to himself, and sat down with them.

Isa giggled as he kept a watchful eye on the eggcup. 'All the rage in Spain, are they? . . . Come on, Samson, eat up; you're not losing weight, are you, only your flies aren't straining at the seams as they usually do. And do let me top up your glass again! — perhaps I should've given you a bucket instead.'

Isa was still wiping her eyes as she watched Pepe anxiously looking down at himself, when Bobby suddenly said, 'By the way, that was one hell of a show you all put on for charity a couple of weeks ago!'

'Oh — you have enjoy it, Roberto?'

'Very much so. Do tell! — how much do you charge for standing in a shop window?'

'Pardon me?'

'You heard! Do you know who rang me that evening? I'll tell

289

you who! Byron bloody Larch!' He stared at his guest with ferocity. 'Let me tell you something. There will be no silly-arse miming at delly Dotchy, and you can tell that to the other two! I know that Martes thinks he's the only begotten son of Saint Cecilia, but he couldn't do a convincing mime if they stuck him head-first into a tank of bloody water!'

Isa said calmly, 'Do shut up about it, Bobby. Of course there won't be any miming!'

He laughed sharply. 'Really? That's what a certain fat cow told the BBC about Seville! Anyway, I've spoken to Bardi about it. I don't give a cow's cock if *Il* bloody *Papa* mimes every blessing in the book, I'm not having delly Dotchy carved up into Walt Disney farcical shit! Translate!'

Laughing, Isa did her best while Pepe rolled in paroxysms on the settee. At length, he raised his hands in surrender. 'You win, Roberto! *Punto entendido!*'

'Certainly,' said Bobby. 'The strawberry or the plain sponge?'

\*     \*     \*

'I wonder what Fazzoletto's doing?'

'When?' asked Isa, checking her credit card and sliding it back into her wallet. 'Right, I think I've got everything.'

'At this moment. I wonder if he is at home?' His hand shot out, held her by the arm. 'Where are you going, *princesa?*'

'I told you – Grosvenor and I are going shopping. He insists that his *mamá* buys something very chic for her wedding.'

'You will go in the car,' warningly.

'Of course, *querido*. Do they allow cars on the third floor in Harrods?'

'Don't be bloody clever, you know what I mean! Car, woman!'

'*Sí, señor.* Anyway,' looking out of the window, seeing a window-cleaner in his pulley one floor below, 'it's too cold for walking.' She opened the window slightly.

Pepe frowned. 'Close it, please, there are germs out there! Or were you thinking of taking a short cut?'

Isa leaned out of the window, shouted loudly to the window-cleaner, 'Oi! You've missed a bit!' and giggling, withdrew before he could look up.

Pepe chuckled, shaking his head, reached for the phone. Then glanced at her sharply.

'Did you say Harrods?' in disbelief.

'I did say Harrods. Where on earth did you think I'd go? Oxfam?'

Outside the hotel, she glanced up at the building then climbed into the car.

'Oxfam, please,' to the driver. 'Kensington High Street.'

\*     \*     \*

'*Saluti*, Sperm Bank!'

A delighted roar. 'Pulgarcito! You in London, *amico*?'

'I am, and shivering with cold. Pio, have you got a few minutes?'

'Sure, sure, I'm having two days' rest. I've finished the film!'

'Oh? Which film is this – another TV commercial?'

'You mean you haven't heard? Pio is now a screen idol! I shall win Oscars for this!'

'You? But you can't act!' he snorted.

'Who says Pio cannot act? I act better than you, you Spanish whore! This is a film of great beauty and great singing – it will be on general release, so look out for it – it's called *Scusi, Luigi*!'

Hooting from the Dorchester. 'Jesus Christ!'

'Go shit yourself, *papo*! Anyway, why are you ringing?'

'Arena della Doccia is why. I'm trying to plan the Contreras main course. The solos, Pio – we did agree four each, didn't we? Look, as you're flogging old *Nessun D.*, how about me going for a bit of *Tosca*, the *Recondita Armonia*?'

Pepe paused, smiling, biro poised. The smile drifted to the left as Pio chortled loudly, 'I'm doing that one!'

'Shit! Oh well, it'll have to be the other number one hit from *Tosca*, then, *E lucevan le Stelle*, unless of course,' sarcastically, 'you've chosen that one as well?'

A guffaw. 'No, Martes has.'

291

'Fuck him! How do you know, anyway?'

'Ran into Buzzer at the airport. He's got a little green notebook now, full of this concert and his ideas, and he told me what Martes plans to do. Hey, get this – Modesto is thinking of opening his *quartetto* with Meyerbeer's *O Paradiso*, only the clever bastard wants to do it in the original French. So Buzzer says.'

A heavy sigh. 'Damn the man, I was thinking of that one, too . . . .So far then, I appear to be doing fuck-all. Anyone doing *Core 'Ngrato?'*

'Christ in a toast-rack, no! This is to be a grand concert, not a musical tribute to Mario bloody Lanza!'

Pepe grinned and scribbled down *Core 'Ngrato*. It was a start, anyway.

*  *  *

From Oxfam, the car took Isa and her parcels to the Drach Agency. The driver looked a little distraught when he saw the cul-de-sac with its piles of bulging black sacks.

'Fifteen minutes,' she told him blithely.

Julie brought freshly-made coffee to them, looking admiringly at Isa and her ring. When she had departed, Bobby said 'I wish that fat cow would put her udders in a sling! It's different with you, you've got nothing to show, but with her it looks like Chelsea having a kick-about under her bloody jumper.' He bent down and fingered the fattest parcel.

She tapped his hand with her foot. 'Where's Jake today?'

'Jake? He's in dear old EC2, trying to find his way through the Barbican. Last time he went, he got lost and ended up in a fucking fish shop. Come on, let's have a peep at what you've bought!'

At her nod, he pulled out a calf-length garment in pale brown lace. Held it against himself, looked in the mirror, and twirled. 'What's this rag for, then? When we go to Sniffer's first night?'

'No!' indignantly. 'That's my wedding dress!'

He looked horrified. Shuddered. 'You'll look like a dish of fucking gravy in this!'

'No I won't, not with a few thin gold chains round my neck!'

'Christ, the wedding of the bloody year! A Jack Russell and a

292

whippet!' He ducked, and then said, 'What about a hat?' and they both cackled. Mina, thank God, would be arriving soon, hopefully with ideas about hairstyles.

'Before I forget, Ezita – I'll pick you up at half-past six. That should give us plenty of time. I'm keen to see this new mezzo Baltasar. And be careful what you eat before we go – we've got to watch Samson push the temple over, don't forget!'

\*       \*       \*

'On the other hand,' mused Buzzer Ahmet over supper, 'it ought to be something Italian.'

'What did, darling?' Fancy looked up from a sheaf of photographs, pushed a dish of soused herrings towards him. He glanced at them, and took a savoury biscuit instead.

'The overture,' he said, munching. He opened his green notebook.

'Which overture?' patiently.

'For the concert. Della Doccia.' He tapped the table with his pen, got up and paced. 'Allah-God says I've got to think of one pretty damn quick . . .'

'Why an overture? Be a bit different – do part of Respighi, his *Fountains of Rome*.'

'No thank you. I don't need waffling crap, I need music.' He reached for another biscuit. 'And not Rossini, either – doesn't feel right for this.'

'Oh be a devil, then, darling, and honour the Mafia!' She chuckled at his blank expression. 'Verdi, Buzz. His *Sicilian Vespers*.'

'And the Mafia come in where, precisely?'

'Sicily, you idiot.'

Buzzer laughed. 'Oh, please, darling! – do give me credit for never being as obvious as that!'

Smiling, he watched her leave the room, shaking his head in amusement.

Then he wrote it down in his book and underlined it twice.

\*       \*       \*

'I told Pepe I'd go round to his dressing-room before he starts to prepare himself,' said Isa.

Bobby was studying the programme. ('They charge nearly as much for this as they do for the fucking seats!') He glanced occasionally around and down at the assembling audience, or cast his eye over the musicians already in the pit and setting out their scores as they chatted. A cellist juddered her bow across slackened strings and spoke to her companion.

'What for?' he snapped. 'Afraid he might be having a quickie with Delilah?'

'Don't be so damn crude!' Too many snide remarks about Bionda Merdina had made her mercifully immune to such wisecracks. More or less.

'I am going backstage,' grandly, and stood up in a sigh of black polyester.

'Don't stay all bloody evening, either! He won't want you slavering emotional shit all over him at a time like this.'

'Thank you for your advice, Robert.' Leaned close to his ear and bellowed 'Twit!'

He jumped high and hard. 'You stupid bitch!'

She was admitted to the dressing-room by a lady in an overall. 'You can go in, duck, I've finished with him,' and she slipped into the larger-than-expected room. She had heard Pepe moan so often about swinging cats and having to sit on washbasins to get a view in the mirror that she was pleasantly surprised.

'Oh, excuse me!' she said, startled, to a Red Indian standing by the dressing-table, 'I am so sorry, I was looking for Mr Contreras!'

The Red Indian scowled. 'That's all I need, your bloody witty remarks!'

Isa jumped. Stared. Moved closer. 'Pepe?'

'Of course it is me!' irritated.

She stifled a snort, prowled round him in disbelief. 'Why are you dressed up as a Red Indian squaw?' and now the giggles escaped. 'I didn't know Samson was an Apache!' and she touched his shoulder-length wig and the narrow red band round his bronzed forehead.

He scowled, and white furrows appeared in the heavy moist make-up.

'Where's your papoose?' and the giggles grew louder.

'Oh shut up!' he grinned.

'Dear God, what have you got on your legs?' and she collapsed on a stool.

'Thongs,' bitterly.

'Thongs,' she repeated thoughtfully. 'Yes. Yes, it makes sense. They go very well with your miniskirt! Oh Grosvenor, look at *Papi!*' and she doubled over.

'Shut it!' he hissed. Then laughed, if reluctantly. 'You damn *cucufato*, stop it! I'm supposed to be psyching myself up now – please go, woman, before I forget the person I am to be soon!'

'Yessir, madam, I'm going! Lordy, I hope Roberto forgot to bring his opera glasses! And don't bend over, whatever you do, beloved!' blowing him a kiss.

*　　*　　*

There was no doubt about it: *Samson et Dalila* was a critical success. Inés Baltasar impressed even the doughty *Times* critic; and 'Contreras,' he wrote vehemently, 'sang in a stratosphere of lyrical concentration which transcended that of his illustrious predecessor in this rôle, Mario del Monaco. This voice will ring forever in our heads and our hereafter.'

And as the critic was thus forming his opinion in front of his typewriter, Bobby Drach took Isa and Pepe for a quiet supper in a restaurant not far from the Opera House.

Before the light meal was brought to them, Bobby said 'Well, Vito – God bless him – would have been green with envy if he'd heard you tonight!'

'A compliment?' and Pepe's eyebrow shot up.

'Indeedy,' Bobby grinned, 'though I must admit, when you first trundled on stage looking like a nancy-boy –'

'Roberto, I am objecting!' as he nuzzled Isa vigorously.

'He looked nothing of the kind, Bobby!' nuzzling him in return.

'Object all you like, children, but it's true. All you lacked, Hiawatha, were a pair of frilly knickers and a velvet garter. And when you bent over – Just what did you wear underneath, as a matter of aesthetic interest?' His eyes gleamed.

'Tights,' grinned Pepe.

'Not that it mattered, really, since your balls seem to be losing weight, as I mentioned before . . . Ezita, don't splutter, darling, that bread flew straight at Bobby – Pepe, pass the wine list, it looks as though I'll have to do the ordering. And put that fucking egg cup away!' glaring at Isa.

During the meal, Pepe crunched celery and asked mockingly, 'So, what did you think to my destructing of the Temple, Roberto?'

'Far too casual, I thought. You only touched one pillar.'

'I am a singer, not a JCB!'

'Yes, but one bloody polystyrene pillar! Still – to more important things, Pepe. How do you rate Inés Baltasar? Good to work with?' And listened carefully to Pepe's opinions and enthusiasm for the new co-star. He nodded, pleased, then said, 'And she also takes on soprano roles, I understand. Good . . . good. Then you wouldn't mind working with her again?'

'Most definite not! She has patient sweet.'

'Whatever the fuck that may mean!' Swept on, 'Right, Hiawatha, think back to Christmas. What did Bobby give you as a gift?'

'Rossini! *Otello!*' they cried, and Isa knocked her fork to the floor in excitement.

'Clumsy mare! . . . Pepe dear, pick it up by the handle, otherwise you'll get tartare sauce all over your fingers . . . Good boy! . . . Right, then. Rossini's –'

'Come on, tell me, for God's sake!'

Bobby looked smug. 'EMI want to record you and Baltasar doing the blessed thing, with Tim Divine and his New York band. This would be mid-June, recording in the Hamburg sonics because Divine and his boys and girls are on a European tour. Well?'

Pepe's eyes were bursting with pleasure. 'Roberto, is *fantástico*, I never thought I –'

'No need to kiss me . . . oh well, if you insist . . . Now, I'm aware that Roberto Junior is arriving around that time, but with a bit of luck Ezita will drop him on the due date and not bugger us all about. You will try, won't you darling?'

And as the chatter and euphoria grew, Bobby smiled to himself and thought what a useful friend Tim Divine was. Even though, of course, he was a bushy-haired oversexed twat.

Later, over coffee, Bobby said, 'By the way, having mentioned babies, may Bobby ask you about your wedding?'

'And what about the wedding?' asked Pepe, still bubbling.

'Guests, Hiawatha, your guests. Press coverage. Telly slot?' hopefully.

'Tell him, *princesa*,' and Isa dunked some celery into the bowl of brown sugar with 'Don't look at me like that, I just fancied it, that's all! What did you say? Guests? Well – you, of course.'

Bobby nodded, closing his eyes fastidiously as she dunked again.

'And Mina, Alfredo, and the boys. Gualterio, of course. And Eve, and Clair.'

She stopped, swallowed some of Pepe's wine before he could protest. Then she looked at him, and they exchanged a smile and a knee rub.

'And?' impatiently.

'That's all. Just loved ones with us. Who were you expecting, the King of Spain?'

'Fuck that lanky sod! . . . Do you mean to say – words fail me! Not even any of your fellow herald angels?'

They shook their heads solemnly.

He blew out his cheeks and regarded them morosely. 'I see. A quiet little reception. Perhaps they're not paying you enough. Tell me, Samson, will your poverty trap open wide enough for champagne for us all? Or shall Bobby order a crate of milk stout?'

# 18

'But Mina, listen to me! It's very important!'

Mina paused in her stride. 'What is it?' Exasperation.

'It's just that I heard . . .' She allowed her voice to trail away; then green eyes gleamed, the brightest things on a grey cheerless morning with rain running like an uncontrolled nose '. . . that there is still to be a wedding.'

'Well of course there is!' Mina let her impatience be heard. 'Look, you'll have to excuse me, Judit, we're due in London tomorrow, and there's a great deal to –'

Loudly, 'It isn't his child, you know!'

'Don't be so silly!' edging her closer to the big door and relieved to see that Ana had taken up her position there.

'I am not being silly! That man could not father –' The eyes suddenly sharpened, and she laughingly pointed the ferrule of her umbrella. 'That's new! Dear old Magda. The face that sank the Armada. Where on earth did you get the dreadful thing?'

Mina turned and looked up at the portrait.

The magic of an ordinary smile. Magda, gazing down at her beloved hall, the entrance to her kingdom.

'Isabel painted it. For the family. We think it's perfect.'

And into the silence said loudly, 'Ana, would you show *Señora* Judit out, please?'

\*　　\*　　\*

I really ought to be pissed off, thought Luciano Bardi as he strolled through the ruins of the Arena della Doccia.

Old towers shaped like rearing snails loomed over him through the rain. His companion slithered silently in the mud. A minion hovered some way behind with a mobile phone and unhappy wet feet. Bardi had known this place since he was six years old, when the family had moved to Rome from Palermo. That had been just after his father was shot in the back of the head. He couldn't recall much about that incident, but he did remember his first sight of the Arena and his awestruck gasp as his elder brother tried to explain how old it was, but couldn't enlighten him about the snail shapes.

Now, thanks to Bardi and several others like him who had banking connections with the Vatican, the Arena was rented out for cultural events during the season at the Pope's discretion or under pressure from potential blackmailers.

This, thought Bardi as rain ran inside his collar, is going to be perfect. The event of a lifetime. As perfect as God, if not better. It would storm the world. He would perfect this even if he had to steal the Pope's ring to create publicity for it. Or steal the Pope, come to that. All would be possible, providing Byron Larch restrained his British whimsicalities and listened to what he, Bardi, told him.

The minion was speaking into the phone, wiping rain from his face.

At Bardi's elbow, Ruggero Ripieno, a high-ranking bank official, slowly turned in circles gazing up at the dizzying towers.

'Fazzoletto,' he said suddenly. 'His voice! Supreme, supreme! It will soar like a dove above the clouds!'

'Only if the sound equipment is replaced,' Bardi said sourly.

'I assure you, *Signor* Bardi, all will be seen to.'

'Like it was last November? The sound boom crashing to earth like the wrath of God, killing two and flattening a valuable camera?'

'That is an unrepeatable tragedy. All will be checked, a thousand times if needs be!'

'Why only Fazzoletto?' Bardi enquired suddenly. 'Don't the other two soar like doves?'

'They're Spaniards,' with a shrug. Bardi stared at him. 'That's the difference,' he smiled.

They strolled on. 'Two orchestras!' Bardi snapped.

'So I am told. Don't worry!'

Don't worry, the man said. The Magia Armonica and the Teatro dell' Orfeo. Unfrocked priests and lesbians in one, would-be priests and tarts in the other. Or so it seemed. Luckily, he thought, Buzzer Ahmet not only spoke reasonably fluent Italian, he also had a wondrous range of universal gestures which he would most definitely need as he tried to mould the old rivals into one orchestra. Still, if anyone could do it, Ahmet was the man. Admirable, if some of the stories were true. The time, for instance, when he outfaced the leader of the American band in Detroit who had wanted to kill him, simply because Buzzer had commented that his bowing technique put him in mind of a baby using a cheese grater. No, indeed, Ahmet was not a man who scared easily.

Still. Could be problems ahead. He sighed, splashing his way towards history.

\*     \*     \*

'Bufido wouldn't like this at all,' said Pau, shaking his head sadly at the cheetahs domiciled in London Zoo.

'Bufido isn't a real cat,' sighed Alfredo wearily, shaking the few bits that remained inside a packet of crisps. He didn't like London. And Pepe was too busy between extra calls and interviews, and vanishing at first light to record the sounds that were intended to bring Lorca and Co. to the masses. The poems were meaningless enough, he thought, without setting them to that bloody dreary music. What he had heard so far reminded him of Schumann just before a suicide attempt.

And Mina and Isabel were too busy, falling over themselves arranging flowers and arguing over which knickers matched that awful thin brown dress; Mina doing her best to straighten Isa's raging hair into neat shiny lines, Isa in tears demanding that something called Carmen rollers be brought to her at once to improve it back to its original mess.

And Gualterio was too busy making himself known to the bartenders in the hotel and environs, or getting himself lost in a place called Finsbury Park because of confusion over the coloured lines on the map of the Underground.

His depression was heightened because he himself was to be in charge of the telegrams of congratulation. About three hundred had already arrived from around the world, and it was his job to select the most important to read out at the small reception. Who, he pondered, do you rank as the most important? The boss of La Scala, or the powers behind the Vienna Staatsoper? A king? Or bloody Martes?

'He is real!' protested Pau.

Oh Christ, not again.

Lluís picked up a stone and eyed the cheetahs reflectively.

'Put that fucking thing down!' snapped Alfredo.

'HE IS REAL!' yelled Pau, and snatched the crisp packet.

'Alright, he's bloody real!' a goaded Alfredo yelled back. 'He's a dead cat that someone stuffed after ripping his sodding guts out!'

Lluís giggled. Pau stared at his father. 'He isn't! He isn't, is he, *Papi*?' and his voice quivered.

A cheetah growled.

'Yes!' snapped *Papi*. 'And put that in the litter bin if you've finished with it!'

The little boy was weeping as he obeyed, staring miserably into the bin with its empty wet cartons and a woollen glove. He kicked the wire mesh in a spasm of hurt rage.

'And stop scratching your shoes! Lluís, take his hand! We're going back to the hotel. NOW!'

'We haven't seen the snakes yet,' Lluís protested.

'Snakes eat little boys for breakfast, or didn't they teach you that at school?'

Unperturbed, Lluís swung round a lamppost. 'It's nearly lunchtime,' he crowed, 'so they won't be eating boys now!'

'Shut up! Pau, stop snivelling! Take Lluís's hand!'

Lluís skipped out of reach. 'Only girls do that!'

Alfredo gritted his teeth and grabbed each by the arm.

'I shall tell *Mamá* what you said about Bufi,' wailed Pau.

Oh God, thought Alfredo. He mustered a smile. 'I was only joking,' he said. Patted his son's head. 'Of course Bufido isn't a dead cat. *Papi* was teasing!'

Pau stopped sniffing, and looked up at his father with a dawning of new and precious knowledge. 'I'm still going to tell *Mamá*,' he said smugly.

\*       \*       \*

301

'That does it!' yelled Isa. And buried her head beneath a towel.

Mina was laughing helplessly on the couch, still holding the brush and comb.

Pepe, grinning, poked his head round the door. 'Everything okay, girls?'

'Get him out of here!'

Mina flapped her hand at him, tears of laughter, 'Go!'

He came into the room.

'Has he gone?' came from under the towel. Pepe tiptoed towards the shrouded figure, ignoring Mina's hissed protest.

'Mina? Has he gone?'

'Boo!' he cried, and removed the towel. He burst out laughing.

'You bastard!' Isa screamed. She tried to grab the towel but he danced out of reach, still laughing.

'Hello, bride!' he gasped. 'Oh *Dios mío*, what have you done? What in Christ's name have you done?' He sat down, clutching his stomach.

Mina's eyes were bright and dancing. 'Leave her alone,' she tittered. 'Go away!'

'I shall kill you!' Isa yelled.

'We were just trying something different,' Mina murmured.

Isa's head was a mass of tiny plaits.

Pepe choked and nearly hit high C. 'Something different? You look like a bloody piccaninny! You can't be seen like this! Mina, is this a joke?'

'Don't blame me, Isa thought it might work, but there was too much hair . . .'

'I wanted to kill those bloody curls!' and she burst into tears of rage.

Pepe put his hand soothingly on her shoulder, and she shrugged it away, 'Piss off!'

Mina said 'Isa, I'll undo them all, every one, then we can try something else. Come with me, *querida*, come with Mina, mmm?'

Pepe patted the topmost lump of plaits, grinning. 'Don't cry, *mi alma*, let Mina do as she says, then have a good shampoo and −'

Isa shouted, 'I've had five bloody shampoos already! Just one more and my bloody scalp will swim out of the bloody door! Just go away!' She leapt from her chair and charged out of the room. A door slammed. Then another.

'*Cristo!*' he said, suddenly anxious, 'Will she be okay?'

'Of cour–' as the door burst open again. Alfredo hurtled in with the two boys.

'*Mamá, Mamá, Papi* says Bufi is a dead cat with his guts torn out!'

'I did not! Good God, brother, what are you doing here? Have they just found out that you can't bloody sing?'

'Hush, Pau, I'm sure that *Papi* . . . LLUÍS! Don't sit there, Isa's left her –' and she pushed her son off the pale brown lace dress, 'God Almighty, she'll have a fit!' and bunched it quickly under her arm, hoping that Pepe hadn't seen it.

'I wasn't singing, *coño*, I was being interviewed!'

'*Mamá*, he did, he said Bufido was –'

'Interviewed? What about? Your views on interplanetary molecules?'

'*Mamá*, he said we couldn't see the snakes, he said they eat –'

'SHUT UP!' They stared at her, shocked. Mina was losing her usually endless fund of patience. Somewhere beyond that door was Isabel, weeping and plaited. 'Take the boys for a walk!' she commanded her husband.

'They've just been for a fucking walk!' he shouted.

'Can we see the snakes this time, *Papá*?'

'What the infernal shit are molecules?'

'*Mamá*, I want to see my Bufi! I want to go home!'

Mina took a deep breath.

'For the love of Christ, GO! GO GO GO!' And, ashamed, added 'PISS OFF!'

They went.

*     *     *

In the darkness of night, in the softness of the sheets, he said gently, 'I'm glad the curls came back.'

'Mmmm?' drowsily.

'The curls,' he whispered, his mouth against her ear. 'I'm happy they are back.'

'Are you?'

'I truly am.'

303

'I was a real bitch today, wasn't I?'

'A very real one,' and he squeezed her hand.

'Sorry, beloved.' Her lips touched his throat. They nuzzled for a few moments.

Then, 'You shouldn't be here!' she said.

A chuckle. 'What are you talking about, mmm?'

'I've just told you.' She struggled to sit up.

'Come back here. At once!'

Protesting, 'A man isn't supposed to see his bride before the wedding –'

'Well, I can't see you – it's dark.'

Doubtfully, 'I don't think it quite means that.'

Silence. Then the muted thunder of an aircraft.

'Bloody Heathrow!'

He smiled into her curls. 'Bloody every airport, in that case.'

'Except when we fly home tomorrow!'

'Of course. So – *viva el aeropuerto*!'

'Pepe?'

'Still here.'

She moved closer, asked his chin 'Are you truly glad about tomorrow?'

'What's happening tomorrow?'

'My horoscope said that I'd be getting married in the morning.'

'Oh? To whom?'

'Some hook-nosed twit who thinks he can sing. And he's as sexy as a castrato.'

'Mmm. Doesn't sound too promising. Will you marry me instead?'

'I'll have to think about that.'

The faint whirr of air-conditioning.

'Have you thought about it yet?'

A kiss missed his mouth. 'I accept your offer.'

'Good! Now go to sleep, Curly. It's very late.'

'That's your fault.'

'No it isn't! You were too strong for me.'

Holding hands, they slept.

\*　　\*　　\*

304

'Did you remember to send the telegram?'

Adriana Fazzoletto sat up in bed and dug her husband in the belly.

'Don't do that, you'll harm my voice,' he murmured.

'I asked you, did you send the telegram to Pepe and Isabel?'

Pio rolled over on to his side. 'I sent it, little one.'

'What did you say in it?'

'I said, arriving tomorrow, meet me at the airport, love, Mother.'

He heard her chuckling in the darkness. 'Be serious! What did you say?'

Pio sighed, scratched his bulging arm reflectively. 'I said exactly what you told me to say, *cara*. Something to the effect of . . . "Go easy, Pulgarcito, don't fuck yourself blind." '

'You said WHAT?' Adriana started to scramble out of bed. 'I'll have to cancel it! Christ, you stupid fat fool, I'll have to stop it, do they work at night, these people?' Then she heard his bellowing mirth, jumped back on the bed, pummelling him.

'What-did-you-say-in-the-telegram?'

'Congratulations and love from Adriana and Pio and family.'

'Ah! Good!'

He stifled a guffaw in the pillow.

*     *     *

Bobby Drach gave a final glance at the late-night traffic below, then slowly let the draped curtain fall back into place. One last drink, then bed.

Father of the bride. That's what it would be, to all intents and purposes, anyway.

He went to the cocktail bar, mixed a stiff gin and tonic, dropped in a slice of lemon. Now why do you always do that, he asked himself. You only have to pull the fucking thing out again and get your fingers wet.

He sat down, rubbing his chin. Jesus, was it only six months ago that a prat called Bobby Drach had asked a scatty mare called Ez Pepper to marry him? He knew, inside, that she would never

305

seriously have taken such a step. But how long had it been, their friendship? . . .

. . . Must be . . . oh, getting on for fourteen years now, since she had tripped headlong over the welcome mat in his old Bayswater office, and, after he'd put a sticking-plaster on her chin, claimed to be a typist with good speeds, and interested in music.

He recalled the scene well. That old Olivetti machine, Ez getting the black and red ribbon tangled round the spool and yards of the bugger in coils on the floor as she tried to straighten it, getting madder and tugging until the whole thing crashed down and shattered. Then the nice man at the office supplies shop in Queensway, selling them a new machine at discount, and her eventual wide smile as she proceeded to type to his dictation and managed three words out of seventy, 'Dear Sir, With . . .'

My Ezita. He'd hired her, of course, since she had already been with him for five hours by then, and because she knew her music. And she laughed a lot and made him feel like a skittish king. He chuckled now, nursing his drink. Remembered her first embroidery for him. God, yes, that black polo-necked sweater he'd bought from Shepherd's Bush market. Just do something to take away the awful starkness of it, he'd said. A slogan, or an intriguing symbol will do. She had chosen one word, the letters in alternate crimson and white. Antidisestablishmentarianism.

And the bloody thing had to be continued round the back and finished up under his armpit.

No use blaming Sniffer for taking her away. No use blaming Ez for going. He sighed, blew a kiss in the general direction of the Dorchester. Then he plucked out the slice of floating lemon and wet his fingers.

*     *     *

There was quite a large and enthusiastic crowd outside the Registry Office in Kensington, plus a TV camera from the BBC and half a dozen reporters.

One of them, from *The Times*, shouted 'Hello, the bleedin' mob's twitching – hey, Freddie, get your camera over that way, don't want to miss the poor 'appy sods, do we?'

306

Shouts began, 'Here they come!'

'Oooer, fancy wearing brown!'

'Isn't he gorgeous? Lucky cow!'

'He's wearing built-up shoes, look!'

'What hairstyle would you call that, Betty?'

'Well done, Peppy, yeeee-HAR!'

'Why ain't she smiling?'

'Don't he look different without make-up?'

Isa was silent, her face pale. She could feel the clench of her stomach, her tiny smile was fixed. Do we have to stand here long, she thought. Please God where are the cars let them come hurry them up.

'HOORAY!'

'Good luck!'

'Isabel, could you look this way?'

Flash flash.

Isa blinked. Don't let it happen here, now, oh please Lord.

'Alright, *mi princesa?*'

She looked at the smiling face, and not even her dread could take away the blazing love in her eyes which made the breath leave him. Then he saw the white face, tore away his gaze, and saw the first limousine gliding to a stop.

'Please, can we get in now?' she asked piteously, and with a frown he elbowed a way for them to the car, Enrique close behind.

Bobby had had to leave his Mercedes by a parking meter two streets away, to his annoyance, and he sprinted off, hearing someone in the crowd say 'Christ, if she was a bleedin' hooker, she'd be on full-time unemployment benefit!' and his fingers clenched. His designated passenger, Gualterio, grumbled and shuffled in the breezy street.

Two more cars arrived, each with a fluttering pennant of Barcelona Football Club, and the crowd was delighted to see a brown-eyed little boy run to one of them clutching his short trousers and shouting something in a foreign language.

Mina shook him when they were settled in the second car. 'Couldn't you have waited?' she snapped at Pau. 'You're wet through!'

In the third car, Clair asked hopefully, 'Is Pepe's brother famous as well?'

'Don't ask me,' shrugged Eve, tilting the brim of her hat carefully over her eye, 'I think Ez said something about him being a chemist. Probably Boots have got branches in Spain. By the way, will you please try to appear cultured and stop asking Pepe if he knows the New Kids on the Block? Can you think classical music for an hour or two?'

'Is Wagner alright, then? He wrote something you sing to, didn't he?'

'No use asking me! If you're not sure, ask Ez, she'll know.'

Alfredo, in the second car, sniffed the air as Mina thrust Pau between them.

'Christ Almighty!' he snapped, 'Can't you wrap him up in a blanket or something?'

'Oh of course! I always carry one in my handbag!' Mina snapped back.

'Bloody hell, he stinks worse than my lab specimens!'

'*Papá*, can we go to the zoo again now?' whined Lluís.

'Pardon me, I thought we were already there!' sarcastically as the cars pulled away and the crowd spilled on to the road behind them.

Mina craned her neck to look at the car in front. 'Didn't you think that Isabel looked pale?' she asked Alfredo.

'Can't say I noticed. Too busy wondering how Pepe could understand all that foreign legal gibberish. He was bloody pathetic at languages when we were at school. Bloody pathetic at Spanish, come to think of it.'

'Pau, sit still! Don't wet the seat more than you can help! No, honestly, *querido*, she did look a funny colour, I thought she was going to faint.'

'Probably worrying about her wedding night,' he grinned.

'But that's silly, they've been sleeping together for ages, how do you think they got the baby? . . . Oh!' Too late she saw that he was teasing, and smiled.

In the leading car, now accelerating, Pepe glanced down at his wife who was in slump position against his shoulder. 'Soon be there, *preciosa*,' he said. 'Hold on – please!' he added pitifully.

308

She smiled weakly. 'I knew it was too good to last,' she said.

This was the fifth consecutive day of morning sickness. If you get it, they said, it will stop in a matter of weeks, then it'll be a thing of the past for the rest of the pregnancy. They said. Including that fount of knowledge, Salvador Meados de bloody Hurón. And she had crowed with delight, the sickness had never materialised. Until now: hiding it, blaming her dashes to the bathroom on pre-wedding nerves.

Until now. She clasped Pepe's large handkerchief to her mouth, glad at least that the car was beautifully sprung.

The wedding guests were a little surprised to see the front car screech to a halt outside the hotel, and Pepe run up the steps almost carrying his bride.

'Christ, he's in a hurry!' sniggered Alfredo. 'I wondered what he was fiddling with when he took his vows. He looked like a little hatstand!'

'Alfredo!'

Isa Contreras was sick on the brown lace dress as the elevator hummed upwards.

'Oh hell!' heaving desperately and trying to avoid Pepe's shoes. He turned his head away but not his arm. She sagged against him, gasping.

'Hush, *querida*, it's okay.'

'It isn't okay! Oh God, why doesn't this bloody lift get a move on?'

She heaved again, felt him holding her, gently bending her forward. Thank God Enrique had had the sense to wait in the lobby for the others.

When the elevator finally came to a sleek halt, Pepe carried her swiftly into their suite, laying her carefully on the bed. Her eyes flew open.

'I don't think Grosvenor Dolores likes getting married,' she croaked.

'Poor little girl, poor little *Señora* Contreras,' and he stayed and soothed her until it was over. Then she scrambled off the bed, tugging the lace dress over her head. 'Give me five minutes!' she panted.

Exasperation. 'What on earth are you doing now?'

'What do you think I'm doing, bridegroom? I'm getting changed to greet our guests,' and a soggy heap of brown wedding-dress was pushed under the bed.

*    *    *

Clair decided almost immediately that she was going to learn Spanish and take singing lessons.

Eve decided almost immediately that she didn't care if she never heard a foreign word again in her life. She only knew one word of Spanish, and that was 'Contreras', and even then Bobby had told her that it meant diarrhoea; so she sat and smiled and nodded and tried not to giggle at her friend's new surname.

Only ten people at the reception, she mused, and yet they made it sound like a thousand. Everyone started to say something, everyone interrupted, there were shouts of laughter and sly jokes; even the laughter was in Spanish, she decided. Then the youngest boy had wanted to climb the wedding-cake; and when that mess had been sorted out, some idiot had given him a toy car to play with. One with batteries. And remote control, she observed owlishly, watching it zigzag along the thick carpet under the table and then revving like a wasp when it got stuck in a furrow.

She wondered why Ez had changed out of the Oxfam dress so quickly, and, if she had to do it, why she had put on a baggy pair of jeans and a shirt instead of a going-away outfit. Eve watched the untidy bride as she capered like a lunatic, and the eldest child giggled and Pepe laughed.

That guitar music from the stereo! – with a woman's harsh voice like Brillo pads in a saucepan, and Pepe's brother singing along like a shrill cuckoo and snapping his fingers. It's a wonder Pepe doesn't scream, when he is so professional musically.

Eve sipped her fourth drink. The big lounge of the suite had looked so beautiful when they first came in, blue and white and tall as a cathedral, flowers growing everywhere especially white carnations, several nice portable fountains that splashed neatly on to marble pebbles. Apart from one, which gave feeble splutters followed by an enormous cascade that had put paid to a dish of eggs *au gratin*. One of the little boys had ended its misery by

310

ramming the contents of a tube of Smarties into the spout. Now it just sighed and dribbled.

Eve wished that someone had thought of getting catering staff. It was only a small gathering, yes, but there should have been some uniformed person there to leap around and fill glasses.

'Please, may I get you something? Another drink, perhaps?'

Pepe was leaning over her shoulder, peering into her glass. For a strict teetotaller, Eve was doing well.

'Oh! Thank you!' and looked up at the deep brown eyes. Christ, and he sang, too.

He took the glass from her hand, sniffed it.

'Blue Nile,' she said. 'Thank you . . . er . . .'

'Pardon me?'

'Blue Nile. My drink.'

'Whisky, lime, lemonade,' sang out Isa. 'Blue Nile. *Nilo Azul.*'

'*Nilo Azul?*' He sniffed the glass again. 'Is with which? Is lemonade?'

Isa grinned. 'And lime. And whisky. God, Eve, why don't you drink Martini?' as Pepe made his puzzled way to the bar, pausing en route to ruffle his nephew's hair. 'He'll probably try to find blue lemonade,' she giggled.

She picked up the toy car and accidentally put her thumb on the switch, making it buzz loudly.

'I like your going-away outfit,' sarcastically. 'You won't see many like that on the plane.'

Isa chuckled, hoisted the shirt to reveal the jeans, open zip over her swelling stomach, the two halves barely held together by a big safety-pin. 'They're Pepe's. They hold up okay like this. Just about!'

'Isabel!' frowned Pepe as he returned with Eve's drink. 'I could not get it into turning blue,' he apologised.

Bobby strolled over. 'Aren't they cute little buggers, those nephews of yours? Ever thought of putting down rat poison, Heart?'

Pepe sniggered, pulled down Isa's shirt.

'Who's cutting the bloody cake?' roared Gualterio. He tried to stroke Clair's long hair, and she hastily moved away, looking for her mother.

311

They heard Alfredo, 'Get! Go on, get! The first one to utter another sodding word gets his throat cut!' And a door slammed. Mina smiled, feebly.

Isa asked her father-in-law, 'How on earth do you cut cakes this size?'

Bobby called, 'Silence, please! The bride and whatsit are about to perform the ancient ceremony of hacking a –'

'Wait till Alfredo gets back!'

Gualterio, after much hunting, handed Isa a knife blade-first, and bowed.

'*Muchas* bloody *gracias*,' she murmured.

'*De* bloody *nada, Señora* Contreras-God-help-me,' and they snorted.

'Where's that randy bugger Sniffer gone?' demanded Bobby.

Behind him, in Spanish, Pepe said pleasantly, 'I'm right here, you son of a she-goat!' and Bobby joined in suspiciously as everyone laughed.

Alfredo returned. The boys were with him, grinning. 'Why do they always want to go at the same time?' he asked Mina, plaintively.

'Let's cut the bloody cake!' yelled Gualterio.

'Yes, why don't we?' from the door.

'Buzzer! By holy God, Buzz, where the hell did you spring from?' and Pepe shot across to the dark-coated smiling man. They embraced quickly, and grinning, he kissed Isa.

'That's the man with the sheep!' yelled Lluís, and they laughed.

'How on earth did you find us?' asked Pepe, pouring him a very amicable Scotch and ginger.

'It was quite accidental,' raising his glass. 'I was in Edinburgh, and decided to stay over in London before going on to Tel Aviv, so I rang Fancy and she told me about your kind invitation to the nuptials – so here I am!' Held his glass aloft again. 'Lots and lots of joy, both of you!'

Eve thought she knew the face, but wasn't sure, even when Isa introduced her. Clair did know the face and grinned widely. 'I thought I recognised you! You look different, though, without your monkey suit.'

Pepe said solemnly, 'Good God, Buzzer, do you conduct

312

monkeys as well as sheep?' Then wished he hadn't, as a slow seraphic smile crossed Ahmet's face and he said 'Not until August. In Rome. Dear boy!'

'CAKE!' came loudly from behind the bar. A glint of light hit the curve of a bottle of Courvoisier as it tilted towards a glass.

'For God's sake, take it off him!' wailed Mina.

'CAKE!'

'We'd better cut the bloody thing before he starts swinging from the chandelier,' Pepe said, and tugged Isabel forward.

'Then the telegrams,' called Alfredo.

'Did Fancy remember to send one from us?' asked Buzzer.

Oh shit. If she did, is it among the ones I've picked to read out?

'Yes! Indeed!' he grinned weakly.

Isa and Pepe surveyed the cake, then looked at each other. The knife was poised. It really was a towering edifice. There were two figures on the very top, one in a dress suit, one in a long gown. Crotchets had been iced around each tier, two had melted into quavers.

'Is that supposed to be you?' whispered Pepe, pointing to the long gown.

'Can't be – no sign of a baby Grosvenor.'

'CUT THE BASTARD!'

He kissed her. '*Mi carita, mi esposa.*'

'I love you.'

'Oh bloody hell!' snapped Alfredo. 'Go and cut the damn thing in bed!'

'Alfredo!'

Laughing, they raised the knife just as something fell out of Pepe's pocket. Isa abandoned the knife, picked up the piece of paper. 'What did you put our marriage certificate in there for?' she hissed, and smiled at it.

'To keep it safe,' he chortled.

Bobby's hand deftly snatched it from her, and he scanned it, his eyes widening. He waved it at Pepe. 'That isn't your real name, is it?'

'CUT THE CAKE!'

'Why, what have they put there, Helen of bloody Troy?'

'It says here that your second name is Maria!'

313

'CAKE!'

Isa grinned. Pepe scowled and the knife pointed in Bobby's direction.

'CUT IT!'

'Papaterio! Will you shut up!'

'Is it? Is it Maria?' and Bobby gave a joyful twirl and began singing 'Maria, Maria, I once met a girl named Maria –' before Pepe snatched the certificate from him. He skipped adroitly away from the knife, bowing to the applause and laughter.

Isa's eyes were wet with mirth as Pepe returned to her side, cramming the certificate back into his pocket. 'Bloody English boot-boy!'

'BEFORE THE ANGELS COME TO GET ME, CUT THE BUGGER!'

And the knife sliced neatly through the bottom tier, Mina instantly bustling around with plates, 'Right, everyone, cake! Papaterio, here's yours, now will you please stop shouting!'

Gualterio shook his head. 'You know I don't like cake, *chica*.'

Alfredo stared at him. 'But you've been whining about the damn thing since we got here! Now eat it before I ram it up your arse!'

'Alfredo!'

Glaring at his evilly-smiling father, Alfredo clapped his hands. 'Quiet, please! I shall now read some of the telegrams. Right – here we go, ladies, gentlemen, Pepe!'

The two boys sat on the floor, wriggling and pushing, while Alfredo began to go through the pile, interrupted by cheers or catcalls and the occasional 'Oh, how sweet!' He hastily replaced the names of King Juan Carlos and Queen Sofia with those of Mr and Mrs Zubair Ahmet, though Buzzer did reflect aloud that Fancy must have been drunk to add 'We look forward to your presence at our holiday palace in Mallorca at the end of August.'

'Ah!' cried Alfredo, sipping, 'here's one from Hot Rod himself – Martes!' Loud cheers. 'It just says *O Paradis*.'

Pepe's mouth thinned. The aria by Meyerbeer that he himself had wanted to sing in the Arena.

'That's nice,' Isa remarked. 'It's French. For Oh Paradise.'

'I know what it's bloody French for!' snapped Pepe, and saw

314

the dawn of understanding on Buzzer's face. The *maestro* grinned.

'And one from Fazzoletto!' Even louder cheers. Alfredo tittered as he read it through to himself. 'Perhaps you'd better not,' said Mina anxiously, looking at her sons' expectant faces.

He ignored her. 'Here goes. It's signed Adriana, Pio and *bambini.*'

'They've got a baby bambi!' cried Pau excitedly. *'Mamá,* they've got a –'

'Either shut him up or throw him out of the bloody window!' grated *Papi.* 'It reads: "Be a devil with your joystick, Pilot, turn the first one into triplets, and don't forget, over and out. When it's over, get it –" '

'Alfredo!'

Laughing, arms entwined, Pepe asked 'How many more are there?' and looked at his watch.

'About five hundred of the buggers. Look, you blest pair of sirens, I know you've a plane to catch – I'll bring this stack back home with me, then you can have a good laugh later. Now – more drinks, everyone!'

The telegram from Judit was in his pocket, waiting to be flushed down the toilet.

*       *       *

Bobby took their hands in his and gazed at them solemnly.

'Look after her, Sniffer. And I mean – look after her. Savvy? And as for you, you crazy mare, take care of this warbling bugger or Bobby's out of work. You hear me?'

His eyes swam as they embraced him. Isa's throat felt sharp and tight.

'Oh, Bobby!'

'Don't start that, you silly cow, otherwise Bobby will wish that he hadn't sent you both such a fabulous pressie!' And, as they stared at him, he said thoughtfully, 'It should be there by now. I expect that Miss Ana has put it in the kennel for you. Yes, it ought to be there, waiting for you!' He grinned sweetly.

'I bet it's Gro-more again,' sniggered Pepe on the plane bound for Barcelona, 'considering how worried he has been about my shrinking balls!'

They were to spend three days by themselves in the house and kennel, while the rest of the family remained in London for a short holiday to get over the wedding.

Ana greeted them, beaming happily.

Then she tittered anxiously.

'A wedding gift arrived for you,' she said. 'We didn't quite know where to put it —'

'Well, it isn't Rossini's *Otello*,' laughed Isa.

'What do you mean, you didn't know where to put it?' demanded Pepe, his hand poised on the tunnel door.

'Well. . .' nervously, 'The men had to put it on the terrace for you —'

'Oh Christ! I bet the bugger's exhumed Rossini!'

And they ran down the tunnel – '*Hola*, Dolores!' – and into the kennel.

Neat, clean, fresh flowers as always. The smell of polish. A cold buffet waiting, champagne swathed in linen aslant in a cooler. Candelabra.

And the daylight from the terrace had been reduced. Pepe turned pink, then white.

Isa collapsed, yelping 'Oh Roberto!'

'What are we going to do with it?' shouted Pepe. 'It can't stay there!'

The six-foot high stone statue smirked at them benignly. It was Ignacio. His suit of lights twinkled in the sunlight; a breeze rattled his ten castanets. The eyes glinted. A card hung from one massive paw.

'Welcome home to my new mummy and daddy!'

# 19

Outside, the streets of Rome were shining black in the rain. But in the eighteenth century hall known as the Sala di Sciocchi, there was a blaze of light and conversation; the frescoes that covered the ceilings up to the dome reflected the patches of glitter from the chandeliers below, and grinning gods with hooves pranced as cigar smoke tried to seek them out.

More than four hundred guests were at the awards ceremony, seated at tables that spread like wheel-spokes from the enormous dais. Brilliant flowers drank in the drenching spray they had received earlier, petals jerking as the drops rolled away.

The orchestra, assembled from Milan, played quietly when no-one listened, and then with vigour as each award was announced and the recipient made his way to the dais with varying degrees of surprise. Keta sat calmly, Pio on her left, Adriana on her right. Pio, dinner-jacketed.

He nudged Keta and said 'What did I tell you!' as the Gigli Silver Plaque and a cheque for a reasonable amount of recently-devalued lire were awarded to the outstanding newcomer of the year. No-one had doubted that it would be Anatoly Sergei Medvetseivich. Already his album *Concerto* co-starring Monda Ballena was riding high in the classical charts. In any case, his only challenger had been a former olive-tree pruner, the tenor Manolo Fulano, who had already blotted his libretto by daubing slogans on the Trevi concerning the Pope's genitals.

Keta heard Vito sighing at her side, heard him say 'If I win, darling, toss the bloody thing in the Tiber!'

She smiled into her champagne. And the bubbles broke on the surface like his sudden laughter. Pio was reaching behind her, trying to attract his wife's attention. As Keta obligingly leaned forward, she saw again the young man staring at her. She had seen him before, of course, when, as the representative of the

317

Reggio Bettino Chorale he had gone to the dais to collect their award.

He was thin, very pale. Exquisitely attired in a platinum-blond linen suit, and blue shirt. His cravat was held in place by a gold pin with an egg-shaped amethyst. Suddenly, he half-raised his glass to her. Unsmiling.

She frowned and turned to listen to Adriana who was complaining about her bra strap.

'I wish I could be like Isa Contreras,' rubbing the sore patch. 'She doesn't give a fig who sees them bouncing!'

Keta smiled. They had been to visit her, Pepe and Isa. A wild-haired girl impatient with pregnancy, longing to meet her baby face to face. They had urged her to go to Rome with them. They wanted, they said, to have a quiet prowl around della Doccia before the tourists began to flock.

So they had gone, the three of them, and Isa had whirled and danced beneath the massive towers and Pepe had suddenly gone full voice and sarcastically sung the final stanza of *Nessun Dorma*, walking backwards looking up at the sky and colliding with his whirling wife.

She smiled now as more champagne flushed into her glass. Vito at her side whispered 'It matches your eyes, gold and bright.'

For some reason, she looked for the young man, but he had gone.

Then shouts of '*Bravo, ragazzo!*' and '*Allora*, Ferruccio!' swam into her ears, and she joined in the applause as the master of ceremonies walked on to the dais to present the Gigli Medallion, the crown of the evening.

Pio took Keta's hand. 'He'll get the Medallion, *cara*,' he whispered.

Vito at her side murmured in response 'Christ, I hope not!' and her smile broke out, the tight lips suddenly younger and soft. 'You will, you know,' she thought-whispered.

Clinks of glasses, the occasional ahem as a throat was cleared, and the dignitary began '*Signore, signori*,' then paused to push away fronds of the spider plant at his side; dramatically lifted his head. 'The Gigli Medallion has been our pride and our honour since its inception in 1958.' His voice faded out as Keta noticed that the young man was back at his table, whispering to his companion. They both looked at her.

'– difficult choice. But this year, ladies and gentlemen, friends, the decision was made for us. The world decided. The world has spoken!'

Pio hissed, 'Does he know there's a wasp buzzing round his crotch?' and those around him tittered.

'– for his achievements, those outstandingly glorious achievements –' holding aloft a white envelope, which most of the assembly knew would have a gold crest and the Vatican seal on the back, '– for his years of sublime music which shook the world by its throat –'

Pio yawned audibly. 'He might be talking about you, you know,' Keta reproved him, and he scowled.

'– who, being in God's almighty favour is now blessedly singing with his wondrous voice in Heaven's eternity –'

Pio looked relieved, Adriana giggled.

'That's what he thinks,' murmured Vito at her side, and she wanted to tap his hand, tell him to behave himself.

'– goes to our beloved and lamented friend, Vito Lavagna!'

Roars of approval, hands clapping themselves sore with enthusiastic approval, '*Bravo!*'

'*Signore, signori, Signora* Lavagna will accept the award!' and the battering hands increased in their fervour, as Keta got dizzily to her feet.

I know what to do. Walk steadily with my head high, to the dais. There are four steps to climb when I reach it. Hold my hand, Baby, I might fall over.

Pio had pushed back his chair, his hand beneath her elbow to steady her. A voice said in her ear, 'Allow me to escort you, *madame*,' and the young man was by her side, hand on hers, guiding her between the stamping feet to the dais.

'Thank you,' she said. And looked into his eyes. Saw in them the dying of Vito. He, too, she thought hysterically. Near to the ending, even as he smiles at me. She stumbled, his hand held her. He reached into his pocket as they neared the dais, and pushed an envelope into her hand. 'Put this in your bag,' he murmured. 'It's from Vito. Don't be afraid – it's all there.'

Only the pandemonium kept her going forward. In a daze, she received the Medallion – flashes of cameras as they focused on her hands and the gold emblem on its bed of white velvet – and spoke her thanks softly.

The orchestra played *Una furtiva lagrima* and Vito at her side shouted Throw the envelope down, tear it up, throw it away, tear it up, throw it down.

She was deafened by his cries. Grateful to see Pio coming to meet her as she returned to the table.

*    *    *

Mimosa walked happily around what the children called The Window Box.

Daffodils, singing to her with zest in the strong wind and rich soil, nearly an acre of them, some wild and welcomed back like old friends, and the crop of new well-bred ones that didn't seem to last half as long. Smaller trumpets, weaker stems, Mimosa thought. While she and Modesto had been in New York for *Rigoletto*, the bulbs had sprouted and shot up under the head gardener's love. His babies, he called them, *mis niños amarillos*, and refused to plant tulips at all.

Mimosa had enjoyed their stay in the apartment near the Lincoln Center; and, since Catalina Lucha had replaced Cherri, there was never any question of her staying at home in Madrid. She went, she told Modesto, as his secretary, doctor, dentist, duvet and security guard. There had been no protest.

The day before they flew to the States, Modesto had received a letter from Australia. He scanned the flimsy sheet eagerly, but his smile neither vanished nor widened.

'It's from Francesco,' he said. 'He says that Cherri should be able to see me when I'm over there. Providing that my tour takes place on schedule.' They exchanged glances over the coffee pot.

After that, La Lucha. Badness was now a memory. Lucha had been met and spoken to, at a small dinner party in Manhattan. Mimosa had kept her glasses in their case so that she would not see the woman too clearly; but Lucha now had a fiancé and didn't flash anything provocatively at Modesto as far as she was aware.

320

The fiancé was a rangy black trumpeter called Eden Krissalis, taller even than Modesto, who had his own combo out in Brooklyn. Mimosa thought he'd make a splendid boxer, and noted that her husband was exceedingly polite to him.

Making light conversation, Modesto had said, 'Catalina began in this business as a gospel singer, darling,' and Mimosa had smiled and murmured 'So do a lot of singing coons,' while Lucha kissed her and thought 'My God! A tame toad!'

Mimosa impulsively bent down and picked some of her old friends, singing.

*       *       *

She lay on her back in the bed, an unlit cigar in her hand, as lights from the Rome traffic swung and dwindled across the ceiling.  No note in the envelope, just the photographs and their negatives. They were now buried deep in her purse. They would go back to the villa, to the music room.

So that was your friend, Baby. That was the ballet-master.

Louis. Very polite, most elegant. You must thank him for me when you see him, Vee. And you will. You won't be without him for much longer.

I shall go into your music room once more because there is no choice. Then –

*Buona notte*, Baby.

*       *       *

Dinner in Rome that evening was eaten at Il Sporcaccione, in the north-west suburb of the city. It was a speedy meal, since Luciano Bardi was due to fly to Ontario to advise the broadcasting authorities there that they could forget any ideas they had (so his spies informed him) about dropping millions of maple leaves on the Arena della Doccia during the concert.

Buzzer Ahmet had arrived in Rome two hours earlier, ready for the meeting next day with his three singers, when hopefully they would finalize programme details. He had also summoned the pianist to attend, just in case time allowed for a run-through of the medley. Now, he looked up from his dish of icecream and *pistacchi* and repeated 'Golf carts?'

'Golf carts,' confirmed Bardi, removing an orchid and some sugar-coated leaves from his peach melba. 'I tell you, they are all crazy!'

Buzzer snorted. 'So what did you tell them?'

'In Italian, *vaffanculo*. In English, to go and fuck themselves. I waste no words, Ahmet, especially not with Yankee retards who think they own the world and all its satellite dishes.' He delved deeper into his dish and discovered damp violets. 'Can you see Fazzoletto in a golf cart?'

'I don't get an immediate picture, no.'

'Tastefully-decorated golf carts, I should add, in all fairness to that prick at NBC. Draped in gold, not a five-iron in sight, just a quiet glide for each nightingale on and off the stage.'

'And what was I doing in the meantime? Conducting them from a tasteful gold toadstool?'

Bardi sniggered, and unearthed a cluster of rose petals. 'You know, now that these transatlantic *stronzi* have caught on to this concert, they want – I quote – glamour and glitz, so that even a hick from Milwaukee will understand the show. Oh, that reminds me, talking of glamour, or rather the lack of it: I have been asked for your services at another concert. Another trio. They would like an open-air spectacular. One week before August 6th. They are what you might call the stealers of thunder. I would call them number one cows, myself.'

'One week before my boys?' exploded Buzzer. 'Don't they know about della Doccia?'

'Oh, they know alright, that is why they want to do it. I'll give you three clues, Ahmet. Lehatz, Bragas, and Ballena.'

'Allah-God! What the hell did you tell them?'

'Ballena gave me the old wide-eyed shit about dear Pepe not seeming to mind when she mentioned it to him. However, considering that he's been honeymooning and must have worn his cock to ribbons by now, whatever was said to him must have registered like custard against an invading army. I told her, and the other tuneless whores, that they could have a date in October and not before. That shut them up! If they can't sabotage *our* bit of

322

world-grabbing dynamite, it would be a waste of their fading top notes.'

He licked his spoon, stood up. 'Must be off, *amico*. Come and see me when you're back here for the orchestra survey – I'll introduce you to Magia's new union leader, militant bastard!'

*　　*　　*

She had lit a small fire in the vast marble hearth in his music room. As the clock chimed, Keta gently placed the photographs on the flames, poking them a little as one slid back towards her.

'Goodnight, Baby,' she whispered. As they hissed and curled, she added the negatives to the blaze. She stayed on her knees by the stabbing mystified flames until only shreds remained. Then she grasped the arm of his chair and levered herself up, stood with her head bowed against the icy mantelshelf.

*Finis*, my Baby. Was it him, I wonder, who told the press about our secret? Somehow, I don't think so.

Tomorrow she would fly home to the States, returning to Italy only for the memorial service. After that, the villa would be sold. Her throat squeezed.

*　　*　　*

*Maestro* Esteban Carrera sat hunched on his piano stool, miserably aware of the draught in the theatre. A pile of scores nested at his feet. The top of the piano was closed, a resting-place for manuscripts and coffee mugs.

'You know what they say about Rome in cold weather like this?' demanded Pio, blowing on his hands.

'No. What?' disinterestedly.

'Dunno. Just wondered if anyone here did.' A thump on the large shoulders, housed today in four favourite cashmere shawls and a striped scarf that swung round his knees.

'Very witty,' and Martes scrutinized his wristwatch. 'It's taking Buzz a long time to get here, isn't it? Christ, he's only lodging across the road!'

'Did you hear what I said?' snapped Pepe, and picked up his notebook.

'Sure we did. Those three tarts want their own wail-along. So what's bugging you, *Señor* Isabel? No contest! – two sops and a bloody pathetic mezzo. I heard Bragas the other day, some recital from Lisbon, and she needs a kick-start to reach A, never mind B flat. So, compared to we three *wunderkind* –'

Pepe groaned. 'God help us, Martes used a German word! Don't say you want to branch out and do bloody Wagner!'

'*Jawohl*,' agreed Modesto.

'So what are you going to do instead of *O Paradis*? *O Himmel*?' Pio grinned, and swiped the pianist's head affectionately with a football magazine. 'Don't worry, *Maestro*, we'll find something for you to do soon! *Dio*, this place is freezing,' and he wandered away, humming.

Then suddenly turned round with an evil smile. 'So what did you tell the girls, Contreras?'

'I bribed them into not doing it.'

'With what, pray?'

Pepe hoisted himself on top of the piano. 'I promised them all my body.'

Guffaws. Even the pianist laughed.

'No, seriously, you clapped-out idiot –'

'I said to Bragas, okay, you drive a hard bargain, darling, but have it your way – two nights it is, and I won't charge you a single peseta.'

Hoots and jeers. 'What's your going rate these days, Pepe?'

'Before or after devaluation?'

Laughter. Pio cuffed him on the knee. 'It's a wonder you've got any bloody sperm left!'

More laughter, and the pianist thumped the piano gleefully.

'Any coffee going round here?' asked Buzzer Ahmet, entering stage left at a brisk pace. *Maestro* Carrera's page-turner hurried off for a fresh pot. 'Oh, by the way, that rival concert that Bragas and Co dreamed up – all a fuss about nothing, you'll be glad to hear – Bardi's rammed a plug in it. Where's that bloody coffee?'

'Oh wouldn't it be nice to see Lehatz with a plug rammed –'

'Thank you, Pio, we get the idea, oh good day, Esteban, is all well, did you have a good journey?'

'*Señor* Isabel won't have to barter his body now,' sniggered Martes, jerking his head as a notebook flew past his ear.

'The next bastard to call me that gets his balls sliced!'

'My humble apologies, *Señor* Isabel.'

'Won't happen again, *Señor* Isabel!'

'Gentlemen, please! Pepe, perhaps I'd better warn you, the penalty for manslaughter in Italy is extremely severe and they don't permit singing in jails . . . Oh good, coffee,' pouring and sipping before it had finished swirling in the cup.

'Right! Let us first check that your solos are agreed, then we can look at the medley . . .'

\*     \*     \*

Mina stared long and hard. Blinked quickly, looked away.

'Well?' asked Isa impatiently. 'What do you think? Was Pepe right?'

Clad in a billowing shirt and a pair of dungarees belonging to Gualterio, she stood with Mina surveying the bear. Ignacio II had been manoeuvred (under duress by Moncho and several cousins) from the terrace to the most overgrown part of the kennel gardens. He stood, now, surrounded by wild garlic and ferns and rocks, naked and brazen.

Pepe had said that he could only stay if he became a proper statue, otherwise Drach would get the bloody thing back and God help him when he tried to think up some good explanation to whoever ran SWI. And, he added, proper statues should not be glittering hazards with castanets that clattered irritatingly in the breeze.

Isa had, therefore, solemnly removed the bear's outfit. He reared over them, smirking. His massive genitals caught the eye at once. Isa put her fingers over her mouth. Mina risked another look, and tittered.

'Suppose someone comes along and sees it?' she said. 'Can't we put a few branches over its . . . er . . . things?'

They clung together, their laughter rising in crescendo.

325

'Mind shifting your fat arse, Pio?' enquired Pepe. 'I'm trying to lean on the piano, if you'd kindly make room. I need rest and a support!'

'Oh sorry, *amigo*, couldn't see you for the coffee pot! Hey, Buzzer, Pepe is worn out, could you find a small bed for his prick?'

Modesto chortled. 'No bed that tiny!'

'So what would yours need, a bloody four-poster?'

Modesto grinned and rolled his eyes.

Buzzer raised an eyebrow, rubbed it with his biro. 'So – are we happy with *Maria*, gentlemen?'

'If she's the Maria I'm thinking of, I'd sooner have her sister,' Pio snickered.

'How about *Tonight?*' asked Pepe, and wished he hadn't.

'You dirty poof!' 'Your place or mine?' Guffaws.

Unperturbed, Buzzer said 'Right, I'll pencil that one in . . . .so, that's two Bernstein. Good. By the way, I'm getting Larry Tremblin to re-orchestrate this lot, and do the linking passages. So, Modesto, will you open with that, the *Maria?*'

'Don't forget it's in English,' Pepe sniggered.

'Certainly didn't sound like it when you did that album, *Señor* Isabel!'

'Who suggested *O paese d'o sole?*' Buzzer, scribbling fast.

'Who do you think?' Modesto snorted. 'You did, didn't you, Air-balloon?' and ruffled Pio's hair. Pio ruffled back with considerable vigour. Modesto scowled.

'I suggest I open with –'

'You, Pulgarcito, have more openings than a ten-legged whore!' Amidst the laughter, Buzzer said to the pianist, 'If you feel like claiming redundancy money, Esteban, I'll sign the chit for you. Gentlemen! To order!'

*    *    *

On his return home, he swung her round, rejoicing in the swell of her stomach against him. 'It's beginning to come together, the concert!' he crowed. 'Nearly, almost!' They kissed fiercely. 'Missed you, missed you! And Grosvenor!' He nuzzled. 'Shall I pop in and see how he is?'

She smiled into his eyes. 'Before or after a glass of wine?'

'Oh. Er . . . after!' He draped his scarf carefully on the floor. 'Anything happen while I was away?'

She held up a wine bottle to the light and squinted at the level. 'I am now training Pau,' she chuckled.

'Training him? In what?'

'He's learning how to be a dog. I throw a stick for him. I shout "Fetch!" He barks, then rushes after it.'

She handed him his glass of wine, saluted him with her eggcup.

'Oh yes – Ignacio II's clothes have been removed, as per your instructions, and Mina has issued a complaint. She would like him to wear either a nappy or a modest pair of jeans!'

He laughed, drained his wine. Then 'Put down that eggcup! I wish to inspect my child!'

\*     \*     \*

The low hospital complex was white, and glittered deafeningly in the hot light.

One of the four car parks was filling up as the afternoon staff began to arrive. The rest were almost unoccupied, lazy trees angling their shadows over the few vehicles standing there. A nurse, off-duty, crossed the tarmac to her car. She wore shorts and a buttercup-yellow shirt. Smiling to herself, a Walkman on her head, rope sandals on her strong feet.

Francesco Giormani watched her for a moment, then let the plastic slats quiver back into place. The sleeve of his cotton jacket caught the leaves of a plant on the windowsill. They jerked, showered dust. The dust crept everywhere.

Cherri sighed, turned her head on the pillows. 'When will Moddie come? When will the Latin bastard get here?'

'His tour starts soon, honey. Don't worry – he promised to be here. You want another drop of water?' and held the beaker to her lips. She took a half-hearted sip and spat it out. 'Jesus, it's like warm koala piss!'

He switched on the TV for her, a screen full of suntanned and

327

darker brown faces, Australia versus the West Indies in a one-day at Melbourne. She slept as her boys were bowled out for 114 without a fight.

*     *     *

'You're late!' reproved Mina, and gestured to Ana to serve the soup.

'I wonder why!' Alfredo guffawed as Isa and Pepe slipped into their seats. Pepe scowled at him, reached for the bread and pepper as Ana finished ladling the steaming liquid into his bowl.

'Well?' demanded Gualterio impatiently. 'You get everything sorted out in Rome?'

'Fairly well, I'd say,' sniffing the soup. Isa tittered, Mina smiled. Gualterio snapped 'What the hell's that supposed to mean? Pompous bastard!'

Isa asked, 'Will it be you or Martes doing the Meyerbeer after all?'

'*O Paradiso?*' He shrugged. 'Modesto. And he's confirmed that he'll be attempting it in French, which should be a lesson to us all.'

Isa enquired, 'Why in French?'

'Because it was written in French.'

'Oh.'

She tasted the soup cautiously. 'So what are you doing instead? The one from *Werther?*'

'No, the *Lamento* from *L'Arlesiana.*'

Mina frowned. 'Why did you pick that dreary thing?' and Gualterio added 'Isn't that just typical of you! Of all the composers in the world, you have to choose that turgid bastard, Cilea. They should've dosed him with Syrup of Figs before he was allowed to set pen to paper!'

Alfredo chortled in agreement. Then said, 'Excuse me for asking, but what sort of soup is this?'

'Tastes like iron tonic, smells like man's spilled seed,' commented Gualterio.

'Yes – what the hell is it?' frowned Pepe, laying down his spoon. 'Don't tell me that Ana's been experimenting again!'

Ana, coming in through the door, bristled.

328

'Ana didn't make it,' said Mina briskly, 'Isa did.'

Spoons clattered. '*Querida?*' pleadingly, 'What did you do to it?'

Isa brandished a chunk of bread. 'It's called *gabacho* soup. It's very good for you,' and she winked at Mina, who winked back.

'*Gabacho?*' frowned Alfredo. 'That's a word we use to insult the French!'

'So what are your other three gut-stranglers to be, son?'

'Isa, what is in it!' hissed Pepe. 'My other three? . . . *Core 'Ngrato* –'

'Christ on a fucking spinning-wheel! *Catari, Catari* . . . such inspiration! Did a bloody tone-deaf angel visit you one night?'

'Alfredo!'

Pepe ignored his brother, burped soup. 'What's that – two? Ah, yes. Then I shall do *Granada* –'

A shower of abuse from Gualterio; who burped soup and flung his spoon on the floor.

'Isa, what did you do, piss in the saucepan?'

'Papaterio!' as Isa choked on her laughter.

'– and finally,' Pepe glanced round at his family, 'I've almost decided on the *Improvviso* from *Andrea Chénier* – you know the one,' and he began to sing '*Un di' all' azzurro spazio*,' while Alfredo conducted him with a knife.

Mina nodded her approval. And 'More soup, anyone?' calmly. Ana giggled.

Gualterio emptied his wine glass. 'What's for the next course, donkey shit? . . . Kindly fill up my glass! . . . Who's doing *Nessun* bloody *Dorma*, then? That fat Italian whale?'

'Isa, stop laughing, what was in that soup?' as the bowls were removed.

'Frogs. Yes, what is Pio going to sing at the concert?' sweetly.

'Fuck Pio! What do you mean, bloody frogs?'

'New frog shop just opened in Sant Moiseps – Mina, can you top up my eggcup while you're doing the honours, please? Come on, what's Pio –' as a hand reached for her throat, '– doing?'

'*O Sole Mio* at a guess, am I right, brother? Jesus, my throat feels like bloody red hot sand! Mina, if you had anything to do with this –'

'Wrong, he's doing *Rondine al Nido* and –'

'*Rondine al* what?'

'*Nido*. Some ditty he learned when he was about six, before he grew a beard. Then *Recondita Armonia* from *Tosca* –'

'We know where it comes from, you pretentious git!' roared Gualterio, and glared at Ana. 'Were you party to this fucking soup farce?'

Ana's shoulders manifested a tiny shake as she proceeded to serve potatoes. They waited for Mina to shout 'Papaterio!' Silence. They stared at her.

'Jesus bloody Christ!' said Alfredo in awe.

'Alfredo!' They breathed a sigh of relief. She beamed, then raised an eyebrow at Isa. 'Shall we tell them, dear?'

'Oh very well,' eggcup clattering against her teeth as she giggled. 'There were bits of fish. And some watercress. And – what was that red stuff?'

'The curry powder you'd spilt; then you decided not to waste it.'

'Oh yes. Plus the remains of the white wine from yesterday –'

'Don't forget that pickled cabbage you found, and the onions –'

'Oh, of course! By the way, has Modesto decided on his own four –?'

'Modesto can go screw himself – what else have I bloody well swallowed?'

'Strips of chicken,' supplied Mina. 'And some Bisto granules. Actually, it mixed together rather well, don't you think? Perhaps tomorrow we could –'

Alfredo said icily, 'I always knew Isa was crazy, but I hadn't realised I'd married her bloody twin sister! You're raving mad, woman! You've flipped! I should have realised it before, when you started calling me Ignacio in bed!'

Three men watched as three women collapsed, shrieking.

*      *      *

'Hey, Buzzer!' and Byron Larch picked his way through the rows of seats which were piled with jackets and instrument cases, scowling at the noise that continued unabated. A French horn blew a raspberry, and there was laughter. Then mercifully the noise eased, violas and violins placed upright on knees.

Buzzer wiped his face with a striped handkerchief and watched his tormentor struggling towards him.

'Five!' he snapped to the orchestra. '*Cinque! Cinco!*' To Larch, 'Can't it wait, whatever it is?'

First flute emitted a high arpeggio.

'There's trouble!' yelled Larch. He made it to the end of the practice hall and looked up at Ahmet on the podium. His resonant voice did not diminish and the orchestra listened with interest. 'It's Frenzy!' he gasped, 'The buggers have gone on strike!'

The members of the Teatro dell' Orfeo sniggered. This was the third time today that *Signor* Larch had dropped by and annoyed their new *maestro*.

'What about Firenze?' sighed Buzzer. Despite his mopping, sweat still glistened.

'They're on strike! I've been faxed by that twit Fica, the Magia Armonica are refusing to play with −' waved his arm, '− this lot! Their new union leader told Fica that −'

'Just one moment,' said Buzzer. He suddenly turned to deliver a gaze at the orchestra as they cackled. They had learned very quickly to watch the *maestro* with attention, and now jerked upright, grew silent.

He stared at them: then gave a brief nod. *Sotto voce*, to his visitor, 'I have been speaking to *Maestro* Fica on the phone. I suggest that, once again, your panic is not in order. The spokesman was making his traditional point at the traditional beginning of a traditional Italian rehearsal. We are, Larch, in Italy. We are not at the Aldeburgh Festival with the London Symphony Orchestra!'

He raised his baton once more, and stared at Larch without a smile.

'Oh. Sorry.' Larch summoned a pale grin. 'Didn't realise you knew.'

'It is my business to know everything concerning my musicians. Now, if you'll kindly let us proceed?'

'Yes, yes, of course. I just thought . . . just in case . . .' He turned to go, then asked pleasantly, 'So − what are you rehearsing at the moment?'

Buzzer's eyes fixed briefly on the ceiling. 'The overture, Larch.'

He shot his cuffs, nodded warningly to the leader. 'Page three, first bar, *celli*!' And, as Larch had not moved, '*The Sicilian Vespers*, by Verdi.'

Larch stared. 'Sicilian, did you say? Ahmet, is that wise? In Italy? With all the Mafia implications?'

'Dear me, that had quite escaped my attention! How remiss of me!' He rapped his stick, 'Ladies, gentlemen: page three, first bar, *The Venetian Vespers*!'

Orchestral readiness in silence, apart from one lady in the second violins who didn't stop laughing in time.

*       *       *

'Sweetheart?' he said as the nurse closed the door behind her. 'Sweetheart!'

'Moddie.' It was a soft croak.

'Dear Christ.' He cleared his throat, lifted her hand and rubbed it against his bristly jaw. His face, she could see, was dewy with sweat. An iron-hot day.

She made an effort. 'Ta for coming. Couldn't have been easy.'

He pretended to misunderstand. 'It damn well was not! First Singapore, disastrous recital; then a bloody airline that decided there were three too many clouds in the sky and the flight was delayed by six hours. And this heat has swollen my toes!'

He sat carefully on the bed, arm loosely around her shoulders, and talked and joked and made her laugh, wanting to howl his rage and grief when she jolted with pain and fought it fiercely. He wished that he was blind, so that he couldn't see her.

He told her about the concert on August 6th, watching her eyes in dark sockets as they listened and heard every mention of the music. He gazed at the basic contours, mentally filled them with flesh and committed them to his heart. He said 'Do you remember our first *Tosca*? In Salzburg, when you were so nervous that you fell against what was supposed to be a solid iron door and it crumpled up, how the audience laughed, and how they *bravo*'d you afterwards . . . Oh my darling . . .' She held his hand.

'Anyway. I'm doing *E lucevan le Stelle* as one of my four solos,' fighting his tears, grinning foolishly.

332

The nurse returned, 'You must have your medication now, Cherri, you can't leave it any longer.'

Modesto wrapped a strand of her brown hair round his fingers, 'Darling, I've brought a surprise for you. Just a small —'

'Give!' she whispered eagerly. He swallowed, glad to look away as he reached for the summer jacket hanging on the back of the chair. 'It was the only thing I could think of, darling.' From a pocket, he pulled out a package. 'For you,' voice shaking.

She silently pulled away the wrappings, and stared at the video. Tears engulfed her, stroking the picture. 'Our *Otello*! It's —' Her head fell back on the pillows, hands clenching the gift. 'Oh Moddie, I never thought I'd be around to see this . . . Oh Martes!'

He pressed his cheek to her wet one.

'*Querida*,' he whispered, 'My darling best. I made them give me this, is the pilot. Is a winner, *cara*, like no other, ever. This way, we'll never be parted, do you understand?'

After he had gone, she held it in her hands even when she slept.

# 20

Over the years, Pio Fazzoletto had invented many feast days of his own. And now, seeing that his diary had a small gap between *Don Carlo*, a recording of Bellini's *Norma*, the Arena concert rehearsals and a tour of the States and Canada with his pet flautist Arturo Gremillini, he invented yet another one.

He decided to call it, simply, Pio's Day.

It would occur, he thought, checking the calendar, on a Sunday. April 20th, to be exact. And he began his adventure by telephoning Azucarero at his home in Ibiza.

The young man was quite impressed. 'Sure I'm game! Do you want the rest of the guys?'

'The rest of which guys?'

'My band, *amigo* – El Pedo Negro.'

'And why not?' Pio said jovially, hoping that the horses wouldn't mind. The new white mare, according to the head stable lad, was a highly-strung and nasty-tempered bugger with big sharp teeth.

'Great, man! So, who else is coming?'

'The more the merrier,' said Pio vaguely. Was the 20th too near the Easter observances? Still, that would have been the week before, and surely to God Christ wouldn't mind? Perhaps they could do a few hymns.

'No, man, I mean who else? Like names?'

'Oh!' Pio scratched his head. 'Names. Well, what about that *hombre*, whatsisname – reminds me of an insect, a stinging one.'

'Ah, you mean Bee-bee! Sure, he's crazy enough to qualify, but I doubt if he'll be out by then – got done for flogging acid to bloody illegal immigrants in London. Still, if he gets remission, I could get in touch with –'

Pio was open-mouthed. 'Perhaps not Bee-bee,' he said.

'Hey, what about Tizania? She's a rave! You'll really pull the

334

crowds and the media if you have that tart flashing her tits! Shit – shame that Lavagna's not around, I could've done another duet with him.'

'Media?' faintly. By the end of the conversation, he realised that Pio's Day was turning into a pop festival of horrifying proportions.

'Adriana!' he screeched.

When she came, he said piteously, 'This concert on Pio's Day . . .'

She laughed merrily. 'On what? . . . Oh, I see, it's another Fazzoletto *festa*, is it?'

He sank his teeth into a large apple and eyed her sternly. 'Concerts for me are very serious matters, *cara*. Not jokes.'

'And so they are for most artistes, but not everyone wants the day named after them.' She laughed again. 'What about it?'

'It will be held here.'

Adriana stared at him. 'Here? Here in Italy? Or – oh no, Pio; not here, in our home!'

He nodded and crunched his fruit.

'What sort of concert, then? Chamber music, quintets, Haydn, what?'

'Not quite, little dove. More of a popular mix of concert. With, well, Azucarero –'

'No!'

'– and El Pedo Negro, and Tizania –'

'NO!'

'– and me of course, and I expect Contreras will join in too.'

She looked at him. 'Have you asked him? Pepe?'

'Not yet, *cara*, but I'm sure he'll find the time for it – I'll offer him *Mattinata*! I also want to do a bit of religious stuff, something like *Ave Maria* –'

She strode to the window. 'Where were you thinking of staging this pantomime?'

'By the stables, dearest.'

Adriana slapped his hand as he reached for another apple. 'The stables? And where do we put the bloody horses, in the garage?'

'I meant the fields near the stables. By the woodland,' pleadingly. 'Lots of room there for all the crowds and the radio or TV guys, and tents, and the cafeteria and –'

'Oh, Pio!' Helpless, she sank on to his lap. 'What would life be without you?'

*       *       *

'But I want to play Fetch!' Pau's solemn eyes blinked at her as she sat at the desk and reached for her notepad.

'Little one,' said Isa gently, removing her pen from his fingers, 'I have to make a phone call. Can't it wait?'

A determined shake of the head. He held out the stick invitingly.

'Couldn't Lluís play Fetch with you?' without much hope. Another shake of the head, swiftly followed by 'He's gone out on his bike. And last time, he threw the stick at me and nowhere else.'

'Okay, okay,' and she pushed herself out of the chair. Frowned as a piece of cotton from her smock snagged on the corner of the desk. All those pesetas, all the additional embroidery, and it was already fraying. Damn Pepe and his 'my wife is not going around wearing my old shirts!' After she had made this phone call, she would put on an ancient green one of his and hope he wouldn't recognise it. 'Just one Fetch, then I must do some phoning!'

Pau followed her on to the terrace. It was mild this afternoon, and she could smell the earth warming up, hear machinery whirring in the distance as though the world had yawned and stretched and propped its door open again.

Pau asked, 'Why do the birds make such a lot of noise, Isa?'

'They're having a party,' she replied absently. He grabbed her hand, 'Can I go to it? Can I?' Dear God, will Grosvenor Dolores be like this? And she smiled to herself. Or, indeed, Floria Isabel Dolores Roberta. She took the stick from him, and he forgot the birds.

'Just one throw,' she warned. 'And when you've found the stick, bring it back and sit quietly here and wait for me. Okay?' He nodded eagerly. 'Right – here we go!' She swung the stick, felt a twinge in her back. Her increasing weight had started making jokes. '. . . . FETCH!'

And she hurled the stick far out into the tangle of shrubbery. From here, she could just see the head of Ignacio II. She made sure that Pau negotiated the steps safely, watched him disappear into the misty new leaves before returning to her desk.

Dialled, waited, listening to the clicks. 'Drach Agency. Robert Drach speaking.'

She chuckled. 'Hello, sexy baritone!'

'Ezita! What a nice surprise – how's the foetus, darling?'

'Growing and making my back ache, thanks!'

'And how is Sniffer? Has he put a padlock on it yet? In this week's *Woman's Own*, it says that preggy ladies shouldn't –'

He enjoyed the sound of her giggles, smiled at the phone in his hand.

'Bobby, two things to mention to you, which you might want to discuss with Pepe when he gets back from New York.'

He observed sadness in the voice. 'Cheer up, it's only *Turandot*, you silly mare, not a bloody walk on the moon! When does he go – Friday?'

'Yup. He won't let me go with him, of course, not on such a long trip, with me in this never-ending state. Ah well – put up and shut up, as they say!' Her voice brightened. 'Right,' briskly, 'first, he's been asked to do a multi-mix evening concert with Fazzoletto, April 20th.'

'Multi who?'

'Mix. Pop stuff, bit of classical, Charity Gala in reverse if you like. To be held at Pio's place, in Bologna. Has he got clearance for this, only he seems to think there's a promotional for the Magda Fund around that date, and he'll need –'

'I know what he'll need, Ez, leave it with me. Next?'

'Monda Ballena wants him for an open-air recital in Paris with the Vienna Phil, this September 7th . . .'

'Oh fuck me!'

'Shut up! Did you hear that, the 7th.' Then solemnly, 'In front of the Eiffel Tower.' She heard the sound of china cup hitting saucer.

'In front of what? The bloody Awful Tower? The Paris Awful Tower?' A bellow of mirth. 'Those two will never get away with it! A sing-song in front of a mob of wine-sodden Frogs? Jesus Christ, one under-pitched top C and they'll hurl him into the fucking Seine!'

Laughing, 'Write it down, Roberto!'

As she replaced the receiver, a doleful voice called from the terrace 'Isa! I'm cold. And it's raining a little bit.'

Laughing with love, she brought him into the study and sat him down, a damp bedraggled little figure clutching the retrieved stick.

'How about a nice mug of Isa's hot lemon and barley, mmm?'

'Oh yes please. Please please! Can I have some of that dark water in it?'

'What?'

'That brown water that *Abueli* drinks. He says it puts hairs where a man ought to have them.'

She stifled a squeak. 'Yes, I'm sure it does, little one. And the answer's no!'

\*     \*     \*

Pepe Contreras had settled easily and happily into the New York apartment normally frequented by Modesto. There had been a stack of invitations waiting for him on an American version of an antique table, plus a fanfare of flowers in Greek vases. And on the imposing mantelshelf in the drawing-room stood a large square of cardboard, on which was printed in Modesto's best block capitals "DO NOT FORNICATE IN MY BED".

Everything in the apartment was cream and beige and dark chocolate.

He told Isa on the phone 'I feel as though I should be wearing high heels and have a couple of Afghans on a lead!'

The apartment appeared to be open house, too. American and second-generation European accents dominated it from the moment of his arrival. He had very little difficulty with the English fired at him from all sides, but a lot of the expressions were confusing. 'On-going Geminism', for example, turned out to refer to the second pair of twins born to the wife of the producer. And music call, to the fraternity, was 'muzz-bite'.

'I have just had my first muzz-bite,' he said proudly to Isa during one phone call.

338

Sniggered, as her anxious voice came over transatlantic miles, 'Have you got any cream to put on it?'

Much to his surprise, he not only enjoyed the general atmosphere, but he almost liked Tim Divine as well. He looked like Schubert's twin brother, bushy hair, rosebud mouth and spectacles so small that they could have belonged to a child of five. His hands, plump hands, waved and gestured at blurring speed as though he were conducting a hundred orchestras, each playing a different symphony. He was overweight, and had the disconcerting habit of giving a smile that converted itself into a snarl in a flash second.

Love Divine, they called him. He had had four wives, an almost-forgotten love child, and a current girlfriend who designed four-poster beds for the fringes of society or for those who had once visited a Scottish castle. He was also, Pepe decided, a complete genius, and looked at him admiringly from two perspectives – *Turandot* and the recording of Rossini's *Otello* which they would do together in June.

Over generous drinks on the first evening, Divine had simultaneously talked, explained, drank, smoked cheroots and analysed the entire score of *Turandot*.

'I hope,' he said, peering steadily at his tenor over small misted lenses, 'that you've had good time to correct that stoopid mistake of yours in the *Nessun Dorma?*'

Pepe's eyes narrowed slightly. 'Pardon me? Mistake?'

'Sure. Mistake. A real *schlimmer.*'

'Yes?' cautiously. This was impossible. He felt a mistake like a cut on the tongue.

Tim Divine watched him, his small eyes bland. When it became obvious that Contreras didn't know what the hell he meant, he widened the bland eyes.

'Libretto,' laconically.

Pepe thought, but I'm fucking word-perfect! 'Yes?' he said again, politely.

'It's in Italian throughout,' said Divine, sucking his cheroot.

Carefully taking a sip of his triple Martini, trying to avoid the long stick and floating flowers, Pepe managed 'Yes. Thank you. I did know –' before Divine leaned forward and patted his knee. 'No offence, Contreras. I suppose on the few occasions I've heard you in this rôle, you've been feeling homesick, right?'

Pepe's bewilderment increased. Homesick? How bloody old does he think I am?

His new mentor was still regarding his sympathetically. He went in for the kill without changing his kind tone.

'Your pronunciation of two words in the *Dorma*. Both of which occur quite close together – mirrors of each other, if you follow me?'

'My pronouncings?' Affronted, Pepe's chin lifted. 'I always in classic music pay my attention to pronouncings and the artistical interpret!'

'I am not talking about your fucking artistical interpret!' The smile was a snarl before Pepe could blink. 'You mean you didn't know? No-one said to you, hey Pepe, you're not on the plains in Spain now, old buddy? You weren't homesick and missing that god-awful payella? So why the shit do you pronounce Italian like Spanish? Two words, pal – *speranza* and *silenzio*.' Snarl flash smile. '*Speranza* the Contreras way is sperantha. *Silenzio* is silenthio. Get me? That's not *italiano*, if you think about it.'

He stood up, raising a hand as he was hailed from behind. 'I'm sure you'll attend to it – just thought we'd get the major errors out of the way before we tackle the lesser ones, right?'

He had thought about this long and hard afterwards. Memories swam at him, Vito laughing at this same error, his feeble joke about his great grandmother being attacked by an Italian kitten. Shit, he thought he'd cured himself of this, years ago.

'*Speran*-TSA,' he breathed as he shaved.

'*Silen*-TSIO,' as he showered.

\*     \*     \*

'But the mare is due to foal around that time!' protested the *capo* of the stables.

'Then move her!' snapped Pio.

The weather was gliding into warmer days, and he was glad to exchange the cashmere for silk. He tugged the bright patterns around his shoulders, and tossed a cigar butt through the open door into the yard.

'To where, *Signor* Pio?' sarcastically. 'To the open fields? Won't your audience object?'

Pio's eyes narrowed angrily. Straw-festooned twat. 'We have other stables we can use for her! What about the pair we use for emergencies?'

'You had them converted two years ago.'

Taken aback, 'Did I really? Into what?'

'An art studio. You wanted to take up painting, you said, so *Signora* Adriana said you could have the spare stables as a studio.'

'Great God, so I did!' Eagerly, 'Are the brushes still there? My canvases? I must go and look!'

'But the mare –'

'Okay, we won't use the field by the stables, we'll use the 500-acre stretch instead for the audience, she'll be fine then!' and he swept out, shawls rippling, anxious to inspect his artist's studio.

The stable boss watched him go, then spat on the floor. A pop festival. And he'd heard that Azucarero was going to sing a religious song or some such idolatry with *Signor* Pio! No wonder the human race was in such a bloody mess.

*　　*　　*

It seemed that the only place in the apartment for privacy and quiet reflection was the bathroom. Pepe sullenly climbed into the heart-shaped tub for the fifth time that day. The door was locked, the key on a glass shelf nearby. He wondered if Martes actually used the hundreds of bottles of cologne up there.

Pepe was haunted by his pronouncings. The more he strived, the worse they became. Divine had congratulated him today on having translated the whole thing into Spanish in such a quick time, and suggested that instead of singing *Nessun Dorma* he did a short flamenco ballet instead.

Not only was he haunted, he was hunted. Hunted by Lucha. Even her bloody fiancé fancied him. He lay back, grinning

341

suddenly, and watched the well-organized water race round his hips.

*Speran*-TSA. *Silen*-TSIO. I hate the sight of this bloody bath.

*     *     *

'Dear *Signora*,' the letter began. Isa frowned. *Signora*? And the letter was in English.

She scanned the single typewritten page, didn't bother looking for an address or a signature. The letter had arrived in the kennel without challenge from Federico, trapped between a stack of music publications advertising new rum-flavoured gargles and sweat-resistant socks.

She had spent the last hour or so embroidering a baby shawl, just managing to restrain herself from adding a border of treble clefs in silver.

'Dear *Signora*, Please forgive a stranger writing to you.'

I will not read this, she thought grimly. I shall throw it in the . . .

'But after much thinking, feel it to be of importance. I have no wishes to hurt you, but I have to give warning. About Contreras. I am sorry, but this is repeat of the first time, and I try to warn *Signora* Martes. But you should know that Lucha does not change her spots —"

She carefully laid the baby shawl beside her on the sofa.

'— and word comes from a friend in New York that she and your man are instantly together, kissing —'

Isa dropped the letter from the worried stranger, pleased to see that her fingers were calm and her mind steady.

'Hey, you okay, birdbrain?' She hadn't heard Alfredo come into the kennel.

'Oh, hi,' turning to greet him, slightly dazed, unaware of her paleness.

'Isa? What's wrong?' Went to her, sat beside her, his eyes roaming over her face. 'Has something happened, *querida*?'

She gestured to the letter. He picked it up, frowned at the English words, stumbled slowly over some of them, reading aloud like a child with a text book. Isa winced at them, put a hand over

342

Grosvenor Dolores curled beneath Pepe's old green shirt.

' "– instantly together, kissing, and –" ' He glanced at her quickly. ' "– and that she has been for at least one night in his apartment." '

Isa's heart froze in mid-air. 'No!'

Alfredo shouted 'Who is this bastard? Who writes to you these bloody lies? Right! We'll see about this!' Grabbed the phone, one hand squeezing her shoulder. 'Police! Be quick about it!' his eyes never moving from the sheet of paper.

Please let the hurt stop. The numbness was wearing off under Alfredo's noise. She knew it wasn't true, of course. Not Pepe. It was not true. And suddenly she needed to get on a plane, be sick in a bag, run through New York in his green shirt and stop the words being written. Instead, she sat there dumbly, until Alfredo took her into the main house and left her with Mina.

*    *    *

After the police, the walk. Through the privacy of the foliage, to the side gate with its thick ivy, and on to the steep downward path to Sant Moiseps.

Mina had held her hand and patted it as Inspector Chanchullo deposited two damp dead leaves on the carpet and accepted coffee. Answering questions, her mind spinning. Had Mimosa felt like this? Of course she had, she now had a gossamer lead around Modesto's neck. Time zones. What time was it now in New York? Her usually quick mind refused arithmetic.

Made a statement, signed it. When they had gone, announced 'I'm going for a walk.'

'Oh no you're not!' Alfredo said sharply. 'You're going to telephone Pepe!'

'Don't be ridiculous,' firmly, 'I'm not going to disturb him with this . . . this bloody rubbish!' Voice stumbling and falling. 'I'm going for a walk.' In his green shirt.

She heard Alfredo say 'Then I bloody will!' and Mina speaking calmly, 'Not yet, let's just consider –'

'Consider what?' His anger bounced after her. 'Consider whether we should disturb him in case he's still in bed with that –'

She ran carefully through trees as knotty as pineapples. There was a deep pothole where the path curved sharply towards the village, and Pepe had scowled and said that if the authorities had brains a quarter the size of that hole they would have filled it in by now instead of paying regular compensation to injured motorists.

Then he had swung her hand high in the air, and they'd danced their way round it, before kissing in full view of a white pigeon.

Now, only recent tyre-marks from the police car. Damp. A cool breeze that went still if the sun came out. The green shirt grew wet with perspiration and loneliness. She went into the white church and sat in the back pew.

*       *       *

After ten rings, the kennel phone automatically switched to the number of the main house. Pepe sighed impatiently. She must be with Mina.

Alfredo answered with a sharp '*Dígame!*'

'*Hola*, brother, where's Isa?'

A moment's silence. Then 'Thanks to you, we don't bloody know! She went for a walk over two hours ago, and hasn't come back!'

'What the hell are you –?'

'The postman's been, brother, with a friendly letter for your wife, an anonymous letter, spelling out that you're up to your old tricks, you whoring bastard!'

'Now wait a fucking minute –'

'Isa has had an anonymous letter, cretin, about you and Lucha! Isa is upset, Isa looked like death meeting itself, brother, when the cops had been! Isa went for a walk, she and that baby of yours, two hours ago, Mina is going frantic – do you read me, brother?'

'Oh dear God! Oh Christ!' The panic was real, the fear heard. 'Find her! Find her for me, Alfredo, for Christ's sake!'

*       *       *

344

The man in grey dungarees sat behind his display of melons and his homemade sun-faded sign and remarked to a friend 'All dressed up and nowhere to go!' and they sniggered in a kindly way as they watched the green-shirted figure walk first on the black glassy pavement and then in the road.

Gualterio spotted her as he stood by the unshuttered window in the billiard room of the *taberna*, a converted barn with ancient sawdust and enormous barrels labelled *Vino tinto* in chalk. He was standing with his cue when he glanced outside and saw the girl in the green shirt, the dampened curls. Dropping the cue, he hurried into the street after her, 'Hey! *Chica*! Isabel!'

She heard his voice, slowed to a halt.

'What the bloody hell are you doing here on your own? Where's Moncho?' He was panting.

She tried to smile as reality faded in. 'I was just walking.'

'I can damn well see that! How many times have we told you that –' He peered at her through the tossed hair. 'Christ in a hen's nest, you've been crying! What's Mina thinking of, to let you – What the hell's happened?'

'Gualterio, shut up.' Her nose was beginning to run again, and she lifted the shirtflap to wipe it.

'Come with me!' grimly, and marched her to the *taberna*, to the *taberna* proper, a dark room where even the loops of sausage seemed to make a pleasant sound. He sat her down on a stool, keeping an eye on her as he reached for the phone on the bar and pulled it towards him. The bartender nodded, continued his work at the sink, soaking labels off empty bottles and rinsing them. A black and white TV on a shelf was showing a Walt Disney cartoon. She sat obediently on the hard stool and watched Bugs Bunny.

Gualterio finished his call, spoke gruffly to the barman, and eventually pressed a small glass of brandy into her hand. '*Una copita*!' he growled. 'Drink it!'

She drank the rough fire, oh please don't let me see Pepe in my mind. Please. Not his face. She choked suddenly, and while they waited for Moncho, she told Gualterio what had happened.

\*　　\*　　\*

345

He came home four days later, and they saw that his face had changed. The skin was tight and pale, and the blue shadow of the jaw and top lip stood out sharply.

There had, of course, been phone calls, the sound of pressure in his voice, the numberless times he called her '*carita*'. Little face. He was sending his arms to her so that they could hold her for him until he returned. Above all, she believed him, but he no longer seemed real. And he brooded in his borrowed apartment; the laughter had left her voice and that he missed above all else.

When he returned, she saw a small healing cut at the side of his mouth, and touched it gently, wondering. He said, 'That was Pong's ring,' and there came a welcome shadow of a giggle. 'Whose what?'

'You remember, *querida* – Ping, Pang and Pong in *Turandot*. I got too close to Pong's waving arms!'

Alone again together, they nestled in the bed of fresh linen. For some reason, Ignacio the First was now on Isa's bedside table. He looked twice as large on the smaller surface.

It was awkwardness. As he stroked the mound of Grosvenor, he asked if all was well with The Baby after the shock, and what Don Salvador had said after her emergency examination. He tried not to notice as she moved slightly from the stroking hand.

'The Baby is fine,' she said stiffly.

She asked if he had seen Keta while he was in New York, wanting to yell at him where has Grosvenor Dolores gone?

'Yes, I saw her. She hopes to see you at Vito's memorial service.'

'And will she?'

'If you feel fit enough to travel,' and his hand fell away from the nameless baby.

'When is the memorial service?' Who exactly am I talking to here, she thought wildly; and he replied 'April 17th. The day before our next meeting with Buzzer. The first rehearsal, actually, musically speaking.' Christ Jesus, I sound like my diary!

'Then the memorial is three days before the pop festival,' tugging her pillow.

'The what?'

346

'Don't tell me you've forgotten! What did Adriana call it . . .
Oh yes. Pio's Day!'

Careful, Isa, you nearly smiled then, he thought bitterly. He
wanted to argue about it, to say cancel the bloody thing. Instead,
he fixed his eyes on the invisible night ceiling and said 'You didn't
believe that bloody letter, did you?'

'Of course I didn't.'

Sharply, 'Just that? No more to say to me?'

Oh, so much, far too much. 'What else is there to say?'

'Do you believe me, Isa?'

'Yes. I think so,' and he felt her arm quiver.

His sudden anger was a surprise to them both. He left the bed
abruptly, pulled on his robe, and without a word left the room.

She heard a glass ring against the nest of bottles on the bar,
then a clatter, more glass on a collision course. His side of the bed
cooled quickly.

Why don't I do what I want to do, get up and go to him? Hold
him, talk.

She lay motionless, occasionally moving her mouth to blow
away a corner of the sheet which was tickling her lip. Her throat
ached with the effort not to cry, then came the memory of Bobby's
voice, 'Come on, you silly mare, your face looks like a fucking
squashed cake when you blubber!' Christ it hurts, it hurts when he
calls him The Baby.

A crash from the other room jerked her back, and without
further thought she leapt out of bed and ran to see. He had
pushed a bowl of flowers off the table. His head was on his arms as
he slumped across the polished surface.

'Pepe? *Mi querido*?' She bent over him, touched his shoulder, the
thick wavy hair. He sat up slowly, and his eyes were wet.

'Oh my beloved!' She was appalled. He pulled her roughly on
to his knee, and she kissed his face all over, light kisses. 'I love you,
believe you, I love you so much, oh Pepe, I –'

'*Cucufato*,' he said, his arms like a vice, 'listen to me. Listen, for
God's sake. The day I stop loving you, and only you, will be when
God disinvents music and we have to start all over again with
bloody plainchant and square crochets!'

She looked into his eyes for the first time since the letter, touched each eyelid. Smiled deeply. 'I love you.'

'More than square crotchets?'

'More than bloody oval minims!'

Then the phone rang.

'Fuck off!' he yelled, and she giggled as he snatched up the receiver.

Pio said plaintively, 'Pulgarcito, will you sing *Ave Maria* with me on Pio's Day?'

# 21

After that, there followed hectic days. After that, they could not bear to be apart ('Isn't it too bloody sweet for words,' said Alfredo), and so Isa accompanied Pepe to Rome for the memorial service which was attended by more than five hundred friends and colleagues, and at which Pio sang *Ingemisco tanquam reus* from Verdi's *Requiem*. The scandal had been buried.

Keta said to Isa over coffee, 'I'd still give a few thousand dollars to find the dung-heap who leaked it to the papers!'

America had given her a new hairstyle, more severe, less red, which made her eyes lively. Not Louis, she thought for the millionth time. His gloats had been private, he enjoyed them too much to share them with anyone. Poor, indeed, Louis. He had died soon after the awards ceremony, a tiny obituary, deep sorrow from the Reggio Bettino Chorale.

Isa touched her hand, smiled awkwardly. 'These anonymous someones are a bloody nuisance, aren't they?'

'Any news about yours?' asked Keta with a crooked grin. And as Isa shook her head and piled sugar into her cup, added 'I reckon we ought to form a club, you and Mimosa, Adriana and me!'

After the memorial service, word came from the Vatican that it planned in due course to inaugurate another award, on a par with the Gigli Medallion. This would be named in honour of Vito Lavagna; and the outright winner of it would be the singer who had achieved the highest accolades for public performances, recordings, and general services to music.

'That should triple Modesto's work-rate,' grinned Pio as they met in the empty Opera House in Rome for their piano runthrough. He smacked his lips as he reached for another pizza. 'Instead of a mere five hundred operas a year, he'll multiply that by ten and compose one of his own each week, then conduct every orchestra in Europe –'

'– the world,' interrupted Pepe.

'*Scusi*, yes. The world. Then a quick day trip to Mars to record a few love duets with himself –'

'A few?' Pepe frowned. The knot of his tie had been loosened, the tie itself was flipped over one shoulder as he sorted through various manuscripts.

'Ah, but don't forget – a few to him means about a thousand to the rest of us,' and Pio bent down in lumbering fashion to pick up a silk shawl. He sniffed it. 'This smells of piss! Couldn't you have waited, Martes?'

'Oh, very hilarious,' Modesto yawned. His donkey jacket lay across his knees, a tablecloth for his *hors d'oeuvres*. 'Unlike some of us, I am not stuck in a bloody rut! My next project is to do all Schubert's *lieder*, then Schumann – all in German, of course – and then a film.'

'What bloody film? God, don't say MGM have signed you up!'

'Can't you see the credits rolling?' dreamily from Pio. 'Starring, co-starring, directed by, produced by, written by and sung by, none other than –'

'Modesto Big Balls!' cackled Pepe.

'At least it wouldn't be called *Scusi* fucking *Luigi*!' and Modesto aimed a kick at Pio's backside.

They were waiting for their pianist. Buzzer Ahmet was patrolling the back of the stage, deep in thought, licking an overspill of mustard on his hot dog.

'Yeah, how's that one going, Sperm Bank? Any release date yet?'

Pio scowled. 'They've approached all the cinema chains in bloody Europe, and nobody's shown an interest!'

Instant jeers. Pepe did a little tap dance to applause.

Buzzer approached, wiping his hands on a serviette.

'Can we make a start now?' Modesto asked plaintively.

'Certainly we can, if the piano would care to play itself,' said Buzzer. 'Esteban should be here in a minute –'

'Hey look, *amigos*! Here he comes, Fats Waller himself!' and there were ironic cheers as the pianist entered from the wings. Less irony when he was seen to be carrying a tray. The tray bore

350

crystal glasses and a freshly-uncorked bottle of champagne.

'Christ, what's this in aid of?' and they watched breathlessly as Buzzer grinned and poured. He raised his glass: 'Happy birthday, Modesto!'

Modesto smirked.

'What? Your bloody birthday? Cheers, happy days!'

'*Viva* Martes!'

Modesto bowed, spilling some of his champagne, '*Muchísimas gracias!*'

'How old are you this year?' demanded Pepe. 'As far as I recall, last year you said you were forty-seven, which means that you are really somewhere between fifty-five and fifty-eight.'

Pio belched as he interrupted 'So – if we subtract ten from . . . what was it you said, Pepe? . . . from something, anyway, that should give us –' His finger busily sketched numbers in the fine dust on the piano. ' . . . .er . . . fifty-seven . . . what comes after fifty-seven? . . . fifty-nine . . . You're sixty!'

'I am not fucking sixty!' howled Martes as they roared with laughter.

'Yes you are! Christ, poor Mimosa, I bet she needs a bloodhound to find it these days! Anyway, happy birthday! *Cantare! Mangiare! Fottere!*'

Ringing cheers, and Modesto smiled. 'I ask you! Do I look sixty?'

'Not a bit of it,' soothed Pepe. 'But I wish you wouldn't leave your pension book on my scores, I've just sorted them out.'

Amidst the renewed laughter, Buzzer grinned 'Okay, gentlemen, to order, if you please! Esteban, not from the top yet, we want a try-out of a song recently added . . .' He flicked through a stack of manuscripts, '. . . this one. Here – the Russian one. French horn intro, then – dum di-dum di, dum di-dum di . . .'

Carrera nodded. Pio bent over his own copy, humming. 'What the hell does it mean? *Ochi* what?'

'*Ochi tchorniye,*' said Buzzer patiently. 'Russian for "dark eyes". Modesto was kind enough to suggest it.' Groans.

Pio sang the first few bars. 'It's jolly. Makes a good contrast to that bloody *Memory* dirge. Yes, I like it. It cheers Pio up, makes him want to smile and shout Hurrah!' and he waltzed round the piano as Carrera played.

Buzzer consulted his notes. 'Yes, very light-hearted. Anyone here know what the words mean?' Heads were shaken. Buzzer read out loud, '"You have been my ruin, dark eyes, you have ended my happiness forever."' He peered at them over his reading-glasses.

'Oh,' said Pio, crestfallen. Then, 'I suggest we ask Boris Yeltsin to go shove his cock in a bottle of vodka!' Laughter.

Buzzer rapped the piano with his makeshift baton, a child's giant fun pencil. 'Are we ready, gentlemen? . . . Esteban? . . . One and two and . . .'

*     *     *

Two separate cars wound their way to the Fazzoletto villa. Adriana and Pio travelled in one, Isa and Pepe in the other. Isa was getting bored with poplar trees and cypresses and blue hills that never came nearer; looked forward simply to the relaxation Adriana had promised. Pepe, on the other hand, knew that he preferred the treescape to what lay ahead.

'Why *Ave* bloody *Maria*?' he had complained bitterly to Pio. 'It'll sound ludicrous in between all that pop stuff!' Pio had responded cheerfully, 'Don't you believe it, *amico*! – when the synthesizer gets going, you'll be surprised how jolly it can sound!'

Isa put her head on his shoulder. 'This is heaven. Being with you, I mean.'

'Better than long-distance calls, mmm?'

'Oh much! I like to see your mouth when you speak, not just imagine it.'

He kissed her satisfactorily. Then 'Shut up,' as she started to speak, and kissed her again. He was about to begin on the third when she struggled. 'What the –?'

She sat up and stared over his shoulder through the window. 'Pepe, what in God's name is that?' and giggled.

They gazed at the giant image of a red rearing pony in one of the pastures. Tiny black figures swarmed over it, ant-style. Endless ropes were pegged around it.

352

'Oh shit!' Pepe groaned. 'Does he have to advertise his bloody circus?'

'But what is it?'

'It's a bloody horse!'

'I can see that, *estúpido*, but what is it for?'

His jaw twitched. 'That, *princesa*, is a sign to the world that here is Pio's pop *fiesta*. I think I wish that I was dead!'

\* \* \*

Gualterio gazed at the portrait of Magda long after Detective Inspector Pandeo had departed.

'Oh,' he'd said, shrugging on his overcoat, 'What a lovely likeness of her!' Stared at it, fastened the top button and forgot the others. 'I miss her very much.' Turned to Magda's father and said wistfully, 'We used to take coffee together, she and I. And lend each other books. I think I still have one of hers. I'll return it to you, of course.'

'Good God!' was all he could think of in response. Magda? And Óscar Pandeo?

Mina breezed into the hall, handing her cape to Ana. 'Who was your visitor? I saw the car leaving.'

'What? Oh . . .' He turned from the portrait. 'That, *chica*, was a gallant detective, making intelligent enquiries about our anonymous letter. You know what he's worked out, and, presumably, all by himself? That the letter was written in bloody English, and that the postmark was Palma de Mallorca! The only other positive thing he did was to have a glass of Alfredo's brandy.'

She laughed. 'Was it Óscar? Óscar Pandeo?'

He stared at her. 'You know him?'

Mina glanced at the portrait, and smiled. 'Of course I know him! He and Magda were good friends, you know.' And before he could bluster, went on 'So what are they doing about it, the police?'

'They think there might be a link between this and the two incidents that happened to Martes and Fatty Fazzoletto,which shows how quick on the uptake they are. And I repeated my own little tale about the hit-and-run driver, just to give the bugger something else to think about. Useless git. He's coming back, to talk to Pepe and Isa when they get home from that Bologna farce. And did you know,' swinging round with a glare, 'that Alfredo has started marking the levels on his bloody brandy bottles?'

He stamped off, and Mina smiled to herself.

\*　　\*　　\*

Miss Tits wriggled free of her sweater and hurled it across the roomy tent that was her temporary home. It was a tall tent, cream on the inside, bright green outside, one of a family of canvas homes that had been erected in a field close to the woodland.

There was a constant hum of generators, and a patch of scorched earth where a fire had been lit by someone because he had fancied a lamb barbecue one evening. The lamb, shorn of playfulness but not of wool, had been rescued by a vigilant patrolman: and, as a gesture of gratitude, Adriana Fazzoletto had given the man a signed photograph of her husband as a younger if not slimmer Duke of Mantua.

Miss Tits (billed as Tizania on the hoardings) sat cross-legged on the sweet-smelling grass inside her tent, and yawned. 'You want to or not?' she asked peevishly.

Guitar riffs and outside laughter were all muted by the thick canvas and Tizania's portable radio which was relaying 'another chance to hear Michael Jackson in concert', via the BBC.

'Why do your boobs look bigger when you're dressed than when they're hanging loose?' asked Azucarero with interest, squatting down beside her. He poked one with his finger.

'That will cost you a million lire,' she said primly. She squinted down at her chest. 'Trick of the light. They're just as big.'

'Bollocks,' he said lazily, fingers plucking tiny stems of grass from the earth, 'especially the left one.' A tiny frown between the eyebrows as she surveyed herself more closely.

'It's like a sick balloon,' he continued.

She touched it cautiously. 'It can't be. It's insured.'

'Christ, you must be paying a hefty premium! What are they insured against? Flood? Fire?' He tossed the loose grass across the breast in question. 'It can't be theft,' he mused. 'Life?' He sniggered, rolled on to his stomach. 'Shit, imagine what they'll look like when you're seventy! They'll be hanging over your bloody knees!'

'I have made a solemn pact,' she said, brushing off the grass, 'that I shall die on my fortieth birthday.'

'Why wait? As far as I can see, you may as well do it now.'

'Piss off!'

He sat up, grinning, his ringlets coming loose from the ribbon. 'Did you know,' he said slowly, making a grab and pressing a nipple firmly with his thumb and making a honking noise, 'did you know that this one is wrinkled down the side?'

'WHAT?' she screamed, pushing him away and scrambling for the mirror.

He lay back smiling as he watched her solemnly turn from side to side in front of it, her heavy blue eyes reflecting acute anxiety. He turned up the atmospherics from London, listening with professional interest.

'This guy's an hysterical tart,' he remarked. 'Couldn't phrase a song if they put pincers on his balls.'

She flounced back and kicked him. 'Nor can you!'

'At least I haven't had a bloody skin transplant,' pulling her down beside him, 'Well, was I right about the wrinkles?'

'Must have been the way you were twisting the bloody thing!' She tugged one of the ringlets. 'Well, are we or aren't we, Shirley Temple? I want my beauty sleep.'

'By the look of you, you need at least a year uninterrupted,' and he rolled on top of her, his foot tapping to the beat of the music.

\*       \*       \*

'Aaaa-ve Maaaaareeeeee-ee-aa!'

The room, vast as it was with arches and a carpet that would have fitted a car park, was no match for the noise. Pepe was laughing so hard that he cannoned into a table and sent a tray piled high with chicken portions flying to the floor and into a cluster of bottles.

'Clumsy bastard!' roared Fazzoletto. 'Pick 'em up!' and the two hysterical tenors fell to their knees and grappled with hot chicken coated in sticky breadcrumbs.

Pepe, holding his ribs, gasped 'We . . . we can't sing that, for Chrissake! We'll be escamoni . . . examunicated . . .' and he fell forward, clutching the howling Pio. Strangled squeaks. The vast mounds of Pio's knees thumped helplessly on the floor.

The maid in the room below shrugged and continued refreshing her mascara.

''S fuckin' awful . . .' and they struggled to rise, slipping on the chicken.

'I've trodden on a breast,' tittered Pepe. 'Or might be a thigh.'

'Ishabel must be a bloody funny shape if you don't know the difference,' and they tottered howling back to the piano. Pio suddenly struck a mighty chord, and the piano shook.

'Right!' he shrieked. 'One for the road! One – more – fucking – time! Go! Aaaaa-veeee Ma-sodding-reeee-eee-aaa!' before letting his head fall with a crash on the keyboard, his laughter echoing through the piano wires.

Adriana and Isa, in a smaller intimate room one floor above, heard the noise and wild laughter. 'I can't hear much singing,' Isa said doubtfully.

'Singing?' giggled Adriana, refilling their wine glasses (the eggcup was in Spain), 'All I hear are donkeys braying!'

'Wonder if they give rides along the beach?' They tittered companionably.

A loud crash from the studio below. Isa jumped.

'Piano lid,' said Adriana nonchalantly.

'Oh.'

They listened. More wild laughter.

'Dirty joke,' said Adriana.

'Oh.'

A very long and protracted scream.

'Pepe,' said Adriana.

'Oh?'

'Pio's just persuaded him that *Ave Maria* stays in the programme.'

'Oh!'

It was not a very Spring-like evening in Dresden. Gusty wind, sudden stabbing showers, and a draught in Modesto's dressing-room. He still wore his jogsuit; loosened the drawstring round his waist, panting after the work-out. A hot bath, and then another run-through of Act IV of *La Forza del Destino* with that meticulous Austrian fart who treated his singers like clarinets.

But, he admitted, the conductor was very good practice. Modesto was here, not only to sing, but to learn more German. His next adventure, after the *lieder*, was to be Wagner. He yearned for Bayreuth, to wear helmets with horns and leap around in mystical boats, to die thunderous deaths. Unfortunately, he had let this slip during a recent run-through of the della Doccia solos, and Pio had started calling him 'Fritz', and every intro was marred by that asinine twerp Contreras shouting '*Ein! Zwei! Drei!*'

The draught suddenly discovered a card propped up on the shelf, and it slid face down. He knew without looking that it was the hospital telephone number.

He would ring after rehearsal, see if Francesco could talk for a few minutes.

He held the card against his cheek.

'I'm very sorry,' said the BBC presenter on Radio 2, 'but we're having a bit of difficulty joining our friends on the Italian network for tonight's special pop concert, which is being hosted by Pio Fazzoletto from his OWN HOME in Bolonyia. I'm hearing through my headphones that . . . yes, there will be a delay to the start of this fun SPECTACULAR, so in the meantime let's have some MUSIC! – here's a taste of the great man HIMSELF, Pio in a well-known number from Pally Archie –'

The trouble had started at one of the entrances, when a turnstile jammed. The good-humoured jeers had escalated into shouts and jostling, and the ticket collectors watched helplessly as the crowd surged and flattened both the fencing and the turnstile and raced over the fields in different directions.

'What the bloody hell's happening now?' snarled Pio, as his dresser adjusted the tailcoat carefully. His view from the window was in direct line with the concert area; but his gaze passed beyond the crowd already assembled there to a multitude of figures racing in the distance, towards –

He whipped round, nearly pulling the assistant off his feet. 'They're going towards the fucking stables!' he bellowed. 'Where in the Holy Shit of God are the guards?' and he stormed from the room, tails swaying, one still displaying the dry-cleaning label.

The concert platform, erected beneath a swathe of trees, was lit in a rainbow spectrum of floodlights. Dungareed helpers wheeled on pots of flowers; rock music howled through speakers to entertain the audience. Azucarero leaned against a tree trunk, smoking and trying to think of a rhyme for 'perpendicular'. Musicians chatted and spat. Miss Tits was in the Portaloo, with a friend.

Pepe sat on an upturned bucket while Isa prowled round trying to find out what the hold-up was. By now, Pio should have been opening the proceedings with *La Donna è Mobile*, accompanied by five acoustic guitars. It was already nine o'clock, and she could see hordes racing across the muddy fields towards the stables. Unfortunately, Pio had decreed that these, too, should be floodlit to enhance the charm of the scenery. Radio announcers from six countries listened carefully to earphones. Several burly Italians moved through the crowd offering protection at competitive rates.

'We're late,' Pepe said plaintively. His head ached from the night before.

'I know that, I was trying to see if I could spot Pio in the crowd.'

'What do you think he'd be doing there? Selling bloody programmes?'

She sat down hard on his knee, and he screeched as the rim of the bucket sank deep. Then 'Pio!' he exclaimed as the giant Italian hoved into view on the stage.

'Take fifteen!' Pio bellowed. 'Take fucking sixty! Some bastards have pitched themselves near the horses and a bloody foal's coming!' His fixed snarl lingered in the air long after he'd plunged back into the heaving turmoil, to the despair of his guards.

'A foal's coming?' puzzled Isa, standing on tiptoe.

358

'I think he means it is being born, *querida*,' Pepe sniggered, watching her.

'I didn't think he meant it was arriving down here on a bloody bicycle,' and she patted his aching head firmly.

Miss Tits, having vacated herself and the Portaloo, pronounced herself bored and tried to swing herself into a tree.

'I can see your bare arse,' observed Azucarero. She slid down again, glad that her dress was the same colour as the trunk of the tree. 'So?' she demanded, 'You gonna write a song about it?'

'Sure – why not? Don't think anyone's written one yet about a clapped-out old tart with a flabby fanny. Worth trying, I suppose.'

'Anything else you like about me?' she snapped. He squinted down at her body, settled on the groin area. Grinned. 'Yeah. There's room inside that for a bloody bull elephant. And a couple of his friends.'

Pepe frowned as he heard the anguished shriek. 'You know,' he said to Isa, 'it is quite remarkable. All this, plus what sounded like a murder. Just for the price of one ticket!'

\*     \*     \*

The young lady in a tweed suit was waiting for him in the wings.

'It's long distance, *Herr* Martes – from Australia,' and he brushed her aside and ran up the stairs to his dressing-room. It was lamp-lit and quiet, the wind had stopped gusting against the panes. He picked up the phone, afraid.

'Modesto? Frank Giormani.' The voice was low and steady. 'Sorry to come out with it like this, old friend, don't know how in hell else to say it. Cherri. A couple of hours ago.'

'Oh God.' Tears bubbled in his throat, a chill intensified at the back of his shoulders. 'I see.' Fucking stupid thing to say. His nose was running, he grabbed a tissue from the box. 'God, Frank, I'm sorry, I don't know what to –'

'That's okay, boy – look, she gave me a message for you. I –' He heard the voice break like a lonely wave.

'Not now, Frank, wait until –' his throat gasped '– until the funeral.'

359

'You'll be coming over? You really would do that? Gee, she'd be so glad, Modesto, she'd be so . . . .' He heard the unashamed pain, reached for his pen.

'Just tell me when and where, Frank, that's all, I'll be there,' and he cried as he wrote down the details.

*     *     *

On the flight home from Italy, Pepe slouched in his seat holding a wet cloth to his black eye. Every time Isa looked across at him, she grinned.

He stared with his good eye at the clouds below. Tips of mountains sometimes poked through like dark swimming incisors.

It had been a pomegranate. It had been in its natural state, and thrown by a brawny arm from somewhere in the front row. He heard Isa tittering to herself, and she buried her head in a newspaper as he looked at her sharply. He wondered why, of all the papers on display at the airport, she had chosen *La Stampa*. She had swept past the Spanish dailies, turned her nose up at *Corriere della Sera*, and headed straight for it. *La Stampa*.

Pio had laughed it off afterwards, stuffing himself with pasta and Chianti, holding his head back and dropping black olives into his big stupid mouth as though they were bloody grapes. 'Don't worry, *amico*!' the fat idiot had chortled. 'Suppose it had been a bullet?'

I almost wish it had been, Pepe thought bitterly. Quick death, and only an unregistered pain. One minute a tenor pelted and abused; the next, a quiet chat with God and a few sympathetic angels.

Now what is she laughing at? His left eyebrow flared, watching the sheets of *La Stampa* shake, a glimpse of jumbled hair as she ducked her head and snorted.

'I need more cold water for my cloth!' he snapped.

A finger appeared from behind the newspaper and stabbed towards the floor: a small champagne bucket, containing water and dissolving ice-cubes.

'*Muchas* fucking *gracias*,' he muttered. Even bending down caused the eye to tug painfully.

'*De* fucking *nada*,' from behind *La Stampa*.

As he winced at the freshly-chilled cloth, a trickle of water escaping and running down his cheek, she peeked round the newspaper. 'Good photo!' tittering.

He snatched it from her. Looked at it, stared at her. 'Read it!' he commanded.

'Do I get danger money?'

'Read it!'

The photograph was excellent. He and Pio on stage together, smiling, Pio with arms in the air, saluting, broad grin. Pepe, hands folded in prayer position just above the midriff, teeth looking polished. Caught exactly, too, the moment when cabbages flew. And the pomegranate, just before impact. Caption: 'AUDIENCE SUMS IT UP!'

Isa peered at him again. 'There are some words I can't quite underst–'

'Read!'

She cleared her throat, choked back a laugh. 'It's dated –'

'Fuck the date! Read!'

He was on the point of howling. For this to have happened now! Now! Jesus Pedro González Christ! He had planned and arranged for a special showing on Spanish television of the Lorca recital, as a surprise for Isa; a showing before the official European transmission, now scheduled for sometime in June. They would watch it together, just the two of them, in his holiday retreat in the mountains. And now this bloody shambles! All those cabbages, and Pio hadn't turned a hair. Just a wolfish grin and a blatant universal gesture to the crowd, plus encores of it: and for that, he had been applauded rapturously. He remarked later that if he could get ovations like that for a mere obscenity, he might turn his back on music for good and become a traffic cop.

Isa said ahem twice, then read aloud ' "The demons of the universe united this evening in giving a demonstration of their powers. They had already invaded the brain cells of our own il-lustrious Fazzoletto by giving him the sad inspiration in the first place. Then they fuelled their wickedness by suggesting he should . . . er . . . combine? . . . combine with Azucarero and El Pedo

Negro." ' She paused to announce that they had spelt 'Negro' with two g's.

'Read!' The cloth against his eye was again losing soothing coolness.

'Er . . . blah blah . . . "Crowd trouble delayed the start of the live radio relay, and fifty youths were arrested. A further delay occurred when the sound system mercifully failed during *La Mattinata*, brought to us courtesy of the Spanish tenor, Pepe Contreras. Unfortunately, the sound was restored for his next offering, *Amapola* . . ." '

'Read!' as Isa mopped her eyes.

' "Contreras was dragged back later by *Signor* Fazzoletto to give a performance in duet form of *Ave Maria* (Bach, arr. Gounod). Eight bars into the item, Fazzoletto burst into hysterical laughter, while Contreras audibly broke –"' and she yelped wildly.

'Shut up!'

Eyes streaming, she continued "'– broke wind several times, sounds which were picked up by the hand-mike dangling from his fingers –"'. She bent forward, gasping, and the newspaper slid to the floor.

'Shut it!' he barked. She choked again. 'I'm going to cut this out and paste it in my scrap-book!'

'You're bloody not!'

'I bloody am! I want Grosvenor to know the truth about his *Papi!*'

*　　*　　*

She was, however, ecstatic when he told her about Lorca and the special transmission, and poo-poohed the idea that he had established himself as a figure of fun.

'That pop festival was a trivial event, your serious work is a glorious thing.'

Somewhat mollified, he sat in the car with her as Moncho drove them home to Sant Moiseps, and decided he felt able to reveal his full plan.

'*Princesa*, there is a small house in the mountains near Barcelona that is mine. Is very lonely, very wild. There is a monastery not far

362

away, and one of the brothers – *Hermano* Presa – is an old friend, from schooldays.' He smiled. 'Who would have thought that old Lusty López would have turned out to be a religious!' He chuckled. 'We have walks together when I am up there. I hope you will meet him, *querida*, you will like him.'

'Your house,' she prompted.

'Ah yes, the *casita*. Is near the village of Puig Aragalls, very famous for its cheese.'

'Definitely! Every time I went into Sainsbury's I'd ask for a pound of Aragalls cheese. They used to cut it off the bone for me, and very nice it w–'

A kiss stifled her. Then, 'Why are you telling me this, anyway? Are we going there some day?' Her eyes shone expectantly.

He smiled. 'On Wednesday!'

A squeak. 'This Wednesday? The day after tomorrow? That's Lorca Day!'

'*Exacto*. You and I, *carita*, need a small holiday together. Before Grosvenor. And I need a rest. So, alone, we shall watch the mountains being busy, and then Lorca. Sounds good?'

Moncho grinned in the driving mirror as the next kiss began.

\*     \*     \*

The car, on its roof, finally stopped spinning.

A dusty road and endless blue sky, the sun turning the bullocks black and gold-rimmed. The dead one, tossed by the impact, lay with a broken neck and one horn buried fiercely in the hardness below the dust.

Inside the car, Buzzer Ahmet was hanging upside-down, suspended by his seat belt. One front tooth dangled with him. His driver, an English itinerant, swore with rhythmic passion, his feet wedged in the dashboard. Buzzer's secretary moaned. The driver of the bullocks, scarcely older than a child, didn't know whether to assist the stricken limo or run after two of his fleeing animals.

Isn't it bloody wonderful what life can offer, thought Buzzer. You come all this way to visit your father in hospital, then find that he's been discharged that very morning, and you end up arse over tip on the road to the family home near Dacca.

363

'Can you see the bloody phone?' he snapped to the driver, his tooth swinging.

'Who'd' you want to ring, you fucking halfbreed? Interflora?'

'858585898986,' muttered the secretary, his jaw in the glove compartment. He added, 'Emergency number,' and fainted.

The driver growled, cautiously fumbling. Then, panicking,'I can smell petrol!'

'Then find the bloody phone! Bloody damn quick!'

The phone was undamaged. While the driver pressed the numerals, Buzzer spat dust from his mouth and the tooth came away. I shall now bleed to death, he informed himself. If I'm not incinerated first. He began to count the lines that patterned his seat belt.

# 22

At about the same time as Buzzer and his companions were awaiting the arrival of the Bangladeshi emergency services, Bobby Drach was dining *à deux* with the eminent British composer, Sir Harry Birdcastle. Might be interesting, Bobby had thought; Sniffer's always on the look-out for something different these days.

Sir Harry had been awarded his knighthood in January, and had promptly started wearing white doeskin gloves at all times; brown doeskin, however, averred his friends, for the more intimate moments of his day. Tall and neat, he was known to all and sundry simply as Tat. He had owned this acronym since May 1967, when his first work − a tone poem for flute, xylophone and double-bass − had been published and premiered. 'Tuneless and Toneless' had been the overall verdict, and Tat he became overnight.

In the tasteful surroundings of the Carlton Towers, picking his way through pork fillet and an Italian salad, he was attempting to woo the Drach Agency with his new opera.

He had hear a rumour that three of the world's leading tenors were to appear in concert together, and was keen to interest them in a new adventure. Quite by chance, and after a few hasty changes, the opera was scored for three tenor voices. He was convinced that it could be a winner. Not as big as *The Barber of Seville*, perhaps, but thereabouts, especially if the three could be persuaded by its glorious novelty.

'So − what's it called?' demanded Bobby through a mouthful of steak. He was not enjoying the meal. The steak was bloodless, for a start. Perhaps the waiter didn't know how to spell 'rare'; stiff-backed prat.

'Ah!' Tat beamed. '*The Stiffwick Princes*. Catchy, isn't it?'

Bobby choked daintily. 'And what's it about?'

'Well, first of all, it's for tenor voice only. Three of them.

They're the Stiffwick Princes.'

'No love interest?' wondering how Ez would go about translating the title.

'Oh of course there's a princess!' smiled Tat. 'But she doesn't actually appear.'

'So how the hell do we know there is one?'

'Because she is hinted at. There's an oboe theme throughout, you see. That's the princess.'

'Makes a change.'

'Oh it does!' eagerly. 'No sordid rape scenes or masochistic mating, nothing so dreadfully unsubtle!' He shuddered, tipped salad onto the pork. 'The oboe, you know – such a clean pure instrument. Does the job beautifully.'

'I assume you're telling me this because of my connections with a certain tenor?'

'Certainly. Isn't Contreras your son-in-law?'

Christ on a chamber pot, thought Bobby. 'No he is not! He's married to my partner. Anyway – go on, what's the plot?'

'Ah yes! Well, the princes, you see, are brothers. And they have a quest.' He leaned across the table in conspiratorial manner. 'For the Holy Grail!'

'What a new idea,' murmured Bobby. Nice wine, this.

'Isn't it!' with enthusiasm. 'Of course, they all die before they can find it. The Grail is, you see, a symbolic yearning within us all for –'

Bobby tuned out the voice. God, the things he did for his bloody clients. He waited until the voice ceased droning, then asked tiredly 'So what exactly do they do, these princes, before they peg out?'

With childlike simplicity, 'They hunt through lots of forests. For the Grail.'

'That should be a real crowd-puller, a stage full of trees and dead leaves.'

'Oh, you won't see the forests, old boy! They're alluded to, in the opening aria. The stage is completely bare throughout. Which brings me to the main point.' He rapidly twisted his fork through the *lollo rosso*. 'This is a set piece for their talents. Sure-fire success!' Hissed, 'Guaranteed!'

'And exactly how do I describe this work of yours to Contreras? A bare stage, an oboe that's a bloody princess, and an unseen Holy Whatsit? Any tunes in it?'

He gestured for more wine, and wistfully prodded the rim of the steak in the faint hope of discovering blood. Nor did he hold out much hope for good tunes. As far as Bobby Drach was concerned, all that Birdcastle's music did was to provide tuning-up practice and getting rid of surplus rosin. He looked up, and saw Tat's eyes gleaming.

'Tunes? Robert, what do they need with tunes? With my opera, they'll never need publicity again!'

'I don't think they exactly need it now,' sarcastically, 'considering that they're three of the highest-paid fucking canaries in the world!'

Tat winced. 'Don't be so coarse and materialistic, Robert! This,' and he scored a faint line on the tablecloth with his knife, 'will be the most expressive work they will ever undertake!' Raised his head and winked. 'Ex . . . pressive.'

Stare met stare. 'How do you mean, ex . . . pressive?'

'Full frontals, dear boy.'

Bobby's choking laughter sent saliva sparkling through the air. Tat frowned with distaste and smoothed his white doeskin hands, waiting for Bobby to regain composure.

Bobby whispered, 'All three of them?'

Tat nodded, calmly. 'They are of course clad at the beginning, to represent mortals of a material world . . . Robert, please! This is serious art!'

'I think I need a serious bloody brandy,' murmured Bobby. Christ, the man was as cracked as a fucking egg! Oh how Ez would love this! 'Do go on, Tat – when do they get down to the striptease?'

'Are you taking the piss, old boy?' He belched gently into the cupped doeskin. 'In the opening scene, they are wearing suits. Then as Act I progresses, they begin shedding parts of their attire as a symbol of their eternalism. Look – I've brought you the synopsis,' and he removed a smart blue folder from his briefcase. 'Perhaps you could start off by having a word with your boy, mmm? See if he's interested in –' modestly lowering his voice, '– making history?'

Bobby was delighted, and accepted the document. He was already planning his first move as the brandies arrived.

*     *     *

Before Bobby Drach had time to do anything about the new opera, however, the entire music world was rocking back and finding it difficult to digest the news from Australia. And the tone-deaf united as one with the rest, donning clothes of shock and grief.

To Pio and Pepe, God had blasphemed.

To Modesto Martes, it was devastating. He stood at the graveside with Mimosa, straight-backed but head bent, staring at the earth but not at the coffin draped in the Australian flag, waiting for its final lowering. Mimosa cast anxious looks at him. Already his morning shave had fled, and his face gleamed with a peculiar whiteness she had never seen before. She squeezed his arm gently, and he aimed a taut smile in the direction of her hat.

His stare switched to the huge sky, large wheeling birds, as the coffin was lowered on blue ropes. Then Francesco, with Cherri's three brothers, sprinkled earth on the casket he had no wish to see. And the deed was done. In a daze, Modesto chatted with the usual bonhomie of funerals, drank the Australian wine which she said was like nectar with piss added, and talked to the brothers with whom she had once wrestled. And much later, when the tall slender lights of the dual carriageway cast a living glow on the nearby cemetery, he and Frank Giormani returned and knelt by the new grave. The husband placed a small crucifix on the mounded earth and prayed silently to his wife.

Modesto's tongue was stuck hard, so his head whispered 'Sleep then, dearest joyful girl. I love you. Christ I love you.' His fingers were thick with clay afterwards where they had clenched through the earth reaching for her smile.

And Buzzer Ahmet, relaxing in his hospital bed in Dacca, bowed his head and remembered part of a hymn he had learned at school: 'And with a well-tuned heart, sing thou the songs of love.'

'Do you or any of your family have any connections with Mallorca?' Óscar Pandeo asked hopefully, as the clan Contreras regarded him across the room.

'We have a holiday home in Deyá,' grunted Gualterio. 'Friends use it from time to time.'

He looked at the detective inspector with narrowed eyes, trying to link him with coffee sessions with Magda. And book-lending. Pandeo had returned, as promised, the last book to pass between them. Which puzzled him even further. *Poultry keeping.* And it wasn't even a library book! He had roared at Alfredo, 'She didn't know a chicken's arse from its bloody beak! What the hell was going on between those two?'

'And what about your ex-wife, Don Pepe? Does she ever use it?'

Pepe laughed. 'I shouldn't imagine so! She hated the place.'

Isa's thoughts had travelled beyond the room and Gualterio's scowls and cigar smoke, had leapt forward to the holiday in Puig Aragalls. She and Pepe were anticipating it with joy. Even Alfredo's chortled references to the casa's cesspit and its overflowing untreated shit, the spiders at least thirty feet across in every room, did not mar their enthusiasm. Together, they would watch Lorca and remember the old battered anthology. And just as important, Pepe had said grimly, no bloody family. Or, as he put it to Alfredo after another fight, 'I'd sooner swim through a tidal wave of shit and spiders if it means a rest from you, you bristle-headed twat!'

Isa tittered behind her hand, remembering, and glanced down at Grosvenor, modestly drowsing beneath a pretty smock that had belonged to Mina.

'What? . . . Oh, I'm sorry,' as Pepe nudged her and Pandeo looked at her enquiringly. Inwardly he was groaning. How in the name of holy hamburgers was this going to lead anywhere? Why the hell had he mentioned Judit, the ex? Why the hell had he been dragged into it in the first place? So far, he'd established that there was a house in Deyá, plus a minor reference to a bomb hoax at Los Culitos just before Christmas; and he was sure they'd caught the bugger who did that. Some transvestite who called himself

Rosa. As for the hit-and-run . . . He shrugged. Nothing. File about to be closed.

He waited for Isa's reply to his repeated question. As he had thought – no, sorry. No, nothing more untoward, no. Then she said, 'The anonymous people seem to be in Turin too! Keta Lavagna is fuming that someone leaked the news about her husband's illness.' She smiled. 'Sorry – I was just thinking out loud. Only Keta said we ought to form a club, the four of us!'

A thought occurred to him suddenly. 'Do you have her address?'

'Certainly,' interposed Pepe. 'My secretary will give it to you. But if you think it's important, you'll have to hurry – she leaves soon for the States.'

After he had gone, Gualterio said 'Bloody odd.'

'What is?' asked Isa. 'About Keta, you mean?'

He frowned, shook his head. 'Him. Coffee and chickens. With my Magda.'

*    *    *

Buzzer settled himself as comfortably as he could on the aircraft bound for Italy. His bruises were still painful. The seat belt of the car had somehow got mixed up in his groin, and to cross one's legs was downright impossible. The tooth was in his trouser pocket, to be retained as a talisman. A new one was now ensconced in the vacant hole, courtesy of an excellent dental technician at the Dacca hospital.

He opened his green notebook as the plane headed for Rome.

Rome. Another rehearsal with the Teatro dell' Orfeo, then the orchestras would come together for the first time, and he would see what progress had made with the Magia Armonica by *Signor* Fica. There had been some interesting reports from him. None appeared to have any bearing on music.

The principal trombone liked eating sardines straight from the tin whilst rehearsing, said they helped his lips and gums.

The Mayor of Florence wanted three hundred free tickets for the concert.

A group of men from Sicily had set up business in Florence and were busily printing tickets for the Mayor. And so on, and so on. Oh sorry, Allah-God, Fica did fax me one musical item. Don't forget – he did say that the orchestra knew *Nessun Dorma* so well that they sang along as they played. That should be interesting, he thought. Pio and a hundred musicians from Florence, in concert together. Perhaps they could encourage the Teatro dell' Orfeo to join in as well.

He grinned to himself, touched the new smooth tooth reflectively.

*　　*　　*

The mountain house near Puig Aragalls was enchantment. Low and hidden, rough stone walls and floors, arches linking the rooms, thick rugs with red fringes, wrought-iron lamps whose bulbs flickered and brightened like real flames. And the inner courtyard: fountain not working, but stone troughs abounding, filled with blue and purple irises.

'Look!' she cried, 'Even Lorca's favourite symbols are here!' and she picked a swarm of them and put them in white bowls around the living area.

It was cold in the Sierra de los Superdesarrollados Blancos, and on that particular evening as they waited for the transmission of the recital, there was a massive open fire piled with logs. The intermittent glow from the lamps turned it into home.

Isa hadn't, of course, bargained for a monk sitting between them on the sofa.

Lusty López, now known as Brother Presa, was a large man.

'Doesn't he look like a monk?' she tittered to Pepe behind her hand as they went into the hall to greet him. Long brown robe ('not dress,' frowned Pepe), a useful length of rope around his waist, thick sandals, and badly-cut black hair. He had greeted them warmly, his voice high and clear like a boy soprano.

He also liked wine.

'I bet he's a bugger at Communion,' she whispered to Pepe as she went to fetch more Chablis. Isa had been allowed a proper wine glass, and she sat scowling at the quarter of an inch meted out to her. Pepe was now being insufferably pedantic about the

371

whole thing; as if he thought a full glass of the bloody stuff would bring forth his son in a drunken stupor, reeling round his cot singing *Sweet Adeline*.

Nor, she reflected as the two men chatted, would it be easy watching Lorca on the fourteen-inch black and white portable, with freak mountain reception.

*Hermano* Presa turned to her and smiled. If he says, just once more, I hope you don't mind my intrusion, I shall pour my quarter of an inch all over his bloody sandals.

She smiled back.

He said, 'So, where will you have the child christened? Sant Moiseps?'

Jesu. They hadn't even discussed it! Would they have to have a christening?

Pepe grinned, over to you, *querida*. He looked distinctly like a fox at times, she thought idly. Thank you, sweetheart. For what you are about to receive . . .

'If the font is large enough,' she beamed. 'I love swimming, don't you?'

*Hermano* Presa threw back his head, laughed heartily. 'I must remember that one! Oh yes, jolly good, love it, Isa, love it!'

Pepe was staring at her blankly. She giggled. The fire crackled happily, and Pepe masterfully removed a cork from a fresh bottle, waggled it. 'Lusty? Drop more?'

'*Oh sí. Gracias,* Pepecito!'

She saw Pepe wince, as though the diminutive conjured up visions of ankle socks and tiny shorts. '*Gracias,* Pepecito,' she tittered and held out her own glass. His mouth thinned as he permitted two drops to escape from the bottle.

'So!' heartily from the monk, 'What are you naming the child? Some family name, of course . . . and perhaps . . .' his eyes sparkling shyly, 'you would do me the honour of –?'

Pepe's snort and hers coincided.

'Oh, we've already chosen the names,' she said swiftly, 'Dustbins.'

'Sorry? Doosbeens?'

Pepe choked.

'Yes,' firmly. 'Dustbins Oddsod Twit María.'

372

*Hermano* Presa looked wonderingly at his friend's contorted face. Isa glanced at the clock. That damn set would probably take ages to warm up. She got up and switched it on.

'Doosbeens. Is a new name to me.'

'He sold asparagus in Brixton,' she said. 'Oddsod was the name of his dog.'

'Isa!' Pepe swooped over to the set and jabbed her in the ribs as he passed.

'And the Twit María is for Pepe, of course –'

'ISA!'

'Yes, dear?'

'Will you shut your –' His attention was suddenly drawn to the blizzard raging across the tiny screen. 'Shit!' and he thumped the set hard, as a monk sat thinking deeply on a sofa. Then he looked up and saw the blizzard.

'I don't think you'll get a better picture than that,' he observed. 'May I perhaps suggest –?'

They turned and looked at him.

'– that you both come to the monastery as my guests? We have a rather decent twenty-six-inch there, tremendous picture, very clear. Remote control, all that scientific stuff.'

'Well . . . that's awfully kind of you . . .' They looked at each other.

The monk stood up, rubbing his hands. 'Good! Might I suggest a couple of sweaters each, there's a very cold wind this evening. Oh – and a nice large bag, if you have one, Isabel. Mustn't forget to take this delicious wine with us!'

Which was how Pepe Contreras saw for the first time the recital that was destined to become a classic and which would pour millions of pesetas into the Magda Fund: seated with Isa on a bench covered with foam rubber cushions, surrounded by fourteen monks and a red plastic bag full of wine bottles.

\*     \*     \*

Keta eyed the two detectives with resolution. Let them try to prove a thing; what she had done, she had done with Vito, at his request. His last wish. They would both deny it absolutely, always.

373

She was taken aback when the spokesman said, after two sips of coffee (which he praised generously), 'Were you aware that the press knew, and would publish, the true facts of your husband's illness?'

'Oh.' Switched off the guilt. 'Of course not! I was devastated when it happened, and so quickly. The doctors had agreed to secrecy, also the nurse who stayed with Vito.' She didn't mention Bobby Drach. There was no need to.

'I understand, *signora*, that you are acquainted with Pepe Contreras?' When she nodded, he went on, 'And with his former wife?'

'Why, of course; Judit and I have been friends for a number of years. She was a great comfort to me when my husband was ill . . . before he died. We talked a lot on the phone.'

'Did you mention the true nature of *Signor* Lavagna's illness to her?'

She smiled sadly. 'I may have done, but I doubt it. I'm sorry, I was just so upset, and it's difficult to remember whether I actually said anything or just thought of saying it.' She shrugged apologetically. 'If I did – well, she's a friend, as I told you. A very tolerant and sympathetic friend. That's all I can tell you.'

She refrained from adding that it was sometimes difficult to understand her friend and the often-disjointed remarks she was prone to make. The booze, she assumed.

They finished their coffee, thanked her politely, and left.

\*     \*     \*

Lluís protested vehemently as his father took him by the ear and ejected him from the room. 'Why can't I stay?' he yelled.

'You're too bloody young, that's why! Push off and find Pau! Go haunt your mother, pretend you're a spider and crawl up her skirt! Just bugger off!'

'Shit to you!' shouted Lluís as the door slammed shut. Mina gave him a hearty smack on the backside as she went past.

'Well, it's not fair,' he sulked, and tried not to brighten when she suggested fresh lemonade. 'That's kid's stuff.'

374

'So what else would you like? A triple gin with a beefburger floating in it?'

'Two beefburgers!' he grinned.

'It's a deal,' said Mina, and marched him off for his lemonade.

Inside the room, its furnishings fortified with a coffee pot and three large cups, Alfredo rubbed his hands, 'Right, *hombres*! Let's get down to the dirty bits!'

Bobby Drach smiled. 'Where's Ez?'

'Having a check-up at the clinic,' said Pepe, 'though who will be checking who, I do not know. Don Salvador is always telling her to exercise something other than her mouth, and I think today was the day she would inform him what to do with his booklets.'

Alfredo poured the coffee as Pepe added, 'It was good of you to bring this personally, Roberto,' tapping the blue folder.

'Don't mention it,' Bobby said, and looked at the cup Alfredo handed him. 'Nice to see you millionaires still shop at Woolworth's.' Sipped. 'Get your coffee there as well, do you?' Relaxed in the armchair. 'No, I was in the area, so I thought I'd pop in with the bloody thing. Saves time.'

'In the area? I thought you were in Rome, seeing Bardi?'

'Exactly,' putting down the cup, looking up at Alfredo. 'And what makes you think it's dirty? Have I said it's dirty? Bobby has not!'

Then he smirked, and passed the synopsis of the new work to Pepe. 'This, dear, is a new opera by Sir Harry Birdcastle, for three tenor voices. Lyrics by Ezra Nehemiah Bates; you'd think the bugger would change his name, wouldn't you, imagine going round being addressed as Master Bates especially as he's well known for it.'

Glanced at puzzled faces. 'Talking of names: Birdcastle has had a provisional acceptance from the English conductor, Ivor Woodcock, though whether that really is his name or the result of a nasty accident, I couldn't say. Known as Timberdick in the trade. You ever worked with him, Sniffer?'

Pepe grinned, shook his head. Then, 'The music is of Tat Birdcastle? Christ!' Alfredo leaned over his brother's shoulder, peered at the title page.

'Stiffwick?' he enquired doubtfully.

Bobby nodded. 'The family name of the three princes.' He began to laugh. 'Jesus, Stiffwicks conducted by a Timberdick!' His mirth intensified as he saw the blank looks.

Pepe's face was smooth and serious as his index finger travelled along the printed page. Looked up, said 'What is the name of the princess? Is not here.'

'Her name's Oboe,' said Bobby. He was ravenously hungry and thought eagerly of La Tasca, lots of blood with meat in it. As Pepe stared at him, he said impatiently, 'She's a bloody oboe! She's represented by one – you know, OBOE! Tootle-tootle . . . You play the bugger! That's the princess – a musical theme, on an oboe. Oh Christ!' as the blank look remained.

Alfredo sniggered. Bobby glanced at him. 'Has he always been as slow as this?'

Alfredo nodded. 'Sadly, yes. It took him three terms to learn how to spell "arithmetic", let alone do it.' He leaned closer. 'Is she really an oboe, this princess? Christ, *hombre*, that's one heroine you won't be able to –'

'Shut up!' Pepe looked nervously at the door. 'Roberto, how the hell can we sing love with an oboe? Is ridiculous!'

'Jesus! You sing, it plays. Though if you felt inclined, I don't suppose Timberdick would object if you clambered into the orchestra pit and gave it a fucking cuddle. Now,' getting up and tracing his own finger just ahead of Pepe's, 'this is the important bit. There – look!'

Pepe's eyes travelled where indicated. A penetrating howl. 'Roberto, is this the sick joke?' and Alfredo grabbed the pages and read slowly, ' "After the shedding of garments, the princes perform a slow sensual dance in symbolic recognition of their bodily and spiritual freedom . . ." ' He stopped, frowned. 'What is this meaning, Roberto?'

'It means that they strip off and give their balls some air.'

Pepe choked. 'Please, Roberto, where is the real manuscript?'

'You're looking at it, duckie.'

Pepe screamed. Alfredo gleefully waved the synopsis above his brother's head. 'I'm going to show this to Gualterio!'

'You're bloody not!' yelled Pepe, snatching vainly.

'Oh dear,' beamed Bobby, 'I hope I haven't upset anyone.'

*     *     *

The monument was his podium. He was Patience, standing thereon. At least, he hoped he was. Patience, in a navy-blue sweater knitted by Fancy for his forty-ninth birthday a few Aprils ago, when she had used a bust of Mozart to wind the wool.

Two hundred musicians were arrayed before him. And a nasty case of love at first sight between the back-row cellist of Magia and the principal double-bass of Orfeo. She, young, solemn as an upright owl. He, in his mid-fifties, pixie grin, and neatly-waved silver hair tied back with a black ribbon. Buzzer eyed them; the bass player had just passed her another note, and she was blushing.

'*Signore, signori!*' Two raps of the stick. '*I Vespri Siciliani, da capo, per favore!*' He didn't really hold out much hope for this first rehearsal. In their separateness, the orchestras were natural rivals. Musical duels had already been fought between the flutes. Imaginary blood gathered in pools round the viola desks, crotchet fought with semiquaver, the air swirled with insults. And after an hour, Buzzer ceased to be Patience; rapped his stick five times. Instruments were laid on knees, or hugged against thighs.

'May I point out, ladies and gentlemen, that I wish to conduct one orchestra. For those of you yet to work that out for yourselves, I say again: you are ONE orchestra for the purposes of this concert. One big bloody happy family! We are not Orfeo trumpets and Magia trombones. We-are-one-single-orchestra!'

He stared into the silence. 'When I wave my wand at the violins, I am indicating to all the violins and not just the bloody Magia violins!' Glared. '*Signora!* Am I to understand that you wish to go to the lavatory?'

The lovesick cellist wriggled again, reddened still further, murmured no thank you *Maestro* sorry *Maestro*.

The rattle of a tin at the back. 'And would you kindly put those bloody sardines away, *Signor* Scoreggia?' Waited for the tittering to die away. Gave his traditional curt nod. 'Right! *Bene! I Vespri*

377

*Siciliani*, page one, bar one! And may Allah-God have mercy on Verdi's soul!'

This raised an appreciative laugh. Silence fell. And they began to play.

*     *     *

'So you don't want to do it?' smiled Bobby, mopping his plate happily.

Pepe glanced up from his stewed squid and said nothing. Gualterio and Alfredo had torn him to pieces and Mina giggled whenever she looked at him. Isa was laughing now, dirtily.

'Okay, okay,' Bobby pretended to sigh. 'So you don't fancy making history. Pity.'

'Making history?' Pepe snapped. 'I do not call parading on an empty stage stark fucking naked to that atonal crap making bloody history!'

'Sssh,' frowned Isa. 'Keep your voice down, *querido*.' La Tasca was quiet this evening; a handful of diners, and a journalist from *La Vanguardia* hoping to catch Pepe for an exclusive interview, following the acclaim for the Lorca recital.

'And you can stop sounding like Mina!' he flared.

'When you stop acting like a bloody three year old!'

'Would you like a black eye?'

'Would you like a kick in the balls?'

'Really, kiddies,' said Bobby softly. 'More *vino*? No? That's good, more for Bobby. Now, if you lovebirds would excuse me for a minute, I must go for a wee-wee.'

He disappeared through the arch, smiling wickedly to himself.

'What was that?' frowned Pepe.

'He's gone for a wee-wee.' Isa moodily dipped her finger into his wine glass and sucked it thoughtfully.

'Stop doing that!' irritably.

'You know something? I think I've fallen in love with Don Salvador,' idly.

Silence. She sighed. 'Spain is a country of flamencos and cretins.'

378

Silence, as he stared at the squid and pushed it slowly round his plate.

She picked up Bobby's wine glass and waved it back and forth in front of his face.

Silence.

'How about me murdering a priest at full moon?'

The fork squeaked on squid.

'I had a dream last night, about Grosvenor,' she mused.

Pepe muttered 'Good,' and gazed blankly at the plate.

'Well, more about Tschaikowski really. He was sitting on top of the cooker, complaining that he'd composed a set of variations but couldn't remember the theme he'd started with *querido* oh Pepe, what's wrong?' Her hand touched his.

He didn't reply immediately. When he finally looked at her, his face was pale and sad. Then, sounding distraught, 'Remember that abscess I had on my neck? I think I've got another one coming. On my arse.'

*　　*　　*

'But Judit's an old friend of ours, don't be ridiculous!' bristled Adriana Fazzoletto.

'This is silly!' Mimosa Martes said angrily, 'I hardly know the woman! We've met on a few social occasions, that's all. I can't even recall what she looks like!'

'Once, that's all. She seemed friendly,' said Isa coolly.

'Well, I . . .' said Mina, flustered.

'She's a bloody nuisance,' Gualterio growled, 'coming round here as if she still belonged to the family, drunken bitch!'

'You are not going to ask my sons anything!' Alfredo snapped.

'Sorry, but I've no idea where she is,' said the *señorita* in the next apartment.

Pepe said 'This is bloody ridiculous! Now, if you'll excuse me −'

Outside, in the drive, Pau ran ahead of Óscar Pandeo. 'My *Tía* Judit is nice! She got Lluís a mountain bike cos his other was stolened. He won't let me ride it!'

'When was this then, boy?' The man hunkered down, face to face.

'Dunno.' Feet shuffled. His brother pushed him. 'It was just before Isa came, and when she came to live with us my *mamá* made *Tía* Judit cry when she told her about it. *Señor* Pandeo, what is a *puta*, Isa's one, *Tía* Judit said!'

Lluís looked at the detective inspector, then grinned. 'Do you know Bionda Merdina? She sings, like Uncle Pepe does. *Tía* Judit says she's written a nasty book about him. Will you arrest her and hang her, *Señor* Pandeo?' And Pau bounced eagerly, 'My *Papi* says *El País* are going to print all the dirty bits about a bonker and Uncle Pepe! What's a bonker?'

'Oh shit on a Tampax, he's coming back!' Alfredo groaned as Pandeo marched up the drive with the two boys.

'Well, it was round about . . . September?' twitched Mina. 'Judit had heard about the theft and bought him a new one, that's all.'

'I was merely repeating what my wife told me about the book!' blustered Alfredo.

'Printing what?' laughed Miguel Yuste, sub-editor of *El País*. 'Sorry, never heard of the book! Anyway, it's not our policy to serialize.'

'Oh her!' sighed Bionda Merdina by the swimming pool of her hotel in Córdoba. 'Me? Write a book? I'm too busy signing contracts, thank you. No, I only met her once, when she was married to Contreras.'

Pandeo, exhausted, drove back to his office. He sat alone, thinking.

\*     \*     \*

And then began the month of May, dragging like a lizard on an unfriendly rock. Even the May blossom had bloomed in April and was now faded and brown. Isa tried to show enthusiasm by singing as she wandered through the spilling vegetation, grinning at Ignacio II, his Things now hidden beneath a tide of creeping weeds.

Pepe was in Milan with his new abscess, wondering why the hell he had agreed to do Massenet's *Manon* in the first place. He was, however, earning reserved plaudits for his unusual interpretation of Des Grieux, a character not normally associated with aggression and foul temper. His abscess, thanks to prompt attention by the physicians, receded then returned with painful regularity.

Isa felt fit and strong, fed up with the unnatural way of walking and sitting. Never mind, young man — next month! And she patted the ridiculous blown belly with a loving giggle. Grosvenor's room was ready; an unused extra study, next to their bedroom.

Pepe went frantic when he was informed. 'They cry!' he shouted. 'Babies cry! At night! What about my sleep?'

'You never bother about your bloody sleep when we come together!' Hot and flushed with temper in the swift heat of May.

'You don't howl for milk! Babies do!'

'Don't be so bloody stupid!'

'He is not going next to our bedroom!'

'He's your child, not a sodding barking dog!'

'No, but his bloody mother is!'

Of course, the tugging abscess hadn't helped. Nor had the fact that Isa firmly refused to consider a nanny. Mina sympathised with this, never having had one for her own children. 'Mothers should be mothers,' she said firmly.

'You really sound quite brainy at times,' chortled Alfredo.

'No nanny,' repeated Isa steadfastly.

'And suppose I want you to come with me when I travel?'

'Then Grosvenor comes too.'

'He does not! I'm not going to be photographed at every bloody airport with a howling baby!'

'Of course not, they won't want two of you in the same bloody photo, will they?'

'A nanny, or you won't come with me!'

'Then you'll just have to do without us, won't you,' calmly dangerous.

Perhaps his new course of vitamins will help, she thought, ducking underneath the branches of a fig tree.

*   *   *

Modesto peeled off his socks, examined the blisters. May in America was lousy on feet, he decided, especially when the air-conditioning in the theatre broke down.

That, and the boots, were to blame. Cowboy boots. He scowled at them: stiff leather, spurred, and silver-chained. Heels that gave him an extra inch and made him teeter around like a drunken mammoth.

'The next time I suggest reviving a Puccini opera, give me a kick in the balls, will you?'

Mimosa nodded. He watched her scribbling. 'There's no need to write it down!'

'I wasn't. I'm writing to Gruñón.'

It was their fifth day back in the New York apartment, and Puccini's *La Fanciulla del West* had begun well. Modesto was having mixed reviews so far, many of them referring to the fact that a Spaniard was singing in Italian and trying to be, at the same time, a convincing Yankee bandit called Dick.

'Any message for Gruñón?' she asked as Modesto padded towards the bathroom.

'Sure. Tell him his old man's got very sick unhappy feet.'

'Don't worry, darling, it's just your age beginning to tell,' and she giggled, hunted for a stamp.

'What do you mean, my age beginning to tell?' He hobbled back to his wife.

Her smile was sweet. 'I was just thinking – when we go to Rome for the concert, why don't we extend the trip and have another honeymoon? A lovely nostalgic second honeymoon. Before your sixtieth birthday.'

He shook visibly. 'Sixty? Will everyone shut up about me and bloody sixty? Christ Almighty, woman, I'm only –'

'Fifty-nine,' she supplied, licking the stamp.

'Forty-nine!'

'Yes, darling, of course you are. And I've also heard that Real Madrid are going to play all their away games on skateboards.'

Muttering, he went to soak his feet.

*     *     *

May stretched forever, as far as Óscar Pandeo was concerned. His fellow officers in Madrid and Bologna and Turin were equally

382

disenchanted and frequently uninterested.

The woman they sought for a few friendly questions and honest answers had disappeared. Her apartment remained empty. Neat. Clothes in closets, everything in good order. The Banco de España reported no unusual withdrawals or transactions. Her passport was in her bureau drawer, together with certificates of birth, marriage, divorce. The family villa in Deyá was tenanted for a month by one of Mina's cousins and her boyfriend.

As far as Pandeo was concerned, Judit might never really have existed.

*       *       *

Only one thing in life bothered Pio Fazzoletto these days. And that was the month of May.

May was the anniversary of the death of his mother, Stefania, whom he had worshipped. There were countless photographs of them both together, displayed in all the family homes, in the numerous biographies. Her death had robbed him of his precious baby dumpling, as he had called her.

May. Ten years ago, baby dumpling had died of a stroke. Adriana knew that, at the chimes of midnight on April 30th, he would take the black armband from his drawer and wear it for the next four weeks.

He also hated May because, like August and December, it signified a long visit to the dentist. He whimpered like a child on his way there, grinned like Spartacus on his way back. And today was the day for his trip to the dental clinic on the hill. He had been winding up for a whimper and nervously exploring a new cavity with his tongue when the phone rang.

It had been Buzzer, with a new idea. 'It's worth a try, don't you think?'

'Well . . .' doubtfully. 'Didn't Pepe say something like that in a joke, right at the start of the planning, and we later discounted it?' He rang a finger round his gums. Christ, they felt sore! Please, Sant' Angelo, please don't let the dentist find a disease! Not today! Not any day, he hastily amended. 'Still, if you think it would work –'

383

'Of course it will work, Pio! The audience will love it, the three of you with a last encore. So, shall we try it out when we meet in a couple of weeks' time?'

Pio frowned testily. Why should the other two cash in on what was virtually his own signature tune? Then he heard the sound of his car arriving outside the open window. It was time! He whimpered.

Perhaps if he agreed, God would – 'Why not, *Maestro*? Let's try it out, as you suggest. The three of us together,' and he went forth to meet his fate.

*     *     *

It had been a fun run, the previous evening. Promising and blood-refreshing.

The emaciated tits and pruned backside were irrelevant. So was the blonde hair which was badly in need of a good wash. As far as Azucarero could see, all that was as nothing when compared to the wondrous green eyes that swallowed him inch by inch.

He was on holiday, four days of it without ringlets or red acne, just soundless music and a good long shag. He hadn't cared if they wore lace body-stockings or suits of armour providing that they arrived and did their job then buggered off without asking for his autograph.

But then came the green eyes. They massaged his face, made it impossible for him even to attempt to cross his legs. And he took her to his apartment for a civilised chat and a few drinks before making love to the eyes on his new water-bed.

Remembering this, Azucarero now rubbed his aching body, kneading the muscles awkwardly as he sat in the bath under a scalding shower.

The crazy cow!

The drunken bloody crazy cow!

Wondrous green eyes turning vacant, shambling around his pad talking to someone who wasn't there, a jug full of cognac in her hand, drinking thirstily, yelling that someone had bombed the building and that there was no floor by the window, vomiting thin black liquid.

384

Shouting at an invisible woman 'Stop shelling my peas, you bitch!' and bursting into tears the very colour of the cognac she was gulping as she picked up the silent phone and said 'Oh he isn't dead, is he really dead, what were the wheels doing on his chest?'

Screaming at Azucarero that some of the walls were chiffon and wrapping round her and she couldn't breathe, it was tying up her throat.

Hitting him with such force that he thought his ribs were cracked in half.

Falling into the fruit basket.

Banging her head so hard against it that even the bananas rolled.

He panicked. Rang the cops, who brought a doctor with them.

They held her down and gave her a small quick jab, and the ambulance came, took her and the doctor away.

The cops asked him her name.

He had shrugged, still shaking. 'Don't know the last one. She said her first name was Isabel.'

# 23

It was generally agreed that the brightly-coloured globe on top of the piano lent an air of distinction to the otherwise drab environment. With one touch of the finger, it slid round and round, one minute the Pacific Ocean, the next Scandinavia.

'I never realised San Francisco was so close to Stockholm!' marvelled Pio, staring at it fascinated.

'Where's Spain?' puzzled Modesto. Pepe stabbed a pencil at a rapidly-disappearing patch as the globe revolved. 'There!' he said.

'That was bloody Iran,' protested Pio, and proceeded to open his lunch-box, which was made of basket-weave and normally housed a picnic for six.

'Close,' said Pepe.

It had been Buzzer's idea. A touch of reality, he said, unwrapping it and surveying his new purchase. As news of della Doccia spreads, many countries are sitting up and taking an interest. A financial as well as artistic interest, he added pointedly. And so (with a shrug) this little globe might inspire us and make us realise the sheer enormity of the enterprise.

'Frightens me to death,' sniggered Pepe.

'It will if you crack that top C again in *Core 'Ngrato*,' Buzzer snapped. 'So far, thirty-nine countries are arguing over TV and satellite coverage. They want it beamed to them on the night. As it happens. Live. Follow me? That means, Contreras, that every missed beat, every fluffed bloody note, will be heard and seen by every bugger with a TV set, be they Dutch, Canadian, or banana-peeling wogs!'

'I have done live broadcasts before, you know,' Pepe said with dignity, wondering why his left shirt sleeve stayed rolled up and the other one didn't. Still, he had no wish to complain about anything; the abscess had finally succumbed, and he was now free of underpants stained penicillin-yellow.

386

A bellow of laughter followed his remark. 'Sure, when you're not poncing around miming, or farting into the mike,' chuckled Pio, rummaging through the lunch-box. 'Look at this! Bloody hotel promised me a packed lunch – one hard-boiled fucking egg and a packet of tomato sandwiches!'

'Gentlemen,' said Buzzer, joining in the laughter, 'we shall have another quick run-through of the medley today, then my arrangement of the final encore. Your four solos can be reprised with full orchestra next month. *Maestro* Carrera will be with us in a moment or two. He is, I understand, settling his stomach.'

'Wish he'd hurry up with his settling, he was farting worse than Contreras an hour ago,' Modesto said from a discreet distance.

Pio popped the egg into his mouth. 'Just had a thought,' he said.

'You've got plenty of room up there for it,' Pepe cackled.

'Shut it, Baby Balls!' He swallowed the egg. 'I was thinking – it's a pity Italy isn't celebrating some big event when we do the concert. Give it the crowning touch, as it were.'

'Such as?'

'Winning a war,' chortled Modesto, peering into Pio's lunch-box. 'No, on second thoughts, that's a bit far-fetched –'

The basket-weave lid slammed down hard on his fingers. Pio glared at him, then said musingly, 'Well – football, say. If Italy had been staging the World Cup, and our concert had coincided with the final, Christ, what a magical day that would have been!'

Modesto said sonorously, 'Italy 0 Albania 24.' Laughter rang through the empty auditorium. Buzzer said thoughtfully, 'I take Pio's point. Just a little extra something to give us that –'

'At least it won't coincide with the Eurovision Song Contest!' and Pepe executed a few steps, mumbling 'Sha-la-la, boomban-gabang, yeah.'

They stared at him. 'Sunstroke, poor little sod,' Modesto said.

Buzzer looked worried. 'I'm sure something's happening on August 6th,' turning round as Esteban Carrera approached them, looking pale.

'There's a shoe sale on in Bologna,' volunteered Pio helpfully.

'Of course, how silly of me to forget that!' glared Buzzer. 'Good day, Esteban, I trust that all is now well?'

Carrera seated himself somewhat gingerly at the piano. 'I hope so, thank you.'

'August 6th is the day of the Transfiguration of Our Lord,' said Modesto looking smug.

A shriek of excitement from Pepe, 'I've found it!' waving his diary.

'Funny place to keep it,' observed Pio.

'Shut it! Look – August 6th – Independence Day in Bolivia!'

And a shower of paper plates fell on him.

The pianist smiled feebly, running his fingers along the keys. Then, wondering if the theatre management would make a fuss about their depleted stock of toilet paper, he broke into a sad *adagio* melody while his singers and conductor sorted themselves out.

Modesto approached him, smiling. 'Isn't that Mahler?'

Carrera nodded. 'Part of the *Kindertotenlieder*.' Modesto smirked and announced, 'Did I tell you? After Schubert and Schumann and before the Wagner, I am going to transpose all of Mahler's *Kindertotenlieder* for tenor voice and record them for D.G.'

'Yippeeee!' Pepe tossed his manuscript in the air.

Pio looked depressed. 'Why take it out on poor old bloody Mahler? Pio's heart bleeds –'

'And so will his throat in a minute!' snapped Modesto. 'I believe in –'

Buzzer whacked the top of the piano with his deputy baton. 'Children, please! Playtime is over. Get out your books and pencils and face the blackboard!'

Grinning, he adjusted his waistband, spread the sheet music in front of him.

'Christ, Buzz, what sort of school did you go to?' asked Pepe. 'Books AND pencils? Your folks must have been bloody rich!'

'And a blackboard!' marvelled Modesto. 'When I was at school, we had to do our sums in the dust with a stick!'

'We couldn't even afford a stick,' guffawed Pio. 'We had to use our –'

'GENTLEMEN! . . . thank you. Now, Maestro, if we could have the intro to *Maria*, please?'

Three throats cleared in chorus.

Esteban said, 'Sorry – if I may be excused?' and fled.

The plump doctor sat down on the edge of the bed, took the woman's hand.

'Hello,' he said to the sluggish eyes.

She thought she smiled up at him. Her brother? Underneath the sheet, her left hand felt her body gingerly. The baby was still there. And she counted four breasts in a neat rectangle. She was now nine and a half months pregnant. Elephants, she thought, and fell asleep.

The doctor stood up and remarked to the nurse 'She's still too far in there. Oh – we've sorted through her handbag, you can put her name down on the chart now. I've notified the police department, but exactly when they'll be able to talk to her –'

He shrugged. The nurse nodded and adjusted the drip by the limp right arm.

*　　*　　*

'Oh hi, Bob. How's it going?'

'Tricky, like the sun on a fucking windy day. Otherwise, fine. Your voice sounds odd, darling.'

'Must be a poor line.'

'The line's as clear as a bloody bell. What is it? Tell Bobby!'

'Oh, it's nothing. A bit of a cold, I think. I feel hot and bothered.'

'Are you in bed?' sternly. And, at the answering 'No,' he snapped 'You silly mare! What are you doing up and about if you've got a bloody cold?'

'Answering the bloody phone, you idiot!'

He grinned. 'I'll keep it brief, then. When's Sniffer due back from Rome? I want a word with him when he returns – see, what's today? . . . June 5th . . . it's about the *Otello* recording in Hamburg.'

'*Otello?* What about it? Please don't say there's been a –'

'For Christ's sake, calm down! The producer just wants to know if he can make it a couple of days later than scheduled, that's all – from what I can see, he's in the clear, but Buzzer Ahmet might

389

have arranged something in the meantime.'

He found himself listening to silence, apart from a faint hum and judder on the line.

'Ez? Did you hear me? . . . Ezita?' Fuck it, we've been cut off. Hang up, Drach, try your luck again later. Workies for you, my boy! You'll never afford a solid gold lavatory pan at this rate.

*     *     *

'Hooray, coffee break!' and they swarmed round the tray.

Esteban Carrera left the piano quickly and disappeared, just as Pio wrinkled his nose and sniffed the air. 'Christ Jesus! What's he been eating, bloody antique prawns?'

Modesto sank into a chair, stretched his arms, folded them behind his head.

'Ladies,' he said, 'I have a challenge to put before you. I am seriously thinking of – What are you doing, Pio?'

'Measuring my foot against yours. Mine's bigger.'

'Oh good. Let the angels bloody rejoice. As I was saying –'

'What about mine? Aren't they worth measuring?' complained Pepe.

Titters all round. 'I bet you even have to stuff your size two's with bloody paper, don't you, Pepita?'

And Buzzer grinned as Contreras shoe connected with Fazzoletto thigh. Pio didn't.

'Fancy grilled prick for supper, you Spanish trollop?' he roared.

'Tuneless barrel of bloody wind!'

Modesto snapped 'Shut up! Stupid buggers! Look – do you want a good intellectual challenge?' And, as they shook their heads, 'Good. Then here's my plan. Let me explain, first of all, that I –' expanding his chest, '– am going to write my autobiography!'

Loud laughter. 'What are you calling it? "My first sixty years"?'

Modesto scowled, eyebrows beetling. 'Once and for fucking all, I am not sixty! Just listen, will you? How about us all doing our autobiogs, and see which comes top of the best-seller list?'

Pio looked thoughtful. 'I think I'd call mine "Life with Pio".'

Jeers. 'So what is yours to be called, Modesto?' asked Buzzer.

'As I was born on a Tuesday, I was thinking of "Tuesday's Child".' He smirked.

'Oh yes, of course, from the nursery rhyme,' said Pepe. 'What was Tuesday's child full of?'

'Wind and piss,' sniggered Pio. Thumped Pepe's arm. 'Go on, what would your title be?' Winked at Buzzer. 'Poor little sod. He can't even spell his own name!'

Pepe said pompously, 'I would keep it exquisitely simple. My book would be called "Pepe. By Pepe."'

Roars of laughter. Pio sneaked up behind him, tipped him off the chair. ' "Pepe, by Pepe!" ' he carolled. 'Come on, lads, we'll have to re-think this concert! Alert the printers! Now it'll be *O Sole* Pepe, *Nessun* Pepe, Pepe *'Ngrato, E lucevan le* Pepe!'

They were still laughing as Esteban Carrera crept back to his piano. The toilet paper was used up. He had had to start on yesterday's edition of *La Repubblica*. It didn't feel the same.

\*     \*     \*

'Brought you some coffee!' called Mina from the little octagonal hall. 'Fresh!'

She listened. Clocks ticked in the otherwise silence.

'Isa? Where are you – in the study?' She bumped open the door with her hip, holding the tray carefully.

'Oh my good God!'

She thrust the tray on to a table, hastened to the desk. The telephone was off its hook, buzzing to itself. Isa lay on the floor, eyes closed, face flushed and damp. The chair was lying down, too.

'Isa! Isabel!' Mina knelt down, forced herself to stop shouting, put her hand cautiously on the swollen stomach. All calm there. A few little movements, normal ones. She laid her hand on the girl's face. Withdrew it sharply, 'Oh Christ!' and slammed the receiver back, picked it up, dialled 1.

'Ana? Ring the clinic, quick! Emergency! *Señora* Isabel – we need an ambulance, *prontísimo*! And get *Señor* Alfredo down here to the kennel as soon as you can!'

She threw the phone back on the hook, grabbed a cushion,

placed it carefully under the damp mass of hair. Touched the heart: beating fast. In contrast to the perspiration, the lips were pale and dry. Breathing rapidly, then halting, then speeding up again.

'Oh Christ!' she said again. Gently stroked a hand while she waited for Alfredo to come and help her.

\* \* \*

Ana stayed at the house with the two boys while Gualterio paced up and down a garden path.

Alfredo and Mina sat on green chairs in the small annexe of the clinic, tense and afraid to move. Outside, the sun shone and was hot on the jasmine. The leather chairs grew damp and sticky as they sat in the heat. Alfredo nibbled his thumbnail, Mina toyed with a silver chain on the pocket of her dress.

Don Salvador came in and regarded them from his swaying height. 'Phone Don Pepe,' he said tersely, 'It's viral pneumonia. We shall have to induce the child or perform a Caesarian if necessary.'

'Pneumonia?' squeaked Mina, staring.

'Induce it? But it isn't due –'

'The telephone is in the next room, the girl is ready to connect you to Rome. Hurry, please!'

'But this virus, is it threatening the baby's life?' Mina, anguished.

'Not yet,' terse, impatient to be gone, 'but *Señora* Isabel is in danger herself. I stress that. Oh, I do indeed! We shall do all we can –' And he didn't spare them the spread of hands and lifted shoulders.

It was Alfredo who ran to the telephone.

\* \* \*

'Whew!'

An exclamation shared by all five participants after the rehearsal of the medley. It had gone reasonably well, indicated Buzzer. *Maestro* Carrera had only left his place twice, fleeing with his mouth screwed up and returning relaxed and apologetic.

He had now reached the sports pages of *La Repubblica*.

Cool drinks had been brought, and they gulped gratefully.

'More work needed on *Memory* and *Cielito Lindo*,' Buzzer remarked.

'Can't you stop bloody Contreras from jerking his head up and down when he does the *lindo* bit right at the end?' complained Modesto. 'It's like standing next to a fucking marionette!'

'Oh shut up, Rommel!'

'Nasty bit here, too,' frowned Buzzer, tapping his score. 'You all fade off at the end as if you're drifting into a coma. For God's sake, I know it's in French, Pio, but you might sound a little more enthusiastic!'

'There's a phrase here I'm not happy with,' said Pepe, pointing to a page, 'It –'

They looked up as feet ran on to the stage, very fast. '*Signor* Contreras!'

A breathless girl. '*Signor*, a phone call for you from Barcelona! It's very urgent, please!'

'Oh Christ!' He turned white. 'The baby!'

And ran, shoulders forward as if they wanted to get to the phone before the rest of him.

'Good luck!' they called.

*     *     *

She frowned, said piteously, 'Why won't they go away? Why are they still there?'

The nurse said as she bent over her, 'They wish to talk with you, *Señora* Contreras, when you are well enough,' and she glanced at the police officer by the open door.

'Don't worry about it, it's nothing very important,' soothingly.

Judit closed her eyes. Not important? Was that what she heard just now? Of course it was important! The tabby cat with its red mouth wanted to say something, she knew that very well. It kept arching its neck, rubbing its side against the door. The other cats just nodded and watched.

393

Ana was petrified. She held the phone as close to her ear as she could, knew that the voice was speaking in English, but in the upside-down day she could make no sense of what was being said. Helplessly, she thrust it at Federico, on his way to the airport with Moncho.

'*Es inglés,*' she hissed.

'Good evening,' said Federico cautiously.

'Thank Christ, at last! Robert Drach here.'

'Oh, *Señor* Drach, I am sorry, things is of bad here, could if you ring possible later?'

'Is that Frederick? What's happened?'

'Is the *Señora* Isabel, she is in the hospital, very sick, I am to go now at the airport to meet with Don Pepe –'

'Hospital, you say? She's in hospital? You mean the baby's arrived?'

'Is not the baby, *Señor* Drach, is a very illness for *Señora* Isa. Is a sick . . .' He hesitated, sought frantically for the English, failed. 'Is *la pulmonía.*'

'Is the what? Poolmo-near? What the fuck is that supposed to mean?'

'Is right, *Señor* Drach. I must go, the car is hoping for me, Don Pepe come soon.'

'Mrs Mina – is she there?' hurriedly.

'Yes, at the hospital. Please – to ring later?' and he pushed the phone back to Ana. Who heard English squawking from the region of her hand, and dropped the phone hastily back on the hook.

*　　*　　*

The baby was borne rapidly away, an unseen item in a thick white towel, the nurse in a hurry, heels slapping in their sandals. Mina called after her, but her voice was faint and the nurse disappeared.

She returned panicking to Alfredo, who was hunched over the phone. He said something quickly, then hung up.

'Federico and Moncho are at the airport,' he said. 'Plane's due in ten minutes.' Then for the first time he noticed the pallor and weariness of his wife, took her in his arms, rocked her soothingly. 'Any news about the baby, *querida*?'

She shook her head. 'They have said nothing! Just took it away,' and tears came.

His voice rose in anger. 'Where's that bloody *papo*, Don Salvador?'

'I don't know, I don't know! Oh Fredo, they won't tell me anything, how Isa is, how −' sobbing into his shoulder.

'They'd better have some fucking answers when Pepe gets here!' and 'Sssh, little *cara*, it'll be okay. It'll be fine, just you see!'

He was glad she couldn't see his own tears.

*　　*　　*

Pepe ran into the clinic, full tilt into Don Salvador.

'Easy, Pepe, take it easy!' and led him into a cool hushed room, propelling him towards a sofa and arranging him into a sitting position.

'Isabel! Tell me!' His eyes glittered, his jaw stiff. 'Tell me!'

'She is no worse. We were in time. It is a particularly nasty virus, you see. It rages, it depletes, but we have been able −'

His head whirled with her name and her teasing '*Cucufato!*' '*Superquerido!*'

'Will she . . . ' He bit his mouth, turned away, and his hands shook.

'She will pull through,' gently. 'She is strong. Strong as a young cauliflower, as my mother would say! Your wife is a fighter, Pepe!'

'Oh thank you, God,' and he sank back, head drooping. Weariness was nothing compared to this. There was a short silence as Salvador poured him a stiff cognac. 'Here, my friend. This is both a medicine and a toast − congratulations!'

Pepe stared up at him. 'Congratu . . .? You mean the baby? It's here? My baby?'

Salvador smiled, nodded, patted the rigid arm. 'We had to induce the child, you understand. Isabel's own fight − we couldn't wait for your son to be born in normal labour. But he is only a few days early in joining us, he is strong and healthy.'

Pepe said dazedly, 'Son? My baby is a son?' Bemused, throat strangling. He was here! Grosvenor! Isabel was a strong cauliflower, and Grosvenor was here!

He wept and sniffed as he drank the cognac.

*　　*　　*

Bobby arrived for a brief visit as the baby thrived and Isa gently pulled back from the virus.

Alfredo said to Mina just before their first visit to see the child, 'And don't start cooing all over it!'

Mina said coldly, 'I shall refrain from cooing,' and drooped over the crib with unpunctuated '*preciosos*' and '*cariños*' and 'Oh, what wonderful brown eyes!' and an exasperated Alfredo said to the nurse, 'A miracle – brown eyes in Spain! Ring the Science Academy immediately!'

Pepe was relieved that Roberto was present, to deal with the re-arranged *Otello* dates; with the Lorca; and with his next major engagement in *Andrea Chénier* at the Theater an der Wien. He could, to his intense delight, concentrate fully on his wife and son instead.

Pale and thinner-faced and fuming, she sat up in bed. 'Why did I have to be bloody unconscious when he was born? Why wasn't I there properly?' and Pepe slyly and rather foolishly said, 'Never mind, *princesa*, next time –'

'What do you mean, next time?' she shouted. 'There won't be a next time! Even though I wasn't there, it bloody hurts! And you can stop laughing, Contreras, I'll paralyse you first!'

A few days later she was home, weak and tired, with a nurse who marvelled at the robust child and the mother's evil temper because she wasn't yet strong enough to hold him. Pepe did nothing but grin, pay his son visits until there was a permanent draught in the room that was now a nursery, the one she had intended for him all along; and ply Isa with revitalising wine.

'Not another one!' she groaned, as yet more Lambrusco was pushed into her hand. She yearned for her eggcup as she saw the brimming glass. Lambrusco! – Pio had sent six cases of the stuff, and even Alfredo was fed up with it.

Cards had arrived by the score, including one shaped like a rabbit from Eve and Clair. Bobby had departed after a final wave to Roberto Junior, and Gualterio bought drinks for the population of Sant Moiseps and told everyone that his new grandson was for sure a bass baritone. And Isa and Pepe opened a bottle of Dom Perignon when they realised that Grosvenor shared the same birthday as Lorca. 'How about adding that to his names?' and they chortled happily.

Then Pepe flew to Hamburg for *Otello*, sending a wire in fluent German to Modesto (after paying a pretty barmaid to write it for him), inviting him and Mimosa to the christening on July 20th, in the church of *Nuestra Señora de Dolores*, Sant Moiseps.

On his return, he was delighted to see Isa prowling around her territory, and three cases of Lambrusco in the drive with a sign which read 'Reduced for Clearance: Apply Within.'

She led him into their sunny sitting room. And Elena served them coffee. Pepe raised an eyebrow as the girl departed with a giggle, fuzzy hair in a plait.

Isa grinned at him. 'Mina's idea,' she said. 'Do you mind if we keep her with us for some of the time? She'll be awfully useful with Grosvenor.'

He pretended to consider. Then, 'I think I can just about afford it if she supplies her own food, wants no holidays, works overtime without extra pay, and lives out.'

She giggled. 'You know something? You, *querido*, would steal a bun from a blind baby!'

'Ah but I've got to think of our growing family, *carita* –'

'It's stopped growing – I told you!'

Pink flush creeping, his finger reaching out, caressing mouth. 'No!'

'Poor old marrow. What on earth shall I tell it?'

'Tell it to get stuffed – oh God, that's one of Bobby's old jokes!'

'Very funny, ho ho . . . ho . . . Mmmm, that's nice –'

'Get off!' wriggling away. Wriggling back. Held close, lights buzzing.

Sadly, 'I was lonely in Hamburg. And, as today is the feast day of –'

'No!'

'– St Cyril of Alexandria –'

A fierce 'No!'

'– I thought he might put in a novena for us like Dolores did,' whispering, hand moving.

'St bloody Cyril can go crucify himself!'

'Never had a Cyril in the family,' he mused.

A shout of laughter. 'Cyril Contreras? Oh God!'

Little snorts, mouths close, each tempting the other. 'Sebastián will be christened soon,' his tongue flexing for an assault.

'I've got so used to calling him Gr–'

'Mmmm?'

'Used to calling him –'

'Good. Now shut up.'

Half-hearted struggle. 'He might wake up and want me . . .'

'I'm awake and wanting you.'

'He's only a baby!'

'So am I. Elena can see to him. That –' curving her into him, '– is what we pay her for.'

'You haven't paid her one damn peseta yet!'

'*Exacto.* She's got to work for it. Now SHUT UP!'

*    *    *

The Lorca recital was launched throughout Europe ('A second chance to see' for Spain, announced Telecinco proudly), and with it the official Magda Contreras Fund for Skin Cancer Research. Within hours, pledges were received from all over the continent; and Pepe made a televised appearance after the screening to give a brief speech. He sat solemnly in a leather armchair, with a table lamp at his side, and wearing a green jacket the family hadn't seen before. ('Look at the bugger, he looks like a half-pissed elf!' cackled Alfredo.) The speech was devout and sincere, sometimes puzzlingly interrupted by anxious side glances to a point off-camera. Towards the end, Pepe blinked and half-turned, muttered 'Right! Yes.' Smiled pitifully at the camera, nodded slowly to it several times.

'And so, to you all, I say many thanks from my heart. The music you have just heard was sung for the soul, the soul of my

398

sister and for all those who suffer from this dreadful illness. Friends everywhere, I beg your support now, and in future years, for the Magda Contreras Fund. God bless you all.'

On his arrival home, he said angrily, 'No-one told me who was going to be responsible for that broadcast of mine! The cue cards were in bloody Japanese!'

*    *    *

Óscar Pandeo had notified the family, of course. And told them that, at present, a visit to Judit – even if they felt so inclined – would be pointless. He himself went optimistically and daily.

On this particular afternoon, the doctor looked up at him impatiently. 'I assure you, we are doing our best for the lady. There is a slight improvement; today she recognised me, addressed me as "Doctor." That is a hopeful sign.'

The nurse interrupted, 'Excuse me, Dr Curandero, she also addresses one of the cats she sees as "Doctor", and she calls me Vito.'

'Thank you, Sister Gilipollas.' He smiled frostily at Pandeo. 'So there you have it, *señor*. A slight improvement.'

*    *    *

While Isa gained strength and started to plan and worry about the christening, and Mina still cooed unabated, Pepe went to Vienna, eager to perform again in one of his favourite theatres. Unfortunately, *Andrea Chénier*, as manifested on this occasion, was not an unqualified success. Eagerness was rapidly negated, not only by the press but also by the cast.

The blame fell squarely upon the artistic director, a lozenge-shaped Belgian, who was obsessed by the 1950s and accordingly re-designed the entire opera to fit in with his dreams. The Italian baritone, Benvenuto Peneleone, tried to commit suicide after the first full rehearsal.

Pepe discovered him just as he was unwrapping his eighth Beecham's Powder, and gently took him for a walk in the fresh air.

'I will not do my ballroom scene in what looks like a bloody

399

coffee bar, with Doris Day and Guy Mitchell smirking at me from the walls,' sobbed the distraught baritone as they drifted around the side streets of Vienna.

'What about me?' Pepe said gloomily. 'Have you seen my tumbril?'

'You have a point there,' conceded Peneleone. The tumbril was a 1953 Fiat with rusty doors and bird-droppings on the roof. Miserably, they finished the four-day run.

'A good laugh,' was the general verdict of audiences and arts critics.

Back at home again, he complained long and bitterly to Bobby Drach, who had arrived for the christening. 'I am almost wishing I had done the *Stiffwicks*,' he moaned.

'Not my fault, Heart,' said Bobby cheerfully. 'No-one told Bobby what the fucking director was going to do to it! Isn't he the peroxided twat who did *Madame Butterfly* with drainpipe trousers and pony-tails? Now! – when do I present my christening gift to my godson?'

'What is it?' suspiciously.

He glared. 'What the fuck do you think it is, a fretsaw? It's a christening mug, of course!'

'Oh no!' groaned Isa, 'not another one!' She came on to the terrace with a pile of small garments, some of lace, some of wool, which she placed on a bench after testing it for dust with the knee of her jeans.

'What do you mean, another one, you ungrateful mare?'

'What I say – another one!' She sighed. 'Sebastián now has two hundred.'

'Pio and Adriana have sent one also; got it this morning, so Federico says,' Pepe said.

'Two hundred and bloody one.' She sat down with the bundle of garments and started picking through them.

'What are you doing, *querida*?'

'Making a boat.'

'Oh, aren't we grumpy!' grinned Pepe. He sat down on the bench and slid across to her side. 'Where did you get this lot from?'

'Mina,' she glared. 'All I said was, what do babies wear for christenings, and she opened about fifty damn cupboards and presented me with this lot! She bought triplicates for the two boys, just in case it rained, got too hot, they sicked up their milk, or the bloody priest spilt something on them.'

The men laughed. She held up a frothy cream shawl, silver and gold embroidery which glistened in the sun. 'What do you think of this one?'

'A bit too small for me, don't you think?' Bobby said, fingering it.

She tapped his hand. 'Get off! What do you think, *querido*?'

'Very pretty.' He ruffled the pile. 'Isn't there anything a little more, well, masculine?' And she giggled, draping the shawl around his shoulders. 'What do you suggest, denims and a hard hat?'

'Something like that,' he sniggered.

It had been a gracefully serene few weeks for Isa. Recovery was swift, apart from a slight breathlessness. There were long days in the gardens with her son, heart-stopping days realising who he was, this placid yet howl-making creature with Pepe's eyes; hers, his, theirs, a small healthy battlefield of names which still had to be sorted out.

And the long hot days under fig trees and palms also meant the frequent presence of Pau and Lluís and a rapidly-balding Bufido. In an unwise moment, Alfredo had suggested that everyone should go down to the village and sort out a few cats so that Bufido could have a fur transplant, and now Pau howled if his father went near it.

On one particular day, the week before the christening, a fine breeze tempered the heat and they gathered in a shady part of the gardens, the two mothers, the three children. Mina had her sewing basket, Isa her notebook.

'Can he sing yet?' Pau enquired anxiously. He was perched on the cracked lap of a kneeling statue, peering into the bassinet. Isa tickled his arm with a stem of grass.

'Not quite yet,' she replied solemnly. 'He needs more practice with his top C's.'

'What does "practice" mean, Isa?' and Mina laughed, then said '*Caro*, don't put your hand in there, it's dirty and Baby's clean.'

401

She looked at Isa. 'When is Pepe going to start calling him Sebastián? I heard him say "Grosvenor" quite a few times yesterday!'

Isa snorted. 'He did that when Pio rang! Have you ever heard a Spaniard trying to explain to an Italian why a baby has the name of an English hotel?' They giggled together, and Lluís sang out 'I know what you can call him, Isa! Call him Carmen!'

'Girl's name, idiot,' mumbled Mina through a length of thread she was breaking with her teeth.

'Well, he looks like a girl, all that long hair!'

'It isn't long!' Isa protested.

'It is, then!' And he danced up and down, feigning swipes at the sleeping baby, 'Come on, Carmen, give us a dance! Show us what's under your skirt!'

'Lluís!' Mina dropped her sewing and raced after the boy. Isa, closing her eyes against the shimmering leaves, smiled as she heard him shout '*Papi* always says that to the lady in the newspaper shop, so why can't I say it if he can? OW!'

*　　*　　*

The small plain church in Sant Moiseps was trying to come to terms with its sudden popularity. Villagers who normally paid it a flying visit once a week and only lit candles when Barcelona had an away game, now jammed inside and outside the squat white building, and filled the main street. The *taberna's* bartender rolled empty *vino tinto* barrels on to the pavement and used them as extra seats.

Mimosa Martes had insisted that they crept into the village without fuss. 'This is Sebastián's day, not yours. No autographs, no arias, if you please. And wear a plain incognito suit!'

Modesto agreed; then ruined her plans by standing up in their open-top car and waving both arms aloft, beaming his famous beam and reaching down to pat heads.

'Oh, for heaven's sake!' from an exasperated Mimosa beneath the brim of a straw hat, 'Who do you think you are, a visiting president?'

'Smile!' he hissed over his shoulder, gracefully catching a flower

402

and throwing it back when he realised it was plastic. In the shadow of her hat, Mimosa stuck out her tongue at his swaying back, and made a puking noise.

Pio and Adriana had arrived minutes before in a fleet of Seat taxis, and quietly disembarked as the crowds surged round Modesto's blue Mercedes; tiptoed into the church, grinning. The priest, Twit Rodríguez, already confounded and confused, hastily sketched a curtsey when he recognised the Italian tenor and conducted them to the very front of the congregation.

'Is that the font or a bloody soda fountain?' bellowed Pio with interest.

Adriana nudged him sharply. 'Language! You're in church, remember!'

'Am I?' He peered round. 'That explains it! No bar and no buffet!'

'Oh for God's sake,' Adriana muttered. 'Pio, behave yourself – say a prayer or something.'

Pepe came across to them as Pio was intoning loudly 'Lord be with us, Christ be with us, angels and saints be with us, Spanish tenors be with us, and let us hope that some 1975 Chianti will soon be with us –'

'Sorry, we've only got Lambrusco for our honoured Italian guests,' grinned Pepe.

'What? You insult us with that cheap piss?'

'You sent us half a dozen cases of the stuff!'

'There you are, then,' and they sniggered.

Adriana smiled up at him. 'And where is Isa?'

'Changing the baby,' Pepe replied half-apologetically.

'Why? Wasn't the other one good enough?' boomed Pio, and the swelling congregation tittered happily.

Pepe laughed, '*Coño*! Anyway, Adriana, I don't expect you will recognise her today. She's –' bending down, 'dressed up!'

In a small side room, with Mina fussing round her, Isa pulled down the frilly christening robe, smoothed it carefully, then held the baby close to her heart.

'Did I do it correctly?' she asked Mina.

'I think so,' frowned Mina, 'but perhaps the eighth safety-pin was an extravagance,' and they tittered together.

Then 'Oh no!' said Isa, catching sight of her white gloves. 'Look at this!'

They began to laugh noisily. The baby snuffled, asleep, warm. 'I can't go out there with this all over my gloves!'

Mina doubled over. 'I hate to say this, but it's on your skirt as well!'

The priest looked in on them, withdrew quickly. He began to suspect that *Deus* was either testing or teasing him. A sudden eruption of noise sent him hurrying back into the body of the church. Modesto had entered and was progressing up the aisle to a torrent of applause and calls of '*Bravo!*'

'Is he riding a donkey?' whispered Pio.

*　　*　　*

Afterwards, in the kennel changing for the reception, Pepe shouted 'No gloves! No hat! A smeared damp patch on your skirt like the map of Europe! If you were going to louse up your outfit, why the fuck did you pick white?'

'No-one noticed,' she said broodily, pulling on silk trousers.

'No-one bloody noticed?' he howled. 'A brown stain that size, and you think no-one noticed?'

'I tried to rub it off, but that made it worse –'

'And what happened to your hat?'

'I sat on it when I was changing Grosvenor,' she said calmly, and tied the sash of her silk top into a perky bow. He looked sinister, she thought, and brushed her hair quickly.

'I can only excuse you, *señora*, on the grounds that you are certifiable, a raving lunatic –' His voice rose higher and she winced '– a cretin and completely bloody brainless!'

'I couldn't help the mess on my skirt, it was –'

'I am not talking now about your bloody skirt! *Estás de atar!*' He came behind her, both of them reflected in the mirror, his mouth damp with effort. 'I am talking about that fiasco, that cock-up, that bloody paralysing roll-call of names you have bestowed upon my son!' Added furiously, 'And stop laughing!'

'I'm not,' she mumbled, pushing her fist into her mouth.

404

He swung away and prowled to the bed. Pointed to it. 'Our next child will be conceived right there! What do you propose to call him, eh? Bloody Slumberland?'

The laughter tore from her, punctuated with squawks. Her head collapsed on the dressing-table, scattering bottles and combs. 'Sl . . . Slumberland!' he heard her hoot.

'Why did you do it?' he shouted.

There was a knock on the door, and Mina peered cheerfully round it. 'Only me! Elena's washed and changed Sebastián, he's all ready for the presentation of his mugs! Do hurry up, Pepe, you can't go to the celebrations in your underpants. Ready, Isa?'

Isa was still paralysed by laughter. 'Slumberland Contreras!'

Pepe stared at his sister-in-law. 'What did you call my son just now?'

'Dear Lord above! The man's just been to the christening and already he's forgotten his child's name! Sebastián, you idiot! He was the one in the lace robe!'

Perplexed, he sat down. 'What about the other names?'

Calming down with an effort, Isa said, 'Oh, those. He won't have to use them all, Sebastián is his first name, after all.'

'And Grosvenor?'

'Er . . . that came fifth, I believe.'

'Ludwig?'

'Third.'

'Roberto?'

'Fourth.'

'Was there a Josep?'

'After Sebastián.'

'Any more?'

She grinned. 'Only Contreras Pepper, beloved!' With dignity, she released herself from his grip. Beamed at Mina. 'Let's leave *Papi* to change, shall we?'

Only after they had gone did he collapse with tears of laughter on the bed. Oh my *cucufato*! Whistling happily, he pulled on his jeans.

\* \* \*

Four doctors stood round the bed, watching her hands describe circles and the vivid green eyes gazing at the movements. She looked up suddenly, said 'I think it was a crushable offence, what he did to me, the old bastard.' Then there was a silence as her mouth jerked with each circle.

The psychiatrist looked at his watch. Six minutes past his luncheon break.

He said briskly to the police officer, 'Sorry. You can see how it is. I shall have to recommend that *Señora* Contreras is committed to the Clínica Psiquiátrica in Sabassa. Physically, she is dried out. Feeding a little, with help, taking liquids by herself some of the time. Mentally, as you can see, she is in a mess. It may take a few months; it may take more than a year. At this stage, impossible to say.'

He straightened his tie. 'I shall be notifying the family this afternoon, and then arrangements can be made for her transfer to Sabassa.'

'I see,' said Óscar Pandeo.

He called to his companion, and they went out to their car.

# 24

The only relative she could claim to be truly her own was a brother, Jaime, long since resident in Colombia. There had been no communication between them for fifteen years; even birthdays had been forgotten, neglected. And so it was that Judit's unwilling and baffled ex-husband and her former brother-in-law went in subdued manner to the Clínica Psiquiátrica to sign her into the care of the medical authorities.

After scribbling his signature on several documents, Pepe watched as the doctor placed them inside a folder which bore the number 344.

On the way home, Alfredo said quietly, 'Do you think that was meant to be Judit? That number?'

Pepe said nothing, and flicked a finger up and down his thumb.

\*　　\*　　\*

'If I hear that bloody song once more,' screamed Mimosa, 'I shall cut off your balls and mince them up for the goldfish!'

'Which song?' he queried innocently, pulling the sun umbrella down to shroud his face and chest.

'You know damn well which one! *You are my heart's* flaming *delight*! I'll be glad when this concert is over!'

'Oh – you mean this one?' and his voice burst forth resonantly. To his surprise there was no further protest forthcoming. He cautiously continued singing, and raised the umbrella a little. Through the knotted fringe, he saw his wife kneeling a short distance away, sharpening the butter knife on a rockery stone. She was muttering.

'Alright, *querida*,' laughing. 'Test me on another! How about *Caminito*, there's a tricky syncopated –'

The sound of honing increased.

'I shall read my book,' he said hastily.

\*        \*        \*

Adriana Fazzoletto was feeding apples to a chestnut mare when Pio came into the yard in his sailcloth shorts and satin vest.

'I can't contact him!' he complained. Patted the mare heavily, 'Good boy!'

'If you mean Pepe, of course you can't, he's in Bonn doing an ad for Daimler-Benz. What's the problem?'

Pio sat down moodily on a bale of straw. 'The reprise of *Nessun Dorma*', he grumbled. 'The way that silly fart Martes wants to play it, we shall end up looking like bloody traffic cops if we have to keep pointing at each other,' wiggling his toes in the dust and eyeing the apples lustfully.

'You've got another rehearsal yet, *caro*. Just calm down and think what fun it will all be!'

She fed the last apple to the mare. Pio's eyes grew round and hurt like those of a whipped baby.

'Bloody della Doccia! Bloody greedy animals!'

\*        \*        \*

Pepe like Bonn. He wasn't exactly sure why Daimler-Benz wanted him to sing *Valencia* for their latest model, a 350 SL Dusseldorfer, but it was a pleasant trip, and he was able to pay a visit to Beethoven's house and acquire a souvenir for Isa. This was a framed cartoon, which showed Beethoven holding a phone to his ear saying 'Sorry?'

He lounged happily in the aircraft taking him home. Four more days; then −

Viva, Roma!

\*        \*        \*

August 4th.

It was an interminably hot day, taxis shimmering as they off-loaded passengers and argued over new ones. Vehicles that revved and screamed and ploughed through the petrol-smelling sunshine.

From his hotel window, Buzzer watched the heat-soaked humanity below. He was morose. He resented coming and going disguised in a fedora hat and sunglasses like a Hollywood conception of Al Capone. In short, Buzzer was now a star. It was all thanks to *La Repubblica,* who had decided to re-print the sheep photograph on the three consecutive days leading up to the concert; and as a result, the foyer of his hotel had been awash with new fans of all ages, plus one enterprising old woman who had set up a stall near the reception desk and was selling little Italian flags on sticks and dishes of scallops to the crowds waiting for Buzzer's autograph. His conducting hand felt sore and stiff, scribbling his signature over those bloody sheep.

And of course Byron Larch and Luciano Bardi were constantly on his neck and worrying about every damned thing, from cameras that couldn't manoeuvre through cables without careering into the cellos, to rumours that the Arena della Doccia had been targeted by either ETA or the Mafia, no-one knew which.

Buzzer's hands gripped the window sill in a sudden convulsion. And now more fuss and bother, which involved Bardi and ultimately himself: the time-wasting trio of tenors now wanted bloody helicopters.

Fazzoletto said that his other one had shrunk, and he wanted to arrive in style in a spanking new one. Martes had never owned one, thought it would be fun to commute from his rented villa near Florence like a winged god. Gruñón had pointed out that helicopters didn't exactly have wings, but his father said stop nitpicking and get on with checking my special souvenirs.

The family consensus about his brainwave had been mixed. 'Will people really want to buy tea towels with your face on them?' asked Mimosa, doubtfully.

'Why me?' wailed Sara. 'Why do I have to walk up and down selling the damn things?'

And now, guess what, Allah-God? Contreras wants a helicopter, too. And it must be pale blue, as that was Isa's favourite colour.

Buzzer poured himself a very magnificent Scotch and ginger. It might soothe his battered hand.

*     *     *

August 4th.

And Isa gave Sebastián a tearful goodbye kiss, Pepe hugged him. Pau held up Bufido, demanding an encore of the tearful kiss for his cat.

'We'll look after Cousin Sebastián for you!' he shouted, satisfied that Bufido had been awarded a tear. Uncle Pepe had declined to bestow anything on the moulting toy, on the grounds that loose fur might fly into his throat.

Lluís giggled, said *Papi* would say it wouldn't make any difference. '*Papi* says you always sing as if –'

'*Papi* can go hoist the Spanish flag up his arse,' responded Pepe, patting his nephew's head hard in farewell.

'Pepe!' from Mina, as the family went with them to the car. All except Alfredo, that is, who was attending a two-day science forum in Bilbao.

Pepe fretted aloud, would his son be alright with Elena and Mina? Then, anxiety flying to other targets, 'Isa, have you got your passport?'

Nonchalantly, 'What on earth for?'

Explosion. 'Because we're going to Italy!'

'Oh – is that abroad? No-one told me,' and she hugged Mina, exchanged titters.

'Have you got all my medical stuff?' he barked.

'Yessir! New nose, change of Adam's apple, twenty kilos of spare –'

'Shut up!' as the family laughed gleefully. Gualterio gave the couple a benevolent scowl, 'By the time you get back, your son will be able to pot the red quicker than his grandfather!' Adding in English, 'Now bugger off!'

Everyone laughed and waved, and Moncho was grinning as he drove them away.

*     *     *

410

August 4th. And Bobby's knee, strapped and throbbing, bulged inside his trouser leg.

Thanks to traffic lights that had stopped working and remained on bloody green on Holland Park fucking Avenue, he was obliged to fly to Rome with two walking-sticks. Mind you, Alitalia were very kind, very patient. Had this been British Airways, he reflected, they would have re-routed and dropped him over bloody Bosnia.

As it was, he reclined regally in his seat and was cossetted; and that nice boy, the steward called Patrizio, was very caring indeed. He just hoped that Bardi wouldn't put him on the top floor of that fucking villa of his this time.

\*    \*    \*

August 5th. Cloudless. Perfumed with diesel and cigar smoke and assorted body lotions, the Arena della Doccia reeled under the heat and the massive odour.   Buzzer had autographed his last sheep, speeding up and onwards to the Opera House in the morning for a final piano rehearsal and the sorting out of a few musical tangles; a quick lunch of *prosciutto* and a giant icecream shrouded in syrup, and then on to the Arena where his two hundred musicians prowled and sweated and fanned themselves with pages of the overture.

The lady cellist and the bass player, deeply in love, kissed greedily beneath the copy of *Corriere della Sera* they had bought at the airport, and were glad that it had so many sections. The deputy leader (the leader herself was in the toilets, changing her Aertex shirt for the fourth time that day) was arguing with a technician about residual cable footage that kept his music stand on a permanent tilt. Various hand and finger gestures were exchanged, no solution found.

A nearby trombone blasted out suddenly, causing Luciano Bardi and Ruggero Ripieno to stagger.

'*Stronzo!*' yelled Bardi. His morning had already been poisoned by a house guest with a bad knee and two sticks who persisted in yelling from the top of the villa that, having already struggled up miles of fucking stairs he had no intention of struggling down again for his breakfast.

A shout from overhead, cables plummeted round them, a boom swung low then zipped away in a wide arc.

'It looks like a fucking war zone,' Bardi moaned. Snapped suddenly to attention, pointing. 'What the hell are they?'

'Monitor screens,' Ripieno replied, turning to stare at the perky backside of one of the harpists. His fingers itched. She looked over her shoulder at him, smiling invitingly, and he saw that she was at least sixty.

'Monitor screens? I didn't authorize any bloody – Hey, you! Out! Fucking *rapidamente*! The press aren't invited in here yet! Oh shit,' catching sight of a familiar figure heading towards them, 'here comes Larch! Do excuse me, Ripieno –' and he fled for cover.

Hammering, banging. Whistling, the occasional burst of song. Sound-testers who pretended they were tenors and lustily yelled *O Sole Mio*. Catcalls. A few cheers greeted the perspiring Buzzer as he came into view, striped shirt darkly damp. A bassoon moaned, someone swore with staccato speed as his stand fell over and distributed sheets of music among his colleagues. A general cry of '*Maestro*, how can we possibly concentrate in all this noise and dust?'

'Good afternoon, ladies and gentlemen,' he called, un-perturbed.

'Ahmet! I want a word with you!' and Byron Larch pushed his way between a heap of unwired microphones and a Datsun truck. 'Buzzer! Can you hear me?'

'Allah-God have mercy,' murmured Buzzer, making a 'sit down' gesture to members of the wind section. 'Allah-God have twice as much mercy as he has shown thus far! Allah-God bear with his servant if he leaps upon Larch with a meat cleaver!'

Larch shouted, 'Buzzer!' Buzzer said *grazie* to an elderly violinist who handed him a carafe of iced water and a plastic cup.

'Buzzer! It's about the press conference! Been re-arranged for five o'clock!'

Buzzer stood and looked at him, face devoid of expression.

'So?', trying not to grin as second violins began to play *Passing Strangers*.

'I was wondering if you'd pass the message to −'

A mobile cameraman on a trial run yelled 'Quick, somebody help, my balls are trapped!'

'− to the tenors, please?'

The orchestra watched the writhing cameraman with interest, shouts of sympathy from the men, cheers from the ladies.

'When I see the tenors, Larch − bloody hell, what was that?' as a loud explosion ripped through the Arena. A viola player shouted, 'Bet that's Emilio! − lighting his cigarette by the paraffin store again!' Buzzer nodded. 'As long as his violin's still playable. Now, Larch −'

'Will you tell them five o'clock, instead of six?'

'When I see them, Larch, it will be to rehearse, not to hand out bloody timetables. I suggest you come back at two o'clock, they'll be here by then. Is no-one going to rescue that poor bugger on the camera?'

'But −!'

'Two o'clock,' repeated Buzzer pleasantly. Allah-God must have gone for a quick paddle to cool his feet. He paused while a crane reared its height above the orchestra and swayed. He held his breath, watching. As it elected to remain upright, he turned again to his musicians.

'*Signore, signori, per favore!* Lucia, please?' and the oboe sounded its obligatory mournful note. One by one, the members of the orchestra joined in the cacophony of tuning up.

\* \* \*

Then came the height crisis.

'Right − cameras ready? We want a panned try-out here, close-ups of the three buggers if they'll kindly form a line on the platform; we'll need this in the medley, three full-face in sequence, no thanks Paolo I've just had a cup, right − come on, Camera Four, you're not on a day-trip to fucking Rimini, pan in on them . . . NOW!'

413

Modesto crossed his eyes and stuck his tongue out at the camera.

Then came a gap, a hazy blue background.

And then Fazzoletto, who picked his nose and waved his finger at the camera.

The producer yelled 'Where the fuck was Contreras?' gazing at his giant monitor.

'He's there, but the camera will have to drop so we can pick him up in vision!'

'Perhaps if I kneel down,' came over the earphones, 'because even when he stands on bloody tiptoe, I only get the top of his head!'

'Oh bloody hell, this is all I need!'

'Perhaps if we hung him by the shoulders from the sound boom, sir —'

\*　　\*　　\*

'What in the name of Apollo are those things for?'

And Fazzoletto strode to a full stop, flat cap rammed over his head, yellow scarf dangling past his knees. The outside of the Arena was in premature darkness beneath the rearing walls and towers, the shadows blackened by spotlights that replaced the setting sun. In the mix of brightness and gloom, the bustling continued, coils of rope, overalled figures, ladders.

'Those,' said Luciano Bardi, 'are Portakabins.'

'I can see that!' snapped Fazzoletto. 'What the hell are they doing here?'

'They are here for you three,' Bardi said with some irritation. 'Somewhere for you to have a rest or a piss or say a prayer, whatever else you do between bloody songs!'

'Jesus sodding whatsisname!' Then Pio caught sight of Martes, neatly-buttoned shirt-cuffs, jumping down the steps of one of the Portakabins, whistling gaily.

Pio grinned. 'Hey, Gipsy Maria! You tell fortunes?'

'Sure,' jovially, biffing Bardi on the head. 'No expense spared, I see, when you put on a show! Right, Fatty, cross my palm with your credit card and I'll reveal what the fates have in store for you.

You seen inside yours yet? They're like bloody rabbit hutches!'

'Dear God,' moaned Pio, gazing at his temporary home. He waved his hand at it weakly. 'Where's Contreras? Has he seen his little nest yet?'

'He came, he saw, he passed out,' Modesto said smoothly.

'I'm not bloody surprised! No room in there for a fart, let alone a shag!'

'May I remind you,' said Bardi icily, 'that the cabins are supplied courtesy of the Italian broadcasting network for a few moments of privacy and rest. Inside, you will find a dressing area, television set, shower —'

'A kitchen? Food?' And 'Shit!' as Bardi shook his head. Pio wandered disconsolately to the cabin indicated as his own to inspect the width of the door.

'WATCH OUT BELOOOOW!' and an oil drum hit the ground, bounced, rolled over.

Modesto glanced ironically upwards. Lots of workmen, lots of scaffolding.

'Aren't we supplied with hard hats as well?' he frowned. 'Oh *hola*, Pepe! What do you think of our holiday village, then?'

'I'd like to drop a frigging bomb on it! Puddles of petrol round mine, and they stink to heaven. Have you investigated the toilets yet? My arse is covered with rivet marks!'

'*Signor* Bardi, *Signor* Bardi, telephone!'

The two tenors drifted slowly into the Arena itself, gazing at the acres of seats and two television cameras doing a *pasa doble*, the orchestra riffing and scraping, humanity moving in all directions.

Pio caught up with them, panting. 'Isn't it fun!' he said viciously, tugging the end of his scarf which had snagged on a plank. 'I was born to sing, not to work on a bloody building site!'

'Is that what you tell your psychiatrist — that you were born to sing?' Pepe grinned. A booming roar echoed round them, a few fat pigeons took flight.

Pio smiled down at him. 'Thought you'd got over your word-blindness, Baby Balls? You're still doing it, you know!' And seeing the puzzled expression, he added kindly, '*Nessun Dorma*, Pulgarcito, *Nessun Dorma*.'

'Oh Christ, I'm not, am I? Not — *silenzio* and *speranza*?'

415

They both nodded solemnly.

'What – even when we ran through it this afternoon?'

They nodded again. Pepe walked slowly away, lips moving, '*Silen*-TSIO, *speran*-TSA,' and they guffawed. Modesto frowned slightly. 'Actually, I didn't hear him go wrong with it today.'

'He didn't!' with a shout of glee, 'Just wanted to frighten the little bugger!'

Laughing, they made their way through the chaos to the vast stage. Esteban Carrera was there at the piano, in case he was needed. The top was down, and he was leaning on it doing the crossword in a children's comic book. He greeted them, sucking his pen.

'Is the English for *gato*, cat?' he asked Modesto.

'It is, *Maestro*. What's this for, your doctorate in zoology?'

'Is it spelt with three letters?'

'No,' sniggered Modesto, 'seven.' Carrera's brow cleared. 'Ah, that's where I've been going wrong! Thank you,' and he began to fill in some of the squares.

'Oh. That's alright, then,' murmured Modesto. 'Any sign of Buzzer?'

'He's up there,' Carrera said, pointing skywards with his biro. 'Something to do with acoustics. I think *Señor* Larch was worried about the thousand-year-old towers being inconveniently placed and distorting the sound of the triangle in the *Vespers* overture. Something like that, anyway.'

Modesto cackled. Pio placed a tall three-legged stool near the podium and hoisted himself on to it. 'Any one of you ladies in need of a good fuck?' he roared to the orchestra, and the females giggled and cheered while their male colleagues made rude noises.

'How much do you charge, Pio?' called a violinist.

'Tonight, is free. Why, do you want a go, Constanza? Mine's the second bloody Portakabin on the left, you can't miss it, it's got one of the Pope's condoms on the door!' Gales of laughter. Modesto sniggered 'Shut up, you fat cretin! She'll be too depressed to play a bloody note!'

Pepe approached, looking moody, his lips still moving silently.

'What's the matter, Tiny? Can't you get it right?'

'Shut it, Sperm Bank! I wish the authorities would empty you

416

along with the rest of the fucking dustbins!'

Modesto snorted as Pio pulled his cap down over his eyes, pretending to sulk.

When Buzzer arrived, everyone was freely perspiring in the heat of the lights and the evening.

'I thought Aertex was supposed to stop all this!' grumbled the leader.

'Try shaving your armpits once in a while, you smelly bat!' called a cellist.

Buzzer tried not to grin. Failed. By contrast, he looked fresh and cool.

'Sorted out the acoustics yet, Buzz?' Modesto tittered.

'Not really, but I did find out what the snail shapes are for.'

'Oh?' interest sparking.

'Most ingenious. They're quite hollow inside, you know. They were designed, Martes, to imprison stupid tenors.' Then he gazed round, '*Bene, bene,* all here,' rubbing his hands. 'Esteban, stay here, we may need you. But first of all, full run-through, *O Sole Mio,* three voices as of.' He stared at the orchestra: suddenly, a vast silence.

'How do you manage that?' said Pio in wonderment.

'Last rehearsal, my friends,' said Modesto thoughtfully. The four of them looked at each other. Then Buzzer raised his stick. '*O Sole Mio!*' he called.

Howls of laughter from the musicians as the violins swooped in with *Core 'Ngrato.*

Buzzer grinned before the frown took command. Rapped hard. They began again. Pio stretched his neck, licked his mouth, waited for his first solo entry.

*　　*　　*

They grew hotter and wearier.

Trouble flared during the reprise of *Nessun Dorma.* Pepe let out a spirited howl. 'Will you stop hauling me around like a bloody puppet, Fazzoletto!'

Pio chortled, and his hands made jerking movements above

Pepe's head. 'Come on, Pinocchio, let's see you kick those little legs of yours!'

'Get bloody off!'

Buzzer sighed. The orchestra drifted into obedient silence as the *maestro* looked at his soloists.

'Sorry, Buzzer.'

A brief nod, baton raised, corner-of-eye glance. All in a neat row, solemn.

Splutter of laughter from Martes. 'Sorry, Buzzer!'

'Hold it, *Maestro*!' roared Pio, and climbed off his stool. 'I am in dire need of a piss!'

And Pepe sank to his knees, laughing helplessly.

The orchestra exploded with mirth.

# 25

Isa straightened the lapels of his jacket, removed a piece of pink fluff from the satin surface. Stared at the fluff on the tip of her finger, blew it away.

With the same finger, she touched his chin.

'Don't say it!' he warned, tightening and relaxing his jaw.

'Don't say what?'

'Mmmm?' Distractedly, he twitched his shoulders, then carefully massaged each side of his nose.

She grinned at him. 'What is it I haven't got to say?'

'What?'

Amused, she stood back and watched him, brown eyes roaming round the Portakabin, then settling on his wristwatch. 'What time is it?' he barked.

'But you've just looked at your – It's nine o'clock, *querido*, give or take a few minutes.'

'Give or take exactly how many?'

She smiled, 'Three.'

'Oh.' He sat down, got up, poured a glass of Perrier. They could hear laughter coming from Modesto's Portakabin. 'Noisy bastard!'

She giggled gently, went to the window, peered out at the dinner jackets and long dresses walking around the cables and ropes and rainbow puddles of fuel, some carrying wind instruments, one man with two violin cases. Pepe joined her at the window. She could see his index finger scraping the back of his thumb.

'Jesus, what the hell's that?' They stared as a bouquet of flowers and a tin of Coke flew through Modesto's door. The laughter had ceased.

Pepe said smugly, 'Good! He's just noticed the time! I bet he's

419

also remembering what Buzzer said to him last night.' He cackled happily.

'And what did Buzzer say?'

Distracted for the moment, he assumed the *maestro*'s favourite stance and intoned 'Far be it from me to criticise your impeccable French, Mr Martes, but shouldn't it be "*le ciel est si pur*", and not "ler seely sipoor"?'

Isa tittered. 'What did Modesto say?'

'Stood there, blinking, staring at Buzzer. And when he did the re-take, he dried up, forgot the whole bloody thing!'

He put his arm around her waist and they watched for a while, but nothing else emerged from the neighbouring cabin.

*　　*　　*

Modesto gargled, spat, gargled again. Then, 'That dream I had last night –'

His son groaned. 'Oh not again!'

Modesto looked at Gruñón reproachfully. 'It could be very significant,' he said, and dabbed cologne on his temples. Gruñón sniggered, handed his father a clean pair of black socks. 'Don't laugh, Child! I am a great believer in the occult!'

'Dreams, Father Dear, are not the occult. Dreams are a sign of a jumbled and restless brain.'

'My brain is neither jumb– Not these socks! The ones over there with the silver whatsits down the side – your mother insists. *Gracias!*' He sat down, brooding. 'This dream. And coming on the very night before the concert! Weird.'

'What's so weird about it?' laughed Gruñón. 'Hello – there goes Contreras, terrified of being last as usual.' He looked over his shoulder at Modesto.'You say that in the dream you were kidnapped?'

'Yes,' with a shudder. Then 'These socks are too bloody big – what on earth possessed Mimosa to get them a size over?' He waggled his foot. 'Go on – you were saying about my dream?'

'You need a shrink, not a son! Okay, then; you were kidnapped. Your hands were tied, they wound sellotape round and round you, but left your mouth free.' Gruñón sniggered again. 'Then

420

they stood you on a chair in a room with pink carpets, prodded you with a rolled-up newspaper –' Broke off as Modesto pulled on his shiny shoes, moaned, and did a practice hobble. 'Father Dear, are you sure you can manage with a bunch of spare sock tucked under your toes?'

Another loud moan, then 'Get on with your analysis! It could be important.'

'Right!' Gruñón waved through the window to Adriana Fazzoletto, who was instructing a man with a large straw basket to go up the steps of her Portakabin. 'So, they gave you a prod and then –'

'Dad, I've closed down the stall! I'm fed up, we've only sold one!' Sara bounced angrily through the door.

Modesto stared at her. 'What do you mean – one? You've been on that pitch I rented for you since eleven o'clock this morning!'

'No-one seems interested in tea towels,' petulantly, 'they're all buying Contreras car-stickers and Fazzoletto dolls and Buzzer sheep.'

'I'll kill those bastards!' he yelped. 'This is sabotage!' He glared at his son. 'I told you that dream portended evil and bloody disaster!'

'What dream?' asked Sara, dropping her carton of towels, kicking off her shoes.

'Father had one last night,' said Gruñón solemnly. 'He was kidnapped –'

'They told me to sing! Ordered me to sing *Nessun Dorma*! In bloody French! And I . . . I couldn't even remember the tune.' Head in hands, he whispered 'And only one Martes tea towel sold, out of four thousand! Give a gold medal to the bugger who bought it!'

'Give it to him yourself,' giggled Sara. 'It was Buzzer. He needed something to wipe grease off his music case.'

*     *     *

'One more!' pleaded Pio. He sat in front of the mirror, white bow tie in his hand, doing mouth exercises.

Stretch, pout, thin line. Stretch pout.

'No!'

'But the last one was only a baby!'

Adriana sighed, passed him the basket of roast chickens, each neatly wrapped in cellophane. She said, 'Can you remember, years and years ago, when you had a waist?'

'No. Can you?'

'I think there's a photo somewhere . . . A bit yellow now, one you had taken when you were about four years old – the first one of yourself you ever started kissing goodnight. I'll see if I can find it, it might bring back memories of the days when your belly didn't begin at your neck and end at your knees.'

He grinned lasciviously. 'Ah, but don't forget the bits in between!'

'Look, hurry up and finish that blasted chicken, there's Modesto already on his way to the starting post! Oh dear – I hope he's alright . . . '

Concern. 'Eh? What's wrong?'

'He's limping.'

'Oh, is that all. Probably folded his cock on the wrong side.' He stood up, still chewing chicken, wiping his hands on a paper towel. Plucked a loose thread from his shirt front, lunged back his shoulders.

'Ah well,' he said. '*Vesti la* bloody *giubba!*'

She stood on tiptoe and flung her arms round his neck. 'I'll be the one cheering and applauding loudest of all!'

'Good girl. And bring that basket with you!'

\*     \*     \*

Buzzer shot his cuffs, adjusted the fit of his tails, and wriggled his shoulders to evaporate some of the tension. 'Time?' he snapped.

'Almost there, *Maestro*. Ten minutes.'

The atmosphere at the back of the vast Arena was high voltage. Workmen, performers, technicians by the hundred: the entire area resembled an aircraft hangar moments before a major scramble.

And in the Arena itself, the resounding chatter and clatter of the audience, late arrivals trying to read their souvenir programmes as they excused-me past irritated shoes and knees, men in casual uniform examining tickets, pointing, explaining.

The orchestra: buzzing and alight, an arpeggio here and there, a trumpet with hurtled notes above the clamour, heads of hair shiny and scissor-fresh, four hundred feet in glossy black shoes.

Buzzer, in the hangar, was poker-faced and impeccable, stick and sheets of music in his hands. He was suddenly enveloped in an embrace from behind, and the baton clattered to the stone floor. Scowled, then flashed a smile as he returned Modesto's hug.

Someone retrieved the baton, wiped it, handed it back.

He nodded to Pio, who was standing patiently while Adriana gave the shoulders of the jacket a final touch and smoothing down.

Pepe squeezed Isa's hand. 'Do you think they've allowed Sebastián to stay up and watch?' he whispered.

'I told them to,' she whispered back. 'I expect Gualterio has dipped his dummy in brandy for the occasion!'

Suddenly, there came the sound of applause – hesitant at first, then louder and faster as the orchestra leader made her appearance. A camera rolled forward from the hangar towards the Arena entrance at the back of the orchestra. Transmission lights glowed.

Buzzer stiffened his back, smiled briefly at the three tenors, and began his no-nonsense stride out of the hangar and into the brightness, down the aisle between his musicians, nodding to them, first one side then the other.

In the hangar, they heard the applause swell to welcoming proportions. Grins were exchanged, fingers were crossed and held in the air.

Silence fell, and breathing stopped.

Then the opening bars of Verdi's *I Vespri Siciliani* flew back towards them.

\* \* \*

'If you don't stop that bloody noise, I'll send you to your room!'

Lluís scowled, dropped a sugared almond on Sebastián's chest.

'I can't see the red light,' frowned Mina, looking at the video recorder.

Pau cried 'Did you see what Uncle Pepe did then? Did you? He blew a kiss at a plane that went over when he was singing!' He hopped round the room excitedly. 'Why did he do that, does he know the driver?'

Gualterio reached out a hand for the boy's collar and pulled him on to his knee. 'God, this is a bloody dirge! I told him, but oh no, he wouldn't listen, would he, pea-brained twat. Bloody Cilea!'

'What do you mean, the red light isn't on?' Alfredo barked. 'Of course it's – oh no! I forgot to put the tape in! Oh fuck it, where's the new video tape? I had the damn thing ready!' He jumped up. 'Come on, where is it? It was on the table! Who's got the bloody thing?'

Lluís said off-handedly, 'Sebastián's got it.'

'Don't be so stupid! What would a baby want with a –' He snatched the video tape from the crib, wiped off a few drops of milk, and slotted it into the recorder. 'I'll skin you, you stupid little shit! The concert will be over before we've recorded any of it!'

'Alfredo, please! Oh look, they're applauding him!'

'That makes a bloody change.'

'*Papi*, why is Uncle Pepe going off so quickly?'

'Probably afraid of farting into the mikes again!'

'Alfredo! I shan't tell you again!'

'Good! Peace and quiet at last!'

Sebastián began to whimper. Gualterio beamed proudly. 'That's a good boy, he's already beginning to appreciate music – you hear him? He cries when Martes comes on!'

Mina giggled. Her father-in-law yawned, tugged Pau's hair. 'I think this calls for a brandy. Go on, girl, pour it! I need something to give me strength to sit through this. Jesus Christ, does Ahmet have to sway around like that, he looks like a bloody ship going nowhere. Pau, sit still!'

Mina said pleasantly, 'The recording light's gone out.'

Alfredo tightened his lips and knelt down again by the video recorder.

\*　　\*　　\*

424

Clair frowned. 'I didn't reckon much to that one. Doesn't his voice sound funny and wobbly when he sings high like that? Bet it drives Ezzie up the wall when he practises at home!'

'Oh, I expect he's got a soundproof shed somewhere,' Eve said sarcastically. 'Look, are we playing Trivial Pursuit or not? If you've had enough, I'll put the damned thing away!' Looked at the screen. 'If Kelvin Cragg says "Coming to you live from Rome" once more, I'll bring up my supper. When's the fat guy coming on? He's the best of the lot!'

'Sooner watch the New Kids on the Block . . . '

'Shall I tell you something? So would I!'

They grinned at each other companionably.

\* \* \*

'Have they found out yet?' demanded Bobby during the intro to *Granada*.

'Have who found out what?' Luciano Bardi picked bits of peanut from his teeth with the corner of his programme.

'Whether it was ETA or the Mafia,' grinned Bobby, and raised his opera glasses to focus on Pepe. 'You know, that sod stands on his toes more often than fucking Margot Fonteyn! And he didn't shave himself very closely, either, his face looks like bloody Epping Forest!' He glanced at his puzzled companion. 'The threats, Luciano. The bomb threats to the delly Dotchy.'

'Oh. Those.' Bardi shrugged. 'There were a couple of car bombs, that's all. They were defused.'

'Christ! Where?' open-mouthed.

'Belfast,' grinned Bardi.

\* \* \*

Keta and her lover Ellie sat entranced, three rows from the front. Keta had a spun shawl on her knees in case the evening began to cool.

She had long ago stopped seeing the tracking cameras and the booms and the television lights. Now, it was just sound, and the sharp flash of light on brass, the gleam of the violins.

Through her opera glasses, she watched the young man with a piccolo dip his whole body forward as he played, the violinist with short dark hair who sometimes grinned with sheer enjoyment. Her eyes appreciated Pio, his unflorid stance, no movements of arms or hands like the other two, simply emoting by voice alone. And she watched Buzzer, who swooped and swung with his feet still in their place, the grin on his face at the end of *Granada* and his quick nod to the orchestra after the final bar which had sounded suspiciously like 'Oooo-lé!'

And now, as applause greeted Martes for his last solo, the *maestro* stood with head back, gazing ostentatiously skywards to see if they really would have stars for this aria.

As *E lucevan le Stelle* began, Modesto stood by a grave in Australia. He heard his throat open fully as he sang. For you, dearest girl.

And he ended the aria gasping, his breath gone, having amazed even himself.

*       *       *

The medley had been an enormous success.

And the medley had been repeated. The applause was deafening, a million bulldozers coming towards them.

'What do you mean, another fucking encore?' Pio gasped under his breath, waving to the crowd.

'I'm fit enough,' said Modesto bouncily, 'Feel as fresh as a lark!' and he grinned at the ecstatic audience, waving his hands aloft.

Heat and perspiration had reduced Buzzer's hair to tight wet curls. His red braces showed brightly against his shirt momentarily as he stepped off the podium to join and embrace his singers. Pio tugged him into line, then grabbed Pepe and hauled him closer.

'You do that again and I'll stitch your balls together!' hissed Pepe, his smile broad and happy for the thousands in the Arena.

'You'd need at least a kilometre of wire for that,' Pio chortled. Then 'Oh come on, let's do *O Sole* fucking *Mio* again, then we can go and get pissed!'

'And *Nessun Dorma*,' Buzzer said firmly. 'Come along, get into a neat line, let's do it while we can still bloody stand. From the beginning – at a risk to art!'

*  *  *

Pau and Lluís lay asleep on the sofa.

'Jesus Christ, how much longer?' Alfredo groaned. 'You don't think they're going to do the medley for a third time, do you?'

Gualterio emptied the last of the Martell into his glass, then peered blearily into the crib. 'Bless the little innocent! Sleeping like a baby. That reminds me, has Pepe said anything yet about his religious education?'

'What?' muttered Mina, opening an eye. 'What made you think of that?'

Gualterio continued to stare at Sebastián. 'Because I want him to grow up believing in bloody God, that's why! Never mind about television and modern crap, just music and fucking angels, thass all!'

'Papaterio, please put that brandy down!'

'Certainly, dear,' and he dropped the empty bottle on to the carpet.

Alfredo screamed 'Great merciless bluetits! They're going to do *Nessun Dorma* again!'

*  *  *

He knew what he had done.

He knew by the way Pio tittered and Modesto covered his mouth and twinkled at him.

And he knew when he saw Buzzer grinning and nodding at him. As the applause rose, deafening and solid, Pepe knew.

*Silen*-TSIO. *Speran*-TSA. They hadn't been like that at all.

Pio said, 'Well done, Baby Balls! Perhaps by the time you retire, you'll have nearly mastered the –'

'Fuck off!' bowing, smiling, waving.

Modesto said with a smirk, 'Who likes to criticise my German, then?'

'Up yours, Martes!'

427

Buzzer hugged them all, grasping hands, waving to his musicians and then to the audience on their feet, cheering. 'Not bad! In fact –' a grin wider than they had ever seen, '– *molto moltissimo* bloody *bene*!'

'Champagne, everybody?' Modesto yelled above the clamour.

'No glasses, just the bloody bottles! Christ, I could drink a river!'

'For God's sake, let's go, we'll be here all night!'

'One more wave to the buggers, bless 'em!'

Finally Buzzer said 'Right, I think that's it!' Trickles of perspiration ran down his happy, tired face. 'Let us retire, gentlemen!'

'You coming, Contreras, or do you want to practise your Italian first?'

Pepe was silently exhausted as they made their way back for the last time through the applauding orchestra towards the hangar, which had already erupted into celebration. He sucked in his cheeks, and his eyes stretched like those of a weary bloodhound.

'His voice has gone,' Pio said solemnly behind him, and hooked his fingers round Pepe's collar, lifting him a few inches off the ground.

His feet kicked and flailed. 'Put me bloody down!' Loud guffaws as Pio dropped him.

Isa came running, precocious hair tangled, face glowing. Pepe stuck his foot behind Pio's knee, and the large man stumbled clumsily. 'You Spanish whore!'

\*     \*     \*

Mina yawned, stretched her arms. 'Oh, come in, Elena, I think Master Sebastián has seen it all! Alfredo, I don't think we needed to record it, after all. Federico was telling me that there was to be an official video of it: and I think Decca said they were going to contribute generously to the Magda Fund if the sales were good.'

He stared at his wife. 'An official video? Of that bloody rubbish? You must have had too much to drink! The recording companies aren't stupid, you know!'

\*     \*     \*

428

In London, Buzzer Ahmet said to the press, 'The four of us getting together again and doing another concert? No,' laughing, 'that was unique. One for the history books.'

In Barcelona, Pepe Contreras said to the press, 'You must be joking! We shall never do another one!'

In Bologna, Pio Fazzoletto said to the press, 'Well, it was fun. But a repeat? No!'

In Madrid, Modesto Martes grinned and said to the press, 'Well . . . let's just say . . . '